Deadly Divinity

Can the world's solutions be found in a bottle?

For information regarding discounts for bulk purchases or promotional applications of this book, contact rob@writeawaybooks.com.

Published by Write Away Books
PO Box 1681, Carlsbad, CA 92018
www.writeawaybooks.com

ISBN number 979-8-9896431-9-6

First Edition

Book design by Danielle Tweedy

Deadly Divinity

Can the world's solutions be found in a bottle?

Can the world's problems be solved from a solution in a bottle? The answer lies within.

In 2024, aspiring artist Sofia Montgomery received the shock of her life when her home—and much of the downtown area of La Mesa, California—was leveled by a series of bomb blasts. Dozens died, thousands were homeless, and the city found itself the centerpiece of a major law enforcement investigation.

Before the dust had settled, Sofia almost suffocated from bleach fumes, quickly shifting her focus from the day's tragedy to her own personal survival. It would be just the beginning of a disturbing pattern of attacks involving bleach and poisoning accidents across San Diego County.

Follow Sofia and the infatuated Damian as they trace the pattern of attacks and its relationship to a close-knit community and its charismatic leader. This story of fear, death, courage and personal growth demonstrates the incalculable value of recognizing that not everything is what it appears to be.

This book is a must-read in these days of blindly trusting whoever grabs the microphone last, and highlights the very real fear of people who will do anything to "cure" those deemed to be different in any way.

♦♦♦♦♦

SIERRA GRUZD had been creating different kinds of art since she was two. She spent much of her youth moving back and forth from her San Diego birthplace to cooler climates, including Michigan and Escalon, California, but always returned to her hometown.

Haunted by a never-ending string of fears and nightmares invading her mind at all hours of the day and night, Sierra translated those visions into any visual and written media as a form of therapy of themes such as grief, death and even monsters. The self-prescribed therapy of taking out her frustrations and angst on a computer keyboard has resulted in *Deadly Divinity*: her first novel.

WARNING

The story you are about to read

is sure to scare

the HELL out of you!

Author's Note

Hello there, this is Sierra Gruzd, or just Sierra G., since my last name is hard to pronounce for some people. I am a cartoonist, writer, and graphic designer who enjoys creating in all media. In addition to writing, I have an entrepreneurial business that makes stickers and other art forms. This story that you're holding is my first novel and I have thought of writing novels for decades. Whenever I read I always wanted to make my own stories for other people to enjoy.

Hell, even at third grade when I lived in the small town of Escalon, my little self made small homemade books with my own stories and drawings of each character. And if my smaller self realized what I have written and achieved to make a novel, she'd be amazed and jumping for joy knowing that her dream of getting her stories out there is finally coming true.

Horror is the one genre of books and cartoons that I simultaneously enjoy and am terrified of. Like Karloff, Hitchcock, and countless others before me, I'm fascinated by the very real fears that flood the subconscious mind as we're confronted with whatever scares us. To confront these fears head-on, I used elements of my dozens of phobias to create scary situations and worst-case scenarios that eventually evolved into this story.

Along the way I had a revelation: written therapy beat the hell out of constantly having these horrors intruding into my dreams and daytime thoughts and becoming a plague for an anxiety-ridden mind. Writing about my fears gave me control over them, rather than having them controlling me.

Simple and logical, right? Only it's not that easy to do it. After all, how can you work on yourself when dealing with the disheartening thought that no one is taking you or your fears seriously? For years, those surrounding me would downplay my concerns, calling me a worrywort, then moving on with their lives without giving me another thought.

Writing was equally difficult, as imagination, inspiration, and that one word you're seeking to describe your feelings can come and go in an instant.

Yet while much of my creativity was fleeting, I found the panic my phobias produced was equally brief at times. Using my fears as inspiration for creative endeavors, while scary, was without question a fascinating process.

♦♦♦♦♦

One of the phobias I've spent a great deal of energy on has been the idea of cults. Despite my best efforts, news reports and stories of The People's Temple (Jonestown), Heaven's Gate, Charles Manson and the rest haunt me, even years after the fact. The idea that dozens—even hundreds—of people could become some hivemind, sharing the same warped view of the world and the so-called 'outsiders' around them, frankly, has been both sobering and scary as hell to contemplate.

Yet I've also learned that some of the most bone-chilling cults appear on the surface to be the most normal. Sometimes they appear in the guise of religion, other times as political movements, but they all say they're there to help the world be a better place.

Most of them, I have found, are nothing more than wolves dressed in sheep's clothing.

Perhaps that was one of the many reasons why I have been so consistently iffy about joining many clubs. I mean, I want to join a group where the people in the room have interests similar to mine so it will make me feel better, rather than filling my head with even more anxiety than when I walked through the door.

All this for a sense of belonging...but the question remains: how can you tell when an organization is—or is not—a cult? Where do you draw the line between the desire to be part of something bigger and the fear of being controlled? Is it possible to always know when it's a mainstream group, rather than a controlling facade?

Take the Duggar family, for example, and their reality TV show "19 Kids and Counting," which aired on TLC from 2008-2015. Were they merely a large Christian family who continue to share their story, faith, and resources on their blog and social media, as their website states? Were they a seemingly ordinary family that so many in our society wished they could have, with a perfect marriage, flawless kids, no "problem children," and consistently good morals throughout?

Or did a more sinister truth escape when it became apparent that the values presented on the show were associated with the Quiverfull movement, which has been described as promoting strict family conformity, male hierarchies and subservient roles for women? Mainstream or cult: you decide.

♦♦♦♦♦

While we're talking about hive minds and cult-like thinking, a lot has been said over the years about Autism Spectrum Disorder (ASD). This condition is oftentimes characterized by difficulties in social communication and interaction; a strong preference for predictability and routine; sensory processing differences; and a need for repetitive behavior.

Though it's been scientifically proven that there is no single cause for autism, there are many in so-called "mainstream groups" who insist it's a product of certain medications or environmental factors, even as professionals in the field repeatedly prove it's nothing more than a spectrum of neurodivergence. Some might even argue that everyone is on the spectrum to one extent or another, and that denying it doesn't change this fact.

I mention this because I was diagnosed at age six with PDD-NOS (Pervasive Developmental Disorder). And despite my being a productive member of society, there are thousands of people who know little about me and less about autism, but would have people like me taking a 'Miracle Mineral Solution' or 'MMS' as a cure. There was a page of the FDA where it warned the public about MMS. But to nobody's great surprise, as I write this for further research, the page had been taken down from the web. Either the link had expired or someone deliberately took it down. Can't say for certain, hopefully it'll be placed back up soon.

This product, which the US Food & Drug Administration warned against in 2010, is actually a toxic solution of sodium chlorite in distilled water, and is falsely promoted as a cure for HIV, cancer, and the common cold, as well as autism. It causes nausea, vomiting, diarrhea, and life-threatening low blood pressure. "Ingesting these products is the same as drinking bleach," said FDA Acting Commissioner Ned Sharpless in 2019.

Meaning these community members and church-goers would have me swallow poison because they don't like me. Should I trust a church because these are "people of God"? Or are they trying to kill me? Clear-thinking or cultish? Again, you decide.

As I've been researching these types of organizations, I've observed they all have one thing in common: a strong, charismatic individual in charge of a body of individuals who start out believing they're doing wonderful things...only to learn their leader has a completely different agenda. And it rarely turns out well.

Which is why, for me, it is increasingly difficult to trust people in general. After all, when you're raised to fear strangers; when you hear countless news stories of people killing their friends, their parents, or their children; when you read stories about people planning to kidnap a governor or kill a president merely because they disagree; or you learn about groups kidnapping someone and the body not being found until weeks' later...well, I don't know about you, but it scares the hell out of me as an adult.

Like the times when a 'rapture' would be declared. Only for people to be either disappointed or left with devastating repercussions, like bankruptcy and dead family members. These are the kinds of thoughts and concerns that have invaded my brain over the past two years as I've been writing this book. But something interesting, and very positive, has come out of the exercise.

Because even though the headlines haven't really changed—and the stresses are just as real today as they were 24 months ago—I actually find I'm less worried about it now than I was before. I guess the right kind of therapy really can do amazing things to set your thinking on the right path.

So, I would ask you to set your fears aside and enjoy this novel from a mind that some say is troubled and others see as benefitting from this form of therapy. It's a fictionalized history in a real-life setting, based in an alternate reality in the recent past. I hope it will give you pleasure, as well as some intensive food for thought.

Finally, thank you for sharing my phobias, and may they give you many hours of satisfaction. If I've done my job well, you will enjoy reading this story as much as I've enjoyed writing it. It's intended as a work of fiction, of course, but who knows...stranger things have happened, don'tcha think?

Sierra Gruzd
March 31, 2026

Dedication

To my mom and dad, I finally made it! Thank you for all the guidance and help, love you both!

To my sister, Savannah, thank you for being my inspiration to write again and create stories like we used to do together with our toys.

For my friends Hoodie and Berkeley, thank you guys for being there for me even if you guys are so far away in other states. You guys are great friends and amazing storytellers.

Next a note of thanks to Rob and Tweeds at Write Away Books for making this novel possible.

And finally to my Ms. Amalia, *the queen of nights*, for great company for long nights, even if you chew on my pencils and sit on my computer like the tyrant you are.

"When we cross the threshold of good to evil, we become deranged."

– H. Meadow Hopewell, Rage Against the Machine

Bleach - Safe or Fatal?

Bleach. It erases stains and makes things pure, mostly by destroying germs. It doesn't politely nudge away dirt—it annihilates it! And my guess is there's a bottle of it sitting underneath your kitchen sink right now.

You already know that smell. You walk into a freshly scrubbed bathroom, and—*bam*—it hits you like a wall. Sharp, almost metallic, with that tang that seems to crawl up your nose and sting your eyes. Bleach is unquestionably one of the most useful, and most dangerous, chemicals you're ever likely to encounter.

It's funny, isn't it? On one hand, bleach has saved more lives than we could probably count. On the other, it's the sort of thing that can land you in the emergency room—*or worse*—if you happen to breathe in too much, swallow it, or even just spill it in the wrong place.

So, let's talk about bleach for a minute. Not as some dry, chemical formula, but as the double-edged sword it really is.

♦♦♦♦♦

If bleach had a résumé, it would be impressive. Hospitals, schools, restaurants, city water plants — everybody's used it.

Think about epidemics in the 1800s. Cholera was ripping through whole towns, and disinfection with bleach was one of the primary things that slowed it down. Even today, when doctors scrub down a hospital floor or clean a surgical room, they're probably using it in some form to do the job most effectively.

Your city's drinking water is probably touched by it too. A carefully controlled amount of bleach makes sure the stuff that comes out of your tap won't give you dysentery. In disasters—hurricanes, earthquakes, floods—aid workers sometimes use tiny doses to make filthy water drinkable. It's not glamorous, but it is lifesaving.

And at home? Well, bleach keeps our shirts white, the mold out of the shower grout, and germs off the cutting board. It's almost boring in its usefulness. *Almost.*

Only things can sometimes go very wrong with bleach, and it will show its dark side. Because the very thing that makes it good at killing germs—its corrosive, protein-busting strength—also makes it brutal on human tissue. The alkaline substance has a shocking PH level of 13...roughly double the level of what's running through your veins as you read these words.

♦♦♦♦♦

Imagine Suzanne is leaning over a bucket, pouring in a healthy splash of bleach, and she starts scrubbing. The bathroom is small, the fan is broken, and the door is shut. At first it's just the sharp smell, which is annoying...but tolerable. Then her eyes start watering and a tickle grows in her throat. Suzanne coughs - once...twice...and soon she's in the middle of a hacking fit, her chest tightening like an invisible band is squeezing her ribs.

If she just opened the door so that fresh air could flood in, these symptoms would quickly ease. But if she keeps working and ignores these signs, her breath will quickly get raspy. As she grows dizzy, her breath would become more of a wheezing, like a broken accordion. And if she just kept going, eventually her lungs would start filling with fluid, leading to a pulmonary edema—the sensation of drowning without water.

The scariest part of this scenario is the bad stuff might not happen for hours, with poor Suzanne suddenly collapsing and gasping for air as her lungs betrayed her.

What a horrible way to go, isn't it?

♦♦♦♦♦

But what if your food was tainted by bleach? Maybe someone didn't rinse off a cutting board well, or worse, deliberately tampered with a meal.

That first bite would undoubtedly be shocking: bitter, metallic, and chemical. Your tongue would burn instantly, like licking a battery. Your throat would clamp down, with your gag reflex firing on overdrive. Of course, if it was just a trace of bleach you'd spit it out, cough, and maybe vomit...before spending the next several hours with a sore, scratchy throat.

But if it was more than a trace, your stomach would soon be cramping like a knife twisting from the inside. In short order you'd be retching violently, the vomit streaked with blood from all the irritated tissue throughout your digestive system. Your mouth and throat would probably blister, and these results would be messy, painful, and immediate.

♦♦♦♦♦

On April 23, 2020, President Donald Trump suggested people drink bleach as a way of curing COVID. This led to a 400% increase in disinfectant inhalation nationwide within 48 hours, as well as attendant visits to emergency rooms.

Mr. Trump's comments had led to a nightmare scenario. Because the moment bleach touches the lips, there's burning—real burning, not spicy pepper burning, but raw, caustic pain, like swallowing fire. Down the throat, into the chest, the agony follows. The stomach reacts violently, trying to eject the poison.

And make no mistake—bleach *is* poison when misused.

♦♦♦♦♦

Vomiting among countless people was inevitable, but here's the cruel twist: bringing bleach back up tore and burned their throats again. And internally it was carnage. Because when someone drinks bleach, the esophagus swells shut, cutting off breathing. The stomach lining gets eaten away, typically forming holes that spill stomach acid and bleach into the abdominal cavity.

That's not just painful; It's *fatal* if untreated.

Even those people who survived were left with permanent scarring inside their esophagus, making every meal a painful struggle. Reports came in that so much as a sip of water felt like they were swallowing broken glass, and many survivors needed surgery—or even feeding tubes—just to keep living.

♦♦♦♦♦

Eyes watering uncontrollably. Coughing fits that left people doubled over in pain. Vomiting so violent it left the stomach muscles aching. Skin around the mouth, reddened and raw. Shock. Clammy skin. Racing pulse. Confusion.

And those who were damaged dealt with paramedics, emergency rooms, surgery, intensive care and comas. Then, with their throats typically swollen shut, there were feeding tubes until the tissue healed...begging for water but forbidden to drink it...and permanently vulnerable and ruined for life.

Obviously, anyone who knew what was coming wouldn't voluntarily do this to themselves...unless they were convinced it was the only way they could save themselves from something far worse. Or if they were on the receiving end with no idea what was happening.

Now, why don't you have a nice chocolate truffle while you settle back and enjoy the story.

Chapter 1 - Fear of Everything

-Sofia-

If I weren't afraid, I would finally speak my mind and not be fearful of the consequences.

If I weren't afraid, I wouldn't stay home and instead take risks by investing in a fuller life.

If I weren't afraid, I wouldn't want to conform to the ideas of others of how I should live.

If I weren't afraid, I would live life to the fullest and welcome death as a friend and not a phobia.

If I weren't afraid, I wouldn't be guilt-tripped into changing myself to please the meaningless desires of others.

If I weren't afraid, I would lose my fear of being touched and defend myself from harm.

If I weren't afraid, I would tell the truth about what's happening in my life and not lie.

If I weren't afraid, I would see failure as a lesson to be learned from and not focus on perfection.

♦♦♦♦♦

I paused to read the documentation of my psyche. Like an inner therapy for myself, I use typing and writing as coping mechanisms to remove my frustrations...but only to an extent. Other things I've written are a basic gratitude list: my sight, living in a stable home, my outdoor cat friends, my mentors or guides, the ability to draw, my bed, food, plants, flower garden, and so many other things.

For me, writing is better than the inevitable job where I feel invisible. That's how it is. That's how it's always been. And yet, I felt comfortable here. Too comfortable, getting the necessities I want and need with no effort due to benefits from a regional non-profit support group. They provide me with things like transportation and help arrange accommodations for my job.

So, I write letters to myself to help maintain some of my sanity and be in a positive mood. It's something that I need to work on, just as I need to work on loving myself, forgiveness, health, art, writing, and recognizing my self-worth.

Deep down I want more from my days than to just stay in my room. I want to have a life that I can enjoy, and stability to engulf myself within my freedom from everyone. But instead I write—reams and reams of stories, scribbles, and poems—hoping the obstacles I face will fade over time. I find it helps to keep me numb from dealing with any more discomfort. It's like an internal tug of war, leaving me chronically unsure whether I want to stay in my comfort zone...or bite the bullet and actually take a risk.

Don't get me wrong. I'm grateful for my living situation. I love my stuffed animals, wear warm clothes, and sleep in a comfortable bed every night. I never go to bed hungry, or even think about where my next meal is going to come from. I unquestionably live a life of privilege, and I appreciate it.

Still, for some reason I'm neither happy nor satisfied. This is the merry-go-round of life, only it just feels a bit mundane right now. I shouldn't need to be a coward in order to stay in this safe—some might say vicious—cycle. It's like...I wanted something new, a change that would make my life less dull.

♦♦♦♦♦

I grabbed my black notebook, feeling the thin leather texture on my fingertips. Grasping a mechanical pencil, I used my thumb to press down on the eraser and pushed the lead out from the tip. A flood of ideas simultaneously flashed through my mind, all demanding at once to be scribbled down lest I forget them. And so my fingers flew, desperately struggling to write down everything churning through my brain, as if writing myself a hopeless poem.

My train of thought was interrupted by a scratching from the other side of my glass door leading to the patio. Pivoting from my bed, I crowded with my favorite stuffies and eyed the curious, hungry felines peeping their heads from behind my patio door and struggling to see around the taupe curtains. As I slid open the door, my ears were greeted with the mewing of the hungry strays, their plaintive cries filling the air. It looked to be a rather nice day today, the sky's palette slowly shifting from orange to blue as the cozy glow of the sun rose up into the sky. Could it be a moment of solace for myself, and perhaps even for the ensemble of strays who are anxious to eat from my plate of discarded breakfast each morning?

The smell of leftover bacon and eggs wafted through the door, enticing the quintet of felines closer. With that I placed my plate before them to encourage the morning feast. Admittingly, it was one of the few most straightforward routines I enjoyed. Feeding the scraps to my finicky fur babies I had taken the liberty of naming Ashes, Mona, Bunny, Fireside, and Lucky Minx. Each name had been chosen with care to reflect their unique personalities and fur patterns.

The one who stood out from the crowd was Lucky Minx, who had earned his moniker due to his scruffy black fur, a missing eye, a chipped canine tooth, and his clipped left ear. This little outcast of the fuzzy group greeted me first with a rugged meow, as he always did, and I found myself feeling that, like him, I too was almost always the odd one out.

♦♦♦♦♦

As a child I was told that you need to have friends to even belong to society; to be a puzzle piece to the massive conjunction of fitting segments, and to form a 'flawless image.' In other words, so you would qualify as another cog in the wheel of the larger machine.

And this wasn't just for simple enjoyment or mingling, either. It had always been that way; the supposed "perfect way" of life recreated to be this corporate garden of Eden.

You see, I've always aspired to be stable in this lifetime and be the inspirational earth angel, despite the unfair, far-reaching expectations of those around me. I don't want to be cast out as

Lucifer and the rebelling angels that followed. Which is why I felt I had to fit into this impossible box I had to create for myself just to fit in.

Plus, I was regularly picked on for almost everything I was doing, getting an earful if someone thought I was eating the same thing every day. Or because they didn't like the television shows I watched. Or when the way I greeted people struck them as incorrect.

From elementary school through college, seemingly every moment of every day, people all around me felt it was their obligation to nitpick about every single detail in my life. And I withdrew further and further into my shell, feeling there was no place where I would feel safe. It got to the point where there was so much noise about all the things that I was doing "wrong" that I couldn't even express myself properly.

All I wanted was to live my own life, without being told everything I did needed to be fixed. And I was told that just wanting to live my life was wrong, too.

I guess I'm the oddball.

♦♦♦♦♦

One day I may decide to pursue a poetry career. Should that happen, I expect I'll be able to finally leave this lifeless box I call my bedroom.

A sudden glint of sunlight spotted from the corner of my eye startled me, causing me to suddenly knock over a small, neatly stacked pile of letters that I had written to myself. I huffed, irritated that something so innocuous could make me so edgy. Picking them up individually, I left the cats munching and nudging each other aside as they huddled over the messy plate.

Stacking the letters as they had been previously arranged, the one in the mint green envelope caught my eye. I opened to its simple message, something I had written for myself right after I had a really bad crashout last year:

> **"Despite everything you did—and the circumstances right now—at least you're still here."**

♦♦♦♦♦

"Sofia, are you almost ready?" It was my mom, calling from the other room.

Damn! It was almost 8am, and I had to catch the trolley and get to my job. Still, it *had* to be better than staying in my room wallowing in self-pity. "Yeah, I'm almost done," I called back unenthusiastically.

Of course I was lying, as I still needed to get my bag ready. I closed the letter of self-motivation before putting it in my satchel, thinking I would use the paper with this mantra scratched on it to get through the day. I also placed my journal and two plastic water bottles in the bag while checking that my wallet, cell phone, and headphones were in there as well.

Oh yeah...and my keys. Mustn't forget my keys, or I'd find myself sitting on the lawn waiting for mom to get home from work at the end of the day.

♦♦♦♦♦

After the cats finished their meal, I grabbed the dirty plate and closed the outside door, bidding my furry pals a fond farewell for now before heading out from my dishwater gray room to meet my mother in the kitchen. Ensuring the water from the tap was hot enough to cut the grease and remove the kitty spit, I rinsed off all evidence that five feline faces had been all over these utensils just moments earlier. The last thing I needed right now was to have my mother once more giving me grief for feeding—in her words—'those dirty strays'.

Her reaction has never been because she hates cats, mind you, but rather because my parents feel that animals living on the street are unclean.

You see, my parents were brought up in a world where they were expected to present a picture perfect family to please others who would otherwise despise them. That's probably where my perfectionism came from; it was *their* generational trauma, and I've found myself permanently warped by it.

Still, I wish my mom would at least give the cats a chance. After all, they're still living creatures, and they deserve as much care as anyone else.

Then again, I guess I shouldn't be surprised by her reaction to my furry friends, since she doesn't really approve of anything, anyway. And if I'm being realistic, I have to recognize that she and my father are never gonna change. I mean, 53 years of being a doormat—without enough self-awareness to recognize the problem and lacking the spine to change, even if they wanted to—well, it's like they're actors in an imaginary play, with fixed roles and a director refusing to let them ad lib. You could almost hear the instructions being yelled at them: "Just read the lines as they are in the script!"

And yeah, I know I could try to tell them how I feel, but that's not gonna do any good, either. They shut me down every time I've tried explaining my perspective, and I learned long ago that I just have to accept it; this is just the way things are. I'll give myself more love and try to be my own cheerleader, but know that they're never going to give me more than they already do.

Sometimes I wonder if I was ever a burden to her like she thinks these cats are. Okay, I'll admit they do make a mess by occasionally knocking over the potted plants, but that's just who they are.

Just like I want to be who I am, though I seriously doubt she would ever approve of me being a poet. And let's not even get into her easily anticipated reaction if I told her I have no desire to ever find a man for myself. Maybe I like girls. Maybe I just want to be by myself.

Oh, the horror! Oh, the shame! Oh, what would the neighbors think?

Oh, who gives a shit?

I've got to confess it; sometimes I hope I can get out of this house soon so I can live on my own and pursue the career I've always wanted. I just want to be living on my own as a poet and writer—nothing more, but nothing less—and responsible to nobody but myself.

What a concept, huh?

♦♦♦♦♦

Once finished, I placed the dishes in the sink amongst all the family's breakfast leavings, knowing a full tub of soap and hot water will provide the thorough cleaning and sanitation my mother so desperately craves for them.

"*CRAP!*" I thought to myself, realizing I had left my cozy burgundy sweatshirt sitting on my bed. Dropping my backpack onto the chair, I dashed back into my room, put on the extra layer, and returned to the living room to grab the bag and head out the door. Pulling the keys from my pocket, I called out "Goodbye!" to my mom before heading towards the trolley station for the only transportation available to get to my job.

I walked past the variety of multi-hued succulents and flora, recognizing they're perhaps the brightest things in this otherwise rundown and humdrum little California town. The vibrant shades of the flowers, the gentle hum of the bees and hummingbirds, and the mingling scents of sweet flowers, garlic, and seared beef from the local restaurants created a sensory symphony.

It was almost like living in paradise. Almost, if you ignored where you actually were.

♦♦♦♦♦

I headed up Fresno Avenue towards Spring Street, briefly crossing the linear street to switch paths and slide beside the parked cars before continuing my trot in earnest. Fresno, running at a 45-degree angle, was always faster than the streets that just ran straight east to west.

Taking this alternate route also had the advantage of letting me pass Moonstone Mystique; the one store that I enjoy visiting periodically. It's one of those places with various kinds of crystals, tarot cards, dishes, pendulums, and other spiritual things that address the needs and interests of a wide diversity of religions.

What I always like about coming to this store are the sometimes-rare finds, such as dreamcatchers of different designs with feathers and raccoon tails. Mind you, I'm neither religious nor spiritual, but I *am* fascinated by things associated with 'otherworldly' practices. I even got a chime from there decorated with wood-carved cats; painted in a range of pastel colors, flower patterns, and a few marbles tied to them.

♦♦♦♦♦

Half a block past Moonstone I turned the corner and hurried down the sidewalk of Spring Street—one of La Mesa's main strips—walking past the Mammamia Market, a professional office building, a recently-shuttered Mexican eatery named Carnitas Uruapan, a women's resale clothing store named Act II—a quirky, community-oriented shop—and the usual collection of dentists, banks, and empty storefronts.

Seeing the psychiatric center's office reminded me that I needed to make an appointment with my therapist.

I couldn't help but notice a few cars that were parked on the sides of La Mesa Blvd. today, hinting that the town had closed off the street to do the farmer's market. The sight of the bustling market; the vivacious colorings of the fruits, flowers and honey; and the lively chatter of the locals, which always combined to bring a sense of community to this small town. It was kind of a shame that I couldn't stick around for that. La Mesa isn't known for much in the larger San Diego region, but it is well known for its superb local fruit and honey prices.

And as I passed by the local library, where I sometimes enjoy spending my free time reading books by various authors and poets of every stripe, thoughts of being able to create something that could touch people's hearts—like the books I read—filled me with longing.

Man, I just wanted to have the opportunity to be like them one day.

♦♦♦♦♦

I shook these wistful thoughts from my head before steering myself into the short walk remaining towards the train tracks draped in scattered rubble and rocks. Finally arriving at the intersection of La Mesa Boulevard, I looked past the papered-over windows and "For Lease" signs on a dozen other local buildings that have been decorating our downtown for nearly a century. Looking for the orange line trolley station, I yawned at the homogenization of the Chase Bank and the California Preferred Escrow office, and sprinted towards my goal—the La Mesa Boulevard station—in hopes I'd arrived before the trolley did.

And as I cooled my heels alongside a crowd suggesting the 15 minute interval until the next trolley arrived was about up, I admired this southern California community and took a moment to appreciate why its many communities have enabled the city to be coined as the "Jewel of the Hills."

Entering the trolley station just in time to hear wheels screeching against the iron tracks, the trolley and I both arrived at the station exactly when we needed to be there. Looking around, I wondered how I could possibly feel like I belonged to this city if I couldn't even understand how to be part of it or feel comfortable living there? I mean, how can you take someone seriously when all they do is judge you based on your looks and beliefs?

♦♦♦♦♦

Buying my ticket, I hopped aboard the train and sought space away from the other passengers. Thankfully, a few seats remained unoccupied in the furthest corner to my left, and I settled in, away from prying eyes and nosy neighbors.

As always, I used this privacy to pass the time, reading through my journal notes, stray writings, and an extensive collection of brain dumps, word vomits, and meandering thoughts.

Looking through my most recent scribbles, I observed that they sounded more like stories than poetry. And I found it curious that this brief writing of some short story had the climax written into it...even before the introduction.

> **What would be the point of that? What would I and everyone else do once they leave their bunkers and enter the barren world? At that point we'll all live in the soon-to-be-land of nothing, where there would be a devoid motherland of much more suffering and a constant struggle to survive. That fate is more cruel than to die a fiery death in moments.**
>
> **I curl myself inward, hot tears streaming down, and my heart is pounding wildly. I sniffle, wiping tears from my face. At this point why should I cower or worry anymore? The important part is that I was able to live a meaningful life—a life that I dreamed I had. And perhaps...maybe that was enough...**
>
> **I came to my senses as if I wiped my eyes and got up from my bed, and placed a CD into the DVD player. Soon, flashing on the screen was the cartoon show I watched in my childhood on television. As the video played, my feet shifted toward the kitchen. I walked to the café machine to brew a coffee before going under the cabinet to grab a glass bottle and add the butterscotch liquor for flavor.**

Fetching my drink, I slowly walked back to the room and sat on my bed, watching my favorite show as I waited for the inevitable. Suddenly a soft mewl was heard beside my bed as my cat, wearing a curious expression, pounced onto the comforter.

I allowed my beloved feline to sit on my lap, stroking her soft, warm fur as she purred. At least I won't be dying alone. I gently raised my glass of spiked coffee brew, giving me a toast to my life, celebrating my success in finishing the multiple decades I had lived through.

Soon the flash of light that gleamed from behind the charcoal curtains from outside alerted my feline friend. I pulled my cat close to me to comfort her, already feeling her long nails piercing my long sleeves and skin. I looked to the ceiling of my room, my gaze softened, feeling the tears of grief spilling over my cheeks, soon to embrace the destruction that can only come from the detonation of a nuclear warhead.

I was proud of this passage I'd created. True, it wasn't much, but it was one of the few short stories I'd written and I think I'm getting better as a writer. Okay, it has a bleak storyline, but even so I think it's wonderful.

Then again, even within the pampered life I've been living, I still feel...trapped. I have little—or arguably no—resources and advantages to help me pursue the life I desire.

Sigh. I guess that's just the existence I'm condemned to have.

Chapter 2 - Sofia

-Damian-

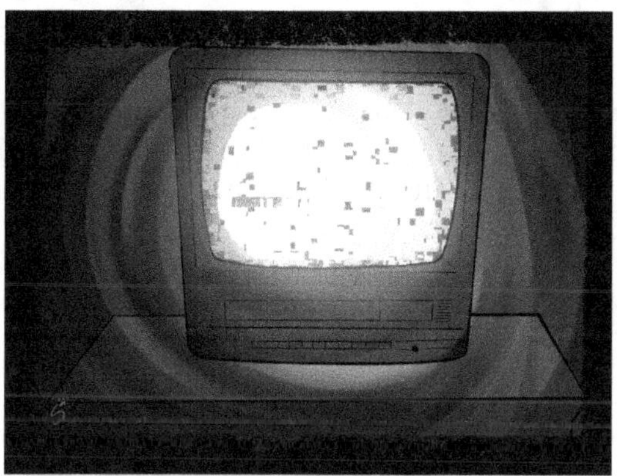

I sat up from my bed, arms outstretched, drinking in the oxygen of my room and sucking it into my lungs. My eyes slowly unblurred as I looked around my room, once more experiencing the dark green walls and shelves loaded down with countless curiosities, stuffed animals, and horror film figurines.

This 1980s-themed time capsule has become my safe haven from the frights of the real world. Nearby stands a messy stack of horror novels, DVDs, and VHS tapes, barely balancing and threatening to topple over at any moment onto my 12-inch box-shaped TV, upon which flickers the remnants of that cult classic Cyborg 2087 that I neglected to turn off before falling asleep in the middle of the night.

I smile, thinking I'll get to see if this movie accurately predicted the future, before considering how I was better off passing out than staying up late and letting my thoughts of existential dread consume me. Such fears always make me question my own reality, while classic cult and monster films give me comfort and lull me to sleep while preventing me from going down an existential rabbit hole.

Of course, a strategy of watching old movies as an escape can't keep me going forever. And while I know I could probably find other options, like drugs or booze, this somehow seems healthier...at least for the moment.

Shifting from my bed, I reached for my cell phone to look through my texts. My ride wouldn't arrive for an hour yet, so I figured I had time to get dressed and maybe to eat something more than a Pop Tart. Sitting up, I grabbed the clothes I'd set out on the edge of my bed to wear today. The fact that the black tee and jeans with silver chains were the exact same thing I wore yesterday was unimportant.

Hey, at least this time I remembered to put on underwear! And it's relatively clean, too.

♦♦♦♦♦

As I got dressed, I couldn't help but think of Sofia; this girl I've been working with. Damn, what was her last name? It would definitely help if she'd sometimes talk about herself a little bit, but instead I'm always left to wonder and to make up stuff to fill in the blanks. I should ask if she's in the mood to hang out with me somewhere, rather than only seeing each other at the clean-up gig.

I mean, we're even in the same biology class in our local community college, and I've noticed that she likes books and poetry.

Well, it's a start, I guess, though that's one of the only interests I know we have in common. I'm kinda grasping at straws here.

Still, beggars can't be choosers, so I'll take that crumb of information and be happy with it for now. I mean, I've always liked poetry, horror movies, gothic punk things, plushies, music and seeing beauty in the most unusual things around me. I'm hoping maybe her mind works the same way as mine does.

I mean, wouldn't it be awesome if we actually had a great deal in common? Or even a few things would be good...because hanging out with her outside of work and college would be nice. I could ask her if we could go to the local library or if she'd allow me to take her to a café, right?

Or is it too soon? I never know how to handle this sort of thing...when is it okay to be aggressive and when do I cross the line into being pushy? Is asking her to go someplace that's public, yet quiet, socially acceptable behavior? Is it neutral territory? At what point does it become obnoxious?

I *hate* this! It's so confusing!

♦♦♦♦♦

I've been watching Sofia a lot lately, and I suspect she's feeling overwhelmed at work. Perhaps, like me, she needs a quiet, peaceful place to unwind.

Watching this scenario unfold makes me wonder what might happen if maybe—just maybe—I could arrange for us to spend a little quiet time alone together. The way I see it, such a setting could allow us—two people who often find solace in silence—to hopefully learn a bit more about each other.

Or maybe I'm kidding myself. So often she seems distant, despite my fantasies that she'd agree to the idea of hanging out with me.

Still, I'm determined to build a connection with Sofia, even if it's a gradual process. I'm content with my sanitation job; it provides me with benefits and allows me to contribute to keeping the city clean. However, I understand that she finds the job stressful.

I don't know. I try talking with her, but she always seems to keep me at arms-length. Maybe our whole "relationship" is just in my head. For all I know, she doesn't like me at all. It seems sometimes like she doesn't even know I exist, despite our working side-by-side. Maybe I'm just being paranoid.

There are many things I'd ask Sofia if I could, like when she talks about her dream of becoming a famous poet. Sometimes I find myself wondering what drives her to seek fame. Why does she feel the need to be recognized for her work? Or does she believe that everyone is out to get her?

Hmmmmm...could *she* be the one who's paranoid?

♦♦♦♦♦

These questions intrigue me, causing me to reflect on both my aspirations and my motivations. I'd like to explore these questions with her, but I need to be patient and not overwhelm her with my curiosity. I need to put her at ease, and persuade her that I'm not a threat; that I really just want to be friends...and, with time, perhaps just a little bit more.

Okay, in my fantasies it sometimes becomes a lot more, and I recognize that I'm getting ahead of myself. I shouldn't bombard her with questions like that - at least, not until we know each other a little bit better. And that assumes such a day will come one day, of course.

Still, maybe I should talk about all that stuff later. For now I just need to prepare for the day ahead of me.

♦♦♦♦♦

My phone began pinging in a desperate attempt to grab my attention. It was a text from my mom saying "Good morning!" and wishing me a great day. Well, SHE's certainly in a good mood today, and a whole lot happier than she was when my dad demanded the divorce and things started to get really ugly.

I typed back to my mom, adding some black heart emojis at the end in what's become my signature response to her. It's become a routine thing we always do, since I live on my own and it tells her that I'm all right. Considering that I'm her only child, I know she worries about me.

At least my mom stayed around after they split up, even if my dad didn't. He decided he'd rather go around the world participating in 'dance classes' with other women, rather than to hang around with me and mom. Gee, Dad—you set a *GREAT* example for your son, as well as leading to the tragic end of my mother's marriage.

What a dumbass!

I'll admit I try to not think about it much, but I can't help but find the whole thing incredibly depressing. I mean, the man actually said to me "Hey, it's MY life!" and conveniently forgot, or ignored, the two innocent lives he was destroying with his selfish attitude.

But there's absolutely no bitterness here, right? I mean, I know it's better to not dwell too much on the bleak history that shadows my family. The past is in the past, after all. And these small communications with my mom always bring a smile and a brief moment of joy into my otherwise complicated existence.

I recognize that I should remain focused on the present, though. Today I would be cleaning with the others by Belmont Park down by Mission Bay, so that's a plus. Even if being a laborer custodian isn't an easy task when it comes to clearing out the most disgusting

things imaginable in public parks, I know that *someone* has to do it. And it pays pretty well too.
Then there's the bonus of being surrounded by the beauty of nature down there, which always improves my mood. The salty breeze from the nearby ocean tickles my skin, and never-ending songs courtesy of the seagulls fill the air as I dwell in that fond vision.

♦♦♦♦♦

Ah, Sofia—I have visions of us walking on the boardwalk and spending hours playing amusement park games as we laugh and enjoy each other's company.

It sounds awesome...only how do I make it happen?

♦♦♦♦♦

I opened my eyes and stretched out my arms, remembering I was still in my room and feeling a profound connection to the unique paintings adorning my walls. They remain a reflection of my distinct interests, featuring acrylic paintings of eerie clowns and zombies, my artistic interpretation of darkness, and the peculiar things that captivate me.

I dunno...for someone so young to have already experienced so much negativity, maybe it's not so strange that I view the world as a dark vision. These artworks, layered atop my collection of horror stories in various media, create a captivating visual narrative of my life. They all combine in my brain and just make sense to me.

What also made sense was that I should prepare breakfast before my transportation arrived. I grabbed my keys, phone, and backpack and unzipped the bag to make sure all my stuff was in there. Wallet, chemistry book for my college studies, my small journal for writing and doubling as a sketchbook, extra pencils and erasers, phone charger, sanitizer, sunscreen, water bottle...

Something was missing...

Headphones! Mustn't forget the headphones! I seized them from my shelf and shoved them into the bag.

Today seemed relatively quiet—maybe a bit too quiet, though I'm sure that probably didn't mean anything. It's usually calm around here during the daytime, with nothing but chirping finches and cooing mourning doves on the windowsill, singing to welcome the rising sun.

Still, I didn't think much of it as I entered the bathroom, which was noticeably cleaner than it had been yesterday. As the guy tasked with maintaining cleanliness in the group home shared with other regional group members, I consider this small victory in my daily routine to be something I can take pride in. I checked that my hair was properly stylized with styling powder and matte wax; a small act of self-care that set the tone for the day. Then I put on some deodorant and was ready to face the day.

♦♦♦♦♦

I met with the other group residents in the kitchen—a space that constantly buzzes with morning energy and quiet contemplation. The sunlight streamed in through the window, casting a warm glow on the table. Taking an orange from the fruit bowl, I peeled it, causing the sweet citrus scent to mingle with the aroma of freshly brewed coffee and creating a comforting, familiar morning ritual.

Ren, one of the caretakers, greeted me, "Morning, Damian."

"Morning, Ren," I responded as I pulled up a seat next to Pedro. Pedro doesn't talk much, oftentimes because he took medication for seizures that sometimes make him space out depending on the size of the dose he takes. Despite his quiet nature, Pedro's presence always comforts me, which makes him good company. He and I exchanged a few words, our conversation a mix of small talk and shared experiences.

Our home has always been a place of support and services to all of the people who live here. Besides Pedro, who needed the most assistance of anyone living here, there was Cristie, my next door neighbor on the second floor, sitting on the table and fixing herself some eggs. Nearby was Bella, pushing 40 and carrying a worn-down plush elephant held close to her body, tucked into the crook of her elbow like a child and using her other hand to shovel cereal into her cavernous mouth for simultaneous slurping, chewing, and gulping.

Then there was Jenny, taking her medication. She tends to be more timid than Bella, and as always was wearing one of the most colorful blouses I've ever seen. Finally, my eyes fell onRoberto, our little community's oldest resident. Visually impaired and resigned to a wheelchair being his only form of mobility, he sat there slowly eating his bowl of oatmeal topped with blueberries, aided by a social worker named Karen.

It's a cozy home, with a great garden where we have our own little backyard garden where we grow tomatoes, corn and sunflowers. And it's a nice bunch of clients—that's what they call us at the support group that pays for our housing; clients—though I just like to think of it as our neighborhood.

It's true that Bella kinda hogs the area more than the others do, and this has led to some back and forth rivalry and disagreements between us, but this is still unquestionably better than the first group home that I used to live at in Chula Vista. That place was horrible, with a puritanical social worker shoving scripture down my throat any time I came up with a fact about cemeteries, neuroscience, or the movies I've watched over the years. Even if the others in the house wanted to hear what I wanted to share, this bitch would shout us down and talk over us until we would finally stop talking...just to get her to shut up.

♦♦♦♦♦

I pulled out my phone and texted my boss that I'd be at work soon. Belmont Park is a 22-minute drive from my home between Spring Valley and Otay, and I sometimes take a taxi to get there. It's one of those accommodations provided to me by the regional center. And while the commute can be challenging, I've learned to enjoy the quiet moments it offers.

I briefly reviewed my journal, my thumb skimming the countless pages of sketches to find the section I've been writing lately. It's not my best work, I'll admit, but I know Sofia and I share a passion for writing our hearts out.

So I'll keep writing, hoping she comes around to liking me when the day finally arrives for me to share this section of writing with her. I usually write inspirational ideas I've gotten from my dreams, anyway, so I can't wait to share this with her, hoping she'll appreciate the effort and the emotions I've poured into it.

♦♦♦♦♦

> The Egyptian carvings are an example of a low-relief sculpture. They were carved within the wall to create the shapes and figures within the stone walls. Though it doesn't seem realistic, the imagery can illustrate the story and create rhythm with the carving lines...

Wait–that's not right. This was my writing for my notes for Art History class. I turned more pages until...aha! I found it.

I remember taking a boat ride at an amusement park, scrunching up my nose at the smell as I looked down at the mildewed water. The glistening blue lights and the faint smell of bromine overwhelmed me, bringing thoughts of a stale, musty scent to this boat ride. However, this imagery felt like I was recovering a lost memory of my fading childhood. It was intense, yet simultaneously so vivid that I could still feel the presence of the reaper looming over the plastic cattails.

In my mind we did a jumpcut to another setting, like you'd do if you were in a movie bouncing from one scene to another. Now it looked like a summer camp from the 1980s. However, this wasn't going to be an innocent nostalgia trip, as I was walking through the forest towards the lake shore.

Unfortunately, it's relatively short. Despite not being able to explain this sad dream, it is a reminder of my brief mortality and a childhood that's faded away as I've grown up. Some dreams seem so real that they feel like figures in your dream could touch you. Sometimes, you could feel them hold you down as if you're bound to the floor, with your mind so stunned that you cannot move despite your best efforts.

That felt really deep! And I suspect—or at least hope—that this section of writing will grab Sofia's attention. Maybe she's a fan of poets like Edgar Allan Poe. She may enjoy reading and writing that contains profound messages.

But I'm getting ahead of myself again. I could write more about this poem and then ask her to meet in La Mesa one day to grab a coffee and actually talk. Of course, I'd need to schedule a ride to get there, but that should be fine, even if I require alarms on my phone to ensure I remember.

And if I can't work up the nerve to ask her today to go out for coffee, I can always ask her the next time we're in biology class at Grossmont College. Either way, I'm confident she'll find this piece intriguing and thought-provoking.

♦♦♦♦♦

I turned to Pedro and couldn't help myself, "What do you think of this writing?"

The older man looked up and read through the poem, like he had read through so many of my writings before. Once finished, his tired brown eyes drifted to me and he just nodded before saying, 'Mhm.'

Pedro doesn't talk much these days, but I am grateful for his taking the time and offering the compliment.

Yeah, sometimes I don't need words to hear the compliment, but more like the person's genuine soft expression that makes me feel well-appreciated.

“Cool...it was written for a friend...”

I can’t wait to see her today. I’m exhilarated just thinking about asking her out for coffee, and can’t wait...I hope she says “Yes.”

Chapter 3 - Safe Haven

-Juniper-

'I'm doing the right thing, aren't I?'

This is a question I always seem to be asking myself. Looking around the safe haven that I call my room, I've typically found myself nervously pulling several strands of my hair out of my head as my mind wanders into that miserable memory lane that first woke me out of such a sound sleep.

Searching for some level of stability, I've examined the blank white walls that surround me. Usually a canvas for sunlight, the perimeter of my cell this morning is just dimly lit by traces of day seeping around the edges of the deep purple curtains that hang so heavily before them. Their weight only permits minimal bits of brightness to pierce through, with the sun's small beams of light filtering through the stained-glass window, its streaks of blue, red, and green just barely peeping through the curtains.

To me it seems to be a light shining on a hidden spot, a beacon of hope or anticipation. It's as if beauty and truth are hiding behind a shroud of obscurity, just waiting to be revealed.

But...to reveal what? Could it just be my imagination and thoughts playing with me again? My mind likes to jump from one thought to another.

I shouldn't worry.

At least it's better than it was ten years ago. That's when I was always staying at home with my parents, living through my tense childhood among the members of that contradictory church congregation that my mother and father thought of as a second family.

Yeah, these were the people who made me unreasonably impatient and resentful, seeing them as Bible-thumping hypocrites trying to force me to live my life their way during those last painful years of adolescence.

I always hated that 'loving evangelical' misery pit. I despised the idea of being told at the age of six that I'd be burning in Hell for all time if I didn't believe in their version of one particular deity. They made me think that I and all the other children in our community were responsible to prevent other people's souls from being sent to eternal damnation.

And I completely disagreed with this attitude, feeling that we should instead be giving the so-called wicked a safe haven for them to rehabilitate in. I kept trying to stay pure for my future husband, even as the pastors would prey on me. And we'd sing songs about the inevitable apocalypse, even taking those demeaning 'wife classes' to learn the secrets of making—and keeping—our husbands happy.

I was miserable, living a life where I wasn't getting the love and health treatments I needed. My parents would just blindly repeat *"pray it away"*.

And nothing I did was ever good enough for them. They would proceed at every turn, convinced that I shouldn't have an anxiety disorder or depression as I was *"too young to feel any stresses of life"* and telling each other it was *"all in my head"*.

Like I could turn off or control those parts of my brain, even when I wanted to.

♦♦♦♦♦

I felt so much resentment towards my parents and the congregation and the preacher that it manifested itself into a boiling rage. When I was living in my old home, my heart would be chronically filled with hatred, even as I was told I should love those who were just like me.

I hated the church members so severely that I sometimes wished I could do something so they wouldn't recover from the wrath I wanted to bestow upon them. That's what led me to the daydream about setting the building on fire with all of them—my parents included—locked inside.

Even knowing it would never actually happen, I wished for it anyway. Because for me, getting that taste of revenge would compensate for all the times they felt it was their right to rule me like I was just another lamb being led to the slaughter.

I mean, who did these bastards think they were? They couldn't live their own lives well, but they felt perfectly comfortable telling *me* what to do? *Fuck* that.

I rubbed my fingers against each other, kneading the bits of hair I had pulled out in a sad attempt to soothe myself before I spiraled further out of control. And I fully recognized that my anger never dissipated...it's just been hidden beneath the surface for so long that I'd gotten used to it.

♦♦♦♦♦

Then came that fateful evening when I couldn't stand them or their hypocritical bullshit anymore. The spiritual prison they were imposing on me was smothering me, and I knew the time had come to go live my own life. I *had* to leave...to go anywhere that wasn't this ridiculously small town of Escalon that I'd known as home for so long. Escalon. I guess that means "Jail" in some language. It certainly applied to my existence there.

Actually, I looked it up once and learned that escalon is a Spanish word meaning "step." Well, these people felt they could step all over me, so yeah...I guess that tracks.

Either way, it was time to get out of there. Only I had no idea where I was going, and I didn't really have much of a plan for my escape. I just grabbed my backpack with a few food items and clothes and headed for the bus depot to get onto the first bus heading out of town. I didn't know where I was going, nor did I care very much. I just wanted to be gone.

Thinking back these ten years later, I realize it was pretty foolish for a 14-year-old girl to go out into the world without a plan...but I just couldn't stay there anymore. *Something* had to change!

That's how I met Aeron Inochi. He approached me at the San Diego bus station, offering me a safe place to sleep and food for my empty stomach. And his offer to rescue me was just what I needed to hear; especially since it included refuge from the horrors of my old life.

♦♦♦♦♦

Aeron saw how well spoken I was and looked past my moth-eaten clothes and the mud-caked sneakers on my feet. He saw what I could provide to him, even as a young teen. I still remember his words that had given me new hope: *"you have potential."*

He chatted breezily with me as we drove the 40 miles from the bus station to what was to become my new home—a complex tucked into the scrub grass in Ramona, California. Along the way I saw the usual landmarks—Walmart, Target, Starbucks—and watched as we exited State Route 67, traveled a block or two on Julian Road, then turned off the main artery onto Magnolia Avenue.

About two miles up Magnolia he made a right onto a street without a signpost, driving down a few blocks that dead-ended at a 3-acre site he simply called "*the complex.*"

This had been a ranch originally, focused on raising cattle and horses, though Sully Knight—the actor who bought it and then "gifted" it to Aeron—saw it as more of a refuge from the world and a place to go off the grid. So he turned it into a farm, investing in solar and wind generation and bringing on the young Aeron Sochi as his assistant.

Sully would disappear for weeks at a time on one location shoot or another, helping to create such cult classics as, "The Incredibly Bad Girls From The Planet Before Time," "Bela; The Man From Lugosi," and other similar films that were messy, cheaply made, and would regularly vie for the title of "The worst film ever made." While Sully traveled, Aeron was in charge of everything; property, crops, finances...the works.

Knowing Aeron as I do now, it didn't really surprise me to recently learn that he had been writing himself two paychecks every week at the time, siphoning off an extra $500 here and a thousand there. And those little bits of petty cash that vanished into his pocket were never missed either.

And by the time Sully figured out that something wasn't adding up, he'd already written Aeron into the will for the property. Then he disappeared shortly thereafter and...well, Aeron just told everyone that Sully had convinced one of the major studios to let him direct the next film and that he'd be gone for a year or two on a secret project.

♦♦♦♦♦

Of course Sully never did come back from that project, and Aeron's story of him traveling the world and living off the royalties of his movies all made sense to anyone who inquired. Which was about when he started bringing on associates to help with the farm and the cooking and the cleaning.

Nobody ever seemed to notice that almost all the staff at the complex were under 25 years old. Like he'd done with me, Aeron would meet teenagers escaping from an untenable situation and were now in need of a place to crash or a hot meal or a friend. He would always be generous, unstintingly giving compliments and gifts, seeking connection with these strangers, and somehow demonstrating a complete understanding of who they were deep inside.

His feel for the potential in almost every newcomer was amazing. As they became part of our family, each new addition would try their hand at each task the complex needed handled, while key roles like administration, legal, and financial matters were only handled by long-time, trusted associates.

Which is why I'm still humbled to be associated with Aeron a decade later as I've moved up the chain of command within the organization. For today I am the mouthpiece of the Purity Syndicate—our official name—using a power that was gifted to me and encouraged by our leader. He and I work together closely; him the brains of this life-changing organization and me the voice of it, sharing our story with the public.

Together, we provided a beacon of hope for the world. And I know I've been a help to the cause, possessing great power through speech and determined to get through to those who need our help the most.

That's why I love this way of life—controlling my days and everything I do—and have long felt that it's better to help those in need. After all those years feeling like I was totally out of control and fighting those who were intent on telling me what to do and when to do it, I'm grateful to Aeron for giving me back my own existence. And I'm only too happy to help those who are still desperately lacking the happiness and satisfaction they need.

♦♦♦♦♦

I knew that I was a better person than my parents ever would be. Ten years after I ran away, I've discovered I barely think of them anymore.

Actually, I doubt they even thought of looking for me. After all, my disappearance had to have made their own existence SO much easier, eliminating the stress that my natural rebelliousness was bringing on.

And the Purity Syndicate, while not a perfect solution to my life's questions, provided an environment that was so much more understanding and empathetic than my parents and their church had ever been. Here at the Syndicate, I'd spent years surrounded by people who loved me for who I am, accepting me and teaching me about the larger world around us. That's how I've learned of Aeron's wisdom, and have experienced the joy of him as my teacher, my leader, and—when I'm very fortunate—my lover.

I guess what it all comes down to is this is now my home, and I'm planning to keep it that way. All that matters to me is Aeron; his vision for a better world, and how I can be an important part of turning his ideas into a larger reality. I know now that all I can do is try to understand my thoughts, feelings, myself, and how I fit in for the good of this organization...and for the world. I work hard every day to prevent past parental influences from polluting my current life's mission.

And y'know...it's funny, but I rarely even question Aeron and his instructions. In fact, I know I shouldn't even question Aeron and his word. He's family to me, and these people of the Purity Syndicate are my community. They're the people who, without question, took me in after I ran from the stench in which I was raised in search of a new life.

It's not like I'm less of a person than any of them, right?

♦♦♦♦♦

I just glanced in the mirror, curious about how my auburn hair appeared today. How do I look? Is my complexion behaving itself? How much concealer and blue eyeshadow do I need for my face?

Nothing else matters to me at the moment except making sure I'm ready for this important day. For a moment I debated making my hair blonde, making a mental note to ask Aaron what he thinks.

I guess that shouldn't matter so much. I am brave and creative with my looks and my tactics on my own. At least that's what Aeron told me. Ever since he let me start sleeping with him, he's been telling me that I am one of his special ones...and it makes my head swim when he tells me that I'm his favorite. He makes me want to do anything and everything for him, and I recognize how much empathy and understanding he has for me.

Still, if I'm going to communicate on his behalf, I should probably know what he's doing. That'll help me understand what I'm doing, and to keep the Syndicate's messaging on track.

Yup, he took me in when I needed it most. I owe him my life. I will do anything for that man—all he has to do is ask.

♦♦♦♦♦

I got all clammy inside the first time Aeron said I was one of his favorites. Living in his home—in his bedroom with him for the first few months as if we were husband and wife—instantly made life so much more warm and inviting than anything else I'd ever known. And he made sure I was homeschooled, given a shoulder to cry on, warm food and a bed in exchange for doing him any favors he asked for. I was taught to do whatever Aeron told me, without question or hesitation.

And if I ever forgot, I knew that the punishment he meted out was both justified and deserved. I needed to be periodically reminded that he was in charge. Which is why, when he called me worthless at a dinner in front of the entire group and sent me off before I'd had a chance to eat, I understood it was for my own good. And that time when I questioned something he'd said and he had me locked in my room for a week with a bucket to pee in—and nothing to eat and barely anything to drink—I never wondered about anything beyond what the hell was the matter with me for challenging him. "*You should know better!*" I reminded myself.

It's a teenager thing, I guess. But once I learned my proper place in his life, Aeron stopped withholding his affections from me. Indeed, everyone in the community became nicer to me after that. And life became better, all the time.

♦♦♦♦♦

One lesson I learned is to always keep smiling, embracing life every day with a smile. Another was to keep on with every task he asked me to do, especially when it came to speaking with the public. I used to be shy before, but over time I became more confident—even qualified—to be the main mouthpiece of this organization.

Which, I guess, prompts the question: why am I so unnerved by Aeron's recent plan? Knowing it's imminent, and will come into action soon, is raising all kinds of question marks over my head.

Is it really such a bad thing to be sacrificing cities so that the rest of humanity will come to us in need? I mean, we'd be shining a spotlight on society's problems by causing chaos and destruction, but that's okay...isn't it?

I must not question what Aeron tells me. He knows what he's doing, right? If he says this is the way, I must believe him.

It's like he said: old drab places would be going out with a bang, but that was necessary for others to come in with a flourish.

Still, something feels "off" about this operation. I've so wanted to ask him about it, but know in advance that the other members will scold me harshly if I ever did. I'm not sure I can take that happening again.

Then again, Aeron tells me I'm his favorite girl in the community, so maybe it's okay to at least ask for a few more details...to question him gently. I'm his pride and joy, after all. I know how much he loves to run his fingers through my hair and hold me close; close enough to feel his heart beat. I don't even mind when he holds me and touches me, stroking my thigh and distracting me like he did that one night while I was writing a speech.

Which reminds me. I need to gather all the papers for the script after the coming chaos blows over. I've made sure that each page was in a logical timeline order.

And I must remember, again, what I learned as the public speaker of this organization. Smile brightly, speak clearly, and keep the positive, hopeful tone in my voice. And state all of the benefits of this organization and what we stand for.

My members have stories similar to the one I had. Destiny came from a broken home where her mom drank and smoked dope all the time, tearing her family apart. Jason had an abusive father and felt trapped most of his life, before escaping on his 12th birthday to live with Aeron, growing into a strapping young man, and becoming the head of security for the Purity Syndicate.

Then there's Brady, who was an orphan living on the streets in a life right out of Oliver Twist. Beatrice and her mother were left broke and abandoned by her father who, in the stereotypical, "I'm going out for a pack of cigarettes" scenario, was never seen again. Mune was a runaway like I was, except he was running from the home he shared with his "funny" uncle, who wanted to touch him in places Mune didn't understand and wasn't comfortable with.

And Jasmine? Well, she recently got over the heroin addiction that had plagued her most of her young life. These, and countless other stories, were told within our small box we called our safe haven. We all recognized that so many of us were alone, taken from unstable families, or are simply orphans that left our foster homes once we hit 18.

We even have had a few new members who joined the community with their parents, siblings, or other family tagging along to see what we're really all about. But that usually doesn't last too long, since after a week the parents are never seen again...almost as if they have abandoned their children and are just hoping it'll all work out for the best.

It's sadly a bit too common for new members who are joining us. However, I take comfort knowing that these abandoned souls, as Aeron calls them, are in good hands with the tutelage and family environment he, I, and the others can provide.

After all, Aeron has helped us so much for many, many years, and none of us could ever forget his countless kindnesses and the sense of belonging he was responsible for bringing into our lives.

♦♦♦♦♦

The Syndicate's rules were neither complicated nor strict. We're allowed to go and explore the world, but only if we spread the good news. And on those days when we're not feeling all smiles and satisfaction? We're to stay behind closed doors—preferably in our rooms, alone so we don't pollute anyone else's positive vibes—until we're over it. And yes, I've had more than a few days like that.

Despite any sad moments, though, overall this safe haven of mine has been a comfort. We get to do many crafts and activities that are calming and fun. Feeding the geese before harvesting their eggs for breakfast; planting and watering flowers; sewing embroidery and making dolls...all simple tasks that are helpful and peaceful for the human mind.

Yup, there's no such thing as stress here. Occasional disorientation, perhaps, but no stress. And certainly no unhappiness.

But here's the thing: I recently started to notice something odd, that I couldn't quite put a finger on or explain.

Was it the new set of rules being put into place by Aeron? Or was it the recent plan he had been brewing for some time. While it could be helpful for our cause and the lives of many other people, something about it just doesn't sit right with me.

Again, I must regularly remind myself that it's probably nothing...just my thoughts of anxiety probing my brain again.

All my life I've been told I think too much...overthinking to the point where I dissociate. That's *got* to be what's happening here, and these questions will go away soon enough.

It will be for the best for not only our organization, but for society as we know it. I'm looking forward to it, and know it will all be for the betterment of mankind.

Chapter 4 - Poetry and Similarities

-Sofia-

"Hi, Sofia!" a familiar male voice was calling to me.

Oh no—it's Damian. That's just fine and dandy.

Reluctantly, I sipped more of my steamed milk and double-spiced chai tea and resigned myself to getting this conversation over with as quickly—and as painlesslessly—as possible. This guy was the *last* person I felt like dealing with—now, or anytime.

The fact is I'm really not in the mood right now to have some pesky guy wanting my attention with the far-fetched intentions of wanting to date me. It feels as if he's been hanging around me just to get something out of me. And, to put it simply, I'm not interested in him or anything he has to offer.

Damian is...how can I put it politely? Well, he's an interesting character. Every Tuesday and Thursday—at 1pm *SHARP*—we share the same chemistry class at our local community college in El Cajon. It's summer school, so the classes are relatively small, ensuring us personalized attention. Only he's always trying to sit next to me, forcing me to constantly move around the room trying to avoid him. Lately I've begun showing up a couple of minutes late so I can scope out where he's sitting...and then pick a seat as far away from him as possible.

Yeah, I know, it's not subtle. But it *can* be effective.

All of this would be bad enough, but then I learned he works at the same place—with the same job I've got—and on the same schedule. So now he wants to travel together sometimes or study together.

Like I need this? PLEASE!

♦♦♦♦♦

Damian's got to be the most talkative person I've ever met. He's the blabbermouth in our group, often asserting his intellectual prowess with his vast knowledge of horror film trivia, science, and chemical bonds of the element table. He completely lacks any social graces or concepts of personal boundaries, constantly stepping too close to anyone when he's speaking at them. Even when his "audience" steps back a foot or two, this guy is so oblivious that he takes that as an invitation to step forward a foot or two so he's right up in their face again.

It's both annoying and obnoxious. I've seen this kind of behavior many times before and understand it all too well, but that doesn't mean I have to put up with it. It reminds me of the time some guy in middle school talked my ear off about his interests, which I neither knew nor cared about. And once he saw I politely stuck around to "listen" —even though I was ignoring him and struggling to not hear a word—, he would try to corner me in nearly every PE class to talk about the latest playable card games he plays while he smelled like morning breath and bad hygiene.

Worse yet, my teachers allowed it, explaining he was lonely and *"just like you."* Like I cared that he was lonely—when did his social life become my problem? When is *anyone's* problem my problem?

Besides, I don't get what they were trying to say, other than that I have special interests too. And I guess that would be fine if he ever asked me about stuff that I like. Then again, even if he did show any interest in me, I sure as hell wouldn't be talking to him about it nonstop.

Where I come from we call that being respectful.

And while I'm trying to be polite with Damian, he just doesn't take the hint. I'm not even sure why I even let him talk to me. Why can't I say no? Why is it so hard for me to assert my boundaries with anyone?

♦♦♦♦♦

Sighing, I turned to face the inevitable. Seeing him coming towards me, I greeted him with as bored and blunt a tone in my voice as I could manage. “Hey Damian.”

“How've you been?” I heard him ask. He's always wondering what I am doing; so much so that it feels like he’s prying. I mean, what does he want to know from me? Details about my life? How I’m doing at school? We are literally going to the same chemistry class together, for God’s sake! Now it’s at a point where I don’t even have to see him to feel his very aura invading my space.

“All right,” I nodded, eyeing something balled up in his hand. I decided to throw him a few crumbs of conversation. “Just studying.” Admittedly, it wasn’t much of a conversation...but at least it was something. I’m definitely not going to sugarcoat anything like my parents would, talking in a cheery attitude that looks sweet enough to give someone a cavity.

He really is clueless about how I feel.

The thing is I’m just not a very conversational kind of person, and I see absolutely zero reason to adjust who I am for someone I care nothing about. Only he had me cornered, and I saw no real way out of feigning interest in his responses. Even though I just wanted to be alone this morning, sipping my warm cup of chai tea and feeling the cool sea air from the ocean. But it felt like I really couldn’t worm my way out of this.

Of course that part I said about just studying wasn’t entirely true. I mean, I look at the past week and I’ve been doing more writing than studying. Increasingly there have been nights where I’ve been finding myself staying up until way past midnight, writing until my brain gets numb and I’m finally forced to close my eyes and settle into some level of unconsciousness.

“Nice,” he replied before displaying to me whatever he was concealing in his grip. Feeling the leather of my own book under my fingers, I bit the inside of my cheek and tried to think of something else to say to him.

I had nothing.

♦♦♦♦♦

I looked at his journal, covered with fading stickers that he kept picking at nervously. It looked more rundown and used than mine, suggesting he'd had it for years and actively used it on a regular basis.

Huh! I guess he wasn't kidding when he said he's also a writer. "I've been studying too," he offered, adding "but I've been writing and thought since you like to write, maybe you can give me some suggestions on how I might be able to improve my work."

I raised an eyebrow, "Suggestions?"

"Yeah, since you're a much better writer than I am, maybe you could provide some criticism to help me improve?" Damian offered me a soft smile that confused me. How am I supposed to be disdainful towards his presence if he's being respectful and asking for my advice?

"I guess..." I said slowly, berating myself internally for saying that. Even before the words were out of my mouth, I recognized that now he's never going to leave me alone until I read whatever he's thrown together.

In truth, a part of me really didn't want to continue this conversation, even as I was simultaneously intrigued. So I slowly agreed to read whatever crap he had scratched into this ominous journal he carried. Reluctantly, I allowed my morbid curiosity to take control, fervently hoping I wasn't going to be looking at a love letter.

"Great, give me a sec." He skimmed the pages of his book before handing it over. Wincing, I hesitantly took it and eyed the small paragraph before me. Reading the passage, I cocked an eyebrow in Damian's direction.

"The Egyptian carvings are an example of a low-relief sculpture." I read aloud, trying to keep my voice steady despite the nervousness of the moment.

"Oh, uh..." he stammered, then laughed involuntarily. "No, not that one; it's a few pages down."

Irritated, I sighed and flipped through the scribbled pages until I found the text in question. It was a passage about a boat ride through bromine-tainted water; a concept that didn't quite click for me. Sure, I knew bromine is a chemical, but chemistry and I just don't get along really well.

I was instantly bored. Yet despite my lack of interest in his theme, I couldn't help but be impressed by his eloquence and choice of wording. A pang of jealousy stirred within me, wishing on some levels I could write like he does. Even his grammar was impeccable. And his handwriting looked like calligraphy, all fancy and impressive.

Jeez!

Stubbornly, I refused to give him the satisfaction of a positive review. "Nice," I stated simply, noticing his smile faltering at my economy of words.

"Is it okay?" he asked. "It's only my first draft."

"Yeah, that's pretty obvious," I said cattily, trying to not let my envy get the best of me. I took a breath, struggling to sound pleasant. "Other than lacking context, I think it's nice."

Beaming, Damian nodded. "That makes sense. This was from a dream that I had last week, so I guess I had a hard time trying to add context. My dreams slip away so quickly when I wake up, and remembering them sometimes seems impossible."

I resisted rolling my eyes. How can this guy be so happy all the time? His life must be better than mine is.

♦♦♦♦♦

Why the hell does Damian stick around with me, anyway? There must be other people he can hang out with. Am I that fascinating? And, for that matter, why do I let him stick around?

He nervously shuffled a bit, obviously wanting to ask me something. I watched his expression carefully, trying to anticipate where he was going next. "So, other than being *'nice,'* are there any other things you like about it?"

I hummed a monotonous tune, struggling to find something positive about his abbreviated work, "I like how you described the water and the atmosphere. But that's all I can say about it."

"So ah..." I heard Damian asking quietly, "I was thinking, but if you want, maybe we can..."

There it was. Shit! He was about to ask something that would place him squarely in my personal space, and all I wanted to do was to run away screaming. I hated that I'd been put on the spot, feeling like I had no other choice but to stay involved in the conversation.

I really didn't want him to say *ANYTHING* about wanting to hang out or go on a date! The last thing I wanted right now was to socialize with anyone. I'll see them in school or at my job, but I'm just not feeling like being sociable these days.

And add to that my mother always warning me about never being around guys when I'm alone. "They only want one thing," she'd tell me ominously. So that's all I wanted; to be alone!

♦♦♦♦♦

It wasn't just guys who I felt invading my space, either, but anyone. Sometimes I just wanted to scream "*LEAVE ME ALONE*!" to whoever was standing in front of me. Boys, in particular, can cause problems because their intentions are...well...usually less than honorable.

I live in fear much of the time, having heard so many stories from my mother about her family members touching kids inappropriately. "I hate them, but need to invite them to family gatherings because they're family," she says, shaking her head sadly before noting "They should be arrested for what they've tried to do."

These are the same family members who look at me in a weird way. Yet when I've said something to my mother about it, she's gaslighted me to say 'they're family' or 'that means they like you' or some such bullshit like that.

No wonder I like neither family gatherings nor the idea of going out on dates with boys! Besides, I'm not the romantic type, let alone being interested in any kind of sexual relationship. I'm not sure why people just don't get that, but when it comes to guys or girls, I'm just *not* interested.

So the question remains: why is Damian always hanging around me?

My train of thought got interrupted as I noticed he'd stepped away a bit. Was it possible he'd gotten the hint that he makes me feel uncomfortable when he's too close to me?

No such luck! His sentence had been cut off by our manager calling us. And for the first time ever, I was grateful that there was work to do. Her interruption has prevented Damian from going further down this unwelcome path.

♦♦♦♦♦

It was time to get our supplies to start the beach cleanup for this part of the boardwalk. I headed for the truck to collect supplies for the next hour's cleaning session.

For the past few hours I'd been cleaning around Belmont Park and across the busy road running beside it. I'd focused on picking up litter from the black asphalt streets and beach sand, certain it would distract me from less pleasant things that usually weigh on my mind.

And I couldn't help but notice how dirty the concrete was, with dried gum and stickers that were stuck on there for who knows how long. My guess was they'd been there for years; maybe decades. Still, it's better to address these black blobs becoming the modern world's urban fossils as an excellent way to keep my mind off of what Damian was just about to say to me earlier.

Yup, it's probably for the best—for me, anyway. All I want to do right now is to just do my job and make enough money to get a new journal and possibly save enough to live on my own one day.

♦♦♦♦♦

There are many people who just don't understand me and my desire to be alone today. Even if the things I've gathered using my trash picker are completely vile, I just want time with them...and nothing or nobody else.

Because at moments like this I find myself happiest when surrounded by crushed beer cans, plastic water bottles, used tissues, aluminum soda can tabs, and even discarded piss-stained unicorn panties left by the dumpster.

I know; it's both filthy and disgusting, the strange things the people of this city leave abandoned on the streets. It's as if they feel they own the local parks and beaches, and can just leave the detritus of their lives laying about, making the streets their own personal trash cans.

You'd think people would keep their word about cleaning the cities and saving the world from pollution. Yet they don't always practice what they preach, preferring that we 'trash pickers' deal with it instead. Sure, it's gross, but to me it's a pretty important job; more important than the public realizes it is. Kind of like being a doctor or a plumber.

Those guys don't want my job, but I wouldn't want to work their jobs, either.

Besides, how am I supposed to write and become a great author if there isn't a clean world left? It's like these idiots are bent on destroying themselves. And overpopulation isn't an acceptableexcuse...at least if you're not homeless.

♦♦♦♦♦

After discarding a whole bag of awfulness into the dumpster, I removed one of my vinyl gloves to grab my phone and check the time. Finally! One of the best times of the day - a 30-minute break to just relax and resume my writing as I eat lunch - was quickly approaching.

I grasped my grabber tool and again filled the trash bag, heading towards that awful smelling dumpster while struggling to avoid the underwear stench drifting downwind towards me. I started making up backstories of the "classy" people who live in America's *'finest'* city and leave junk like that for me to pick up for them.

The stories weren't pretty!

And I don't care if I get paid for doing that kind of thorough cleaning of the urban streets; I refuse to pick up some of the biohazardous waste these dumbshits leave behind. Period! 'Cause dealing with shit like that just makes me puke.

So I walked away from that awfulness to avoid the smell before I lost my appetite by being near it.

♦♦♦♦♦

I headed back to the group, first detouring to the bathroom to quickly wash my hands. Once finished, I grabbed a lunch bag that my manager provided, then parked myself on the concrete ledge.

This afforded me a beautiful view of the beach, the sky filled with melodies of the crashing waves below and the seagulls above.

Hey, this job's gotta have *some* perks to it!

I slowly chewed my sandwich; peanut butter and grape jam as always. My mind was filled with a melody spontaneously composed from the sounds surrounding me that was simultaneously overwhelming, yet sentimental.

There were a few moments of peace as I enjoyed my lunch and the attendant view. It was one of those amazingly rare occasions where I just felt serene, halfway between the boardwalk and the ocean. I looked past the sand and sea, admiring the bluish hue of the afternoon sky.

Yeah, when I'm in this frame of mind, I don't care about the people laying on the beach or about watching their kids play on the shore. I barely even hear the joggers and bikers passing by. All that matters at the moment is feeling the very warm, welcoming beams of light from the sun shining above me. It envelops me with love, happiness and comfort. It just feels nice.

No, it's more than nice. It makes me feel grounded in the present moment, like I'm drifting in an actual moment of tranquility, allowing my eyes and mind to wander while enjoying a meal.

♦♦♦♦♦

"Sofia?"

Goddammit! My serenity was disrupted as I turned to again see Damian standing right next to me. Why must he do that? What must he have that's so damned important he had to interrupt my personal quiet time at the very moment I'm finally enjoying the day?

At first I stared at the ocean, refusing to look at Damian. Out of the corner of my eye I saw him standing there like a curious puppy. Was there still a question stewing in his mind?

Finally I gave up on this stand-off, recognizing I had to speak again...or at least it felt like I had no other choice. I swallowed the bite I'd been savoring in my mouth before I spoke. "Yeah? What is it?"

I studied his expression, noting how concerned he looked. Crap! Now what's happened? What IS his problem? He glanced left and right before timidly asking, "Is it okay if I sit next to you?"

I raised an eyebrow at the question. Why is he asking me this? He never asked me if it's okay to be near me whenever he's around me, so this new behavior was rather odd.

I'd concluded that Damian's a social golden retriever compared to me and my anti-social ways. Except he's more of a golden retriever that wants too much attention, and comes off being practically touch-starved.

I opened my mouth to respond as he added, "I mean, it's fine if you don't want me to."

I gave him a puzzled expression, feeling confused, awkward, and annoyed all at once, "No, it's...it's fine." Yeah, this was definitely something he would never do. Why is he asking me so hesitantly? Why is he confusing me, even as I'm intrigued. I mean, I simultaneously want him to leave *and* to hear him out.

FUCK!

"It's fine if you want to," I lied. In truth, I wanted to be by myself. Inside my head I was screaming "Are you such a fucking moron that you don't understand this?", even as he refused to hear me.

Of course he wouldn't take the hint; I was too busy being polite, telling him it was okay to sit with me. It wasn't okay, only now I'd committed myself. What the hell is the matter with me? Why do I do this to myself?

"Are you sure?" he asked. "I can sit somewhere else if you'd rather."

"No, it's okay," I said with a deep sigh. I guess I'm not very good at hiding these things from others.

So in my head I'm blunt, but my outside acquiesces, stupidly saying *"Yes,"* even as my mind is screaming at me to say *"NO!"*

Yeah, I've got to do something about that!

♦♦♦♦♦

I can't stand it! Why do I always give in? Even more importantly, why is he so concerned about me all of a sudden? Was it my blunt answer? My body language? My very presence? He's not very direct, though it would've been so much more helpful if he just said what he wanted, rather than these vague conversations. Like c'mon, man!

Damian sat down, just a few inches away from me. He briefly glanced at the ocean before shifting his gaze to the ground before us. He looked nervous, sitting next to me as I watched him cradling an apple in his hand like it was a priceless gem.

Only he was WAY too close! Those couple of inches between us definitely felt like an invasion of my personal space, and I found myself wondering what is with this guy.

He cleared his throat. "So, uh, how's lunch?"

Now, if you're looking to get a girl's attention, this is probably the most mundane, hackneyed cliché you can ask, and ranks right up there with, *"How is the weather today?"* I mean...*"How's lunch?"* What kind of a ridiculous question is that? I don't understand! Why is he like this? Why am *I* like this?

"Fine," I nodded, shrugging. "Peanut butter and jam again," I responded with a dull, blunt answer...as if he was too stupid to understand. Yet even this bit of conversation made me uncomfortable. Not just because he had intruded into my space, but also we were having the most bland conversation imaginable. *YEESH!*

♦♦♦♦♦

We stayed silent for a few seconds. God, why does this have to be so awkward? I just wanted to eat my PB&J, because it's probably the only food my stomach can tolerate on a day like this. Anyway, it's certainly much better than eating mayonnaise sandwiches all the time like some people I know.

Yet just having Damian nearby struggling to talk to me made me cringe to my core.

I usually get more lunches from my manager than I bring from home, mainly because my parents are much pickier about what I eat than I am. Of course, my mother and father typically choose foods that I despise—stuff that tastes awful and has a genuinely icky texture. So can anyone really blame me for finding peanut butter and jelly the superior choice?

But that's not the point: what is this conversation? And why are we having it?

"Nice," Damian said softly.

And that's when I noticed he wasn't as loud as usual. Once again I was simultaneously confused and panicked, wondering whether he finally got the hint that I don't want him around. Did he waltz over to my secluded spot to apologize, then to be on his way?

Yeah, right. I should be so lucky!

♦♦♦♦♦

"So how's your writing going?" I heard him ask. "Any stories coming along."

An odd question, but okay? What is he asking me here? What is the context? What does he want from me?

Oh...right! That was a tactical error on my part. I told him about my book earlier when we were sitting in chemistry class, and he's been following me around like a curious puppy ever since asking for updates and status reports. It's like he always wants to know what's going on in my life. I mean, what's so important about that? It's not like I'm that interesting a person, after all.

Other than my writing, of course. But what is really important about me? What does he see in me? I'm just a simple dreamer, after all, and not much more than that. I just want what other people have, and dream of having a successful career that makes me feel like I'm worth something more.

I want to not be afraid; to not be held back. To not be limited....I need something to define me. To confirm that my existence means something more than just being a simple girl who writes and is little more than a forgotten cog.

What does Damian even see in me? What makes *me* interested in him? Does he want to hang around me so much because he has a crush, or because he's that interested in my work?

Maybe he's just lonely too. Could both be true? Or even all three?

♦♦♦♦♦

"It's all right, just some passages I've written; a few poems here and there," I responded dully. "Why do you ask?"

I'm still wondering where he's going here? Why is he nervous with me all of the sudden? Is it something he wants to do with me? As those questions ran through my mind, Damian said something that finally caught my interest.

"Just curious," he shrugged, adding "Did you know there's a program at the La Mesa Library that's hosted by a local writing club? Maybe we could meet up with each other there sometime."

I blinked as he mentioned the writing club in La Mesa, glossing right over the part about hanging out together. Since when was there a local writing club? Have I been so busy journaling that I didn't even see the flyers announcing this new resource? How could this be? Could this be what I've been looking for to finally achieve my breakthrough?

Yes, I know that sounds cliché, unrealistic and a bit over the top, but maybe this could be it; my way to finally leave this mundane life behind and creating some freedom for myself. Perhaps I'm on the verge of finding that special something that can define me and my career, making me more than just a girl who's alone writing in her journal all day!

"Writing club?"

He nodded enthusiastically. "Yeah. It will actually be starting in September, if you want to check it out. We can even grab a coffee or something and we could..."

I rushed in. "Is there a contest or something?"

I didn't really mean to cut him off, but I was so excited and curious that I really needed to know this information quickly, and I didn't have time for the non-essential stuff. All I wanted was every detail; every timeframe. Hell, anything that could point me in the right direction could be helpful.

"Ah...I think so? Something about writing the best horror experience or stories like that, but that's not until October, I think. I guess they're trying to time it for Halloween."

I blinked: *NOW* he tells me this? Now he tells me about this opportunity? Why hasn't this dummy spoken up before? I gripped my sandwich hard as ideas flooded my mind. At last: a real chance to escape this hell of a dreary existence to finally become the person I wanted to become!

"And like I said, we could always go out to the café or something. I just need transportation to..."

THAT'S PERFECT! I thought to myself. The perfect time. I just hoped my parents wouldn't notice that I'd disappeared when I walked over there.

"It's a date, then!" I responded suddenly.

It wasn't my intention to respond so enthusiastically, but the topic had gotten me very excited. It was as if my dreams were suddenly materializing in front of me, and Damian was my ticket out of an otherwise dead-end life.

♦♦♦♦♦

Looking at me as if I'd suddenly grown three heads, Damian's eyebrows shot up in a combination of pleasure, thrill and surprise. "Wait...Really?"

He looked stunned that I'd given him the answer he'd dreamed of for so long. A 'yes' to his offer was a fantasy come true, even as he remained blissfully unaware—or willfully ignorant—of the real reason why I would be coming with him.

It certainly wasn't going to be a *'playdate'*, if that was what he envisioned.

I nodded curtly. "Yes, I want to go. I think after fall semester starts on September 1st, okay?"

I supposed that would be the best time for me to go. At least my parents would think I was going to study rather than doing something else. Because heaven forbid I would go anywhere other than to study! I mean I'm in my twenties, for Chrissake! Why should I need to have a curfew?

♦♦♦♦♦

Damian was stunned into momentary silence—a reaction I greatly enjoy. "I..." he swallowed hard, his eyes never leaving me for fear I might be an apparition brought on by too much time in the sun.

Finally he nodded, and I realized he probably had expected me to say no. Given that I typically treat him like an annoying kid brother, I guess his reaction wasn't really too surprising. "Yeah, after 4pm sounds fine."

"Good. Since I live nearby, I will walk and meet you there."

I carefully avoided telling him where I was walking from, because the very last thing I would want is for him to know where I live. But the library is only a few buildings away from my home, and I've walked up and down the main drag many times before, so this would be easy.

Meaning I just boxed myself in, leaving me no choice but to meet him there. Still, at least I'll be able to go to this library, rather than having to deal with major transportation issues.

"Yeah, that sounds great!" Damian practically shouted, beaming with delight and nearly dancing away.

♦♦♦♦♦

This was going to be the *furthest* thing possible from a date! Sure, that was the word I had used, but that was merely a technicality. I mean, if anything remotely suggested getting me out of this dump of a town, I was going to grab it and hang on tight.

And this could be just the chance I'd been seeking to get into a better place, physically and mentally. To be someplace where I'd finally be able to express myself properly, become known and escape my home and everything else that had been holding me back.

Yeah, yeah—I know it sounds harsh that I'm using Damian to reach my objective, but it's like that old saying: "Desperate times call for desperate measures." And it's not like we're friends or anything, let alone it being anything more.

EW!

Yup, this is my chance, and I'm gonna grab it regardless of the cost. Even if I have to wait until September; well, that's just around the corner. Like the change from summer to autumn, this will symbolize my transition to the next step of my life...and my escape.

♦♦♦♦♦

“Hey Sofia?” Damian said softly, interrupting my train of thought. “I think Mrs. Mullens said lunch is almost over. Are you going to finish?”

Why does he bother showing concern? This isn’t going anywhere.

I looked at my sandwich before wrapping it up in the crumbled paper, placing it in my bag, and zipping it up. “No. I’ll just finish this later; I’m not that hungry anymore.” I stood up, brushed the crumbs off my lap, and prepared for my next big adventure.

“Well, I’m glad to know you’ll be coming with me, Sofia. I'm very excited, and really appreciate it,” he beamed. Is this goth-looking goober for real? Is he that dense and typical?

Even this conversation bored me. “Yeah, yeah. Of course,” I said, trying to appear nonchalant. His gratitude was *way* over the top, making me wonder if he was really that desperate. He’s obviously lonely, but that’s his problem, and I won’t let it become my problem.

Yup, all that matters is my ability to take advantage of this chance to improve my life. I’m finally going to use my talent to build a better life. And about time, too!

Until then, though, Damian and I need to head back to our respective piles of belongings, sitting next to tools waiting for us to clean up the beach litter.

♦♦♦♦♦

This *had* to be the leftovers from a frat party. That’s gotta be where the piss-stained unicorn panties also came from. It took us the next hour to clean up everything these slobs left behind, and through it all I couldn’t help but notice Damian sticking close to me. Worse yet, he had a sickly smile plastered on his face, as if this was the best day anyone had ever had.

What is it with this grinning idiot? I mean, it’s just a get-together at a club with a contest where I’ll finally be able to submit my work. It’s a chance for me to become noticed and well known...but nothing more.

Okay, it’s a real chance for me to be taken seriously as an independent adult, rather than as a 25-year-old autistic doormat.

Meaning I won't allow *anything* to stand in the way of this plan - this transition in my life that I'm certain will come off with a bang.

"Sofia?" I turned towards Mrs. Mullens, who wore a rather worried look on her face, the bright screen of her phone just inches from her right ear.

I felt unnerved, though I couldn't say why. "Yes?"

She handed me the phone. "It's your mother. Something has happened to your home..."

Chapter 5 - The Town of Nothing

-Juniper-

It was another ordinary day in La Mesa, as cliché as that sounds. But that's what it's always like here whenever my clan and I drive by. Sometimes the local farmer's market would be packed with consumers, other days it would be sparsely populated.

Friday afternoons were probably the busiest days. That was when the farmers' market would take up the two blocks between Palm and Fourth and there was always a big crowd around. And there was also the OktoberFest in the fall, where the games, dancing, beer, and dachshund races would typically attract around 100,000 attendees over its three weekends.

There have even been a few times where I struggled to get past the mob of people to deliver the message of peace our community offers to one and all. Just last Oktoberfest it was a total zoo, with countless cars parked on the curbs and the crowds sloshing into stores, food stands and the main biergarten all at once. And with all this activity, nobody was really interested in hearing what I had to say.

We parked in the parking lot where Mune paid the fee for extended parking. Aeron suggested I stay behind with him, figuring having us all scoping things out at the downtown stores might be overkill.

I watched through the car window, waiting in anticipation. This was going to be one of the greatest favors yet, and our way of giving back to the larger community. It was, as Aeron said, "A blessing." I sat quietly, despite the surge of adrenaline pumping through my system, and watched my fellow devotees exit the car.

What I found curious was that each of them carried a plain white box. They all lacked labels and markings of any kind, leaving it to the imagination what they were and what they contained. Aeron's comment that they would generate a reaction and stir up the interest of the locals temporarily pacified me.

From my perch in the passenger seat I noticed Brady going into a taco restaurant, Mune heading for the mystic shop, Destiny walking further down the street towards the library, and Beatrice wandering into the cremation center.

I thought their choice of locations was odd, though I assumed these were all high-traffic facilities that would be amenable to sharing our message. Personally, I would have opted for the horror-movie themed record place down the street from us, but that's just my style. The mystic shop probably has a community better suited to our objectives.

And I'll confess I was curious to know what use these packages would be put to. Assuming they contained promotional materials, the natural assumption was the local citizenry would be asked to place them throughout their respective buildings.

Waiting. Anticipating. I shifted in my seat, watching Aeron as he observed the road before him. He was silent, patiently expecting who knew what.

♦♦♦♦♦

The air felt heavy, with my guts in turmoil and chaotic visions dancing before my eyes...but for no apparent reason.

"You all right?" Aeron asked. I jumped from my seat at the sound of his voice.

"Yeah, I'm fine," I nodded. Only I wasn't. I had a bad feeling about us sitting there, though I was damned if I knew what was bothering me. "Why are we here?"

“We’re just spreading the word, putting up a few flyers to grab their attention. We’re letting them know that our group provides them with an explosive opportunity to change their lives.”

Aeron sounded like he was struggling to keep a straight face as the words left his mouth.

I nodded, leaning back in the car seat and looking down the pretty street as Aeron muttered, “don’t worry your pretty little head about it.”

♦♦♦♦♦

La Mesa looks like a nice place, even if it is a bit run down. I’d heard recently that they're redeveloping parts of downtown to make the stores more appealing to merchants. “Gentrification,” someone told me the process was called, which to me was just a fancy way of saying they’d be jacking up the rents and bringing in still more high-priced coffee shops. Because seven Starbucks in one community aren’t enough, right?

A murder of 13 crows flew overhead, heading south. I followed their lead and enjoyed the clear summer skies before shifting to consider some of the antique cars trundling down the road and crossing over the railroad tracks, then heading over the hill towards another event. Several of them stopped as the orange trolley rushed to pick up the next queue of people heading downtown from El Cajon. For all these folks it was just another busy day, scurrying from here to there to address details of their lives that they deemed, at this moment, to be so critically important.

I guess the question for so many people has to be whether or not they have their priorities straight. Is it that 9 to 5 job, going home, having dinner, sleeping, and doing it all again tomorrow? To me that vicious cycle would be living death. Family. Relationships. The Purity Syndicate. These were the important things in life!

I mean, without them - without my members or Aeron - well, I’m certain I wouldn’t even be here. I’d never have had a chance to positively impact the planet, and probably would’ve committed suicide or been sent to jail long ago for burning down the churches I grew up in.

And Aeron—well, there was a guy who already had made a huge impact on the world, and was obviously destined to do so much more in the future!

He wants to shake up the world, and some might argue he already has.

♦♦♦♦♦

My gaze shifted, first up the street, then back down. Behind me our members were reconvening and were now arguing about who knew what. I sat patiently and focused on five more crows flying by, wondering what that meant spiritually.

Looking at the dashboard clock, I debated how long it took to hang flyers and hand out packages to help spread the word.

Suddenly they were all running back to the car, everyone in a rush. They simultaneously dove into the van, doors slamming behind them, and Aeron hit the gas before Janet's door was fully closed. He floored the pedal and took off in a cloud of dust, scattering rocks and glass from the street. I swear it felt like gravity instantly tripled in the car, pushing me back deeply into my seat. All that was left behind us were the imprint of our tire treads as we peeled out doing 85.

What the hell...?

♦♦♦♦♦

We sped down La Mesa Boulevard, Aeron hustling east to get out of town and heading straight for Mount Helix before turning southwest and back towards our complex. In his haste, he even came tantalizingly close to sideswiping a silver Honda and a blueberry-colored Toyota, their drivers cursing us and gesturing rudely for the intrusion into their day's peace without even the courtesy of a turn signal.

I'd never driven so fast! What should have been a 15-minute trip to cover the five miles to the Mount Helix parking lot took half that. Tires screeched as we tore in, kicking up clouds of dust, then stopped to catch our breath. And I sat there, wondering why we had been in such a tear-ass hurry to get out of town.

Aeron shifted in his seat, turning to speak to me directly as he patted his pockets in search of something. Pulling pulled out a folded piece of paper, he handed it to me and stated "You're going to want this when you speak to the reporters."

Well, this was unexpected. "Is this a speech?" I asked.

"Kind of. This is the script we keep handy for when there's a crisis," Aeron replied.

Imagine my surprise to learn there was a crisis taking place. Still, I nodded and took the folded paper from his fingers and saw a pre-written paragraph for me to recite.

"The Purity Syndicate is a local non-profit dedicated to providing shelter, food, and support to those most in need. We recognize there is a terrible situation that has just taken place, and wish to offer our condolences, our thoughts, and our help. Anyone seeking support or counsel should contact us at..."

That and a phone number and email address and I'd be done. No questions were to be taken, which was good since I had no additional information to provide.

Of course I'd acted as the Syndicate's Public Information Officer many times before, offering support for people in need during a crisis. Such exposure gives the public a chance to learn about us, accept our help, and perhaps even join our sanctuary. We'd certainly never object to having extra help and having them be part of our growing family.

Only, why was I saying it now?

♦♦♦♦♦

In the distance I swore I heard a loud boom, but saw nothing untoward and chalked it up to jets from Miramar Air Base doing some kind of exercise. "Probably an air show or military training," I told myself, shrugging it off.

Returning to the pre-printed script, I took a pencil from my pocket and tweaked the language to sound a bit more like me. I read it several times, refreshing my memory in case I needed it anytime soon.

Looking up, I noticed a large column of black smoke rising over the mountain, coming from the southwest. Sitting here in a parking lot on the north side of the mountain, it was difficult to determine the source of this smoke. Then again, it seems to always be wildfire season these days—an unintended consequence of global warming.

Contemplating how many area homeowners would be driven out by yet another wildfire, and whether we'd have to evacuate the complex to avoid the trouble, I heard Destiny ask Aeron. "You think we were spotted?"

I didn't understand what they were talking about, and eavesdropping felt rude. Still, wasn't being spotted by the media the point?

Aeron's answer was equally cryptic. "Nah, I doubt they knew we were there."

I'll confess I had no idea what they were talking about, nor did I really care beyond wondering why they were worried about being seen in public. I'd have argued the whole idea of our community is we're supposed to get attention from the larger society.

♦♦♦♦♦

The door slammed suddenly as everyone in the back seat scrambled to get out of the car. Mune was doubled over coughing...and vomiting.

Rolling down the window, I called "Is he okay?" Brady shrugged, watching his roommate's nonstop retching as Aeron continued monitoring his news feed before finally looking up. "He's probably car sick. We'll stop at CVS and get him something to soothe his sour stomach after this is behind us."

He pointed towards the crumpled paper in my hands. "You mean when I read the script?" I asked.

"Not just that," Aeron shook his head, scanning the horizon as the expanding column of black drifted our way and turned the vibrant sky into an ugly gray. "There's something else I want you to do."

"Of course," I nodded "What is it?"

His hand shot to the radio, turning on KOGO 600. "These guys are usually on a story first," he muttered. He tuned in as news anchor Dan Plant read this announcement:

> *"This breaking news just in. A massive explosion ripped through downtown La Mesa - the Jewel of the Hills—shortly before 5pm today, polluting half of the*

neighborhoods near Spring Valley, Mount Helix, and Fletcher Parkway with ash and smoke. "

"The primary commercial strip along La Mesa Boulevard is currently engulfed in flame, with firefighters and emergency equipment already arriving from as far away as Carlsbad and Escondido to put out the fires and help the injured. Ambulances have already taken several hundred victims of the attack to area hospitals."

I froze, stunned into silence. I—we—had been sitting right there just an hour ago. I turned to Aeron, searching for guidance. "Weren't we just there?" Aeron didn't answer as he listened almost a bit too attentively to the radio broadcast.

"The cause of the explosion, or potentially a series of explosions, are being variously attributed to gas leaks, a chemical accident, or a local terrorist attack. Authorities have closed all streets and highways coming into the area, and are strongly recommending local residents to evacuate from La Mesa and surrounding towns."

"So there's been a terrible accident, huh?" Aeron said softly to himself. "I'm guessing these good people are going to need help when the fires are brought under control."

"You think people died?" I asked nervously, pained as I considered the worst possible outcome.

"Well, based on this report it's difficult to say," said our leader, adjusting his burgundy sunglasses over his eyes. "But what I do know is that they will need our help now more than ever."

♦♦♦♦♦

I felt helpless watching the massive clouds of smoke drifting over us. The acrid blanket had expanded exponentially within minutes, making it difficult to see the growing fleet of news helicopters. The water bombers arriving from Miramar Air Station dumped fire retardant on the surrounding lands, hoping to minimize collateral damage.

One helicopter, straying too close, ended up with a windshield of fire retardant and had to land unexpectedly on the northern side of I-8.

Panicking at the desperation unfolding around us, I jumped into maternal mode. “Should we take up a collection and make a donation?” I asked Aeron.

“Sure,” he said, adding “That would be a nice thing to do. But first,” he tapped the crumpled paper in my hand “you have to deliver this message to the press after the fires have been brought under control.”

Even as we absorbed the news of the disaster in nearby La Mesa and the possible need to evacuate our own home, Aeron calmly looked past Mune, still tossing his cookies beside the vehicle. Everyone - with the possible exception of Beatrice - was nervous, but the boss was surprisingly relaxed.

Perhaps he was in shock? Or had he become so numb to the chaos in what was laughingly called society that nothing surprised him anymore.

Still, given that our little community was supposed to be dedicated to helping the larger world, I found his reaction to be more than a little troubling. I wondered if talking through his sadness about the desperate situation in the world might help him feel better. Because, like I’ve always told him, “Two shoulders, no waiting!”

♦♦♦♦♦

We’d been sitting in the parking lot for a while listening to the same story being repeated on the radio when Aeron leaned back, his eyes closed and his hands clasped behind his head. By the look on his face, he could have been relaxing to Beethoven’s Moonlight Sonata.

> *“...local officials at this time can not isolate the cause of the explosion and fires. Even as firefighters struggle to get the fire under control, overwhelmed paramedics report as many as 60 people have died, with the count expected to increase significantly over the next several days.”*

Aeron switched over to KFMB radio, only to hear almost the exact same story. The radio news outlets had become an echo chamber about this tragedy, parroting one another while the emergency team worked on presenting a Public Information Officer to help coordinate data and details.

Silently I prayed that the people over there would make it out safely before saying, to nobody in particular, "So uh...do we go down there now and..."

Aeron shook his head. "No, no. Not yet," he assured me softly, as if noticing my worry for the first time. I felt his hand on my shoulder, with that familiar comforting pat and a squeeze to the back of my neck that he reserves for special moments. "When the fires are put out, we'll be able to offer help that really means something."

I nodded, realizing he was probably right. He almost always is, after all. Going there now would mean risking our own lives, plus we'd be getting in the way. Besides, all the entrances to La Mesa had been closed off, so...

So I hoped the fires wouldn't get any worse and sighed. "Okay. I know you're right."

"Trust me, it'll all be okay," Aeron said to me softly. He rubbed my shoulder in a familiar, comforting manner. It was his touch that I liked so much and had never gotten from my family. It was comfort that I had always needed, been denied by my cold and distant parents, and deeply appreciated now. "I'm sure it's not as gruesome as the news says it is," Aeron continued. "Those guys will take anything and inflate the story to make it worse than it is and get people to listen to them."

Well, I knew he wasn't wrong about that. It's like Paul Simon said in a song once: *"I don't believe what they say in the paper; they're just out to capture my dime."* These guys in the news business would seemingly do *anything* to milk out any tragedy or even scare the crap out of people, just to keep the attention on themselves.

The list goes on endlessly when it comes to milking out the tragedies of celebrities. Stories of children who are missing are countless. And if you think about the way these guys act, none of them have any real empathy, regardless of whatever they may say. Not a reporter alive really gives a damn about you.

I mean, how many times has the internet sparked conspiracy theories? The media - not just one side or the other, mind you, but all of them - they take the news about super volcanoes exploding or meteors passing earth or the latest election and twist it into some existential story about the end of life as we know it. And countless millions of people take the bait, every single fucking time!

Just like people rubbernecking at a roadside accident like it was a carnival show, news of pessimism and horror gets so much more visibility than the more wholesome, optimistic stories in the world.

It's both sad and disgusting, when you think about it.

♦♦♦♦♦

So I leaned back and tried to relax like Aeron. It's really all we could do for now, I guessed...just wait offstage, at least until Mune stopped throwing up. Man, how much can one person vomit? It's like every time he seemed ready to stop, another wave of nausea would overcome him. And through it all, Aeron never blinked...or for that matter, looked.

Once my friend caught his breath, I figured, we could head back to our safe haven to help him out. Sure, I was incredibly worried about La Mesa's casualties, but nothing we did now could help people get out of there safely.

I just hoped reciting the script to the public, telling them how the Purity Syndicate could help with this situation and providing comfort to those most in need would have some value to the larger populace. I wanted them to accept our aid - shelter, food, clothing, and things they'd lost in the fires - and our friendship, and with no strings attached.

It was one small thing that I knew I could do to meet the moment, and I just hoped it would be enough to demonstrate we were the good guys.

Besides, Aaron had access to a wide range of resources - food, water, and money - that could probably last for years if need be. True, none of us really knew where he got them from beyond his clipped response of "donations," but I think it's great that so many people were willing to donate to us so that we could donate to others.

♦♦♦♦♦

I'm really hoping this isn't some accident, like a gas leak from SDGE. Maybe someone accidentally ignited a Shell station by dropping a lit cigarette when they were filling up their car.

Still, the news *did* say there was a possibility of it all being caused by a local terrorist attack, right? Maybe I mis-heard, but that sounded downright creepy. I mean, what kind of people would blow up a town - any town - let alone one as pretty as La Mesa seemed to be. And why would they do it?

Regardless, my job would be simple: since the explosion was now a fact of life, I needed to ensure that people received word about us and our willingness to help them get out safely to begin rebuilding their lives.

The winds continued making the smoke plumes bigger, and the stench of burning wood, plastic, metal, and flesh was enough to make the rest of us want to also hurl. A few speckles of ash flew aimlessly among our crew, gracefully landing on the dry soil and resembling greyish snow in the middle of summer. It was going to be a long afternoon.

Chapter 6 - Sifting Through The Facts

-Juniper-

It was less than an hour since the smoke had begun to clear when I found myself being driven down the only open road leading into downtown La Mesa, and one of the few in the area not sealed off in the wake of the explosion.

As we descended the hill, the full extent of the devastation unfolded before me. Entire blocks were charred, gutted...even skeletal. Seemingly half the city had been scorched down to its bones, and I could see why everyone except first responders was being directed back from the police line. Streets, highways, and services had all been shut down by the overwhelmingly massive damage and, though most of the fires were well on their way to being extinguished, their breath still lingered.

This once thriving community now resembled the carcass of something vast and significant. Buildings were reduced to blackened frames, their ribs jutting into the sky. All signs of vegetation had evaporated into a powdery ash, and not even the weeds had survived.

It was as if the town had exhaled one last time and collapsed in on itself.

Even looking down from the 35-foot cross atop Mt. Helix, I knew the view would be unbearable—just miles of ruin, bleeding into the distance. Saying there was nothing left of downtown La Mesa somehow seemed trite, despite the truth of the statement. The vibrancy of the rundown streets was gone, and the life of this little city near the sea had been extinguished...gone with the fiery winds of the countless explosions that had shaken the community to its very core.

Since the moment I realized what had happened, I was sickened just thinking about it and didn't even want to imagine being in the shoes of those who had just gone through what can politely be called a calamity. Whether it was someone who survived the explosion or the fire fighters and ambulance drivers witnessing the horrific brutality of seeing everything in shambles, I just knew there was no way anyone could come out of this without being negatively impacted.

As we neared the bottom of the hill, I saw scorched earth, blackened swaths of dirt and shattered stone...all that was left of the city's once-lush and vibrant patches of green. Chunks of buildings lay tossed across the hillside like the aftermath of the German blitzkrieg on London.

I wanted to cry. Or vomit. Or both. But I did neither, because I had a job to do. Aeron had given me a mission, and for that I had to be strong, even as everything inside me was unraveling.

Meandering down the mountain path, the stench of death all around me in growing clouds with each arduous step of my journey, my nausea became a constant companion. Even as I began asking myself how Aeron knew I'd need this speech today, I absorbed the nightmare around me. I didn't need to know anything more than what I saw, because it was obvious that something unspeakable had happened here.

♦♦♦♦♦

I needed to just stay calm and try to at least get these images out of my mind. As I approached the smoldering remnants of this historic town, the firefighters were still putting out the fires from the seared restaurants and touristy gift shops. The crematorium now looked like it was the city's primary industry.

Hitting all my senses at once, the whole crime scene was truly overwhelming. Ambulances wailed hauntingly for the wounded, even as the meat wagons lumbered through the streets to take away the remains of those who had already passed on. The charred smell of flesh lingered in the air as the sky presented as a mottled red instead of the typical yellows, oranges and purple hues of a southern California dusk.

I looked around at a scene straight out of Dante's Inferno. The 360-degree view was a hellish nightmare...or at the least the vision one wakes up with after having one. From every corner, as well as under piles of rubble, there was crying, gasping, and choking on the thickened air. Cries and voices from every direction rose like smoke, disjointed and desperate, as the streets filled with the injured, some on makeshift gurneys cobbled together from crates and wooden skids, others simply lying on tarps or blankets—whatever the still-standing could find. The ambulances kept coming, but the injured were coming faster, with nowhere left to go but the pavement.

♦♦♦♦♦

The road beneath my feet glistened with what I hoped was overflow from the fire hoses, still hissing and screaming their way through the flames.

And I continued to believe it was just water until I saw the chunks - red, torn and meat-like. I squinted, unsure what I was looking at, then quickly pointed myself in another direction as my imagination connected the dots.

"I *really* don't want to know," I told myself as the bile rose into my mouth.

♦♦♦♦♦

Down near the intersection of Date and Alison I spotted a makeshift morgue where countless bodies were laid out, covered with dirty white sheets and more or less concealed from public view. The corpses were various sizes, and as I sped up I saw a small black foot. This was the animal morgue, where the pets and wildlife who were caught in whatever had taken place here were being set aside and taken to their final resting place.

Those that had not yet been accounted for and still lay bare on the street were acting as food for the flies: dogs, cats, parakeets, crows, squirrels...even a tortoise and a couple of lizards. Off in the distance were the remains of a deer that had been caught nibbling old Mrs. Sanderson's hostas just as all hell broke loose.

Talk about being in the wrong place at the wrong time!

I guess what struck me hardest was the realization that things were MUCH worse than I had thought they would be. Sitting in the car with Aeron, I'd wished the news reports were exaggerating the damage done, but now - in the midst of it - it was obvious they'd been right about the massive extent of the destruction.

One could even argue the news stations had under-played the reports of damage so that they didn't cause widespread panic throughout the San Diego region. Given what I was now seeing up-close, that may not have been such a bad move.

♦♦♦♦♦

Approaching cautiously, I determined to avoid getting in the way of those managing the crisis. Triage nurses coordinated with doctors as ambulance workers shuttled back and forth, sometimes narrowly avoiding the hearses clearing away the remains from under those dirty sheets.

Through it all an acrid smell permeated everything, leaving a bitter taste in my mouth that persisted long after the wind shifted. The stench made me ill, and only the thought of fulfilling my promise to Aeron—spreading the word for our cause—kept me going.

♦♦♦♦♦

The squat man chomping the cheap cigar between his teeth pulled his crushed fedora further onto his head as he came through the broken doorway of the ruined restaurant. He shuffled through the crowd of ash-covered medics, firefighters, and corpses, coughing periodically—both from the smoke and his cigar—and at one point stopped to spit in the street.

I watched as he wiped the dribbles of spittle from his oversized mustache. Rubbing his two days of stubble with his left hand, he shook his head in disbelief at the chaotic scene. He was a cynical man by nature, but even he was obviously trying to not be overwhelmed as he poked here and prodded there.

Wincing as I approached him, I noticed how even the overwhelming layers of death surrounding us weren't enough to mask the stench of tobacco wafting from his clothes. Layered atop the foul odor from the explosions and the hanging curtain of doom and finality surrounding us all, it was almost too much for any one person to bear.

And though he wore a lanyard around his neck that bore some official imprint, the man looked pretty unprofessional; his disheveled appearance a stark contrast to the seriousness of the situation.

Something about him screamed 'Reporter.' Not the *"I'm a professional here to spread the word and inform the community for the greater good,"* type of reporter, but the *"I stand around looking through keyholes all day, trying to uncover something I have no business seeing"* type. To me, he was only there to talk about the latest scoop and the drama of it all, monetizing death and tragedy.

Behind him was his cameraman Tim, schlepping 55 pounds of field camera and assorted equipment, and these two were looking for anything, or anyone, who would potentially give them an edge over the competition.

And I realized they were perfect for my objective. I stepped forward, calming myself by repeating my mantra. *'State the report, tell the newscast what we were doing, and then leave. That's it. That's all.'* This was my entire task, though my mind was so wracked with pain over what I had just witnessed that I couldn't think straight.

This disheveled little man mumbled as I approached him, his words overcome by the unrelenting *"shhhhhhhhhhhhh"* of the water gushing from the fire hoses a dozen feet away. Still, I made out a snippet of his instructions to the camera guy, referring to 'potential crime theories' or something similar.

As I approached the two men eyed me with a disinterest they usually reserved for tourists. "Can we help you with something?" asked Mr. Spittle-flecked mustache in a dismissive tone.

"I—yes," I said, offering a small, practiced smile. A gentle gesture, one meant to ease suspicion and plant the seed of trust. "I'm here to provide assistance."

The mustache man snorted. "Well, you're a little late for that. What'd you do, bring marshmallows? Firefighters are handling things just fine without any extra hands flapping around, sweetheart."

I let the sarcasm roll by untouched. "Obviously, there's little I can do in terms of...containment," I replied, careful and calm. "But I *am* in a position to offer comfort. Kindness. Stability to this devastated community."

They weren't buying it. Both raised their eyebrows, exchanging glances like I'd just stepped out of a padded van.

"Listen, lady," Mustache man snapped. "You can't just sashay into a disaster zone and play humanitarian like some girl scout. People are hurt. People are *DEAD*! You want to help? Go volunteer with the Red Cross. Otherwise, stay out of the way of the professionals doing the real work."

As this obnoxious little man preached, the cameraman quietly stepped back and switched on his camera with a soft click...in case I actually said anything worthwhile.

My words would be immortalized, and I felt the weight of it. "But—" I started, voice faltering. I cleared my throat and steeled myself. "I didn't *sashay* into town," I said with deliberate sharpness. "I'm here because my organization—*the Purity Syndicate*—was called upon to offer aid, compassion, and guidance to those in need. I would think, in times like this, that you'd be more interested in *helping people* than dismissing those willing to give it."

I stopped for a reaction, recognizing that if it came down to choosing between being a 'little girl scout' or a bitter man whose most important accomplishment each day was scratching himself when he rolled out of bed, which one I'd rather be. And as I waited, I realized how much of a struggle it was to string together a decent sentence without the chaos around me crawling back into my head like smoke under a locked door. The carnage, the stench...it was clinging to everything. I felt the nausea surge again, bile once more threatening to rise into my throat until I forced it down. *Keep it together. Stay focused.*

I steadied myself and began again. "It just so happens we're here to—"

"Of course," Mustache Man interrupted me before suspiciously demanding "And what *is* the Purity Syndicate?" His theatrical tone suggested he saw himself as the hero in some B-rated drama uncovering a secret cult.

♦♦♦♦♦

I straightened my posture and swallowed my frustration. This was the scrutiny and misunderstanding that Aeron had warned me about, and once again he was right about everything. All my rehearsing was now paying off, allowing me to deliver my lines with practiced ease:

“The Purity Syndicate is a local non-profit dedicated to providing shelter, food, and support to those most in need. We recognize there is a terrible situation that has just taken place, and wish to offer our condolences, our positive thoughts, and our help. Anyone seeking support or counsel should contact us at...”

The cameraman cut me off before I could share a phone number or an email address, and I suddenly realized he was also a reporter. He cocked an eyebrow and with a slight smirk asked, “So you guys are, what? Some kind of sanctuary?”

“Of course,” I said through gritted teeth, struggling to stay on-message. “The Purity Syndicate provides comfort for those in need. We’re here to help in tragedies like this.”

The cameraman’s tone was more than a bit condescending, and I knew neither of them were really taking me seriously. However, Aeron had asked me to deliver this message, and I was determined to fulfill his request. I tried to maintain my composure, wearing a thin smile made brittle by my inner conflict of annoyance, confusion, and fear and heightened by the obnoxiousness standing before me.

Taking a deep breath, I resolved to push through the tangle of irritation and anxiety knotting in my chest. *This was bigger than me. This was for Aeron.*

♦♦♦♦♦

Mr. Mustache picked up the thread of the conversation. “So I guess you’re one of those outreach programs helping the homeless. Like any number of organizations trying to keep kids in hospitals smiling or single moms off food stamps?”

“Well yes, we also help those people,” I retorted. Internally, I struggled mightily neither to annoy this irritating little man or let him get under my skin.

"Really?" he said. His tone was loaded, as if he was daring me to trip myself up.

"Yes. We provide food to shelters. We offer emotional and spiritual support, as well as naturopathic remedies for trauma, grief, and burnout."

"Oh," he said, nodding like it was all finally clicking in his head...though his smirk never faded. "So, this is like typical Christian evangelical stuff? Or is this more New Age-y crystals and sound bowls and that kind of thing?"

I clenched my hands behind my back. I don't mind curiosity, but I *do* object to mockery.

"Well...no. We're not Christians, exactly," I said carefully, "But we are spiritual."

He leaned in, eyes gleaming with the scent of a story. "Mysticism?"

"I"-

His fedora started falling off his head and he grabbed at it to prevent it landing in the ash. Temporarily distracted, all he could say was "Very interesting," as his voice dripped with condescension and sarcasm. "Very informative. Thank you for stopping by and sharing with us."

♦♦♦♦♦

I forced myself to breathe and to keep my smile steady. I could feel the heat rising in my chest; a quiet rage twisting beneath the polite mask I struggled to maintain. Why was he so rude? So callous? It was as if none of this suffering and destruction mattered to him. From his reaction, I might as well be a clown pitching a circus act.

Clearing my throat, I took a breath and managed, "What's your name, sir?"

"Pete Ross," he stated blandly, straightening his back. He gave the impression of a man whose career washed out long ago, whose best years were definitely behind him, and who probably peaked in his senior year of high school. I half-expected he'd pull the *'Don't you know who I am?'* routine on me.

Keeping my voice even, I said "Mr. Ross, what I'm trying to explain is that we, like most organizations, provide vital support to the community. But the Purity Syndicate is different—much more than just being another San Diego County nonprofit. I hoped you might help us spread the word about the work we do and the benefits we bring to people throughout the region."

He shared a silent smirk with his cameraman, which made my teeth clench.

Stifling a laugh, he started "I—look. You seem sweet, and I'm sure you're sincere. But we're not here to help advertise some random nonprofit. We're here for the story of the disaster."

He unclamped the cigar from his mouth, tapping it to drop some ash onto the ground, and crammed it back between his yellowed teeth. "We're only here for the main event, sweetheart."

I bit my tongue to keep from saying *'Yes, it's quite obvious that's all you care about, so you can parrot it like it's the latest internet trend.'* Thinking better of it, I instead opted for, "And we're here because of the disaster too. We just want everyone to know that we're providing shelter to those who need it. Shelter, food...whatever you need you can get from the Purity Syndicate. And it's all free."

"Housing, huh?" Pete hummed, the interest barely flickering in his tired eyes. "So, you're like a shelter?"

"Of course."

"Big operation then. Must be a wealthy organization to afford property around here—even in this." He swept his arm indicating the dry hills and the scrub brush.

"Yes, we even put up flyers before the explosion." I retorted.

That caught his attention. His expression shifted, a thin spark of interest beneath his cynicism. "Before, huh?"

You could almost see the gears turning in his head. And this was a good thing, right? I mean, this little man had barely acknowledged what I was saying before about the Purity Syndicate, and now I'd caught his attention...*FINALLY*!

He leaned over towards me. “So if you were in town just before the explosion, I’m guessing you saw some of the supposed suspects, right?”

Genuinely surprised, I blinked. “Suspects?”

He shrugged, “Well, that’s what the survivors are saying. Something about a group of individuals in white sneaking into the local eateries and stores and dropping things in the back or in the bathrooms. Nobody recognized the pattern until...*‘boom’*. The flames engulfed the places, one by one. Then people started comparing notes and...”

HOLY FUCK! I listened to his description of the day’s events and suddenly felt nauseous. He continued before I could choke out any response. “There were people who witnessed everything. They’ve been whisked to the hospital, but before they left a few of them said something about potential local terrorists.”

Suddenly he was passionate about the story. “Of course, if we’re being totally honest, that explosion could have been caused by *anything*. Sure the explosion could be a potential gas leak, but hearing these rumors seems pretty intriguing.”

He made air quotes when he said the word rumors before adding “We’re hoping to find more folks that could confirm the claim, or if not, point us in another direction.”

He spoke as if he was telling a campfire story, pretty much desensitized to the horror around him. Yet while he probably didn’t take any of this seriously, I found the whole story incredibly unnerving.

♦♦♦♦♦

I stood there for a few seconds, though to me it felt like an hour. “Pretty gnarly huh?” said mustache man, snapping me out of my shocked trance. I felt so ill from what I saw that I doubted I’d ever be able to watch horror flicks or slasher movies ever again.

The words in my head felt jumbled. There was so much I needed to say, yet I felt the words sticking in the back of my throat. I wasn’t even concerned anymore about speaking for the Purity Syndicate; I just wanted to have a voice of my own.

Why was this one simple task so hard?

I nodded wordlessly. For him this was just another story, and his lack of empathy was astounding. The truth is I really didn't want to talk to him for fear I'd become equally jaded. "Poor bastards," he went on, speaking of the day's victims. "They never knew what hit 'em."

"Yeah," I agreed softly, momentarily forgetting I was there to promote the Purity Syndicate and the services we do. Cautious and dreading his answer, I felt I had to ask; "And you say there were descriptions of the people responsible?"

Mustache man nodded. "People wearing white, but that seems to be all that anyone can recall. Nobody even remembers how many of them there were."

From the corner of my eye I saw my white blouse poking out of the edges of my blue sweatshirt. I quickly tucked it under, afraid he'd see it and get ideas that I was somehow involved in today's horror show.

♦♦♦♦♦

The cameraman glanced at one of the investigators coming toward us carrying what looked like a broken surveillance camera. The look on his face suggested he had more questions than answers about the object in his arms.

Searching for a clue, Pete Ross kept his focus on me. "Right now we know very little. Those responsible could honestly be anything: hippies, terrorists, foreign agents, political extremists...the list is truly endless. I'm kinda leaning towards this being a Timothy McVeigh case myself, if for no other reason than because it would make a *MUCH* more intriguing story for my bosses than a gas leak."

Like all American school children, I had learned about Timothy McVeigh; the American domestic terrorist responsible for the Oklahoma City bombing in 1995, in what is still considered one of the deadliest terrorist attacks in U.S. history. He killed 168 people, including 19 children, and injured over 600 others.

I knew that McVeigh was executed by lethal injection for his crime which, in hindsight, he maintained was a justifiable political act against the 'tyranny' of the government. The irony was only the innocent civilians of Oklahoma City were impacted by his gruesome act of violence. I shuddered at the idea of anyone involved in today's incident being met with such a punishment.

♦♦♦♦♦

Ross was still talking. "You've gotta admit that this is a brutal story, no matter how you slice it. Over a hundred people were injured in the attack, another 60 people are dead, and that death toll is sure to grow if the people in the hospital start pushing up the daisies. But this kind of story gets people talking, just like the 1999 Columbine shooting did. It was huge then, and stories like this will always get people's attention. That's just how it is."

"And when you get down to it, that's just what it's supposed to do."

I opened my mouth to try to tell him off, but kept coming up empty. I wanted to tell Pete Ross exactly what I thought of his sick little game—his callous attitude, his morbid fascination with the carnage as if it were just another action flick for his highlight reel. But before I could speak, his cameraman's voice cut through the tension like a knife.

"Pete, we've got something!"

The cameraman stood near the soot-streaked investigator, his own clothing stained with ash. In his gloved hands he held the melted, blackened remains of the surveillance camera. With a cracked lens and metal and plastic casing warped by the searing heat, it looked as dead as those sixty people Ross had just been talking about.

But like a cockroach, it had survived the blast.

Ross dropped his idle chitchat and became all business, striding over to the two men examining the camera. The investigator, still brushing soot from his gloves, glanced at Pete. "Yeah, found it barely hanging by the cable. The city council is gonna be pissed; this thing was just installed last week, and hasn't even been paid for yet."

Ross leaned in, eyes gleaming with sudden interest. "Last week? That's convenient."

In an instant a dozen thoughts flashed through my mind. A cold sweat prickled at the back of my neck as I considered the flyers we'd put up and Aeron's insistence we establish a presence before the event.

And the most obvious question: what story did this camera have to tell?

My heart raced as I tried to inconspicuously stay in the background. Pete Ross was already firing questions at the investigator, his tone shifting from bored disinterest to hungry excitement. I caught snippets of their conversation: "Footage recovery...timeframe...investigative priority."

A chill swept through me. Whatever was on that camera, they were going to find it...and I needed to know what it showed before they did.

I had to tell Aeron what was going on.

♦♦♦♦♦

Tagging along behind the three men like I belonged there, I quickly found myself standing beside a police panel truck that had been brought in especially for this investigation. Inside I could see a massive nest of wires and appliances for securing the scene, analysis, and collecting evidence, all crammed in beside a fancy black computer. I trailed behind them, recognizing I wouldn't be welcomed to see their evidence, but fully aware that Aeron was counting on me to learn as much as I could as fast as I could.

The three men hunched over the camera's remains, desperately seeking a nugget of information that could guide them towards something—anything—resembling an answer. As they considered their options, I looked at the extensive range of specialized equipment in the vehicle, including body armor; crime scene tape; forensic kits; and bomb disposal robots.

These guys were definitely ready for anything.

♦♦♦♦♦

The investigator was frustrated at the condition of the camera. Melted plastic was fused with the metal base, blocking access to the ports and making it difficult to plug in any cables. After strenuous effort - and more than a little cursing - he succeeded in chipping away enough of the carnage to enable him to plug in a male cable into a female outlet. The computer booted up, and the investigator somehow cajoled a "*WHIR*" from the unit.

The fact that he was showing it to these media slugs suggested to me they had bribed him to get first shot at the story. And though it took a while, he finally got enough pieces of the puzzle into place, allowing them to see some grainy images on the truck's computer monitor. Fast-forwarding through several hours before the explosion took place, the three of them watched, transfixed, hoping against hope that the truth would reveal itself.

Now all but forgotten, I gratefully hung back. These three oversized male backsides huddled together hogging the view as if monopolizing a trough. But for once my slight stature proved to be an advantage, giving me a clear line of sight to the action unfolding before me.

♦♦♦♦♦

"Okay, so this is about 11am from today...so far not much suspicious activity," said the man at the computer as he scanned the dull, partially blurred footage from the instantly aged device.

As the video forwarded, he reported, "12pm, and still no activity."

He then forwarded the footage again, "But here, as we're getting close to 12:45..."

"Well?" Pete asked.

"This van has appeared, but the license plate is blurred," the man behind the computer answered as he adjusted his glasses.

I involuntarily stepped a little closer to see the screen. Looking at the right side of La Mesa's main commercial strip, I spotted a car that looked familiar. The man at the keyboard increased the size of the image on the screen, even as he involuntarily inched closer to the computer to get a better view of the image. "Yeah, there's no license plate either. All I can tell you is it's a burgundy van."

I blanched. That's...that's *our* car...

The four of us watched the monitor closely, afraid of missing even the slightest clue. The time punch in the corner of the screen reads "12:47 PM" as the footage showed the *'people in white'* exiting our car.

No....No! Those are the other members of the Purity Syndicate. There was no way to deny it...*we* were responsible for what just took place in La Mesa! There HAD to be a mistake!

♦♦♦♦♦

"By God, those people ain't lying," Pete mumbled to himself. For while his initial instincts were that the survivors he had interviewed so meticulously were too close to matters to provide a realistic analysis, he now concluded that they were right on the nose. I stepped back, nauseous as I watched each of my members enter the various buildings. *"This is a mistake,"* I told myself. *"It has to be some kind of misunderstanding."*

And though part of me wanted to say *"Oh, those are just members of my organization; not terrorists,"* a little voice in the back of my head told me to keep silent. They'd forgotten I was even there, and I figured I *had* to be better off keeping my mouth shut.

Only...all those members of my *"family"* were all going into the buildings that I watched them going into, and in my heart I knew the answer. I didn't want to admit it...but I knew the answer.

We did it...and Aeron had to have known it was coming.

The man at the screen—Charlie, according to his name tag—reported: "One is going in the library. There goes another into the mystic shop. #3 is heading for the taco place. And there," he pointed at the screen, "that last one is walking into the cremation center. Each one carrying...what looks to be a package...can't really tell for sure." He leaned closer trying to see the shape of the object. "I dunno."

"That's where the explosions took place," reported Pete's cameraman, firmly gripping his equipment and sensing the footage's eeriness. "At least that's what the survivors were saying."

♦♦♦♦♦

A few minutes passed with no activity before the film showed the *'people in white'* hustling back into the burgundy van, only to quickly speed off. Trying to look at this scenario from an outsider's perspective, it struck me that them leaving in such haste suggested they knew the explosives would detonate at any minute.

Even the way the car departed was exactly how Aeron drove off. I recalled the van nearly hitting a few cars as we passed the trolley tracks and the bank. I stared in disbelief, desperately wanting to believe this was just a bad dream, but I knew...and couldn't look away from the nightmare unraveling before me.

There were *far* too many questions. Was this part of Aeron's good cause? I mean, 60 people were dead so far, and that count was sure to rise. How could that result ever be part of a *'good'* cause?

I prayed silently, hoping against hope this wasn't what it appeared to be and that my members were being set up. Still...why would Aeron cover his license plate? Why would he ask Mune, Destiny, Brady, and Beatrice to go into those places. And they were carrying the care packages we had all just put together the night before. They were supposed to encourage people to join our community.

"Tim, this is huge," Pete whispered to his cameraman, "This is irrefutable proof of a full-blown terrorist attack taking place *right* under our noses! Has anyone else seen this?"

Tim shook his head. "Then we've got the exclusive on it," Ross cackled, adding "Suck on this, Channel Seven!"

♦♦♦♦♦

A bright light emitted from the recording, followed instantly by a single, monstrous crack that instantly split into four thunderclaps — raw, glass-shattering, and bone-deep. The air seemed to tear, and windows rattled into dust. Reminiscent of the sonic boom caused by an oversized airplane speeding by overhead, everything on the recording seemed to vibrate on a low frequency that even we could feel in our teeth, while jagged high-end shards of sound snapped like oversized gunfire.

All of us were caught off guard as the explosion ripped through the air with a deafening roar, generating a second wave and a sharp crack that echoed off the walls. This was then followed by the clatter of shrapnel and the shattering of glass, as a shockwave seemed to make the virtual world on the television screen before us tremble.

We continued watching, on a basic level unable to recognize that this had actually happened. The reality check came only when we saw the camera filming itself toppling over and showing colors of bright rustic red before presenting the very carnage the explosions had caused.

It was a surreal feeling, like we were inside a nuclear mushroom cloud.

♦♦♦♦♦

Still disbelieving, I couldn't help but watch the cars being tossed aside like plastic toys. Clouds of commercial papers and paper money exploded and disgorged from the bank, even as tables and chairs blasted into pieces as they got tossed out of multiple doors by the force of the explosives. The glass of dozens of windows, reduced in an instant into millions of slivers, were blown from their frames as easily as if a giant being had sneezed.

One by one we watched the flames engulf each building. The pedestrians were vaporized, their faces and hair liquified from their skulls before they could even see the blast coming. The singe of the blaze melted whatever was left of their bare skeletons as the explosions shook anyone and anything within reach.

Like rubberneckers approaching a car wreck on the freeway, I couldn't stop myself from watching these vibrant community members being reduced to bloodied slime. It was all I could do to not lose my lunch as I imagined I was smelling the giant barbecue that my family had been responsible for. The four of us watched breathlessly until nothing was left but the skeletal cages of what seconds before had been human beings just living their lives and going about their business.

It was as if we were looking through a scene of a nuclear war film...only this wasn't any stage play, nor was there a script. It had really just happened.

And I knew who had caused it to happen. One moment little Susie was living her life and it was just an ordinary day, the next moment she had ceased to exist. She and the others had no time to comprehend what had torn their world apart. Their screams rose like a grotesque symphony of anguish; the kind of sound that curdles the soul. Some wailed from the searing agony of their own mangled bodies, caught in the blast's fury - others keened for what they had just witnessed—loved ones obliterated in flashes of carnage so visceral, so horrifying, it defied the limits of human imagination.

Men. Women. Children. Animals. All reduced to a mass of soot, ash and bloody viscera that gave the ugliest color to the streets. All thanks to the Purity Syndicate. All thanks to Aeron Inchon.

Yeah, it was a glitchy video recording. But anyone watching it could still clearly see the holocaust lying before us...and because of us.

♦♦♦♦♦

My mind had gone blank watching the butchery of the people who had been on this street. This lively little town was suddenly nothing more than a wasteland decorated by flames, ash and charred meat, the bones strewn about like a skeletal display at Halloween.

I couldn't move; couldn't even think beyond what this video displayed to me. I froze. The newscast—or at least what the survivors were caught saying on the video—was much different than I had imagined it would be.

Looking up, I noticed something almost unbearable in the expressions of those three hardened men. Even Pete Ross—that slimebag—wore a mask of dread, a flicker of humanity surfacing for the first time in what had probably been an eternity.

A few harrowing seconds passed before Tim stumbled out of the vehicle. He stood there, trembling and gasping for breath, as if trying to claw his way back from the abyss of the abomination he had just witnessed.

"So uh...I..." Pete stammered, breaking the blanket of silence laying over us all, even as sounds of firetrucks and water gushing from hoses threatened to interfere with our very private thoughts. "I guess that confirms it...." he said. His voice was monotone, even as his horrified expression verified that he had just had the most traumatic experience in his life.

And I didn't know what to say. Part of me wanted to insist this was a mistake. After all, the Purity Syndicate would *never* do this. *Aeron* wouldn't do this. There had to be a reason, right? Those packages contained fliers, not bombs. Somebody had gotten their story twisted!

Even now I doubted the others in the family could have seen this coming...how could they? None of us, in our community of love and hope and helping others, would have knowingly subjected anyone to something like this. This was obviously...obviously what? A terrible, unthinkable accident? A moment of chaos that spiraled out of control?

There had to be some justification, some explanation...anything to keep the blame at bay, anything that didn't cast shadows over my members—*my family*.

My family couldn't be responsible for this. It couldn't be them. It *COULDN'T* be!

Still, here was undeniable proof before me. It's...I didn't really know what else to say other than wishing this was some nightmare that I could wake up from. After all, I'd been there. I'd seen them taking the white boxes into those places; the members running pell mell; the driving and almost hitting people in our haste to get out of town. But feeling the hot wind driven by the fire...the bits of ash blown into my eyes...the sickening smell of burnt wood and barbecued citizens...made it impossible to hold onto that wishful thinking.

Even as I hung onto hope that it was just a nightmarish fantasy—knowing the alternative was just too frightening to consider—I recognized that there was no escape. This was *way* too real!

Any question remaining in my mind was eliminated by the scream of the sirens and the neverending *WHOOSH* of the fire hoses washing away the blood. This was no Hollywood production, but a reality guaranteed to haunt me to my own dying day.

♦♦♦♦♦

Assuming the video was an honest accounting of what had taken place, then the question remained; Why? I'm supposed to be the public face of the Syndicate, but all Aeron had told me was that we were in La Mesa to "*spread the word*."

And if this was the strategy for us "getting the community's attention", as Aeron had put it, then we'd definitely succeeded...just not the way I'd envisioned.

I was torn, recognizing the horror but still forcing myself to believe the Syndicate hadn't really been involved. Turning to the reporter, I cleared my throat. "So, uh...about my organization? Can you..."

"What? What do you want?," he huffed.

I'd run out of steam. "Never mind," I mumbled.

Trying to regain the dispassion his profession demanded, Ross dully responded "Whatever..." and turned away in search of his cameraman.

♦♦♦♦♦

Tim remained doubled over at the curb, trying to prevent himself from throwing up again. And unable to promote the Purity Syndicate—to not even recite the speech touting the many benefits of our small society that I had practiced in the car—I figured quietly disappearing might be my best move. Because I obviously wouldn't be able to itemize the ways we could make someone's life better; the food for the hungry, help for those with addiction, and making handmade crafts as we all bonded as a found family.

It was probably the first time in my life that I didn't do exactly as I was told to do.

True, it was the family that I was now questioning, but I still recognized that I had a responsibility to them. And I'd made a promise to Aeron; the one man in the world I'd do *anything* for, if only he'd ask!

Besides, if I couldn't promote us to Pete Ross—the reporter—maybe I could convince someone else here what a valuable asset we were to the larger community.

Glancing up and to my left, I saw Charlie continuing to mess with wires and cables in a valiant effort to improve reception on the video. To the right I watched Pete and Tim walk off without so much as a *'thank you'* or a *'goodbye,'* mumbling that they needed a drink at some bar in Coronado. And, despite his warnings about how dangerous everything was at a disaster site like this, Pete Ross—that grand humanitarian—had left me behind in the aftermath of the destruction, fending for myself once more.

♦♦♦♦♦

As I considered vanishing from the crime scene and skulking back into the shadows, I noticed a gathering at a charred home. Half of the house was blown off, revealing a cavity of a suburban home. A group of people held flameless candles; the fake kind with LED lights that they probably bought at a local convenience store. Though it was beyond me why they thought it was too soon to have an open flame to honor what had been lost.

I approached these people to offer them the Purity Syndicate's services. Inching up to the mourners as they softly wept about their friends and loved ones falling victim to the fires. Trying to ignore the overwhelming guilt that had piled up within me, I expressed my condolences.

Other groups were also gathering in memoriam, drawn to the site of a former home or where a fellow citizen had died. They stood lighting LED candles, holding children's drawings and photos of people lost to the tragedy.

I made the rounds offering a few words here, a pat on the shoulder there. All around I could see the devastation that we'd left in our wake, but I'd always quietly disappear before I accidentally said the wrong thing. I even thought I heard the cops telling the mourners to leave the crime scene, as it was still too dangerous to be in this part of town.

I suddenly remembered a VHS cassette I'd found sitting in the bottom of my bag. It was an old VHS of Aeron's first and only advertisement he'd ever done to promote our organization. The original plan had been to have it placed as a Public Service Advertisement to get the word out to the public, but Aeron had scrapped the video, saying we needed better quality equipment to shoot it properly.

So even if I couldn't get a reporter to tell our story, maybe I could get this video out into the public conversation. It was a small gesture, I knew, but I figured it was better than nothing. And with the cops now chasing everyone out of town, I went into the empty cavity of a house, placed the videotape on the floor, and left with my fingers crossed.

♦♦♦♦♦

As I walked back toward the hill that would lead me back to our vehicle - that burgundy van I just saw in the video – a text came in from Aeron. "*Is everything okay down there?*"

I swallowed, knowing I needed to respond quickly or he'd become suspicious. "*Yeah, it just took a little longer than we thought it would. I'm heading back right now.*"

I started up the hill, my thoughts tangled in a haze of confusion like I hadn't felt in years. A deep, gnawing sadness—close to depression—weighed me down. I desperately needed answers, because something was happening around me that I just didn't understand. I was being shoved into the spotlight, expected to be the voice and the face of a story I barely understood. And I couldn't tell our story unless I knew everything that was going on.

I had a bad feeling about all of this. Yeah, I still hoped for a faulty gas line being the cause of the problem. But in my gut I knew better.

Chapter 7 - Panic Attack!

-Madelaine-

Many people don't realize that what they have that is dear to them can be gone in the blink of an eye. This reality applies to those we love, of course, who could slip in the bathtub or get hit by a bus, but what most folks don't recognize is that this truth impacts virtually everything in our respective lives.

And it doesn't matter how long you have had these meaningful things, either. The home you live in, a bed with clean sheets, clean water to drink and bathe in, food on the table—even your rights just to exist—can all vanish overnight.

I should add that I love my job as a fashion designer. But ensuring all my ducks are always lined up can be stressful...especially when I'm at home with my two kids. They, of course, are my primary reason for being, and making sure they're okay is what keeps me going.

Yes, even when they do something that makes me nuts.

Which is why I've always worked hard to make certain all our needs were met at home. And I've busted my ass at work to ensure that all the designs were in place for the latest fashion trends or the next show on the catwalk.

Naturally, keeping all my firm's investors happy is always top-of-mind, because without them we'd be out of business.

Admittedly, running a San Diego-based design studio keeps me much busier than the job I had in Sedona, but I prefer it here. There's significantly more creative freedom and the pay's pretty decent. And by choosing to live in a community that's less than an hour's drive to the beach, I'm finding it's a bit less expensive to live here by the coast.

Plus I have bonuses built into my package that I expect will be a huge benefit come the holidays.

So I'm working at a job I'm good at—scratch that—I'm *GREAT* at it! I enjoy what I do, and my kids are now living a more fulfilling life. Sedona's attitude problem towards tourists was starting to get on my nerves, and the people here are unquestionably both more diversified and nicer. I prefer the politics here as well.

Throw in the fact that my two children are getting a decent education and are now positioned to take advantage of the Golden State's college system and this shift west comes out looking like it was absolutely the right decision for me.

♦♦♦♦♦

As a rule, I try to focus on the positives of life—routine and the small, quiet comforts of life—and ignore the chaos that seems to constantly hum just beneath the surface. I've always found this approach to be preferable to wallowing in fear or grief day after day. Even with the bombing in La Mesa still fresh in the news cycle, I try not to get too invested in the story. Like politics and the stock market, this shit can be overwhelming...even depressing at times.

So I don't talk about it much, and especially when the kids are around. The way I figure it, they don't need to hear it on repeat, echoing through every screen and conversation.

Then again, there's only so much I can do. Which brings us to the evening when my carefully balanced world fell apart. The warm scent of spaghetti and meatballs drifted through the house. Garlic bread baked in the oven, and I juggled business and personal tasks by simultaneously taking calls, wiping down counters, and checking oven timers.

Yup, just another Thursday night.

As I passed by Jason's room I glanced in. He was perched on his bed, hunched over his phone, murmuring into it between bouts of typing. The room was dim, lit only by the screen in his hand casting a ghostly glow on his pale face. His wavy, violet-dyed hair fell over one eye. Dressed in black from head to toe, he looked like a shadow tucked into the corner of the house.

"Jason," I called over the thrum of his music, "who are you talking to?"

He barely looked up. "Private."

I flicked on his light.

"Well, while you're chatting with your boyfriend," I said, raising my voice over the static of a rickety ringtone, "why don't you help your sister with her homework? I need to take this call."

Jason sighed, dragging himself off the bed with the dramatic weariness only a teenager could summon. He gave me an exaggerated eye-roll as he shuffled out of the room.

At the kitchen table Claudia sat with her head bent over a scattering of algebra problems, her pencil hovering midair in silent distress. Jason slumped into the seat beside her without a word, earbuds still in, his phone clutched in one hand.

And just like that, another evening unfolded—threaded with tension, silence, and the ordinary noise that fills a house doing its best to pretend the outside world isn't burning.

♦♦♦♦♦

I answered my phone, wandering into the living room to separate myself from the music blasting from my son's radio. It was just a voicemail following up from a reevaluation for my daughter's autism, as well as an accommodation for the meetup.

I hung up the phone. As I was about to return to my tasks it rang again. This was a call I hadn't been expecting, and the tone of my co-worker Serafina's voice immediately set me on edge. "Madeleine, have you seen the news?"

Distractedly, I asked "What about the news?"

"There's been a huge accident in the Creative Minds Center."

Involuntarily I raised an eyebrow, taking in this unanticipated jolt and instantly concerned about how severe the situation might be. "What do you mean?"

For the moment I was just trying to take it in stride. After all, there are accidents every day, right? It could easily be one of those situations that the media blows up just to get another headline, and was nothing really out of the ordinary.

Still, this was the regional center that I often took my daughter to. Was there something to be worried about?

"It's bad, Madeleine. *REAL* bad." Her voice was tight and she was obviously choking back her fear. "Probably a dozen people died there; maybe more. They're still pulling people from the building, it's flooded with tear gas."

"*WHAT*?!" The words hit me like a gut punch as my mind scrambled to process the enormity of what my friend had just said.

I ran to the side table, grabbed the TV remote and clicked on KUSI News. I stood, transfixed, as their helicopter flew over downtown La Mesa over the brewing smoke clouds, showing half the building on fire and plumes of smoke snaking out of the gaping holes.

Dozens of emergency vehicles—more than I could possibly count—were streaming in from every direction. Fire trucks from La Jolla, ambulances from Chula Vista, and police cars from San Diego joined with La Mesa's first responders. The camera panned over East County CERT volunteers directing traffic in a valiant effort to prevent lookie-loos from getting too near the scene lest they be added to the victim count.

Putting out the fire and sorting out the mess looked to be an impossible task and an absolute nightmare. Everything was scorched black, and the remains of what had once been a charming—and thriving—regional center were now reduced to ash and rubble in this modern-day war zone.

For a moment the edge of the camera frame showed the impromptu morgue that had been set up on-site...and I got nauseous at the sight of the bodies. Dozens of them, motionless and each one shrouded beneath a stark white sheet. I was horrified and desperate to look away, but unable to stop myself from searching for signs of life—or gore—or maybe both.

♦♦♦♦♦

The accident last week had obviously been a rather nasty explosion, and this once vibrant, close-knit community town was now little more than charred remains. The reporters danced around the questions of fatalities, though we all knew what they didn't want to say; the number of dead was sure to rise...perhaps significantly. So seeing the familiar building that had provided so much help for my daughter was just shocking.

"They don't know who did it, but there's already some debate whether or not it was an accident. Someone may have done this on purpose..." Serafina added uneasily.

I kept my eyes fixed on the screen, absorbing the morbid images the media was laying bare, and I shrugged. "C'mon...who would do something like that on purpose?"

"I don't know, but something seems to be very wrong. There's no way a gas leak causes *that* kind of devastation! Unless the entire civic infrastructure was a ticking time bomb, there's no way this was an accident."

"I'm thinking this was a terrorist attack!" she declared.

"Serafina, why would anyone send tear gas to a small place like that? It's not like it's a US landmark. Nobody important is coming to town, and it's not like we're really known for anything, either. It...it just doesn't make any sense!"

♦♦♦♦♦

"I'm sure this will clear up soon," I thought to myself, knowing that's just the way these kinds of things work. I mean, anyone who's ever paid attention recognizes that the news is like that: a big story pops up, keeps viewers and readers titillated for a few days, then something new comes along and pushes it off the front page and into the background.

Of course, a relentless churn of never-ending news cycles is needed to feed an insatiable public. Because that next big story will hit, making everyone breathless, and then it also gets pushed aside. That's just the way the system works as people get bored and tragedy becomes content.

Still, the one thing that remains consistent with every news story of a school shooting or kids committing suicide is that those reporting the story don't really care about who's grieving and what's impaired; they just want an engaging tale designed to glue people to their screens, making viewers so desensitized to the world we live in today. They feed us heartbreak dressed up as headlines, wrapping tragedy in a shiny, consumable package. They milk it for all it's worth, riding the emotional high it sparks in members of the public.

And then, when the rush fades and a new story emerges, the pain they were peddling is discarded—forgotten by the masses until the next tragedy surfaces in a hauntingly familiar fashion.

Personally, I think it's disgusting!

♦♦♦♦♦

"Were you near the area? Are *YOU* okay?" I sighed, rubbing the back of my neck in a vain effort to lower my stress level.

"No, I'm fine; I wasn't there. My cousin and his side of the family have been grieving for the past week, though. Their store was blown up in La Mesa and they can't figure out why. They have no enemies; hell, everybody in the area *LOVES* their store!"

"Oh my God..." I sounded breathless, trying to understand just how far this whole thing went.

She continued "It feels like someone has targeted La Mesa for destruction. And my cousin doesn't know what to do because, despite the savings they had, they're trying to figure out how to save more money to fix the damages, let alone plan funerals for some of the coworkers who were there when it happened."

"They've started a GoFundMe campaign that's already raised ten thousand dollars, so that will help," she added. "But still..."

"Jesus Christ..." I stroked my face and glanced back at my kids, who were just talking through Claudia's algebra problems, oblivious to what was on the television. I knew it would be better for them this way. Ignorance is bliss, and all that.

"What can I do?" I asked Serafina, even as I doubted my ability to actually do anything worthwhile to help her or her family. But I could at least make the offer of support to these good people who had just been dealt such a cruel hand and been forced to watch their prized business and their co-workers die in one fateful moment.

“I...I honestly don’t know,” Serafina sighed, reflecting how she was just barely holding it together. “I’ll...I’ll call you back later tonight, if I can...alright?”

♦♦♦♦♦

With a soft click Serafina was gone, leaving behind a dull tone in my ear and a void in my heart.

“What the fuck was *THAT* all about?” I muttered as I brewed some tea in a bid for a return to normality. Pouring the hot water over the tea bag, I watched as the tea swirled and bled into the water, staining the clear liquid a dark red brown. My eyes followed the steam as it rose in delicate, twisting shapes, swirling and dissipating into the air.

Shifting my attention back to the television, my attention was caught by the reporter interviewing a witness to this most recent tragedy. Distraught and distracted by Serafina’s call, I only half-listened, drifting back to how the media could be more helpful if they wanted to be.

I mean, what a fuckin’ concept, huh? They could provide a centralized location of resources for those in need...rather than just seeing news stories, videos and digital posts as commodities and fodder for lining their own pockets. For God’s sake, these were peoples’ lives we were talking about!

But no, they just went on blabbering endlessly, repeating the same story again and again and accomplishing little more than hurting the public they purportedly served.

What a bunch of leeches!

♦♦♦♦♦

Consumed with thoughts of helping Serafina, I wondered how the pair of back-to-back tragedies would be discussed in school. I sighed, realizing I couldn't shield my children from all the devastations life could throw at them, and scrolled my Facebook feed aimlessly, hoping for some reprieve from the dark thoughts my mind kept conjuring up. *‘They’re going to have to face the world eventually’,* I thought, the pang of concern for their future cutting deeper than I cared to admit.

I couldn't shake the feeling that the schools would be closed tomorrow, and probably for a few days after that as well, and part of me was relieved at the thought. Because even though this news story would eventually fade, the ever-present dangers of the outside world haunted me. *'Schools,'* I thought grimly, *'No matter how many security measures they have and the education they provide, are not as safe as they once were. There's always going to be danger and ignorance.'*

I sighed, just as the sharp beeping of the oven timer yanked me from my thoughts. The garlic bread was done.

Setting my phone aside, I slipped on my oven mitts and moved toward the oven, the heat and the rich scent of garlic butter wafting into the air as I opened the door. I gently placed the hot tray of freshly baked garlic bread out on the counter for my kids to chow down on before dinner.

"Wait until it cools down before you dig in," I called to the kids as I stepped away, leaving the bread to rest. I smiled, adding, "And be sure you leave some to go with dinner, please."

♦♦♦♦♦

Even though I knew better, I reached for my phone again when I returned to the living room. My thumb hesitated over the screen, fighting the urge to lose myself in the endless spiral of doom scrolling, but the temptation was too strong. It always was.

A little voice in my head told me to look through my list of contacts. I wasn't even really sure what I was looking for, but I proceeded to flip through the countless numbers I have for clients, family members and such.

That's when I saw '*Mr. Whitney*', a name I hadn't heard in quite some time.

His full name was George N. Whitney. He was, in fact, both an old friend and a client, though we hadn't talked much lately; not since he'd hired me to design that beautiful dress for his wife for their 30th wedding anniversary party and vow renewal.

I thought fondly of the tawny fabric with deep orange and umber patterns and blotches that would be a homage to a leopard's fur coat. To this day it still remains one of the favorite designs I have ever created. And it was one of Whitney's favorite dresses in his wife's collection.

♦♦♦♦♦

Whitney had always struck me as an upstanding kind of guy. A naval petty officer, he had been assigned to the Naval Criminal Investigative Service based out of North Island in San Diego. The two of us had met the day he was the guest speaker at my Rotary club and we struck up a conversation while ladling plates of scrambled eggs. I'd been so struck by his charm and his smarts that I moved from my traditional seat by the window overlooking the golf course to the head table, just so I could hear better and hopefully learn more about this fascinating man.

It's not that I had any designs on him, mind you...at least none that I was aware of. But he was a great conversationalist, told funny jokes, and was one of the better speakers we'd had in the club in a while. And after a steady diet of charlatans trying to sell time shares and similar "entertainment" that was really just people trying to reach the captive audience and the disposable income that a Rotary club represents, I was ready to meet someone who really knew his stuff and was only interested in imparting his knowledge to those around him.

So we met a couple of times for coffee. And I was struck by how much of a—what they call in New York a *"Mensch"* —a person who always strives to do the right thing, regardless of the situation, that he was. He impressed me as the type of person one always wants to have on their side in a fight. But there was no chemistry beyond friendship, and he retired from his last position at the Coronado base after 20 years of service around the globe, and we'd just kind of lost touch.

♦♦♦♦♦

I glanced at the news again, unable to stop myself from gazing at the carnage. The buildings oozed smoke, even as the flow from the fire hydrants made the torched hulks look like they were bleeding into the streets. The steady drumbeat of horror acted as a broken record spewing mind-numbing platitudes and baseless theories. The reporter didn't care—that was pretty obvious—and I unconsciously compared the newscaster's professional disinterest with George Whitney's celebrated passion for everyone and everything he'd ever encountered over the past several decades.

Whitney had always been a straight shooter; the kind of guy who never beat around the bush. Though he was now retired, he seemed to never be off-duty. He spent his days volunteering at the Point Loma United Portuguese S.E.S., helping Portuguese immigrants who were new to San Diego. His goals aligned perfectly with the organization's: finding better opportunities for immigrant families.

"I wonder if he still spends his weekends fishing with José or planning his family's vacations."

Suddenly, Whitney's lamentation that he needed real challenges to hold his interest jumped into my brain. *"Crossword puzzles and raffles will only keep me going for so long,"* he'd confided over our last coffee, before adding *"If I don't find something more complex to think about, my brain will turn to fudge."*

♦♦♦♦♦

The US Navy has a 6-month program for transitioning from active service to civilian life, and many of their newly-minted civilians use this time to develop an idea suited to their particular interests, write a business plan, and hang out their own shingle. In Whitney's case there was a problem, in that he hadn't known what he wanted to be once he left the service...and just kept working on his service job full-time until about three days before he was released.

Now what?

His wife, Elisabeth, had suggested he sleep in and catch his breath before figuring out his next move. But they both knew that travel wasn't going to be high on his list. After all, once you've spent years traveling the world, seeing the best—and the worst—of humanity and war, the idea of going somewhere as a tourist is guaranteed to hold *very* little appeal.

Yet there had to be something he could do. The man had interests, and value, despite what society might say about folks who've retired just giving up.

It was José—his longtime friend—who presented one possible solution during an unguarded moment aboard a rented fishing boat within sight of Shelter Island.

Whitney had investigated—and solved—many cases over the years, such as murders and thefts, and typically in under a week. Being slightly removed from the emotion of the moment, José saw the solution was about as easy as it gets: find the evidence, send it to the authorities, find the person, collect the reward, case closed.

And so with a little prodding from José and Elisabeth, George N. Whitney had gone into business as a private detective. The new firm even operated smoothly for a while, if you ignore the challenges one usually encounters as a small business owner.

Indeed, to George it was almost as if he'd never stopped his Navy career...only now he had to go hustle new clients all the time instead of them coming to him.

Perhaps that's what made his name and the news report connect in my mind. If anyone would be able to answer the question of who caused the explosion in downtown La Mesa, it would be Mr. Whitney.

♦♦♦♦♦

My legs shifted as I headed to the couch with my cellphone in hand. Facebook. Twitter. Instagram. It seemed as though everyone was talking about today's news. But like I said...you kind of expect that from a tragedy like this.

In the background I thought I heard my son calling me for something, though the only thing that really reached my ears was "Mom, we'll be right back!" before he left. I figured he was probably going to take out the trash or something, but by now my nose was stuck to the screen looking through the texts of past messages from clients.

My thumb fell on Whitney's number again. I hesitated. Maybe he's already working on it? Or he's at Shelter Island or the Portuguese hall with José. "*Actually*" I thought "*Today's Thursday. That's Bingo Night at his church.*" I leaned back into the soft sofa eyeing the phone before clicking it off, displaying nothing but the black mirror before setting it down.

God, I'm exhausted! Today really took it out of me.

For some reason, the couch felt impossibly comfortable today, as though it had conspired to swallow me whole. Was I really that drained? Between the fear and the lingering unease from this sudden chaos, my body felt like it had reached its limit and was completely burned out. The relentless pace of the past few weeks, juggling commission after commission through the long, sweltering summer, had finally caught up with me. My limbs felt like lead, and my eyes grew heavy as I drifted into the arms of Morpheus. I sank into the cushions, and all I could think was *I'll just close my eyes for a minute...*

♦♦♦♦♦

It was hours later and I awoke with a start. The TV was playing *A Night To Remember*; that 1958 classic about the sinking of the Titanic. I'd neglected to turn it off, but figured one of the kids would have done it for me. Really? I was annoyed—it wouldn't kill either of them to think of someone else once in a while.

I took a deep breath, had a good long stretch, and looked at the clock ticking quietly above the kitchen sink. 10pm? Had I really passed out on that sofa for three hours? I briefly worried if I'd be up all night and...

Wait! It was too damned quiet in this house. I sat up suddenly, instinctively knowing something was wrong.

I willed myself off the couch, my tiredness instantly forgotten. As I approached Jason's room, its eerie silence struck me, as did the open door and the darkness emanating from within. Switching the light on, I scanned the room and saw everything as it typically was; messy.

Clothes that I'd asked him a thousand times to fold sat in a crumpled heap, ignored and serving as a platform for his in-room dining habits. His music was still playing from his small radio, and his bed still hadn't been made despite my incessant nagging.

In fact everything was exactly as it normally was...only he wasn't there. "Jason?" I called tentatively, expecting an answer from under the bed covers. His phone was even there...untouched on his pillow. *Odd* I thought, knowing Jason almost always has his phone with him.

Why would he be in such a rush that he forgot his phone?

♦♦♦♦♦

Claudia's room was brighter and neater, and was sure to hold the answers I sought. I counted on Claudia to be the level-headed one who, though young, had a nature that bred trust in her decision-making capabilities. As I approached the light illuminating her soft pink bedroom walls, I anticipated she'd know where her brother was.

Only Claudia's room also lay empty before me, with just a handful of anime characters and illustrations of kittens and bunnies there to greet me. Her desk wasn't cleaned either, but her bedspread was folded. No Claudia. No Jason. Just the words *'Mom, we'll be right back!'* echoing in my ears from what seemed like days ago.

I forced myself to not panic. *Maybe they're in the basement.* That made sense—they were always sneaking off there to play board games. I hurried down the hallway, opening the door to reveal the narrow stairway descending into the dim, musty cinderblock space below. I called their names again, struggling desperately to keep my voice steady and not sound like the hysteric I was quickly transforming into.

Running through the kitchen, I saw the untouched garlic bread and the spaghetti and meatballs sitting on the counter, the spaghetti sauce congealing on the untouched platter. Dashing out to the garage, I practically tripped over the clutter of old storage bins chock full of holiday decor and half-forgotten junk. Shadowed and still, the silence loomed and the horror piling up in my gut threatened to consume me. They should be here. They *had* to be here. It was past their bedtime—they wouldn't just...

No, they wouldn't just vanish. They should be here. They *HAVE* to be here!

Only...where were they?

Don't panic! I kept reminding myself. My mind was spinning into overdrive, debating where they could have disappeared to. They couldn't have gone that far. Unless...the patio! They had to be there looking at the fireworks, I reasoned, even as that little voice in my head reminded me that the fireworks display must have ended by 9:00 so that the old folks in the neighborhood could go to sleep.

♦♦♦♦♦

NOW it was time to panic. I ran back upstairs frantically, through the hallway back to the living room and retraced my steps. They could be outside at this hour, of course, but what in the world would they be doing?

Admittingly, I'd be pissed off if Jason went out at night with his friends for some frat party...especially since I don't know how to reach any of his friends other than Jeremy. I quickly dialed Jeremy's number, instantly relieved at hearing his voice. My relief was short-lived.

"Hello?"

"Jeremy? Hi, it's Jason's mom," I said with a fake happy tone in my voice. I was struggling to not scream *"WHERE ARE MY CHILDREN!?"* The thought they might be missing was already too much for me to bear.

"I was–uh–I was wondering if–uh–is Jason with you at your home? I know he sometimes walks to your house at night."

"Um...no, sorry...I haven't seen him since three."

My heart dropped. "Are you sure? C-can you call Ben o-or Axel?" I asked as a tsunami of fear washed over me.

"I mean I can...but Axel's going to a musical play and Ben's at a football game...why?"

"I, uh..." I swallowed bitterly, "I can't find him..."

Genuinely concerned, Jeremy asked "Have you tried calling him?"

"N-no....he left his phone on the bed....I...." It suddenly dawned on me that Claudia didn't have a phone, and Jason had left his phone behind. There was absolutely no way I could contact either of them, and the alarm in my brain was screaming a four-alarm fire alert.

"I've gotta go!" I announced, desperate to figure out what would happen next.

"Wait, what's going on? Where"–

I hung up the phone, my mind too frantic to even comprehend the reality I saw settling in around me.

♦♦♦♦♦

Opening the patio door once more, I again called my children's names. The cool night air blew over the tears streaming down my cheeks as I glanced left to right, my eyes trying to adjust to the blackness that had settled over the neighborhood. I scanned the community, my eyes struggling to adjust, taking in the faint glow of distant city lights and the fading reddish haze of the clouds overhead.

There wasn't a sound beyond the buzz of cars driving by on neighboring roads, driven by people going about their lives with no concern for the disaster now unfolding in mine.

"Claudia? Jason?" I called out louder this time, desperate for any type of response. I strained for the smallest sound—a laugh, a footstep...*anything*—and was greeted by deathly silence beyond the occasional truck rumbling by on the highway and the ceaseless chirp of crickets in my yard.

My heart pounded in my chest, going a mile a minute. *WHERE ARE MY FUCKING KIDS?*

"Claudia! Jason! It's after 10, and you guys have school tomorrow! Come back inside NOW!" I shouted again, the words tearing from my throat.

But the silence was deafening. An owl called out nearby, saying "HOO!"

I burst into tears, shouting at the owl "My kids, you flea-bitten piece of shit!"

The darkness pressed in, threatening to suffocate me as my heart raced faster and became a sickening thud in my ears. Despite the cool breeze, sweat stains had drenched the armpits of my blouse. Where the hell were they?

I tried banishing the growing dread, but that quickly became a useless exercise. I was way beyond logic now, and my reptilian brain had taken over my thoughts. My voice broke as I screamed their names into the night.

"JASON! CLAUDIA!"

♦♦♦♦♦

This had to be a fucking nightmare. They can't be gone, they can't! They can't! THEY JUST CAN'T!

I stood frozen in the grass, my breath shallow and ragged, my mind spinning into a dark, uncontrollable spiral. The world blurred around me, distant and unreal. I staggered back toward the living room, my steps clumsy and unsteady, barely able to keep my balance as panic gripped me tighter with each passing second. Reaching the coffee table, I snatched my phone, my hands trembling so violently I nearly dropped it. My hands shook as I dialed the one person I knew who could help.

He had to. Goddammit, he *had* to!

Chapter 8: Dazed

-Whitney-

I leaned against the cold, smooth wall of the banquet hall, letting the muggy Shelter Island night settle over me. A faint cloud of cigarette smoke wafted from the smoker's outpost nearby, mingling with the sweet, savory aroma of barbecue that lingered in the air. The hall at the crossroads of Shafter Street buzzed with life, hosting one of its many Portuguese events.

Children's laughter filled the night as they dashed around playing toss games, scribbling on tic-tac-toe boards, or devouring handfuls of buttery popcorn. I looked to the crescent moon, presenting its gleaming white glory before the clouds began to snuff the lunar light, as they clustered into a thick blanket in the sky.

Checking my phone for the umpteenth time, I watched as yet another internet headline about today's La Mesa explosion scrolled by. Tragic and enigmatic, the story gripped me. Theories abounded—some called it a bomb, others whispered about a local terrorist attack, and still others dismissed it as a terrible accident.

But this case defied simple explanations. It felt as though the truth had scattered with the wind, lost in the same blaze that consumed what many called the "Jewel of the Hills."

♦♦♦♦♦

Stepping back into the hall, I was met with the quiet creak of the old wooden floorboards and the pristine white walls that framed the space. The television mounted above a display of Portuguese artifacts played muted footage of the explosion's aftermath. Though silent, the imagery of destruction spoke volumes as the news replayed the carnage of the 'bombing.'

The table before me was already perfectly set up for the next dinner party. Topped with a glass vase filled with white roses complementing the light blue hydrangeas, the only thing out of place was the television remote sitting at the table's edge. Next to the vase sat a bowl of cherry cordials; those damned confections that I almost always found to be irresistible.

Pausing, I debated scarfing up a half-dozen of them...then remembered stepping on the scale this morning and my resolution to begin dieting to shed twenty pounds or so.

Distracting myself with the news, I turned up the volume to hear the latest reporting which, to nobody's surprise, was the exact same story I'd already heard a hundred times in the past couple of hours. It was like a parrot repeatedly squawking the exact same phrase. Soon, another broadcast cut the current news short as it sought to provide updates and the latest scoop or rumor.

> *"We interrupt this program as we bring you this special report. At 8pm tonight The Creative Minds of La Jolla regional center experienced a rumored gas leak in one of the classrooms, poisoning many employees, caregivers, and students attending an evening class. The Creative Minds of La Jolla regional center serves and empowers persons with developmental disabilities and their families to achieve their goals with community partners. It helps their clientele to live productive and satisfying lives as valued members of their communities."*

My heart sank. Christ, as if things couldn't get any worse in this rotten city. America's Finest, my ass! What the fuck was going on?

> *"Many of the victims were younger than 13 years old, and we observed many who were being taken to the hospital appeared to be intoxicated. At this time the authorities do not know who or what was responsible for this horrific incident, and they are pursuing multiple leads."*

Are you kidding me? Now I really wanted—no, *needed*—to find out what the hell was going on. My thoughts were interrupted by another buzz in my pocket. I pulled out my phone, squinting at the screen: *Madeleine*. I hadn't heard from her in a while, and seeing her name appear in my life right on the heels of this news unsettled me. I answered quickly.

"Madeleine?"

She was practically screaming. "George! Thank God—something's happened. I..."

I'd always known Madeleine to be calm, cool and collected. Frantic and panicky were two words I'd never have ascribed to her...yet here we were.

I tried to keep my voice calm despite my concern. "Hey, it's alright. Just take a deep breath and tell me what happened."

She was choking on her words. "I-It's my kids...they're gone!! I can't find them ANYWHERE!" "After they finished their homework they went outside to watch the fireworks. I woke up from a nap...and they were gone! *THEY'RE GONE, GEORGE*!"

♦♦♦♦♦

Her sobs choked through the line, strangled and raw. I clutched the phone in my hand, overwhelmed with guilt that I couldn't be over there to give her comfort. All I could do was ask, "Madeleine, have you called the police yet?"

"Y-yes, I did, but please, George—*please*. Can you help me find them?"

"Alright, alright I'll see what I can do. Just take a few deep breaths, okay?" I assured her. "I'm sure they can't have gone that far."

My mind raced as I spoke. Two kids: one a teenager, the other a preteen—disappearing on a summer night? My gut told me they hadn't gone far. Maybe a couple of friends showed up with a tempting offer: *Let's hit the beach, have a bonfire, maybe sneak a beer*. Teens being what they are, they were just being carefree and thoughtless. It probably hadn't even occurred to them to leave a note or wake their mom.

Madeleine took a few deep breaths, trying to regain her composure. I couldn't blame her for falling apart like this: a single mom, two kids gone—who wouldn't be frantic?

"Stay put," I told her softly. "The police are on it, and so am I. I'll keep you on the line so you aren't alone, okay? And do you have recent pictures of them? That'll help the police."

I knew I had to get into this before the police did to help her navigate her way through the system. Even as I headed towards my car, I kept Madeleine talking in a vain effort to calm her down...or at least keep her from spiraling down further...until I reached La Jolla.

Connecting to my car's bluetooth, I dialed up Google Maps and kept her talking, providing a steady stream of updates, theories, and snippets of news as I learned about them from the police band I monitored. And, knowing how sharp he was when it came to identifying DNA samples and analyzing evidence, I decided to bring José into the conversation. I trusted he would be able to help with whatever kind of shit show this situation was about to turn into, and she was gonna need all the help she could get. José was sure to be a huge asset.

♦♦♦♦♦

"José," I called, motioning him away from the kitchen where he'd been deep in conversation with a couple of chefs. Speaking to the others in Portuguese, he excused himself quickly before following me with a curious look. I noticed him grabbing a towel as we walked outside, his hands still dusted lightly with flour or maybe sugar—the ever-present sign of the kitchen professional.

"What's going on?" José asked with a concerned look.

"We have to go to the precinct in La Jolla; something happened to Madeleine's kids," I said quietly. Given the crowd around us and the blaring of the local band playing on stage, I was unsure how much he'd heard me say. Then again, there wasn't much more detail to give him at the moment.

José raised his eyebrows and nodded. Turning back towards the kitchen, he called out to the other chefs "Eu tenho que ir cuidar de algumas coisas. Voltarei mais tarde esta noite." *—I have to go take care of a few things. I'll be back later tonight.*

With several boxes of chicken breast still to be shredded, they waved their understanding and continued their work as José and I headed towards the car. Driving towards Rosecrans Street, and despite the lack of late night traffic, we still had a half-hour drive and one understandably hysterical mother awaiting us.

Noticing I was still on the phone with Madeleine, José asked "Is she alright?" Still trying to comfort her, I couldn't immediately answer.

Periodically I'd remind her to breathe, hoping she didn't pass out on the line. But even as I kept reassuring her, I turned to José and silently shook my head 'no.'

♦♦♦♦♦

I'd been on the line with Madeleine for over 30 minutes during the drive from Point Loma to La Jolla, and I was prepared to stay with her this way until we arrived at her door. Instead she assured me that she would meet me at the police station...or in the worst case scenario, one of the area hospitals.

I didn't want to tell her that the real worst case scenario would be the morgue, and hoped we wouldn't need to have *that* discussion. Hanging up, I turned to José for a more in-depth conversation. "Madeleine's flipping out. She thinks her children were kidnapped."

"Kidnapped?" José glanced at me sharply.

"Or, with a little luck, they just ran away. Neither of them drives, so unless someone gave them a ride they can't have gotten that far. I'm just hoping that's the case."

At least this was my working theory; that it was just kids fooling around by sneaking out at night with friends and hoping for the best...rather than the worst case scenario that Madeleine was struggling not to envision.

Then again, there are a lot of sick degenerates out there. Long ago I'd learned that no matter how safe the suburbs can look and feel, someone always seems to be out to get you.

I'd been on the phone with Madeleine for almost 50 minutes when we pulled up to the Eastgate Mall's police precinct. I knew it was too soon to file a missing persons report, but thought nosing around a little over there might shed some light on her kids.

♦♦♦♦♦

Sheriff Jimmy Bart and I were old friends, and he was pleased to see me walk through the door. "George," he called out cheerily "It's been a while." "Jimmy," I nodded as José followed me in through the door. We bantered back and forth a bit, and I reminded him I hadn't forgiven him yet for that snarky *'Old man Whitney'* comment from our last encounter.

Yet before I could tell him my purpose for being there, I spotted Madeleine sitting on the bench by the door, shaking and sobbing. Next to her was another officer trying to comfort her. Sighing, I suggested we find a place to speak privately.

Jimmy saw my glance and his cheeriness instantly faded. "Right!"

Recognizing the extent of this horrid attack, we both knew we could engage in our usual banter sometime later, and instead headed for his office. José followed closely behind, closing the door after us to avoid the possibility of Madeleine accidentally hearing anything we said and getting even more upset.

"So any luck?" I asked.

Frustrated, Jimmy shook his head and mumbled "No." Clearing his throat, he added "The kids haven't been found yet either, and Madeleine is just barely holding it together out there."

"Any evidence?" asked José. "Maybe the kids dropped something along the way?"

Shaking his head, Jimmy wiped sweat from his forehead. "Nothing yet." I could tell he was as puzzled as the rest of us about the whole situation. "I just don't get it sometimes..." he muttered.

♦♦♦♦♦

The phone on the desk jangled loudly, yanking us all from our thoughts. I'd never seen someone move so fast as Jimmy grabbed it. "La Jolla Police. Sheriff Bart here."

His expression instantly transformed from gloom to delight. "They found them?...who?....okay where are they?"

I was afraid to ask, fearful I'd be reporting to Madeleine that her children were injured...or worse. "What's going on?"

"A jogger found them up in the hills near La Jolla Cove. They were unconscious. There was a guy with them, but he fled when the jogger confronted him. The K-9 unit is up there now trying to track him down."

"What did the jogger report?" I blurted impatiently. "Any descriptions of the attackers?"

"Wearing...white? That's all?" Jimmy asked, adding "Okay, Charlie. Thanks a lot," as he hung up the phone.

Jimmy turned to me and José. "They're over at Scripps Memorial hospital. It's three minutes up the road—let's go!"

♦♦♦♦♦

Jimmy and José drove to the hospital in a squad car, while I guessed Madeleine would be in no condition to drive and I guided her towards my car. I had José buy her a cup of coffee while Jimmy and I went into the ER to investigate the situation.

The nurse at the front desk pointed us to room thirteen, second floor to our right. As Jimmy and I entered the room, we paused to see the one thing no parent should ever have to experience: two children hooked up to tubes dripping who knows what into their veins.

And though it felt like an intrusion, I needed to know what was going on and if these kids were alright. Jimmy spoke with one of the nurses as I cautiously approached the boy's bedside.

Looking back and forth between the two, I instantly saw their eyes were blank and red-rimmed and knew something wasn't right. My first theory—perhaps they'd smoked a little too much pot—fell apart as soon as I got a whiff of their clothing, which reeked of bleach rather than marijuana.

Quickly reviewing his chart, I knelt down next to the young man and waved my hand over his eyes. "Hey Jason. Ya feeling alright?" His eyes remained glassy and bloodshot, and his only response was a thousand-yard stare at the ceiling.

So while the good news was that they'd been found, it was horrifying to see them up close. I tried to figure out how to spin this for Madeleine so she wouldn't bounce off the walls when she saw them.

♦♦♦♦♦

My mind swirled trying to figure out what could have gotten them into this state. Did a "friend" sneak some kind of cleaning chemicals into their drinks? Or was bleach the newest thing kids were huffing nowadays, not understanding it will deteriorate their lungs and burn their throats beyond repair?

I started thinking about when kids all over the internet started eating dishwasher pods like candy as part of the "Tide Pod Challenge" a few years back. And the "Cinnamon challenge" a few years before that. And...

SIGH! I know we're supposed to let children make their own mistakes, but sometimes—and especially in these days where social media makes such a big impact on their not-fully-formed brains—sometimes it's painful to watch as the next "high" or cheap thrill comes along and so many of our young people fall victim to it.

All I could hope was that the poison control team could make a better, more educated call about the problem. I looked at the girl lying beside her brother and saw she was in the same condition. "You all right, Claudia?" I asked. "Can you hear me?"

Claudia lay there, as dazed as her brother, but she managed to say one word in a hoarse whisper: "Pure..."

I leaned in closer. "Pardon?" She stared blindly into the distance, her eyes bright red and unfocused. "What did you say?" I asked again softly.

"...Am I pure yet?" the girl croaked.

I blinked. "What?"

I looked up at Jimmy and the nurse, hoping it made sense to at least one of them. One look was all I needed to recognize that neither of them had a clue about what her question meant. They looked on, their faces both masks of worry.

"...Am I pure yet?" The question sounded ominous. After all, the word 'pure' suggested she was clean and unscathed. At age ten I presumed this girl was sexually uneducated, so I cautiously went forward on the assumption we were talking about something else.

Besides, the trancelike state didn't square with someone wishing to regain her virginity.

♦♦♦♦♦

I rubbed my face as I looked back at the kids. My heart ached, both for them and for their mother. Nobody, least of all children, should be in a horrible condition like this. But there was no way to soften the agony Madeleine would experience upon learning what happened to the two most important people in her life. The screams were sure to be blood-curdling, and just thinking about it made me want to head for the nearest bar.

I was tempted to just hoof it out of there and spend the rest of the evening drinking alone. Damn all those years of training, forcing me to be civil and sociable around other people. Especially Madeleine.

But none of that mattered now; there were *much* more important things to deal with at the moment. Pushing my desire for escape aside, I knew I instead had to find out what happened to these kids and who was responsible; to learn the truth of the whole ordeal, and to keep their mother from going batshit crazy.

Plus I now found myself wondering how many other Jasons and Claudias there might be out there? Because one thing was crystal clear to me: this *wasn't* an isolated incident!

"This is how they were found?" I asked Jimmy, my eyes never leaving the two children.

"That's what the initial report said," he nodded. "The deputy said the jogger saw someone, but the only description of them was someone wearing white. That's all we know right now."

I sighed, my heart heavy and fearful, and studied the kids' expressions as Jimmy added "The K-9 unit is looking for anyone that smells of bleach. And we're waiting for a lab analysis to see if there were any other chemicals these kids might have been exposed to."

♦♦♦♦♦

Chemicals. The word echoed in my head along with the girl asking if she was *'pure.'* It was as if those two words were combining to describe this disgusting crime; using chemicals to make these children pure.

These beautiful children, who hadn't lived long enough to need to be made pure.

Yet some disgusting individual had apparently taken it upon themself to 'clean' the minds of kids with chemicals, as if they were nothing more than a bathtub to be cleansed with bleach.

Well, *fuck* that! These were Madeleine's kids, and that made it personal for me. Whoever this sicko was...

My mind wandered back to the news I had watched earlier about the regional center being attacked. I found myself wondering if there was a connection between that event and the state these kids were in, and the very idea made my stomach churn.

Was this a hate attack of some kind...or was there something bigger going on?

As these thoughts went through my mind I heard the nurse speak. "Why would this stranger be carrying bleach to attack kids?"

"We don't know," Jimmy confessed, adding "but that's our current theory." He rubbed his temples, barely holding his composure.

Given the steady stream of horrors throughout the city that he had to deal with for his job, I couldn't really blame the guy.

"Is it time to call for an official state of emergency? This is getting out of hand," I suggested.

"And what should we say?" Jimmy huffed, obviously still shaken up by the drugged state of the kids. "You want me to announce that San Diego county is being targeted? That we think we may have a Nazi cell gassing our regional centers? Talk about starting a media frenzy...and a panic. As if we don't already have plenty of those made by people who cry wolf just to get the attention. No thanks!"

"Besides," he added a bit more softly "We don't have nearly enough evidence to prove that claim."

♦♦♦♦♦

"That evidence is out there somewhere, Jimmy," I earnestly reminded him. "And we're going to find it...even if it means hiking up security in school for the Special Ed. students and for the summer festivals this coming week."

Of course it's one thing to think such a thing, but quite another to say it out loud. There were July 4th festivals coming within days, and we suddenly had a bigger security problem than I'd previously realized. I felt sick, even as I cleared my throat to continue. "The last resort being, we may have to bring more security and precautions to the events."

"Events?"

"The Midsummer Festival is coming a mere ten days after the Independence Day celebrations. I'm starting to think that adding even more security to events like that one would be the smart move. Better safe than sorry, and all that."

The room fell silent beyond the machines beeping from the heart monitors. Jimmy rubbed the back of his neck, averting his eyes from the children before he spoke again. "Whitney, you should be the one to tell Madeleine what happened."

Chapter 9: Pure

-Madelaine-

Whitney telling me to meet him at the police station confirmed my worst nightmares. Even as I drove there, my hands shook so much in fear and terror of what we might learn that I almost drove off the road. Twice.

And how I made it unscathed through that red light is still a mystery. I was crying so much, I could barely see that the light had changed.

At the station I paced, sat down, got up and paced again...though whether my pacing was driven by nervous energy or anxiety, it was hard to say. Despite the sheriff's assurances and support, all I wanted to know was: where was George? Because the sergeant at the front desk wasn't telling me anything, and I knew they were waiting for him.

But for the love of Christ, these were my children we were talking about. The only two people on the planet who gave my life—my existence—meaning. And the cops were standing on ceremony?

I was reminded of the promise I'd made to my late husband on his deathbed; that I would always be there for our children, no matter the cost. It was a promise I had always kept...and I wasn't about to stop now.

Only here I was feeling like the worst mother in the world. I'd blown it, allowing not one, but *both* of my kids to be in trouble. Were they injured? At death's door? Whatever it was, I was obviously a shitty mother and a lousy widow who couldn't even keep a promise to the love of her life as he lay dying in a hospital bed, mere hours after being hit by that God-damned drunk driver.

Jonathan would have been heartbroken to see any of his family like this...and I wouldn't have blamed him.

Where did my kids go? What had happened? I was desperate for the slightest scrap of information, and the cops were refusing to answer me, leaving me to beat myself up on that bench with a cup of coffee and a uniformed cop being my only comfort as I waited for George. *Where are my children?* Why did I leave them alone? Why the hell did I let them stray from my side for even a few hours while I slept?

I was in the bargaining phase, promising God or whatever supposedly watched over us all that I'd never make a mistake like that again, given the chance.

I wasn't convinced anyone was listening.

♦♦♦♦♦

When George and Whitney finally showed up at the police station, I had figured I'd get some fast answers...only to have them disappear behind closed doors for the most excruciating half-hour of my life. And George taking my keys away to drive me to the hospital behind José and the sheriff did little to improve my mood.

José even bought me a second cup of coffee, but that was obviously a distraction. What were these guys hiding? And what's a girl got to do to get some straight answers?

Deep in my soul I was praying as hard as I could that my children weren't severely harmed or even...I couldn't even think about finishing that sentence. I was trying to cling to any sliver of a silver lining—*anything* that would give me hope that they would both come out of this in the same condition as they had been in yesterday.

These fucking cops weren't helping with their unresponsive attitudes. Didn't they realize how much pain I was in?

My heart skipped a beat as I finally saw Whitney and Jimmy coming from the far end of the hallway. I leapt to my feet, almost involuntarily rushing towards them. "Whitney! How are they? Are they all right?"

Fear and grief had numbed my mind, making it impossible to even think of staying calm.

"Well, they've been found and they're alive..." I cut Whitney off before he could finish.

"Oh, thank God! How did you find..."

"Madeleine, wait....you didn't let me finish...they're alive, but they're not okay."

My blood froze as his words washed over me like a bucket of ice water. I willed myself to stay both calm and coherent, even as my heart sank to unimaginable depths. "W-what do you mean?"

It couldn't be good, and judging by the looks of dismay and confusion on both men's faces – and of the police officer sidling up behind them—I knew this was going to be the longest night of my life. "They...they were taken by someone—the only thing we know about the suspect is he was hooded and dressed all in white, apparently dosed with bleach. The K-9 unit is still looking for whoever is responsible."

♦♦♦♦♦

In an instant I was nauseous as my world tilted. Suddenly I was standing in front of these two men talking, but not hearing anything they or I said. Everything blurred around me as I stopped breathing, convinced this was—hoping this was—a nightmare.

Closely watching my horrified face, José moved just before I fainted, catching me by the shoulders and guiding me to the nearby chair before I could collapse into a sodden heap. The room spun, the edges of my vision flickered, and I sank into the seat, trying to keep the darkness at bay.

♦♦♦♦♦

I don't care what any of the books say about how you're supposed to be stoic—you know, stiff upper lip and all that—in this kind of situation. That's bullshit. We were talking about *my* children being kidnapped and poisoned by some psychopath, and how I wasn't there to protect them. I wasn't there when they left the house.

I didn't see how it was anyone else's fault but mine.

The guilt was suffocating, coiling around me like a hungry python, but beneath it burned something darker: *rage*. A seething, simmering fury at the thought of the vile, selfish creature who had done this. What kind of monster would hurt them? *Why?* I needed answers—no, I *demanded* answers!

"You...you don't know who did this?" My voice was barely steady.

Whitney shook his head solemnly, "Not yet, Madeleine. We're working on finding them now."

A bitter, hollow laugh escaped my lips before I could stop it. Of *course* they didn't know who was responsible. I should have been thrilled and delighted that my kids had been found alive, but that infuriatingly predictable response only stoked my brewing wrath. It took every ounce of my willpower to stay seated; to not bolt from the room and tear the world apart while looking for the maniac responsible for causing them this pain.

I wanted revenge—I wanted *BLOOD*—and I wouldn't be satisfied until I had it.

♦♦♦♦♦

I swallowed, the bile rising in my throat, my voice sharp and cutting when I spoke again. "Where are my kids now?"

Whitney and José hesitated as they looked at each other, both suspecting how I would react and trying to head off further trouble before it hit.

"*Please...*" My voice cracked under the weight of desperation.

Whitney sighed. "Follow me..." The dread in his tone sent a shiver down my spine.

Still feeling unsteady, I struggled to hoist myself from the seat and follow Whitney. I even laughed involuntarily when I saw they were in room 13. Of COURSE it was going to be Room 13...

Stepping inside slowly, I barely kept my unsteady legs in their proper place. The room was dim, the hum of machinery and the sterile scent of antiseptics suffocating. Curtains draped around the beds obscured my view, but the sense of foreboding was crushing.

My vision blurred and the walls tilted, making the world look like something from a Tom Petty video.

I faltered again, my nerves frayed and my breath struggling to get past the rising patch of bile caught in my throat. This time it was Whitney who was ready to catch me.

"Mama?"

The small, trembling voice pierced through my haze. My heart stopped. It was Claudia.

"Baby?" I croaked, my voice barely audible, raw with emotion.

"Is that you mama?" her small voice asked again, her words frail and broken.

My heart screamed at me to get up, to rush to her, to pull her into my arms and shield her from all the pain in the world. I wanted to wail and cry my eyes out at this moment, trying to move to my daughter and son. But my legs betrayed me, trembling and weak. I could only sit there, paralyzed, calling out to her as best as I could. "Yes, Claudia, it's me baby..."

I strained to see through the curtains, to catch even the smallest glimpse of her, but the hanging sheets blocked my view. I didn't even know which bed she was in—or where Jason was. But her voice was enough for now; a fragile thread tethering me to hope.

♦♦♦♦♦

An unexpected surge from the air conditioning unit created a momentary breeze, pushing the thin white curtain aside just enough to give me a glimpse of her red swollen eyes. I struggled to stand, wanting nothing so much as to run to her and hold her close.

"Where are you?" Claudia croaked out.

"Right here, honey...just listen...listen to my voice, all right?" My breath hitched as I swallowed hard, the words like jagged glass in my throat. "Where's your brother?"

"On...on the other bed, next to me," Claudia said weakly. "I think he's sleeping."

I closed my eyes, biting down the sob threatening to escape. “Okay,” I whispered, my voice cracking. “Do...do you remember what happened, baby?”

“Madeleine,” Whitney interjected before Claudia suddenly answered: “a man...in a white robe and a mask...saw us.”

Silence fell into the room, with no other noise but the beeping of the heart monitors. “Did he approach you?” I asked, even as I feared for the answer.

“Yeah...he approached us...when me and Jason saw the fireworks...”

“Do...do you remember what he said to you?”

“I...” Claudia’s voice trailed off as she struggled to describe the memory. I held my breath, unsure if she was in shock or if it was hurting her to speak, “It’s all fuzzy...but he offered us some candy.”

“He offered you candy, baby?”

“And I started to take it, but Jason stopped me from eating the whole thing. He figured out something was wrong...I didn't really see it all...but Jason pushed the man away before we ran...I did remember him saying things...”

“What?”

“He...wanted us to be...*pure*...”

Another wave of shock, confusion and nausea swept over me, and my courage wavered as I asked, “What do you mean *pure*, Baby?”

“I don’t remember why...Jason was pushing them away...it was blurry,” Claudia mumbled under her breath, “then I tasted something...*funny*. Jason was fighting two guys with white robes.”

I felt broken as my daughter described the incident that remained stuck in her mind. A never-ending stream of hot tears poured down my face as I trembled from the tsunami of nausea, wrath and horror boiling within me. It took all my strength to not faint or scream at the top of my lungs, and I felt Whitney’s hand rubbing my back in soothing circles.

It wasn't nearly enough to ease my pain as I processed what Claudia had just said. “He had friends with him…”. There’s more than one. *MORE* than one person had attacked my children. “I…I see…” I croaked. I reached down to kiss her head, suddenly getting more than a whiff of bleach. My daughter smelled like the stuff I used for cleaning the toilets, and I had a hunch.

Moving over to the next bed, I put my face up against Jason’s hair, only to be stung again with the stench of too much bleach.

And I started to boil over as I realized that someone had tried to kill both my children…with bleach.

♦♦♦♦♦

As Claudia dozed off, I rushed from the room determined to find and punish the shitheels that had done this to my children. And though I had no plan, per se, I knew I needed to do *SOMETHING.*

I stared at the sanitized floors of the recently mopped hallway. Until this horrid moment, I’d never thought I would hate the *‘clean’* smell of hospitals.

But now it was serving as little more than a haunting reminder of the circumstances my children and I were in. I felt my stomach churning, fighting the overwhelming desire to be sick amid the heat of rage radiating inside me and around me all at once.

I wanted revenge. I wanted blood to be shed. I thought of my ten-year-old Claudia lying there helpless on a hospital gurney, and determined to find whoever had done this to my little girl and make them pay.

♦♦♦♦♦

“Madeleine?”

George’s voice was breaking through the noise of my inner turmoil. Taking a deep breath, I released it like air slowly escaping from a balloon. “Yes?”

“We have some clues of who could have done this, and figure they can’t be that far away,” he softly explained.

I let out a scornful laugh and shook my head. “Sure, that helps a whole bunch!”

This didn't sound like me. Snarky and obnoxious had never been words used to describe my personality or my attitude, and I knew he was trying to help. But it was so hard to comprehend any of this...this disgusting thing that had happened to my family. Looking at George plaintively, I asked "How the hell can I be relieved by that when my kids are in there?"

A storm of emotions was sweeping over me, building by the moment. Even as I was trying to stay reasonable in my conversation, fantasies about locating whoever did this to my Jason and my Claudia and carving them up, piece by piece, were playing out in my mind. Nothing mattered to me right now more than making these fuckers suffer and know just a fraction of the pain they had caused my two beautiful children...and heaven only knew how many others like them.

Intellect no longer mattered; pain needed to be inflicted. Retribution needed to be visited upon this scum. I wanted to know the address and the name of the person once they were caught by the police. Better yet, I wanted to find them myself. I started thinking about spending more time visiting my friend Peter in Sabre Springs, just so I could start taking lessons at the Poway Weapons & Gear Range.

Nothing was going to stand in the way of my getting justice for my family, and laws against that sort of thing be damned! I was hungry for justice. My little girl needed to be avenged.

Driven by the volcano of rage just beneath my surface, I tugged at the tangled ends of my hair and struggled to keep my breath from shaking. George read my thoughts—I guess I was either more transparent than I'd realized or he'd seen this movie before—and he placed his hand firmly on my shoulder. Was he trying to calm me down, or hold me back?

"Madeleine...I know this hurts right now, but you have to let the police do their job. They *will* find the criminals, and I'm going to help them. I promise."

"But," he continued, "I can only do my job if *you* promise you won't do anything rash or that might get you into danger."

Looking deeply into my eyes, Whitney urged me back to some level of sanity. "*Please.*"

I looked at him desperately. “How are the police going to find them? There are well over three million people in this county and we don't even know who is doing this. Are we going to wait until another tragedy happens in *more* areas where children are playing?!”

“No, absolutely not!” my friend said more firmly. “We’re going to find the man and his friends and shut down their operation, no matter what it takes.”

♦♦♦♦♦

I’d been holding my breath without realizing it, and with a shaky sigh I desperately tried to not break down again. Because George’s reassuring words aside, there was absolutely no question in my mind that the piece of shit responsible for this heinous act would strike again. Whose kids would be next? And would they be as lucky as mine had been to survive the attack?

To make matters worse, I was convinced the public wouldn't even know about any of this until the news caught on to the story. And because it didn’t impact them immediately, most people would likely brush off the issue as a minor inconvenience, rather than being the emergency I knew it to be. It would be just the fentanyl crisis all over again. And the countless stories of people’s lives ruined by mental health issues, whether they hurt themselves or caused crimes that hurt others.

Besides, you just knew that this situation wasn’t going to get any better anytime soon. I mean, I may not know much about the police, but how in the world could they find one man in a white robe handing out candy and trying to poison innocent kids with bleach when there were so many people, and so many places to hide?

It seemed like a pretty impossible task to me.

"Okay," I said softly, feeling the bitter weight of defeat settle in my chest. "I won't do anything drastic...yet."

♦♦♦♦♦

My friend wasn’t convinced. He could see the fire in my eyes and sensed the itch under my skin. Plus he knew me well enough to recognize that I wouldn’t ever truly back down from this.

And he was right. I wasn’t going to stop until I found the fucker who had done this.

"Madeleine...please." His voice held a quiet desperation. He knew me too well, knew the thoughts racing through my mind before they'd even fully formed. "Hunting them down on your own won't solve anything," he added, his words laced with worry. "I can't risk you ending up in a hospital bed too."

I sucked in sharply, the cold air stinging my lungs. I hated knowing he was right. If I went after them now, there was every chance they'd get to me before I got to them.

And yet, I glanced towards my kids lying helpless in their hospital beds—I just didn't care. The urge to act, to retaliate, to make these bastards suffer as my family was suffering, burned too hot to ignore. Even if it meant walking straight into the fire. Even if it meant dying to take them down with me.

Still, if I couldn't do anything reckless, then I had to be smart. I had to find enough proof to force George and the world to see what had happened. To make the news speak on it, to stop them from brushing it aside like another footnote in their endless cycle of tragedy.

More people needed to know. Not just in San Diego County. Not just in California. *Everyone.*

After all, the best way to step on cockroaches is to shine a light on them. Whoever these people were, they needed to be dragged into the light.

And if that didn't work? Then I'd drag them myself straight to the depths of hell!

Chapter 10: The Cassette

-Sofia-

The fires had long since died down, each ember smothered beneath the steady hands of the first responders. What remained was a bleak, lifeless ruin—a blackened skeleton of my hometown, stripped of all its warmth and familiarity. My cats, their gentle purrs and soft warmth, were lost to the darkness. Even my poems—those fragile pieces of myself scrawled in the quiet hours and too sacred to share—had been claimed by the smoke and ash.

It was all gone. My sanctuary. My history. *My home.*

The old houses within the confines of downtown La Mesa had all been abandoned, and I instinctively knew that a quick search on Google would have revealed that countless more on the surrounding streets had suffered a similar fate.

The once vibrant plaza was dead, the firefighters crawling like bright yellow carpenter ants stripping the decaying wood and a facade to allow the next round of scavengers, cutters and harvesters to clear out anything of value, raze the current structures, and lay the groundwork for a new generation of life in a valiant effort to resurrect our little city. Coyotes, crows, and other opportunists scavenged, one step ahead of the looters and other opportunists. Little color remained, save Mount Helix looming nearby and casting a silhouette over the former grandeur of the Jewel of the Hills.

All of which became even drearier as the evening shadows merged with the charcoal gray skies, bringing with them a drizzling summer rain to soak everything in its path. It was an oddly fitting setting for this place of memorialization: abandoned, with only the occasional bygone snatch of music echoing through the bluetooth speakers that still operated and picked up whatever tune was playing from the cellphone of the stray passerby.

My cleanup crew had sent me back to the scene of the crime in hopes that I could salvage the last remnants of belongings for several grieving families I'd never even met. Why it was me they chose was anyone's guess, as I had no special salvation skills, nor insights into the neighborhood or the people. In fact, all that we had in common was that we'd all recently lost our La Mesa homes.

I was in no mood to be here, yet here I was nevertheless. UCH!

♦♦♦♦♦

The loss that we had all just suffered weighed heavily on my mind. Trudging through murky puddles and feeling the cold water splashing on my boots and jeans, I wished I had better clothing for this weather. My burgundy hoodie, thin and worn from years of use, was absolutely no match for the chill that bit through me down to the bone.

I trudged through the abandoned businesses and catering shops, picking my way toward the main strip of downtown. For though the dead had all been moved to a more appropriate setting, the corpses of the shops and homes, piled atop the devastated landscape, was best described as surreal. They lay there in pieces resembling something from one of those old, bad Japanese dystopian future horror flicks, waiting to be consumed by nature, with none of them in even the remotest condition to be refurbished. Rather than trying to fix them up, I figured we'd all be better off just knocking them down and starting from scratch.

The house with the enlarged cavity—my old house—lay just ahead, and I continued shivering every step of the way. The wind was relentless, knifing through my clothes as if I was wearing nothing at all. Above me the drizzle grew heavier, soaking my hair and trickling down my face. Each step was a plea to the clouds above: "*Don't thunder. Not yet.*"

My heart pounding, I slipped beneath the caution tape while praying the police wouldn't spot me. My eyes scanned the wreckage, clinging to a fragile hope that I might find something familiar and intact—just *one* of my stuffed animals, or maybe a notebook filled with visionary writings from countless sleepless nights.

♦♦♦♦♦

The good news was that it was finally safe for me to walk through the area. The sidewalk was no longer littered with the bodies of the recently deceased, though the stench of death still lingered heavily, permeating everyone and everything within reach of the community strip.

Thinking I might retch, I halted mere steps from my home, finding myself faced with an unbearable sight. The ossified remains, blackened and brittle, stood as a pitiless monument to what had once been my refuge from the world's cruelty.

Now I had nothing. My house had been devoured by the explosion, and everything of consequence to my life had been reduced to kindling. The thought of my feline companions, almost certainly lost to this needless destruction, twisted like a knife in my chest. Had the fire claimed their gentle lives, too?

I clung desperately to a sliver of hope, imagining them scurrying to safety, their instincts guiding them away from the flames. But this scrap of prayer felt thin and fragile, even as I beseeched whatever higher power might hear me that the explosion hadn't extinguished my innocent friends—the quiet, comforting quintet who had never asked for this and certainly didn't deserve it.

♦♦♦♦♦

Dodging layers of horror that had once been home, I wended my way towards the empty room where a memorial had recently been held. The mourning crowd had dissipated, leaving me to stand there, alone and shivering.

Inside was neither warm nor inviting, and I eyed the small shrine made for those who had died. Only a few LED candles remained lit, the others as dead as the people they were supposed to honor.

Within my home, of all places.

There was food there, too, though it wasn't in much better condition than its surroundings. Perhaps meant as a celebration of life, or as comfort for the children, the remnants appeared to have been nibbled on after drawing the attention of critters as desperate as the people they were stealing from. The children's drawings remained, washed out and faded by the weather or trampled under the boots of the first responders coming back to finish their work, resulting in wet, crumpled, useless scraps of paper.

All of which both sickened and saddened me, though I was briefly cheered by finding one of my stuffed animals in relatively salvageable condition. I instantly decided that—despite the singed fur on the blue easter bunny's ear and the missing glass eye—Mr. Carrots was coming back with me. The other stuffies were little more than dust or frayed limbs of stuffing and fabric...and one glance persuaded me that my written musings had most certainly not survived the maelstrom.

This was the reality of what had so recently been my shelter from the world; a pile of charred wood, leaking walls, and faulty wiring. The furniture was shot, the gaping holes in the walls disquieting. And while the CRT television seemed relatively untouched, I had zero idea whose it was.

The television looked like something Damian would have had at the foot of his bed—one of those old battery-operated models that a company called Radio Shack used to sell—and I suspected it was the neighbor's that had somehow survived the detonation. I figured that, a Twinkie, and the cockroaches would be all that was still intact in this community.

Looking at the television, I wondered if someone had brought it along to keep the kids entertained while the adults discussed the next moves for our neighborhood. And I questioned if it would even work, or if it was even worth trying to find anything else of value here.

♦♦♦♦♦

Turning to leave, a spot of light caught my eye – the reflection of a video cassette under a dirty napkin, tucked into a remote corner of the room. With the looters cleaning out anything of value, I found it odd that nobody had taken this...or the television, for that matter.

Something deep in my core told me to tuck this video into my bag and take it with me. Maybe it was a film Damian would like to add to his collection, or something classic like *Casablanca*. And it looked to be in pretty fair condition.

A little voice in the back of my brain urged me to unravel whatever secrets this little surviving oddment might hold.

My eyes turned to the boxy TV set a few feet away, noting there was a VCR just beneath it.

I shuffled my feet towards the old box, ignoring the occasional drip of dirty water falling onto it from the ceiling and hoping it wouldn't short circuit if I was able to actually make it operate. "That would be miraculous," I muttered to nobody in particular...only to realize there is no wire attached to it.

I was stunned to see that pushing the cassette player's power button generated a positive result. Inserting the video, I found myself wishing for a warm room, a blanket, and a cup of tea, perhaps in front of a roaring fi...

SHIT! What was I saying?

The machine whirred, clicked, and sprang to life, and with a bit of effort I turned the knob of the vintage set and silently watched as it sputtered to life. The light flickered on the screen for a few seconds, eventually solidifying into an actual picture.

♦♦♦♦♦

There was to be no Humphrey Bogart movie for me, though. The scene I was peeking in on seemed to be a sermon of some kind, undoubtedly from a local church. The screen colors were muted, and the sermon started with the blaring of a pipe organ.

It was painful, sounding as if the poor instrument was protesting the idea of having to play at this service. Its multiple brass throats squawked through the television speakers, only to bounce off the walls around the spot where I stood before finally settling into my ears.

Standing over the pulpit was a middle-aged man with long dark hair desperately in need of a washing. He wore a papal robe that had unquestionably seen better days.

But it was the organ that kept drawing my attention as it played an extended melody that didn't lift, but rather loomed, heavy and ominous. And the man, despite his ever-present smile, seemed to be studying the congregation with predatory intent.

My stomach tightened as I got the distinct feeling that something just didn't smell right about the scene before me.

♦♦♦♦♦

It took just a few seconds more for the sans serif text to appear on the screen, displaying the presenter's name as Aeron Inochi.

His voice was smooth – maybe too smooth—yet I found something about it all that I couldn't name was off-putting. The slight distortion from the aging VHS only added to the dreary effects of listening to him. I leaned closer to the flickering screen, the grainy footage pulling me into his peculiar message.

> *"Hello, friends of the world," he began, his grin unwavering. "Have you ever had an illness that seemed incurable? Have you ever wanted to find something that could help those things disappear? Naturally, you'd want it to be a cure that doesn't cost you a fortune and put your family into the poorhouse. And it should be something that isn't addictive, so you won't be prey to big pharmaceutical companies."*

I blinked. This *had* to be a commercial, but, as the old saying goes, something was rotten in Denmark. The tone, the presentation—they were too personal, and almost too conspiratorial. Yet, like an accident on the highway, I couldn't look away.

> *"Well, there is hope!"*

The camera abruptly shifted to a close-up of white bottles of varying sizes, their stark labels emblazoned with the same bold font screaming "The Miracle Tap". Around the bottles, cartoon flowers danced awkwardly in the screen's corners, as though pulled from an outdated clipart library.

Miracle Tap? I thought, furrowing my brow. The name sounded ridiculous, like a gimmick you'd find at a flea market. The footage itself seemed ancient, maybe from the mid-nineties judging by the grainy quality. A VHS timestamp popped up briefly in the corner of the picture with a 1995 date, confirming my suspicion.

Was this just some relic of a bygone era of telemarketing? And what was it doing in this place, waiting for me to watch it?

The man's sonorous voice resumed.

> *"The Miracle Tap is the holistic answer you've been seeking for the health and mental issues of your loved ones. Whether you want it in capsules or liquid, Miracle Tap is the perfect tool for all the diseases western medicine tells you can't be cured."*

The screen abruptly shifted again, this time to an absurdly literal visual—a sparkling set of cartoon teeth. The teeth gleamed so brightly, they bordered on parody. "This product is so great it can even clean the user's mouth," he added enthusiastically.

The next cut was jarring: a montage of smiling people clad in crisp white shirts and blouses, waving stiffly at the camera. They looked like cult members in a poorly scripted infomercial, with smiles that were too wide and eyes too vacant.

The man doing the voice-over now moved in to close the deal.

> *"Miracle Tap is made locally by our holistic community in Ramona, California...right here in San Diego county," he boasted, adding, "And we guarantee we will get your life back on track...or your money back, no questions asked."*

BZZZZT!

The television sparked from the unseen puddle sitting underneath. I jumped back from the sudden glitch, even as I watched the screen temporarily return to normal.

♦♦♦♦♦

I froze. Ramona. In San Diego? A chill swept through me. This wasn't some fictional ad filmed in a distant, far away place; it was rooted in my reality. The mesmerizing voice continued:

> *"The Miracle Tap is made with only organic ingredients, along with a wide variety of important vitamins and minerals that your body needs to fight off various illnesses and other genetic defects."*

Genetic defects? The phrase bounced around my brain ominously. Defects of what? Of whom? By whose standards? Something about this entire production, from the outdated visuals to the eerie cheerfulness of the presenter and participants, just felt wrong. "Something stinks here," I muttered to myself as I heard Aeron Inochi continue his pitch.

> *"Customers say they have been cured of early stages of cancer, HIV, AIDS and mental illnesses such as depression, schizophrenia, narcolepsy, autism, ADHD and other ailments too numerous to list."*

The cassette crackled faintly as I caught my breath. Despite my skepticism and my best efforts, I was getting sucked in deeper into this unnerving narrative. I blinked, trying to process what I'd just heard—autism on a list of ailments alongside cancer and AIDS? My disbelief gave way to mounting anger, horror, and suspicion.

> *"Just take this tasty cherry syrup twice a day for a week,"* he droned on in an unnervingly cheerful voice. *"And you'll see a rapid, positive, impact on your life. Use this amazing product for 30 straight days and you'll see a complete turnaround from an impressive list of medical woes."*

> *"I'll personally guarantee that you'll have terrific, ongoing results, or you'll get every penny of your investment returned, no questions asked." "And,"* he chirped *"If cherry flavor isn't your thing, Miracle Tap also comes in grape, orange, lemonade, and chocolate. It's so tasty that kids love it, AND it's good for them!"*

I grimaced, the word "investment" doing somersaults in my brain, and I felt sick. This wasn't just some gimmicky scam—it was a direct assault on the most vulnerable, masking its malevolence with sugary promises.

> *"And if you call now for this $19.95 offer,"* the man continued, *"we'll also send you a box of locally made cordial chocolates absolutely free. So call now to order..."*

♦♦♦♦♦

The tape stuttered, the screen twitching with static. Stepping back for fear the television was about to explode, I couldn't help but stare at the snowy flicker, half hoping it would glitch back to something—anything—that was remotely normal and made sense. But after a few seconds the image returned, worse than before...if such a thing was possible.

This time the footage showed a woman seated in what looked like a modest playroom. Her hair, the color of old honey, was tied back in a sagging ponytail. Cheap rose lipstick clung to her chapped lips, trying—and failing—to cover the exhaustion etched deep in her face. Behind her a toddler babbled incoherently, stacking soft foam blocks and blissfully unaware of the camera—or what was being said. The woman spoke directly into the camera:

> *"Emmy wasn't the easiest child to raise. She'd have meltdowns, throw fits...and it got to where we couldn't even keep her in daycare. They said she was disruptive."*

I froze. The toddler behind her—was that Emmy? The little girl was oblivious, stacking brightly colored blocks as though nothing in the world was wrong—her innocence contrasting so violently with what was being said.

> *"There was a time..."* The woman's voice cracked, but only faintly. *"There was a night I sat in my car for fifteen minutes, engine running, Emmy in the backseat. The meltdowns, the fussing, all the crying—there was no peace in my life. I seriously thought about driving us off the Coronado Bridge."*

My breath caught. This wasn't an ad anymore. It was something far more sinister, preying on despair and exploiting people's deepest vulnerabilities. And the worst part, I knew, was that there were people—parents—who would buy into it.

> *"It wasn't until I found the Miracle Tap that things changed in all our lives,"* the woman's voice rang out from the TV, her words as hollow as her painted-on smile. *"After a week, my daughter stopped her tantrums. She started to sleep more, and in turn, I was able to relax. Today we're both much calmer than before...and I couldn't be happier!"*

> *"And...cut,"* said another voice off-screen, likely a director or cameraman. *"That's very good."*

The camera stayed rolling, though. What came next wasn't scripted.

> *"I'm still getting paid for this right? No one will suspect what I did to..."*

> *"No, no..."* the offscreen voice interrupted, *"you're doing great, they won't know anything about how Emmy's..."*

The unfinished sentence was drowned out by the sudden, sharp cry of the toddler off-screen. The child's distress was raw, cutting through the flimsy facade of the staged commercial. *"Damn it,"* the woman muttered under her breath, her smile faltering as she glanced in the direction of the cries. *"Might need more than two of those Miracle Tap things,"* she added with a forced, plastered smile.

At this point I couldn't tell if she was smiling to herself or just putting on fake joy for the camera. What could those things possibly contain that would make it believable enough that it would 'cure' autism, or any of those other medical maladies?

Because for all I knew her daughter was just a two-year-old child being her childish self. Her mother may have just been one of those people who shouldn't have had children, not having grown up well herself. But here was her mother wanting to "cure" her child of the terrible twos.

Yeah, good luck with that!

Besides, how could anyone claim to have the power to "cure" a part of someone that doesn't even need to be cured? How could they do that to their own child? Or to any child, for that matter?

♦♦♦♦♦

There were so many questions left unanswered by this tape, and I obviously needed to learn more about this stuff and whoever was putting it out if I was going to solve this puzzle. I inadvertently leaned closer to the screen, hoping to notice every little detail as the tape played on. Then, the toddler's cries intensified, the sound warped by the old television's speakers into a haunting, grating wail. I jolted back, covering my ears against the piercing noise, my breath catching in my throat.

"I don't feel so good!" the child wailed, her voice shrill and gut-wrenching.

I didn't realize how loud the television was until I heard distant footsteps coming closer. My instincts kicked in. I lunged forward, fumbling to turn off the television. The screen flashed blue as I ejected the cassette. The old machine whirred slowly, agonizingly, as the tape emerged from its slot. I heard a sizzle from the undercarriage of the old unit and knew its days of useful service were done.

Right as the cassette was ejected, I grabbed the thing and bolted out of the dilapidated house. Running through the puddles from the recent rain, I nearly slipped after a few steps...before catching myself and running. Just running, trying desperately to get out of there.

I was so confused and scared of what I had just witnessed that I didn't even bother looking back. The last thing I wanted to know at that moment was what might have been following me.

And my brain rebelled, refusing to accept the possibility that what I held was a true representation of something terrible happening so close to my homc. Gripping the cassette, I ran through the familiar streets of La Mesa's once-colorful community, heading back towards where the cleanup crew's truck remained parked. I forced myself to not take a glance back at every step I took, as the child's cries echoed in my mind, a harbinger of nightmares still to come.

Chapter 11: Purity and White

-Claudia-

Even before I'd opened my eyes, the lights were blinding me. I woke up feeling weird and fuzzy-headed, and every square inch of my body ached.

This place, with the white curtains surrounding me. Panic. People wearing white. Where was I? Where are my plushies, my colorful walls and drawings? This isn't my bed. Why am I here? Why are there curtains around me...*I WANT MY MOM!*

The weird machines nearby made steady beeping noises, and I sat up a little bit. The non-stop tone just made my headache worse as the sounds echoed in my head, bouncing around inside my skull like it was a pinball machine. No other thought was clear in my brain except wondering where my mother and brother were. The nausea and the sore throat weren't helping...and what time is it? The bright light from beyond the curtain suggested it was daytime...maybe afternoon. The last thing I remembered clearly was the fireworks. Then there were those two men in the white robes and...

I couldn't tell, but staring at the light made my eyes hurt. I laid my head back down on the pillow, turning away from the light. Anything for relief from the feeling that someone was driving a chisel through my eyes and deep into my skull.

♦♦♦♦♦

There was a body on the next bed, hooked up to a bunch of tubes and giving it an alien look, like an oversized insect. This *HAS* to be a nightmare!

Still, there was something vaguely familiar about that body. The clothing...the hair...the shape of the face...

"J-...Jason...?"

I called to my brother, weakly and quietly, my voice strained by a throat that was on fire. But he'd saved us from who knows what fate, stepping in to fight those two men off. All I saw was the candy they were offering us.

I needed to call him, just to see he was okay.

Jason lay there, unmoving other than the steady rise and fall of his chest. A mask covered his mouth and nose, fogging each time he exhaled. He obviously wasn't dead.

"Jason..." I croaked. Why did my throat burn so badly? It felt like I'd swallowed a sheet of sandpaper.

"Hey, are you alright?"

The voice belonged to an older man whose demeanor immediately suggested efficiency and wisdom. His face was long and lined, with deep creases crossing his forehead and fanning from the corners of sharp pale gray eyes, sitting behind rectangular glasses that slid down his nose whenever he leaned in to read a chart. His eyebrows—bushy and silver—matched his thinning hair.

As he leaned over me, I saw he was thin and wiry, with shoulders sloped from carrying years of responsibility for other peoples' lives. His pale skin bore a faint undertone of fatigue, and the backs of his hands were marked with prominent veins and sunspots. His face wore the stubble of a day or two without shaving, and he was moving a bit stiffly, as if his knees were protesting years of rushing down hallways.

As he navigated the room with practiced efficiency, I tried to ask for my mother, but all he said was "Shhhhh." His suit jacket barely covered a scruffy tie, and my mouth parted a little but nothing came but a small pained cough. Speaking felt like an impossible task, my vocal cords protesting the abuse they'd recently received.

“Don’t strain yourself...” he said softly, the worried look on his face speaking volumes. “I’m George Whitney; a friend of your mother’s.”

“M-mom?” I rasped, struggling to understand.

“Shhhh. Yes, I’m a friend of your mom. My wife and I worked with her. Just take it easy, okay?”

I coughed again, feeling my body clench in pain as my breath wheezed in and out. I groaned as shuddering tears stung my red-rimmed eyes. This was all too much to understand. “Where?” I whispered, though I wasn’t sure what I was asking of this stranger. Where was Jason? And my mom? Where was I? What happened?

Despite my inability to verbalize my questions, my brain kept screaming them. And between that and the harsh light of the fluorescent bulbs in the ceiling above me, I felt like I was going to retch.

A hand wrapped around mine in a comforting grip. “Shhhh, shhh, you're okay, just take it easy...you’re safe,” he smiled at me gently.

♦♦♦♦♦

“Where’s M-mo-m” I whispered, my words coming out like I was gargling.

“She’s alright, don’t worry. She’ll be back soon,” he promised.

Sighing, I struggled to lay on my pillow and relax. My throat was killing me, my chest was a massive ache, my head felt like someone with a tiny jackhammer was digging up the street inside my brain. And I could once again see my brother on the next bed, wired up to a bunch of machines but never once moving. To call it overwhelming would have been a massive understatement, but I just couldn’t even think straight anymore.

Mr. Whitney just sat with me, holding my hand. He seemed nice.

“Your mom is out right now looking for something for you and your brother, and she asked me to keep you company and to be here if you woke up. You inhaled some bleach, but fortunately it wasn’t a lot. You got hurt, but you’re both going to be okay.”

“How...long?” I asked.

He hesitated. “14 hours.”

“By bleach...?”

“M-hm...” he nodded.

“Bleach...” I repeated. Lying there, I closed my eyes, only to be confronted by a flood of memories from last night. Everything was still hazy, but I remembered the overwhelming discomfort, the fear, the pain from that encounter.

I swallowed. “They said it was something else....”

Whitney leaned in curiously. “Who said that?” he asked softly.

“The man and woman who gave it to us,” I explained. “They were dressed in white...”

“Yeah?”

A fit of coughing tumbled out, my throat burning with each hacking breath. “Water?” I pleaded.

“The nurse says you can have ice chips,” he said, reaching for a cup. I nodded that that would be acceptable as he patted my arm in an attempt to comfort me. “You don’t need to say anything if your lungs hurt,” he suggested.

“It's okay,” I croaked. “It’s just my throat.”

“Burning that bad, huh?”

I nodded weakly. “She held me down and he tried to shove it down my mouth...” I recalled, wincing from the memory. I cleared my throat softly. “It happened real fast. I don’t even know why they did it...”

“Do you remember how they approached you?” Whitney asked. “Where were you and your brother when it happened?”

“Jason and I just...wanted to see the fireworks outside, someone was setting some off near our street.” I looked at my pale fingers, eyeing the pink nail polish my mom painted on my nails the day before, now scratched-up and ruined from the incident. “We didn't even go that far from our house...”

"How far away were you? A block away? Two? Three?"

"We were in the back yard and Jason wanted to get closer to see the action. So, he told mom that we would be back and we walked out from the gate and went down the hill...they were so loud, yet so pretty..."

♦♦♦♦♦

Whitney shifted in his seat. "Did anything happen during the fireworks show?"

I furrowed my brow as a hazy memory surfaced and began blurting out anything that came to mind. Most of it made little sense to me, but I said everything I could think of to be sure someone else knew before the memories faded away. It was like waking up from a dream and recalling the images I'd seen during my sleep.

"We were sitting on the side of the hill watching the fireworks when two people approached us; a man and a woman. I didn't hear much of what they were saying, as they were mainly talking to my brother and asking him a lot of questions. I was just staring at the smoke in the sky after the show had finished..."

Feeling a little stronger, I reached for more ice chips and cleared my throat before continuing. "Then Jason told me we needed to go home. He was pulling me to my feet so we could leave..."

"What did the two strangers say to your brother?"

"First they offered us some candy, which I was happy about. Then they said something about 'purifying,' but I wasn't really listening that closely. But Jason sounded nervous."

"Nervous?"

"Uh huh...then it just...happened so quickly...one of them pinned me down, and I heard my brother screaming..." I winced from the memory, both clouded and nightmarish. The more I talked about it, the less real it felt. "They were wearing masks covering their noses and mouths—white masks that matched their clothes—so I couldn't even see their faces. One of them told me that the thing pressed on my face would help me be pure...then I tasted something funny, and it hurt..."

"I'll bet it did..." said Whitney. He was visibly angry, even as he tried to remain solemn.

"It was like I was inside a big cloud and I heard more screaming. There were lots of blurred shadows...and then I woke up and found myself here..."

Mr. Whitney brushed back his grey hair and looked bewildered. He cursed under his breath before pinching the rim of his nose. It took nearly a minute of silence before he spoke again.

"I'm....I'm sorry, Claudia..."

♦♦♦♦♦

I shifted in my bed, feeling partly scared, partly damaged. Violated, perhaps, was a better word. This emotional purgatory ached as much as my burned throat did. I swallowed, still feeling the ache. "I...I don't even remember if anyone saw us...I don't even know what happened to us..."

"You..." Whitney sighed before speaking again, "You were attacked, Claudia, by the lowest kind of scum in the world," he said sadly. "You kids were lucky enough to survive, thanks to the good Samaritan that found you."

I nodded that I understood, then glanced at my still-unconscious brother. Indicating the tubing attached to him, I asked "Is Jason...going to be okay?"

"Well, he'll eventually pull through...at least physically," he said, the last part whispered. I wasn't sure what he meant. Yet despite the searing ache in my throat, my eyes felt heavy. I took a deep breath, and started to drift off.

"Claudia?"

"Hm?" I opened my eyes to see Whitney.

"Just...know that you're going to be alright. I'm going to find the people who did this to you. I want to make sure they can never hurt anyone again."

Glad he was there to help, I nodded and gave him a weak smile. "Promise?"

"...I promise..."

My breathing grew easier as I again closed my eyes and heard some woman—a nurse, I guessed—walk in to talk with Whitney. I drifted off, trying to sleep despite the soreness pulsing throughout my body. Because there was something comforting knowing Mr. Whitney was there to help me, Jason and Mom. He just seemed like such a nice man.

Chapter 12: A Rude Shock

-Sofia-

Why am I at the Sunset Coast Regional Center? I mean, I've just survived a goddamn explosion. My home is ash, my memories reduced to rubble, and I've been displaced into my aunt Bruna's house, where everything smells too clean and nothing feels like it's mine. And now my mother acts like it's any other Tuesday, rather than a time when the world has been split open, dragging me into this sterile little building.

TWO WEEKS! She expects me to spend two full weeks here, playing along like I'm fine. Like my world hasn't just been gutted. As if normalcy is still something I can touch.

What could she possibly be thinking?

It's humiliating, really—being shuttled into another family home like a stray with nowhere else to go. And they all treat me like I'm fragile glass, or worse: like I'm too young or too stupid to understand what's going on. No one seems to realize I'm an adult. That I see things. That I *know* things. That I'm just as much a witness to this collapse as they are.

Charming, isn't it? Every part of my life—every routine, every inch of safety I once had—has been turned upside down. I can't even let myself wonder where my alley cat friends ended up. They're gone, probably scattered to the wind like the rest of my life. I tell myself not to care, but my chest tightens anyway every time I think about what's been going on around me.

This? This is just the cherry on top of the shit sundae. And somehow, I know it's only going to be the beginning.

♦♦♦♦♦

I was seething internally as I stood at the front of the regional center, probably within spitting distance of Kearny Mesa. It's exactly like the twenty other regional centers throughout the state of California, providing support services for adults who sometimes need a little extra help socializing and communicating with others.

Of course, actually getting that help, or a job, or re-homed, can sometimes feel impossible. Each is a long process and, as I've been learning firsthand, it's even been a process just to get myself re-evaluated for autism.

Then there's that disturbing cassette I found yesterday. It's now hidden away in my guest bedroom so that no one else will find it, though I'm still not quite sure why I did it. I mean, I could've just thrown it away, but something—that little voice in the back of my head—told me to hang onto it.

♦♦♦♦♦

Seemingly the only person interested in gaining access to the center, I waited until the bus arrived and I spotted several cars pulling up. Within minutes there was a small crowd of people huddled around the door, many in wheelchairs, others operating under their own steam.

I figured I might as well go into the building with these people, even if they didn't know me. The last thing I needed was for someone to try and strike up a conversation, as I didn't have answers for anything right now—not even for myself.

Judging by the expressions on the faces around me—tight jaws, darting eyes, quiet trembles—I wasn't alone. There was something heavy in the air; something unsettled. It was as if everyone at the center was waiting for another shoe to drop.

And honestly, I couldn't blame them. Two catastrophic accidents within days, barely miles apart, made it all feel anything but random. It felt like there was a pattern forming, and I couldn't help but wonder how long it would be before I was to be the next name buried beneath a headline.

Was this to be my fate? Just another casualty? A statistic. An afterthought in a city that's forgetting how to breathe.

♦♦♦♦♦

The blast of air conditioning hit me the moment I stepped into the hallway. Cool and dark, it was a stark contrast to the blazing sun outside. I followed the slow-moving crowd, all of us drifting toward an open door about fifteen feet ahead.

There was something unusual about the space today. It felt too structured and formal, like a place where executives in stiff suits would gather to make deals. This was the last thing I expected in a place like this, but I just shrugged and found a seat.

Reaching into my bag, I pulled out my writing journal—now my *only* journal—and flipped it open, gripping my pencil tightly. I needed to write—anything, everything—just to drown out the chaos in my head. For years writing has been my anchor and my therapy, and right now I needed it more than ever.

But what was there to say? That I lost my home? That I'll probably never see my stray cat friends again? That I might not have my own room for a long time? That I feel like I'm drifting, alone in the world, surrounded by people who don't understand—who *can't* possibly understand—what I'm going through?

I tapped my pencil against the page, swallowing hard. Maybe I didn't know what to write...but I knew I had to start somewhere. Taking a deep breath, I had a moment of inspiration where a plot jumped into my mind, fully formed, and I immediately started writing, trying to immortalize the idea before it faded away.

> ***The Fox and Raven fled from the fiery blaze. They had been running for some time as the flames engulfed the once luscious fields. They knew they had to keep fleeing for their safety, lest the inferno claim them.***
>
> ***Oh? What's this? The Fox found something; a hole, I think? Could it be that their only way to escape is to just go deeper into the earth? It seemed so, as the Fox dug with his strong, flexible paws into the soil: it's an escape to safety!***

The Fox burrowed as the Raven followed, trailing behind the vulpine as they dug further beneath the earth until they reached...a door? 'Why would there be a door in the ground?', they wondered to each other. The Raven then remembered they'd been holding a key that could get them to where they needed to be. The Raven perched over the Fox's red fur, inserting the key into the lock, and with her shiny black beak turned the key until she heard a loud "click!" The door opened, giving the animals, to their relief, an opportunity to enter inside and escape the immediate danger.

The Fox and the Raven looked around the area; it was cool, damp, and dark. Had they stumbled upon a cave previously unknown to the two in their quest for relief from heat and threat? Sniffing the air, the Fox sensed moss and stone surrounding them. Should they stay here, or seek a way out? The creatures of the forest weren't sure where to go.

Then the Fox spotted something. A box; no—a chest! They both grew curious as they approached the old wood and iron chest, with the raven flapping above it as the fox cautiously padded up and nudged it with his snout.

Still, there was that key the raven held firmly in its beak. She tilted her head, flew face first into the front of the box, and inserted the key in the slot.

AHA! The box opened to reveal...a pistol? The animals looked at each other, confused, before the reynard picked it up, stepped on it the wrong way, and accidentally pulled the trigger.

As luck would have it, the gun's barrel was pointing towards the cave's ceiling, ensuring the blast made holes and ventilated their temporary safe haven. Almost instantly there was more light from the fires above—bright, hot, orange, and streaming in from the heavens.

Drip! The Fox felt a drop of water on his nose. The droplets became more frequent, soon forming a small puddle at their feet.

Plip!

Another drop, but...where is it coming from? This CAN'T be good!

The Raven and Fox examined the holes made by the gun firing, the water dripping like blood from an open wound and, at best, an odd sight to behold.

Only one drop can quickly lead to two...and four...and eight...and...

And a small stream, which in the blink of an eye can become a torrent.

Thus it wasn't long until the water was gushing into the cave, pooling at the animal's feet and setting off a panic as they faced a sudden—and unexpected—flood.

It seems this 'treasure' they had found was actually responsible for a disaster, leaving a trail of destruction and chaos in its wake. And as the torrent of water grew, the pool climbed up the cave walls. The Fox tried to climb higher, following as best he could as the Raven dodged this way and that above his head.

The end seemed imminent as the two companions considered their alternatives. Their only means of escape was cut off, and their options were increasingly limited. Where could they go? The fires of chaos—a symbol of the external threats and dangers—continued to rage above them, while the flood of despair and absolute desperation was quickly rising beneath them.

This was all, of course, a metaphor for the internal struggles and emotional turmoil I was facing. The pistol was the trigger—a traumatic trigger. The Fox and Raven were painted as misfits, yet they were the victims of the burning fires of hate and the flooding of emotional instability. And they had no idea which path their destiny would lead them down.

♦♦♦♦♦

"Sofia?"

The voice jolted me from my thoughts. I snapped my head up, locking eyes with a woman who looked like she probably worked at the center.

"Yes?" I managed, my voice tight.

"The meeting is starting," she said, her tone clipped but polite. "I hope you'll pay attention."

I blinked. *Shit!* "I...yeah, sure. Sorry." *Dammit...why was I apologizing?*

I glanced down at my journal, realizing I must've gotten lost in "The Zone" again—that trance-like state where time slips away, and nothing exists except the words flowing from my mind.

Maybe I got too lost. Still, I *wanted* to be lost in it. I wanted anything that would keep me away from reality.

I shifted in my seat, forcing myself to at least pretend to listen. But the words swirling around me quickly blurred together, turning into little more than background noise. My gaze drifted to the wall, and soon all these voices became muffled...like a distant radio I didn't care to tune into.

God, I just wanted to drown it all out.

The self-important tone of that woman grated on my nerves. She was so fucking condescending, acting like she knew better than us about everything life had to offer.

Like I wasn't already sick of people talking down to me.

I clenched my jaw, biting back the words I *wanted* to say. There was no real point to making trouble...only I was too angry to relax, and too frustrated to sit still.

All I wanted was to go back to writing—to let the words pull me under and shut out this *bullshit.*

♦♦♦♦♦

It was the same old therapy circle where we just discussed our feelings. And I supposed it was an opportunity for me to talk about my feelings regarding what's been happening recently, only...what can I say? What *is* there to say?

For that matter, why does she want me to bare my soul in front of people whom I've never met and who don't have the remotest clue who or what I am? I mean, like they're really gonna care what I have to say?

Screw that! I'm certainly not going to be coerced into being vulnerable around a bunch of strangers. Thinking about it silently for a few long seconds, I stood up and asked to use the restroom.

♦♦♦♦♦

The anger bubbled and brewed inside me. I couldn't think, and just needed to get out of there. While walking out I thought I caught a glimpse of Damian, only to realize it was just a guy who kinda looked like him.

Why am I even thinking about Damian? God, I can't *think* straight. GET OUT OF MY BRAIN!

It really didn't matter; I just needed to get away. I grabbed my journal and writing tool as I headed towards the women's room, taking deep breaths as I tried to calm down.

I passed a woman dressed in white carrying a package. Cleaning supplies? A birthday gift? I didn't know, nor did I really care. After all, how much attention do any of us really pay to the cleaning lady carrying bleach to clean the next bathroom? She's just doing her job...no big deal.

So I walked past without acknowledging her, pushing the bathroom door open and, happily, finding it empty, without a soul in sight.

Slamming the stall without thinking, I winced as the door bounced back and forth, the sound reverberating around the room. I huffed and puffed, sitting down hard on the toilet seat and feeling queasy. Grasping the side of my head with one hand, I clutched my journal close and chalked the whole thing up to being tired, angry, and wishing people would just understand that...and leave me alone.

Yeah, it's true. I yearn for true empathy, rather than the hollow sympathetic platitudes that most parents give their three-year-olds.

Then there was that video cassette I had taken home with me. The images I'd seen on it kept swirling through my brain, and it wasn't making me feel any better. I was just so exhausted from it all, and staying in the bathroom until the meeting ended was infinitely preferable to having to spill my guts to a bunch of people I neither knew nor cared about.

Yeah, that would be much better...provided nobody found me here, seething and consumed with emotions. I just don't know what to do with any of this anymore.

♦♦♦♦♦

I opened my journal again and looked through the passage I had just written, reflecting on the words and imagery I had put on paper, and it helped a little bit. That's when my new reality struck me; that not even writing poems and stories like this down on paper will ever bring back my old room.

It all still felt painfully unreal to me...especially knowing the old home I lived in had been charred and ruined, and possibly had a corpse or two in there from the force of the explosion. I shuddered, trying to remove that horrid image from my head; to not even think of what happened to those people who were caught in such a painful and violent death.

And with all the uncertainty in our little corner of the world, who was to say I wasn't next? Scared for my life? You're damned right! Because I'd be lying if I said I didn't imagine myself as the next victim. I'd thought about this far too often—lying awake, worrying over the number of ibuprofen I took for cramps, wondering if I counted wrong. Or the unease before a road trip, the long silences during a plane's ascent, the quiet grip of dread in my chest. My parents have always said plane crashes are rare, that accidents "almost never happen."

Still, *"almost never"* isn't never.

♦♦♦♦♦

One thing I've learned in my short life is that anything can happen, and at any moment. Maybe that's anxiety. Maybe it's just realism wrapped in fear. But the reality is that another day of life is never guaranteed. We keep telling each other "it's safe" until it gets you. After all, no one gets a warning before their name becomes a footnote in someone else's tragedy. We say it's safe until it's not. We say "everything's fine" until the smoke's already rising.

I sighed. "...It's going to get worse for me, isn't it?" I softly said to myself. Because in my heart of hearts, I don't think things ever get better for people like me. Not when the world moves on without you. Not when everyone else is busy chasing dreams and I'm still here, trying to make peace with fears that never stay put.

And it's never as simple as "just pushing through." Not when you live with a brain that tangles itself in loops of worry. Not when saying "I'm autistic" makes people look at me like I'm less of a person than they are. Or like I'm some small, harmless thing that needs constant supervision.

They never say it aloud, of course, but I see it—the way their eyes shift, their voices soften like I might break if spoken to too plainly.

It's exhausting dealing with this shit!

♦♦♦♦♦

I still remember the day at age six when I was diagnosed with autism. My memory is a bit vague, but my parents' reactions stick out in my mind.

They were both generally confused; scared, even. And not the kind of fear that comes from monsters under the bed, but the silent kind...where no one knows what to say, and everyone's suddenly walking on eggshells.

Because they didn't know what autism was. Not really. And I guess, in many ways, they still don't. That's probably why they never seemed to understand my frustration—why they would drag me along to family parties and crowded gatherings, expecting me to smile and behave and pretend like none of it overwhelmed me. As if my diagnosis was a technicality, a fine print detail they only remembered when it came time to schedule group therapy.

To them, I wasn't someone with sensory struggles or an unusual way of processing the world. I was just...a misfit. A burden wrapped in a label. Someone they couldn't quite mold into the picture of who they wanted me to be.

And maybe that's what hurt the most: the quiet resignation in their eyes. As if the moment they heard "autism," they started grieving the version of me they thought they were supposed to have. And all the things that make me who I am—my routines, my reactions, my need for space—became things to fix. Or worse, to ignore.

What kind of freedom can you hope for when even your own family sees your future as a compromised version of their own?

Over the years I've tried to make peace with the whole thing. With the way they love me awkwardly, inconsistently, and always with conditions. But sometimes I still find myself wishing—naively, maybe—for someone who could just understand without being told. Like the raven and the fox in the old folktale: strange companions who still found a way to co-exist.

But wishes don't hold much weight when everything's already crumbling. And understanding, no matter how much I crave it, doesn't rebuild what's already gone.

♦♦♦♦♦

Sitting in the stall and deep in thought, I stared down at the tiles. My field of vision was confined to the door, three walls, and the floor tiles, so my options were limited. Taking a minute to look through my other old journal passages before finishing up and heading back to the meeting, I jerked my head up as a strong, sharp odor assaulted my nostrils.

Bleach?

Was the custodian cleaning the stalls this whole time I'd been sitting there? Had I been that absorbed in my own thoughts that I hadn't noticed another person a few feet away from me doing her job?

I stood up, gently opened the stall door, and looked both left and right...but saw no one. All the stall doors were open, and the bathroom was decidedly empty.

Odd.

The overwhelming stench of the chemicals made my nose crinkle. Was it me? Was I overthinking the smell? Because it was starting to *really* bother me. I glanced at the closed bathroom door, wondering if the wave of liquid nausea was coming from out there.

The smell grew stronger, burning my nostrils and threatening to overwhelm my senses. Covering half my face with my shirt, I contemplated making a mad dash for the door. Self-preservation took over, removing my brain from the equation and putting my feet in motion.

Tightly gripping my journal, I desperately tried to hold my breath and not smell the fumes. Slowly, I edged away from the toilet and looked over my shoulder at the other stalls—all empty.

Coughing at the fetid stink, I carefully approached the door and cracked it open, quickly slamming it shut again as a wall of chemicals from the hallway burned my eyes. Yelping, I stepped back and coughed harder, even as the smell continued seeping in through the gap at the door's base.

♦♦♦♦♦

What do you do when there's no way out of such a dire situation? There were no other doors in or out of this tiny room, and no windows that I could smash. *SHIT*.

My mind raced. What was happening? What could I do?

I tried to calm myself and think clearly. Maybe there was a gas leak. Maybe someone spilled bleach in the furnace. Maybe that cleaning lady accidentally spilled a gallon of bleach on the floor outside.

My mind wouldn't stop. There were so many possibilities of what caused the problem, but only one recognizable solution. Because without any other exits, reality beckoned: there really was only one way out of this mess.

I shook all over, struggling to muster the courage to open the door again. Intuition urged me to run, but fear kept me from moving another inch. Yet every second I stayed rooted to the spot left me surrounded by a stronger reek of bleach...until I finally knew I had no choice.

Opening the door, I bolted. Though my face was still covered by my thin shirt, the burning chemicals forced me to squint my eyes almost shut. And though I tripped over my own feet, I kept running, searching, panic-stricken, for clean air,

Holding my breath. Panicky instinct for survival. Hall foggy. I headed towards the light of the front door, only to be greeted with the blaring of the alarm that was somehow activated, albeit very belatedly. I tried to push the front doors open, only to find them locked.

THIS IS A NIGHTMARE! There *has* to be another way out. And where were all the people who had been in the therapy session? Hadn't anyone even noticed I was missing?

♦♦♦♦♦

Someone was walking from the meeting room down the hall, and I saw vague silhouettes through the smog. Crap! Do I call for help, or listen to the voice in my head screaming at me to hide?

That inner voice won the wrestling match. Something about this unexplained situation wasn't adding up, and logic insisted that keeping hidden would help me to save myself.

Spotting a nearby doorway, I bolted inside before any of those shrouded figures could see me, turning the latch behind me. Hiding there shivering, I focused on making myself small and unobservable. My breathing came in small gulps as I hoped to minimize more of the bleach that had apparently overtaken the rest of the building.

Footsteps coming closer, then...a knock. The knocking continued endlessly, insisting I must be there...even as I somehow knew my only chance of survival was complete silence. I desperately wanted to scream for them to leave me alone, opting instead to bite the side of my hand in a desperate effort to control myself and not give away the secret of my existence.

BOOM. BOOM. BOOM. My heart had jumped into my throat, beating loudly inside my eardrums. Thinking I might go mad, I covered my mouth to mask my panicked breathing.

There was silence, but it felt more like the calm just before a storm began in earnest. I didn't budge, suspecting something more was coming. After what seemed like an interminable wait, there came a loud bang on the door, nearly breaking it off the hinges, followed by footsteps creaking against the old wooden floor.

♦♦♦♦♦

I pressed myself against the rear wall, my breath shallow, my heart a trembling fist in my chest. The only thing still anchoring me to sanity was the fractured reflection of daylight bouncing off a metallic surface—a glimmer of hope, a promise of escape.

For a second, I believed in it. Then the footsteps returned.

I swallowed the rising panic, forcing myself to remain as still as possible and shrinking into the shadows as someone slipped a key into the lock and opened the door. Two figures entered the room. I could make out their silhouettes—both clad in white. Not the crisp sterility of lab coats, nor the casual white of a painter's overalls. No, these were hazmat suits.

And worse, they both wore gas masks.

Their voices were muffled, reduced to the hollow drone of insects speaking through a thick veil of fabric. Pressing my ear close to the floor, I strained to make out their words...only to discover the clutter of brooms, mops, and a rag basket obscured my view. Now I could barely see them, let alone decipher what they were saying.

Only two phrases emerged clearly: *'We should leave'* and *'before the cops get here.'*

♦♦♦♦♦

Footsteps walked past me and into the hallway. I sat there silently, torn between cracking the door open to take a quick peek and remaining in hiding until there was no question that the coast was clear.

Yet even as I debated whether the ordeal had ended, my body shuddered from continuous fear and a notable lack of oxygen. I sat there shaking at the very notion that someone would break into the center and try to poison the residents.

The overwhelming silence suggested they had been successful, though they had obviously missed their chance to get me.

I watched their shadows fade as the pair of assassins walked out of the building, unaware that my rubbery legs made it impossible for me to move beyond the relative safety of the closet. Frozen in place, I held my breath—literally and figuratively—until I heard the front door open and close with a loud *'click'*.

Then, as if a cord had snapped inside me, I moved. I bolted out of the closet, away from the poisoned air, away from the door they had just exited. My lungs burned, but I didn't stop. Because one thing was certain...

I was NOT going to sit there and let the bleach mist carry my soul away!

♦♦♦♦♦

An open window invited me to leap through it, and I took the offer. The two-story drop was brutal—with my body twisting mid-air—I landed hard on my side, the impact rattling through my ribs. Pain flared up, sharp and immediate, but I didn't stop to assess the damage. *Run. Just run.*

My legs carried me on pure instinct, my mind severed from the rest of my body, operating in a blur of motion and desperation. I didn't dare look back—I didn't want to know if someone was chasing me, if those masked figures had realized their mistake, if they were sprinting after me through the poisoned air.

I just wanted to get the *hell* out of there.

I veered off the path, diving behind a massive tree, its thick trunk wide enough to swallow me whole. My breath came in jagged gasps, each inhale a desperate attempt to purge my lungs of the poison I'd been exposed to. But it wasn't just the mist that suffocated me—it was the sheer, unrelenting terror.

My eyes burned. Had the bleach seeped into them? Was I blinded? I wiped at my face, only to realize the sting came from tears. Tears I hadn't even noticed forming, leaking silently from the shock, the fear, the horror of it all.

I crouched, hugging myself as my body trembled uncontrollably, unsure what else to feel besides panic and shock. All I wanted to do was hide until sundown so that no one would be able to see me until it seemed safe to step out. My mind felt split between the immediacy of survival and the creeping unreality of what had just happened.

A sudden cough ripped from my throat, raw and violent. I spat onto the ground, my saliva tinged with something acrid, as if my insides had been scraped raw with steel wool. More coughing followed—heaving, gagging, desperate to rid my body of whatever traces of that mist still lingered. I doubled over, my nails digging into the dirt, my entire body convulsing with each ragged breath.

The forest swallowed the sound of my wheezing, my rasping, my choking.

I was alive...but for how much longer?

♦♦♦♦♦

My breathing eventually became less erratic, softening and slowing, even as my mind remained in a dazed overdrive. My vision stayed focused on the clouds, the soft shades of the stratosphere and even a few birds that fluttered by, as that little voice told me to relax.

I don’t know how long I sat on the ground hugging myself, but it didn't really matter at this moment. I couldn't really think of anything but the quiet sounds emanating from the surrounding nature. It calmed me, and ordinarily would have lulled me to sleep if I hadn’t been so afraid I’d never wake up again.

And though the distance sirens were disturbing, they were little more than background noise at the moment. I remained in my own trance until...

A set of hands were on my shoulders before I could react. The grip was firm, grounding, but I could feel the way his fingers trembled ever so slightly.

“Sofia?” he repeated, still hoping to get my attention. “Are you alright, baby? I’ve been worried about you.”

My father had shown up at just the moment I needed him most. He continued, speaking softly. “Talk to me. What happened?”

I opened my mouth to respond, but my throat burned, raw from the bleach and my ragged coughing. My lips parted, but no words came out—only a faint wheeze. My breath hitched, and I clenched my fists into the damp grass beneath me.

I didn’t know how to explain. *I found a tape. There were men in gas masks. I almost died.* Every thought collided in my mind like a car crash, each one more fragmented than the last.

The sirens were getting closer. They weren’t just background noise anymore—they were coming here.

My father followed my gaze, turning toward the distant flashing lights. His brow furrowed. “Sofia...what did you—?” He stopped himself, exhaling sharply, then knelt down, his expression shifting from panic to quiet concern. “Okay. Okay, you don’t have to talk right now. Let’s just get you out of here.”

I barely registered his arms wrapping around me, helping me to my feet. My legs wobbled like they weren't my own, my body still in shock, still caught in the crosshairs of fight or flight.

But I didn't fight. I didn't run. For now, I just let my father hold me up.

♦♦♦♦♦

My father's presence was the only thing tethering me to reality. His hand on my shoulder, the weight of his arm as he guided me to my feet—these were enough to keep me from spiraling completely out of control.

Still, my mind swirled with lingering images of the tape. The gas masks. The eerie, saccharine voices promising miracles.

"Let's get you home," he murmured, his voice steadier now, as if anchoring himself so I could do the same.

I wanted to say something—to tell him what I'd seen, what I'd barely escaped—but my throat still burned, and my breath still came in uneven gasps.

"Shh, just relax and take deep breaths, alright?"

I nodded wordlessly, struggling to breath in the cool air flowing around me, even as I feared further exposure to that noxious cleaning chemical. I shivered as I leaned into my dad in a cheerless effort to ground myself again.

All that really mattered right now was to ensure I wasn't still in that gas chamber of a building.

♦♦♦♦♦

For the first time in a long time I was thankful that I was returning to my aunt's house at the end of the day. Silently trudging down the darkened hallway, I skipped the pleasantries like saying hello to anyone in the household, grabbed my sleepwear, and headed to the bathroom. I needed this day to be over.

I'm pretty sure I took two baths in a dissociative haze—washing vigorously with a bar of soap, shampoo, body wash and hot water—rubbing my skin raw in a desperate attempt to excise that awful 'death' stench of bleach from every square inch of my body. Yet despite my best efforts, the basic chlorine scent remained stuck in my nose for hours after those horrid events had taken place.

Finally deciding this was as good as it was going to get, I dried off and silently dumped the full collection of clothes reeking of bleach into the laundry basket. You could have burned them for all I cared.

I headed back to the guest room where I was staying and sat on the bed without a word. I longed to get my mind off the day's events...to get out of this nightmare. *Anything!*

I pulled out my journal, grateful that the smell of bleach wasn't as strong on the paper as it had been on my clothes and backpack. I pulled out a pencil and wrote, struggling to get my thoughts out.

> ***Booming fires***
> ***Lingering memories haunting me***
> ***Eternal horrors in my head***
> ***Accident or not it happened***
> ***Catalyst of the darker days***
> ***Horrible, horrible outcomes coming soon.***

....Well, that didn't help at all. In fact, I think I just made everything worse for myself.

♦♦♦♦♦

I set my journal and pencil down beside me, only to hear a sharp *clunk* as something knocked against the bed frame and fell to the floor. I flinched instinctively, heart skipping, then glanced down to see the object lying askew on the hardwood.

The VHS tape. My stomach dropped.

I swallowed hard. I'd watched the video once, back in the wreckage of the house, and figured once was more than enough. Still, something about it—something unspoken, sinister, unresolved—had wormed its way into my inner being.

Why did I even take it? Was it panic? Compulsion? The shock of seeing something I wasn't meant to see? Maybe it felt like proof. Maybe it felt like a curse. I just wasn't sure anymore. All I knew was it was here now, and it felt heavy in a way that had nothing to do with its actual weight.

My gaze drifted to the corner of the room, where a squat little box TV—dusty and faintly humming with old static energy—sat in silence. It was one of those ancient units; the kind that hums even when it's off, like it remembers every story it's ever shown.

That little voice in my head urged me to throw the tape away. Burn it. Snap it in half. Stuff it into the garbage bin. Forget it ever existed.

Instead, I sat paralyzed, observing the tape as if it might move of its own accord.

What if it means something? Could it be a harbinger of darker days ahead? If so, was this really something I wanted to be involved with?

I shivered with anticipation of bad things to come. After what I'd just experienced in the bathroom, I didn't feel like tempting fate again. Not tonight.

♦♦♦♦♦

The truth is I didn't want to know what else could be on that tape, or what I might have missed, or what might be waiting in those distorted frames. Trapped in 'fight-or-flight' mode, I'd already seen *way* too much, and it was far worse than anything I could've imagined just 24 hours ago.

The pictures now stuck in my head felt like I was watching rot spread through something once alive. Did I really need to relive that bleach-filled horror again?

No! There was no logical reason to subject myself to that ever again.

Still...just as I was leaning away from the thought, a cold, prickling, creeping sensation slid down my spine.

Wait a minute...

I stopped breathing. Standing dead in my tracks, my blood froze.

The unscripted part of the video jumped into my mind. This Aeron guy...he mentioned bleach, didn't he? Or was I remembering it wrong now that trauma was inextricably tied in my brain to the mere mention of bleach.

That pesky little voice screamed at me to watch that damned video again to see if I'd made a mistake, even as my body refused to move or even shift off my bed to do my brain's bidding.

I inhaled sharply, grateful to be smelling dinner cooking, and not deadly chemicals. Leaning down to grasp the cassette, I used sheer force of will to move. My body begrudgingly rose from the mattress to lumber over to the small box television.

And unlike in the past, when I thought it quaint for us to have a VHS player for such antiquated technology, I now was grateful for it. Pressing the ON button, I watched the machine whir to life and inserted the cassette, grimy with soot from the scene of the crime. Half of me hoped it would work, while another part of me hoped it wouldn't.

♦♦♦♦♦

The television clicked on, the fuzzy blue screen making me wonder if I should get my eyes checked, and the word PLAY appeared in the lower right corner. I squinted a little, watching as the screen turned black and gave out a mechanical cough.

The now-familiar jingle started playing as the camera focused on a sermon in a church-like setting. And there before me was the psychotic man who apparently was behind it all. A part of me really hoped it was some long-lost horror flick. "It's crazy to think this shit is real," I mumbled, reassuring myself of my sanity.

Forcing myself to watch the video again, I kept the volume just barely audible so that no one else would hear me. And it felt eerie watching the scene unfold before me, just as it had before. Suddenly I felt obsessed, skipping the talking bits and trying to find the clip that I remembered; the unscripted part where he talked about bleach.

♦♦♦♦♦

I pressed the forward button, forcing the player to skim through the tape's contents. Flicking pictures and sound whizzed by in milliseconds until the segment I sought appeared. Again pressing PLAY, I leaned into the speakers, struggling to catch snippets of the conversation.

> *"In several years' time, yeah, when the world is desperate enough."*

"But with bleach? Isn't that a bit risky? Especially at the regional centers."

My breath hitched. My stomach twisted. The confirmation of my worst suspicions sent a wave of nausea through me. My eyes widened, pulse hammering in my ears. *No...this can't be real.*

Only—when was this video made?

"They'll probably just blame it on faulty wiring or a chemical spill. Probably the most reasonable explanation, but if they did suspect anything we'll just have to keep it low."

A shiver crawled up my spine. *No. No. No. No. No!*

I fought against the rising dread, my mind scrambling for a logical explanation. *Maybe I misheard. Maybe I misunderstood.* But deep down, in the pit of my belly, I knew the truth.

This was real. This was happening, and apparently it had been in the planning stages for QUITE a long time.

♦♦♦♦♦

"Let's be real, do people even care about them? This society isn't made for them. You've heard the stories, the experiences of the parents raising those kids. It's an illness, something that can't be cured...or at least it shouldn't be."

Unsure what to think or say, I shuddered as this heartless man's words spilled out of the speakers and I remained, unable to disengage. It felt as if I was listening to the emotionally dead confessions of a serial killer or the matter-of-fact plans being laid out by a potential dictator.

Here was a man who could easily be both, coolly plotting a genocide of thousands of his neighbors. That little voice in my head speculated whether this man could be behind it all, even as a corner of my brain struggled to argue I was overthinking it all, and this had just been an accident.

Of course, it was possible my imagination was just working on overdrive and assuming the worst. It wouldn't have been at all surprising to learn that paranoia and delusions were a normal byproduct of the lack of oxygen caused by exposure to too much bleach.

Still, this "delusion" did include two people in gas masks and hazmat gear seeking to escape before the police showed upl...

♦♦♦♦♦

> *"It must feel nice to lie dead in your bed and the heaviness as your body shuts down. I'd imagine having all the organs in your body halting at once to be quite a surreal feeling, yet so welcoming to the senses. It's like...succumbing into a very good, very long nap. There would be no worries, and no sense of time; just drifting into the abyss as your consciousness fades away, finally feeling pure joy...and then nothing at all. Perhaps it can be a mercy for them after all, so they don't have to live with that illness."*

A sudden knock at the door caused me to jump. "Yeah?" I called resentfully.

"Sofia, it's me."

Realizing it was my dad, my eyes widened as I turned off the television set. Pressing a button to eject the cassette and hide it among the rest of my VHS tapes, I responded "Yeah?"

"Are you alright?" he asked. I sat turning that phrase over in my mind, realizing this was probably the only time he had ever asked me that question. I was both impressed and genuinely surprised.

"Uh-huh. Yeah. I'm fine." I responded, fidgeting from the warmth of the tape I'd just held in my hands and feeling dirty from what I'd just been listening to.

"Dinner's almost done. We'll be waiting," he said, just before I heard footsteps walk back down the hallway.

Was it possible that he was sympathetic to what I'd just been through? Could it be that maybe he was in shock too?

Or not. That kind of a reaction was actually pretty unlikely. I mean, in all the years I'd known him, empathy was one emotion I'd never known my father to exhibit.

The tape sat carefully nestled on the shelf, and I couldn't help but to sit and stare at it intently. Waves of fear, as if I were looking at a cursed relic from the tomb of King Tut, washed over me as I considered my discovery.

And that little voice in the back of my head convinced me to hide it...for now, at least. I needed to figure out what to do with this thing; either keep it or find a way to turn it in to the police or something, and preferably without getting more involved than I already was.

I really wasn't sure of my next move, and was just too much in shock to even think much of that or anything else. Thoughts of what might make me feel better, what I might write, or what I'd do tomorrow all swirled around me.

I just didn't know what to do anymore, or who to turn to.

-BZZT-

I glanced down at my phone sitting in my handbag. Today's events had driven it clear out of my head, and now it was forcing itself back into my consciousness. Grabbing the device, I shuddered as I realized even my stupid phone smelled disgusting from the bleach.

A text greeted me from Damian. Of course. Did he know about the events at the regional center that I had just barely survived? The text was both noncommittal and concerned:

> **"HEY! It's Damian. I just want to check in and see how you're doing? Are you alright?"**

I bit my lip, not really sure how to answer, other than "I'm fine."

Chapter 13: Ruby Ridge

-Aeron-

I filled my lungs with cigarette smoke, tasting the burning nicotine before breathing it out softly. It had been a few months since I'd promised myself I wouldn't smoke again, yet here I was...trying to be a good role model here for my legion, and failing miserably...at least on this count.

I hunched over the mahogany table littered with countless yellow sticky notes, scribbles on napkins, typewritten reports, and notepads. Nearby sat a lump of old plans, crumpled but not yet tossed away. My office was little more than four white walls with a single pane of stained glass providing color with a polychrome light. My hair, oily with sweat, kept falling over my eyes and I struggled to keep it held back with my left hand while holding the burning Marlboro with my right.

Quietly, I sat and watched the smoke dance into the air like a hovering cloud, moments before the ceiling fan made it slowly dissipate.

Thinking about it all made me realize I probably looked like a meth addict, dirty and pale from lack of sun. Somewhere in the back of my mind I recognized I'd probably have to take a bath sometime soon, though I was more focused on the lingering memory of the girl that got away.

Ruby Ridge. The girl next door. Her bright strawberry blonde hair reflected the desert sun, and the thought of her still plagued me to this day. That gorgeous hair contrasted against her eyes, green as a flawless cut peridot ring. And there was her skin, soft and decorated with tawny freckles peppering her cheeks and dappling those same shoulders peeking through her summer dresses.

She was every man's dream girl, and at least for me, she was my wet dream.

♦♦♦♦♦

I'll never forget when I met her for the first time in high school. We were the graduating class of 2000, and it was the fall of our senior year. A transfer student from Boston, Ruby had moved to this desert hell hole I called home when her father got a new job in one of the new biotechnology start-ups in the region.

Ruby was the woman of my wildest dreams—*and nightmares* that manifested from traumatic memories of the last time I would see her. She was in my biology science class taught by Mr. Parker, and the moment Mr. Parker introduced her, my hours instantly became brighter. Then, when she was assigned to be my partner for one day during the segment on frog dissection, our fates seemed to be forever intertwined.

She even lent me a pencil during the first hour of the lesson when I had forgotten to bring one, convincing me of her generosity and patience. *This* was the woman for me.

Then there was the floral perfume wafting off her soft skin. It was so delicate, yet it was strong enough to overpower the stale, piss-like smell of preserved amphibians pinned down on our table. The scent of the frogs reminded me of visiting my grandmother in the old folks home.

Every guy in the class wished they were me that day, and I understood why as I stole more than a few glances at Ruby's hair grazing over her shoulders and face. More than once I watched her brush the hair away from her face, her thin, peachy fingers struggling to counter the misbehaving strands that seemed determined to cover her eyes.

And each time she brushed them away, she revealed those gorgeous emerald green eyes that lit up with every word she spoke. Her voice was soft, sweet, and golden, almost ever-glazing like honey from a beehive. Even the memory of the window blinds projecting the sun's beams and giving her a halo remained fresh in my mind, as if it had all happened yesterday.

I had loved her from the moment we met. Years later, I still did.

♦♦♦♦♦

I fondly remembered the moment she handed me that pencil. From the instant our fingers touched, every fiber of my being needed to know everything about her. I'd observe her from a distance, never able to screw up the courage needed to go speak with her or—God forbid—ask her out on a date. So I watched her eat lunch, go to class, and walk home, me following a half-block behind.

Over time I learned she wanted to be an accountant, lived a few blocks away from me, and had a laugh that made her eyes dance and could bring a smile to the most hardened members of the community. Ruby was nothing short of angelic, and deep inside I recognized that this girl—this amazing woman—meant so much more to me than just being a professional contact.

Even the dessert she ate was beautifully unique—pumpkin pie topped with strawberries and whipped cream. I'd watch, mesmerized, from across the room in one of the rundown restaurants around town, my eyes never wavering as I imagined being one of those luscious strawberries blending in perfectly with the shade of her red lips with each bite. Desperately stealing glances, I'd pray she wouldn't see me each time I dared to look up and wish for the nerve to taste her lips and make her hungry to taste mine.

Oh, the glorious memories of sneaking out nightly to stand on her lawn and watch her getting undressed in her pastel bedroom. It felt like she was leaving the blinds and the window open just so I could get my fill of her beauty complemented by the flowery designs decorating her room's turquoise walls. Every dress she owned would call to me from her closet, and I'd send her mental instructions on which dress to wear the next day, as I thought she'd look particularly pretty in it.

Sometimes she even did as I requested...or so I hoped.

♦♦♦♦♦

Then came the night when, while causing a ruckus in the darkest corners of Indio, I realized I really had it bad for her...and I was in trouble. That was the moment when I realized that Ruby was like a drug to me, and I couldn't get enough of her.

Now it wasn't just the sight of Ruby *always* making my night that was the problem. And it wasn't just that it was becoming impossible for me to stay away from her despite my parents' admonition to steer clear.

No, I now knew that I couldn't live without this girl in my life, and if I couldn't find a way to make this idea a reality, I was going to lose my fucking mind.

And it wasn't just that I so admired her beauty. True, even from a far distance she was my beauty to admire, and it felt like she only smiled for me. But even as I followed her to and from school during those last days of high school, Ruby had become an obsession for me.

Looking at her, and listening to her, and loving her from a distance, I couldn't help it. I'd been trying to muster up the courage to ask her out, but even with all the small talk, the fumbling around, and the occasional eye contact, she never took the hint.

Damn her! This was all extremely frustrating, and she left this earth before my first days of college...taking my future and dreams of happiness with her.

My divinity...My deadly divinity. My fixation on her had turned me into a dangerous man.

♦♦♦♦♦

I never got my chance with Ruby because of that horridly bleak summer night when she hung out with a bunch of kids who were different from most of us—certainly different from me—and she never came home again.

It was a couple of days later that the rumors started. Some of the kids in class speculated that Ruby ran away with these kids or pulled a Thelma and Louise with one of them. Then, finally, the truth came out; she had been murdered by these fucking derelicts.

What had started as a *"Let's go out into the desert, light a bonfire, and drink some beers"* kind of evening had ended in disaster. There were six of them, all drinking too much. And with the other two girls passed out, the three boys had raped Ruby repeatedly. Then, out of fear she'd rat them out, they slit her throat and buried her in a shallow grave under the sand in the desert, about halfway between an ecological preserve and the Agua Caliente Indian Reservation.

At least that's what the newspaper reports said, though I had trouble focusing on a lot of the details. Because in one instant these animals had taken Ruby's life and destroyed my dreams of a future. Something inside me snapped, and I knew my life could never be the same.

♦♦♦♦♦

They disappeared after murdering her, of course, but only for a few days until the police were called when they tried to skip on the bill at the Desert Lodge up near Cabazon where they'd been hiding.

Only Ruby never got anything resembling justice. These fuck-faces practically got away scott free, thanks to them having a good lawyer— and being able to use their mental ailments as protection from responsibility.

Devastated and heartbroken, all I could do was mourn the reality that she'd been ripped from my arms and my dreams. Day and night I'd alternate from an intense need to cry to screaming to full-throttled anger, frequently within the span of a few seconds. The longing for what might have been between us, and the recognition of what those fuckers had stolen from me...from *us*.

Not even a therapist could help me get over the devastation, because what could they know about what—who—I had lost?

Over time, my own sense of being grew dark as that memory continued pinging around inside my skull. All I could think of was Ruby's pale, sandy corpse on a gurney being loaded into an ambulance, knowing I'd never see her face, her smile...her bright freckles...ever again.

After the ambulance drove off, I broke down in the dirty alleyway behind the local pizza joint. I was angry, and now—realizing my chance at perfection had been stolen from me—I had regrets. The very embodiment of perfection had been lost forever in what could only be described as a senseless death.

Sometimes I'd even touch myself at night, over and over, lying there just thinking about Ruby and trying to resurrect her in my mind. If only I had held her corpse one last time just to feel her soft skin and smell her floral scented hair. Because I knew she was about as close to satisfaction as I would ever have, and now she was gone...all because of the wretched, mentally disturbed boys that took her away from me.

♦♦♦♦♦

I had always wanted to go into politics, and one of the driving forces behind that dream was to make things better—to try and right the wrongs of the world. Because even if I could never get Ruby back, I was determined to make sure that the freaks of this world—the horrors that society chooses to protect—would all become a thing of the past who could never hurt anyone again.

It was a simple vision: make sure everyone is flawless through a stream of laws. Only a dream like that isn't going to be very easy to implement, and the number of sickos out there seems to be multiplying.

♦♦♦♦♦

I had come to understand something over the years—something most people refused to admit. We're just animals. Dressed-up, self-important creatures clawing at the edges of a world we don't deserve. No one really cares about climate change, about the poisoned oceans or the choked forests. No one truly cares about the suffering that festers in every darkened corner of civilization. We eat, bicker, breed, steal and destroy. That is all we do.

It seemed Hamlet had it wrong after all. *"What a piece of work is man,"* he said, marveling at human reason, our divine potential. But from where I stood it was all a farce. There is no infinite faculty, no god-like apprehension. We are not angels in action—we are maggots, writhing and mindless, feeding on the carcass of a world we have long since ruined.

It's always been like this, this species of ours. Why play along with the illusion of civilization when the truth is so much simpler? No matter how much we dress ourselves up in ethics, religion, or progress, we're still just animals. Breeding. Consuming. Fighting over scraps like dogs in a gutter.

And for what? Some illusion of civilization of false promises? Some lie about human worth?

We're nothing special; just primates with WiFi.

And, I figured, if people insisted on behaving like beasts, then they should be treated like beasts. Herded. Managed. Put down when necessary. It's not cruelty, but mercy and efficiency.

Let's face it; the weak drag the rest of us down. They're the ones who can't keep up and refuse to evolve. So I say let them feel the cold hands of nature guiding them toward the only mercy left to them: the abattoir—the slaughterhouse.

♦♦♦♦♦

While we're on the subject, why stop there? Why not take those who are worthy and make our world into the best society that there will ever be? With my chosen few, I expected to achieve this very soon. The chosen would be much more flawless than the heathens of the rest of the world. They cry "natural selection," yet bring along with them the people who drag us down.

The future belongs to the worthy. The clean. The intelligent. The chosen. The pure.

I'd dream about it sometimes. A perfect world—sterile, orderly, righteous. No more chaos. No more broken minds cluttering up classrooms, hospitals, or sidewalks. This disaster of Ruby's death had taught me that the world doesn't need more noise. It needs clarity and purpose.

But dreams aren't enough, and if nature wouldn't finish the job, then I would. I mean, this is a simple solution, like culling a diseased limb before it spreads. That's all this is; Nature's work—just sped up.

Ultimately, that's the bottom line. You can dress them up however you like, calling them "autistic," "neurodivergent," or "special." You can slap diagnoses on their foreheads and build little playgrounds for them to stumble around in, but deep down you know. *EVERYONE* knows. These people are a mistake, and can't be part of the future.

Mistakes must be corrected.

♦♦♦♦♦

Placing my cigarette into the ashtray, I peered at my litter of yellow sticky notes on my desk. They resembled little graves of half-baked plans and final decisions; scribbled reminders, names, addresses, and times.

One reminder caught my eye. Peeling it off the polished wood, I read La Mesa Fire Plan.

Staring at it for a moment, I grabbed the red marker from the mesh cup overflowing with pens, like bones in a cage. With a flick of my wrist, I slashed through the words. Red ink bled into black.

Done.

The paper fell softly into the tin trash can like the last leaf of autumn drifting down from a maple tree. And I knew what the next step would be. They'd call it a tragedy.

Of course they would; they always do. Then the news cycle would rinse it clean, and in two weeks no one would remember the name of the town, let alone the people who had burned in it.

HAH! But I'd remember.

I just wish they could understand. I mean *really* understand what I knew, and what I'm building here. If only they could see my domain, my design...only they had no vision to understand why only the chosen are allowed in.

Because they got it. Having grown up in filth—beaten, broken, doped up and discarded—those who were chosen had nothing left to lose. They recognized that I gave them purpose. I gave them myself—my leadership, wisdom, and love.

I let them be a part of me...and they were grateful.

Of course, the side benefit is that people who have been raised in rot are easier to shape. You show them kindness, control, and order, and they'll follow you into the fire.

Ah, but violence...that *ALWAYS* gets the message across. You can whisper truths for decades and be ignored. But one explosion—one act of beautiful clarity—and suddenly the world listens. They watch. They *learn*.

I know the law in this country. I know how it bends for the rich and breaks for the rest. Ruby's killers walked free because their parents had money. *BIG money*. That was enough.

But I don't forget. And I don't forgive.

So, I built something better—a world where no one slips through the cracks, because I burned the cracks shut. A world where everyone thinks the same, loves the same, follows the same light—*my* light.

I figured if I can't change them with kindness, I'll change them with fire.

A text came in from Destiny. "Fifteen new ones just arrived. They're waiting."

A small smile tugged at the corners of my lips. Fifteen. That's more than I expected today.

Maybe—just maybe—there are a few with brains among them. Or better yet, ears. Willing ears. Open hearts. The kind of people who wouldn't flinch at the truth, who'd understand that change is painful, but necessary. That obedience is necessary.

Because there could be no question that the world needs to change and decrease the population. This world is broken, bloated, and bursting at the seams. Earthquakes. Floods. Fires. None of it is random. Mother Nature is telling us that humanity is a disease, and that's why we're having these disasters. People are an annoyance. It's not 'climate change,' it's the planet trying to shake us off like fleas.

And me? I'm just helping the planet achieve its goal by cleansing the rot and removing the undesirables. I'm thinning the herd so the worthy can thrive. The bleeding hearts pretend that this sounds harsh, but even they know it's way overdue.

♦♦♦♦♦

I shifted off my leather chair, brushing off the bits of ashes from my outfit. Damn—it's still warm from the last time I burned it. I paused, inspecting the fabric. A tiny hole and a bit of soot remains, but it's nothing that Mune couldn't repair and scrub out later. For now, I had souls to greet.

Leaving the white walls and stained glass of my office behind, the hallways of our sanctuary—lit with soft lanterns—echoed faintly as I padded towards my newest recruits. Our home, hidden deep within the chaparral hills of San Diego, offered more than safety. It offered *truth*. It was a sanctuary, yes, but also a chrysalis.

This was only the beginning. When our numbers grew, so too would our reach. One sanctuary would expand into two. Two would become ten. It would turn into a network...a movement...a cleansing.

This is our church. This is the new world.

And it will be beautiful.

Chapter 14: The Miracle Tap and Cordials

-Juniper-

Located within the cities of Del Mar and Solana Beach on the north side of San Diego, the Midsummer Fair always took place during the dog days of summer. From July 30 - August 15—almost three solid weeks—it was *the* place to be day and night from 11am to 11pm.

The ocean—a mere half mile away—ensured a cool breeze wafted over the fairgrounds much of the time.

And people came in droves, with the fair typically welcoming around 1.5 million visitors each year. It was probably one of the largest annual events in California, offering a wide array of attractions, including rides, concerts, food vendors, and exhibitions.

Despite my being a veteran fairgoer, it was still kind of overwhelming. Row after row of booths hawking fried food, candy, turkey legs, and boba drinks that were displayed for the manufactured consumerism of the public. The smell of the cooked food lingered in the air, making me hungry for this and that as I walked by, far south of the amusement rides and games crowded by suckers thinking they could actually win against the house. Hundreds of people sloshed their way through the walkways where kids and adults alike sweated their way through the high season heat.

In hindsight I realize how different this year's event was. It wasn't just the theme, which changed from year to year, but rather the overall tone of the place. There were many more guards this year than one typically saw around the festival. It was odd, as I'd never seen so much security. Given the proximity to the explosion a few weeks ago, I guess I shouldn't have been surprised.

All things considered, I was kind of surprised that there wasn't more security around the Midsummer Fair. Then again, maybe there was, but they were in plain clothes. I'll never know for sure.

♦♦♦♦♦

Several years ago, in an effort to expand awareness, the regional centers had set up a booth each year during the Midsummer Fair. There a team of their marketing professionals would spend 12 hours each day giving out canvas bags, pens, hand exercisers, and information about the services they provide year-round to a wide range of citizens needing a little extra help.

Today the San Diego County Regional Nexus Center—the SDC-RNC for short—was sponsoring a bake sale, which meant *we* were going to be incredibly busy.

Naturally, they were delighted when we expressed interest in volunteering.

♦♦♦♦♦

Fifteen members of our family headed from the back lot to set up our booth in the pavilion where hundreds of small business vendors were selling delicacies and crafts of every possible kind. Casting a curious eye over the coffee shops, knick-knack stores, art displays, and other nifty collectibles that were offered for public consumption, I noted how industrial the space was. "Still, it's better than standing out in the heat," I reminded myself as I helped Brady set up the boxes of chocolates we'd need for the day's event.

I'll confess now that I felt more than a little guilt-ridden as I set things up as I recollected the recent memories of making and packing all the candies before arriving this morning. Even as I tried shouting myself down about feeling guilty, I kept thinking about the secret ingredient in our 'therapeutic' treat...that one little detail I was pretty sure would raise eyebrows if the public knew about it.

Bleach.

♦♦♦♦♦

There's one thing that's consistent about the effects of bleach: it burns. It will burn the germs off your toilet, or your skin when you touch it. And if you swallow it, it burns the lining of the stomach and intestines.

Still, it kills bacteria in water, so I figured it can't be that bad when used in small controlled amounts.

Of course, considering that 73% of the average human brain is made up of water, introducing bleach into the human body is arguably not a good thing. This is why there was such an uproar when Donald Trump, as president of the United States, suggested that drinking bleach could treat or prevent COVID-19. His recommendation was not only dangerous and completely false, but caused severe harm, including damage to the mouth, throat, stomach, and internal organs, in countless numbers of his followers.

In some cases it proved to be fatal.

The number of bleach-related exposure calls to public-health agencies rose by about 77% immediately after he made this suggestion.

Which is why, to make the presence of the bleach less obvious, we diluted the dosage with sugary liquor. The way Aeron figured, if it was diluted it would be enough to help 'rewire' the brains of the people who ate it, without hurting them in any way.

♦♦♦♦♦

I'm pretty sure Aeron tried this idea once with a rat he had gotten from a local pet store. As he fed the rodent the bread and cheese without the Miracle Tap—our other product laced with the same chemical—there were no effects, like he expected.

Then he gave the rat more bread and cheese, but this time with a few drops of the Miracle Tap.

At first there were no effects. So, all in the interests of science—of course—, he gave the rat another portion. This time with a higher dosage of the Miracle Tap.

Success! The poor animal showed a few symptoms, convulsed a little, and wobbled slightly in its step. But still very much alive.

An hour later, after recovering from the last encounter with Miracle Tap, Aeron gave the rat a fourth piece of bread and cheese, only this time it was soaked in a heavy dosage. Naturally, the creature greedily sucked down what he thought was lunch, only to find himself convulsing and lying on his side within seconds, kicking and foaming as it struggled to breathe.

It was as if the Miracle Tap was seeping into its brain, probing its chemicals into his nerves.

The rat quickly went limp.

♦♦♦♦♦

To Aeron it was a success, but I wondered...was it *really* a success? All he had succeeded in doing was to kill the animal in a merciless poisoning. It couldn't vomit it out. It couldn't even breathe. I didn't know what curing them meant if it looked like that.

For that matter, what was Aeron hoping to cure the rat of?

All of which meant addressing a bigger question: how would our formula—our gift to humanity—affect humans who ate it? Would the reactions be different in a human versus a simple rodent?

Plus I keep thinking about the words he said in the last congregational meeting. They struck a chord within me, but not in a familiar or good way.

If I'm being completely honest, his words left a really bad taste in my mouth.

> *"We need to make it look like an accident, even though it will be used to address the many undesirable things humanity must deal with, like curing cancer, fixing autism, and growing limbs for amputees. There are SO many empty promises given, but I know I'm doing them all a favor. Why? Because in my world people with diagnoses like autism and ADHD wouldn't even exist."*

The promises of a new world and a paradise—you'd think he'd be practicing what he preached. But when he said this stuff about people with autism shouldn't even exist...

I mean, is paradise even worth it if there are those who are different from the mainstream and are denied salvation?

Could it be that I was misinterpreting his words?

Then there was a bigger question: in good conscience, how could I stand by this cause if the reluctance to support it outweighs my trust in Aeron?

Sure, I may be overthinking the whole thing. After all, it's true that not everyone deserves to be saved, but what about those whose only "wrongdoing" was just being born differently?

Yeah, I'm sure there's nothing to worry about. Aeron knows what he's doing, and I trust him.

♦♦♦♦♦

My phone alarm interrupted my train of thought, telling me the cherry cordials in the freezer were done cooling. Pulling on my latex gloves, I opened the freezer and pulled out the icy metal trays of countless 'medicated treats.'

Dozens of brown and cream-colored desserts lay before me, each one meticulously crafted with the exact dosage of the serum used to help our clientele. The ethical considerations—the ingredients, the process, and the precise dosage of the serum—all reflected our unwavering commitment to the well-being of those we served, and the paramount importance we all placed on their health.

The process of creating these treats was also a delicate balance. We'd start with cleaned maraschino cherries, dipped in fondant and flavored with a hint of 'liquor'. But the real magic would happen when we added a half eyedropper-full of our working serum. This would ensure that the taste of the sweet liquor invertase wasn't overpowered.

Once stirred, we would hand-dip the individual cherries in powdered sugar until they were fully covered. The next step would be to encase them in chocolate which, once cooled, would give the cherries a hard coating. We'd wait for the invertase to take effect, making the sugar into fructose; a chemical process that typically takes about a week to complete.

♦♦♦♦♦

As I pulled the trays out of the fridge, I eyed the three different batches of chocolates. It was a simple set of flavors to start with, but it would do the job.

Shifting gears, I pulled over the rouge, pre-folded box and set about filling it, my gloved fingers plucking each candy from the tray and setting the chocolates into neat rows of white, milk and dark, lined up like little soldiers off to war. I even eyed the candies for a few seconds, tempted to try one to ensure quality control.

Shaking off the temptation, I tucked the top half of the box over the bottom half, sealing it with gold-colored glue circles and sealed it tightly.

Mechanically, I repeated the same task, slowly filling the dozens of vacant boxes stacked before me. Eventually, everything was ready for our big public debut.

I stood back to admire my work: 1000 dark red boxes. They'd be a bit tricky to transport, but certainly would be enough for the event. Carefully stacking the boxes four high, I placed them flat in the cardboard carrier boxes scattered around the floor, all fitted snugly and ready for sale.

♦♦♦♦♦

I was filled with the satisfaction of a job well done and the pride in properly completing my task as I prepared the treats for the event. These feelings were a testament to my team's commitment to ethical food production and the joy it was bringing us.

Again I toyed with the idea of scarfing one down, wondering what would happen if I tasted it. Would it really cure my worries and fix anything that troubled me, either physically or mentally? Would eating one wipe away intrusive thoughts that sounded contradictory to my core beliefs and morals?

Of course, I could always ask Aeron if I could have some of them myself, only...what would I say to him? "Oh, Aeron, I have second thoughts about selling these to the people at the Midsummer Fair. Can I have a couple of them to calm my nerves? I don't even feel like a girl at the moment. Can these help me out so I can feel better?"

I mean, how was I supposed to even bring this up in conversation without sounding suspicious? I didn't know how to bring it up without sounding obvious, and I'd hate to upset him.

I didn't like seeing Aeron when he's upset, and I really hated the idea of what he'd be like if he got really angry with me. I know I have to do what he says, and there's really no discussion about it. After all, I owe him my life and for taking me in. So to even think about questioning his authority is unacceptable.

No, he said it's the right thing to do, so it must be the right thing to do.

And yet, this whole idea of the Miracle Tap and its curative powers sounds so *off*. But if I second-guess Aeron or refuse to do his bidding for any reason...well, what does that make me? Ungrateful. Selfish. Homeless. Unloved.

I can't even think about it. I...I don't know what to think...I...

"Juniper?"

I flinched at the sound of someone calling my name; the only sound in this silent, dark room. "Almost done?" asked Destiny. She stood by the doorframe, already dressed in her flawless white robe, and was gathering up the other members so we could go to work.

I nodded. "Yes, they're ready to be transported."

"Great!" she grinned.

♦♦♦♦♦

A case of apprehension took over as I arrived at the fairgrounds. My guts twisted nervously, and my inner turmoil intensified by the moment. The growing throng poured in through the open gates, and the very sight of them—and the knowledge of what we were about to do—only added to the pressure.

"I must stay focused," I reminded myself. Aeron would expect nothing less from me, even as I struggled to keep my composure and not let my doubts show.

The crowds grew by leaps and bounds, and I watched as a few of them wandered by our booth. "Just keep smiling," a mantra I found myself repeating often. I knew if I just trusted the process, everything would be okay.

Watching the day's visitors, I noticed many were parents. A tired looking woman wearing a blue blouse and a blond bowl haircut approached me, the tired bags under her eyes screaming to the world that she was a working mother. She held hands with a child who looked no older than five.

I swallowed hard.

"Are these chocolates sugar-free?" she asked in a voice sweet enough to give me cavities.

"Ah...no, but uh" my eyes turned to a second pile of boxes at the other end of the table. The carrier boxes clearly stated *'sugar free'* and I smiled at her. "But these are."

"Oh good! Great! I wouldn't want anything with sugar for my son; you know how kids can be," she guffawed.

I chuckled a bit, trying to sound as if I was following her conversation, rather than being totally immersed in my own thoughts of guilt and confusion. I knew I needed to focus on the task at hand, but I was finding it so hard to think.

The wall of people bearing down on us, the cacophony of noise echoing off the walls, surrounding us and cutting us off from our own thoughts, made the very idea of concentrating on what had to be done to be laughable.

♦♦♦♦♦

I just needed to do this for Aeron's sake. He had asked me to do it, so I would do as he asked. Especially since lately he has been acting a bit peculiarly. I didn't know what the problem was, but my instincts told me he was hiding something.

Maybe he's sick. I could make him some soup to help him feel better. Or rub his feet, or something—anything—to help him get over it.

I was kind of at a loss trying to figure it all out. Maybe he wasn't himself because it's almost the anniversary of his girl's death. Or could it be that he's just as nervous about the bombing incident as I am?

No, that can't be it. Aeron is strong enough for all of us. He lets us worry, knowing that worrying is for the weak. Still, somewhere inside I heard a little voice telling me he's brushing it off just a little more easily than he should be.

I thought it over some more and began believing it was remembering his girl dying that made Aeron sad. Ruby Ridge was *his* girl, after all; his lifelong love and fantasy girl. And I remember that night two years ago when he vented to me about the horrors that had befallen her...and how heartbroken he still was.

He started crying as he described the bruises and torn clothes she was wearing on the gurney. She'd obviously fought for her honor and her life that night, only to lose both in that tragic scene under the desert moon.

Aeron said he eventually recognized the men who took her from him—or at least days after the body was found. Late at night, the devastated teenage Aeron would vandalize the streets of Indio, trying to work through his anger, and lovesick with an illness of the heart that would never be cured.

And he recounted how the poor girl had been assaulted and killed by these vermin before they took her somewhere in the middle of the desert to be eaten by the coyotes and ignored, as if she'd never existed.

To make matters worse, the police refused to even let him see her corpse in the morgue. Something about him not being immediate family.

All he could do was stare through a glass window at his beautiful Ruby Ridge, lying half a room away. Cold, lifeless, and him unable to even get close enough to touch her hand or kiss her goodbye.

Then there was the final insult, when these bastards got away with it without a lick of punishment. Not even probation. They just walked out of the courtroom, laughing. One of them even caught Aeron's eye and winked as he strolled out towards the street.

No wonder my leader was a bubbling cauldron of raw emotion.

Yes, I must always stay strong for him. Because he needs to have someone he can vent to, and I'm happy to be that support for him...just as I vent to him about how screwed up I am because of my family.

It's nice that we're able to support each other like that. In that spirit of support, I must focus and get this over with for the good of the organization...and for Aeron.

♦♦♦♦♦

I cleared my throat before adding, "The only flavors as of now are milk, white and dark chocolate, all with the cherry in the middle." I gestured, to the other assortments of bottles we had, about twenty of the supplement variants. "We also have capsules or liquids in various flavors. These sometimes make it easier for kids to swallow."

"Oh yes and a very good price too, and this sign says they've got some kind of supplement in them?" she said, pointing to our homemade banner above our tent.

"Yes, they actually help people with different ill-... I mean neurodivergent kids and adults to help them out with their health. It also works with people who have BPD, PTSD, and possibly even anxiety. It's actually a holistic kind of candy, if that makes sense," I said, hesitating as if backtracking something I almost slipped out. I hoped no one had heard that from the raving crowds now flooding the building.

I bit my lip, trying not to say the wrong thing again, and stood stock still. The other family members noticed and came to support me. "Hey Juniper, are you okay?" Destiny asked, adding "You look pale."

♦♦♦♦♦

I didn't really hear Destiny or any of the others through the buzzing in my skull. The noise from the crowds was bouncing off the walls, growing more intense by the moment and making me feel like I was going to faint. My chest felt like it was going to explode from a combination of impending doom and claustrophobia. Here I was—bottled up in a tight space, unable to avoid the screaming crowd around me—and feeling like I was rooted to the spot where an airplane was about to crash. A freight train was bearing down on me, and there was nothing I could do to get out of its way.

My heart pounded mercilessly as I began to sweat. *'What's wrong with me? What the hell is wrong with me?'*

“I...I need to use the bathroom,” I stammered, walking past the confused woman and the other members. As I sped up, I couldn’t look back at them for fear I’d scream, or cry, or throw up.

I sped up, brushing past countless couples, senior citizens, parents and their children. Nobody noticed as I started to pull my hair from its roots. I stood there for a moment looking at clumps of hair that I’d just yanked out, with these images of carnage still bouncing around in my brain. I was desperate for it to stop, but I couldn’t get it out of my head.

Rooted to the spot, I silently screamed, grabbed my face, and hid my eyes from everyone I stumbled past until I finally reached the women's room.

Seeing there was no line to the shabby room, I gratefully ran in and hid from the outside world. Throwing myself into the nearest empty stall, I slammed the door and locked it in a desperate bid for a moment of silence and solitude.

Still firmly grasping my head, I began hyperventilating while vainly trying to calm down. Blessedly, the noises were muffled in here, though the relative calm was of little help.

My eyes welled up with tears, burning as if they would pop out of my head if I didn’t hold them in place. The images of the fire engulfing all those innocent lives still haunted me, and I couldn’t forget them, no matter how hard I tried.

♦♦♦♦♦

Sitting on the toilet seat, I lost all track of time as I focused on pulling my hair until my scalp ached. I was numb and held the strands that moments before had been in my head, gripping them as if they were a lifeline.

I couldn’t shake myself loose until I got a text from Destiny. I hesitated, looking through my pockets for my phone and not really sure I wanted to find it.

“Hey, what's up? Are you feeling okay?”

I bit my lip hard enough to make it bleed as I debated whether to answer. “Yeah, I'm just feeling under the weather today. That's all. I should be coming out soon.”

I was *such* a mess! I mean, I knew I had to get back out there — if not for me, then for Aeron. But the very thought of returning to the table and acting like nothing was wrong just made me nauseous.

My face was sweating profusely, and this damned humidity wasn't helping me to lower my stress level. Anxious, I took another deep breath, preparing myself to get back out there, and knowing that whatever I might want, I just HAD to force myself to do what Aeron had asked of me.

♦♦♦♦♦

BAM!

The bathroom door slammed open and a gagging woman ran into the toilet three stalls down from me. She vomited violently, her heaving and the liquid hitting the water making me cringe as it echoed all around that damned filthy bathroom.

The poor woman puked endlessly, crying out and whimpering as if there were a rabid rodent twisting around inside her, gnawing and clawing in a desperate effort to get out.

She upchucked again, then went silent. I stood stock still for a few seconds, waiting to see what would happen next, only to hear a loud and ominous thud.

I remained on edge, wondering what would come next. After losing her lunch like that, with her body rejecting whatever it was that disagreed with her, she HAD to be okay now. After all, people overeat at these kinds of fairs all the time, right? And those turkey legs did look kind of sketchy. She probably stuffed herself or got food poisoning. Or she ate a greasy sausage before going on the Tilt-A-Whirl, which was virtually guaranteed to make you go WHOOPS!

Finally, I screwed up my courage, stood up from the toilet seat, cautiously opened the stall door, and poked my head out into the room.

Silence. There were no other sounds there but the muffled roar of the crowds outside in the stifling heat. My conscience screamed at me to check on her.

♦♦♦♦♦

The stall door was open at a very odd angle and despite my misgivings, I forced myself to move towards it. I swallowed as I inched closer to the stall, my heart stammering and a new set of sweat running down my face. Gently, I opened the stall door.

My bathroom companion sat on her knees hunched over the toilet, remaining completely still. Her once vibrant curly brunette hair looked mangled and drenched with sweat, her skin mottled, clammy and dull—especially when compared to the brightly colored blouse she had had tucked into her new blue jeans. She looked to be in her early fifties, and was slumped over as if her face was hiding inside the bowl itself. She looked limp and lifeless, but I still wanted to believe she had just eaten a bad corn dog.

“Excuse me, ma’am?” I asked cautiously. “Are you all right?”

She didn't respond, though I was pretty sure I heard some gurgling sounds from her throat.

“I...I just wanted to see if you're alright. I mean I get it, the corndogs and fried avocados aren't that great, huh?” I tried to make a joke to ease the tension. But her silence made it even more awkward — even scary.

“Ma’am?” I asked again. Part of me wanted to approach her or at least tap her back to get her attention, though I didn’t want to come off as being too intrusive. Should I get the others? Should I ask the security or medics of this fair to come get her. Should I–

It took a few seconds before my eyes caught something red dripping from the rim of the toilet bowl. I blanched, backing away. Maybe my eyes were playing tricks on me?

So I took a breath and spoke again. “I will...I will come back to bring you some water,” I lied, quickly exiting the bathroom. I just needed to get out of there. My mind had to be playing tricks on me. I just needed to get back to the booth—and fast.

But I hadn’t gone six paces when a twenty-something blonde with a blouse matching the woman in the stall stopped me. She had silver hoop earrings and her lips were a soft shade of mauve.

“Excuse me, is my mom in there? I was looking for her, she has the same blouse as mine, she looked pale and ran off somewhere and I can't find her.” The slightly panicked expression she wore spoke volumes, and resembled the way I was feeling at the moment.

I gulped as I only gave her one answer: "In there." I said as I pointed to the bathroom where the woman lay.

She thanked me before she headed into the bathroom. This was my cue to run back to our booth, trying carefully to not push anyone or dash off into the unrelenting crowd.

I had almost made it back to the booth when a shrill scream pierced the air. Nobody else in the crowd seemed to notice it, but I definitely heard it...and it was coming directly from the bathroom. The moment I heard it my worst fears were confirmed: that woman hadn't just been sick...

♦♦♦♦♦

Arriving back at the booth, Destiny immediately confronted me. "Where were you? Are you alright?"

I nodded. "Yeah, yeah. I'm fine. I just got too hot and overwhelmed is all," I lied, hoping that would be enough to satisfy her. Destiny looked at Brady, confused. I thought for a moment about telling them what happened, figuring they'd stop worrying. "*Later*," I told myself.

We continued selling boxes of chocolates to the fair's patrons, many of whom looked to be desperate parents wanting to help their kids. Interestingly, they didn't really specify what ailed their kids, other than them having 'outbursts' or sensitivities they couldn't control.

I tried not to dwell on it too much...at least until 10 minutes later when I noticed a few red and blue lights flashing at the end of the hall. They were coming from outside the main door, and I saw two people in white uniforms pushing a gurney into the women's bathroom that I'd been in just a little while ago. My heart dropped as they eventually pulled out the gurney, this time with a body draped in a white cloth. I thought I saw a bit of red staining the end of the sheets.

♦♦♦♦♦

I glanced back at the table, trying desperately to focus on something other than the vision of that gurney, and fixed my eyes on the steady supply of chocolates being sold. The images of these delicious treats danced on the burgundy boxes, taunting me. Still, they helped me avoid the accusatory gazes from the crowd, with patrons and lookie-loos alike halting and jostling to see the gurney being pulled away.

A few people close by sobbed into each other's arms, holding on tight for support, and I had a horrible sinking feeling that those were the woman's family members. Some were stuck in a shocked trance after witnessing such a gruesome death.

Then there were the gaggle of teenagers who pulled out their phones to record the whole thing. Jesus Christ, is nothing sacred to these kids?

♦♦♦♦♦

The walkie talkie in Brady's pocket crackled. He clicked the button as he walked away in search of a quiet spot.

"Hey, what's going on out there?" he asked with his lips close to the device. I couldn't hear much of what he was saying, but felt he was talking to the other members at the front of the colorful, retro-looking entrance to the fair, decorated with neon shapes and designs resembling the aesthetic of the 1980s. I was pretty sure they were announcing the presence of our table, guiding visitors in our direction. I swallowed hard, wanting to listen more to what he was saying, but noticed an influx of foot traffic walking closer to our booth. I sighed, put on a tight-lipped smile, and hoped this would soon be over.

But here was the curious thing. Even as I sold yet another box of dark chocolates, I thought I heard Brady saying over the walkie talkie; "We may have to leave after this patron we have here. We don't want any suspicion cast in our direction for that death in the park."

Chapter 15: Fatal Aromatherapy

-Damian-

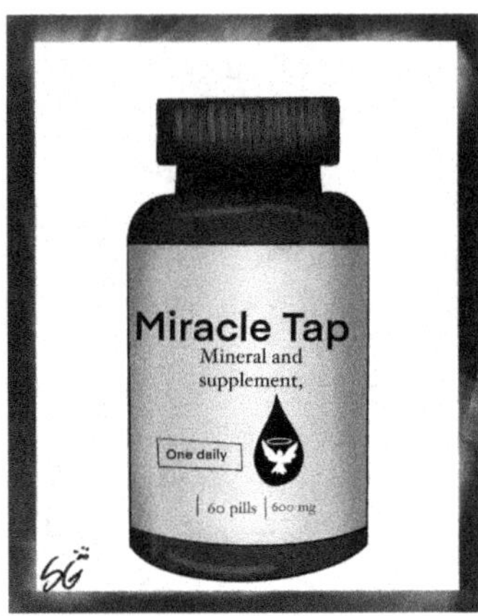

Hopping out from my last ride of the day, I paid the cab driver and gave him a tired "thanks" before he pulled away to pick up his next fare. Then it was down the hill toward the group home, the familiar slope under my aching feet a quiet reminder of how long this day had been. I was dead tired. *Bone-tired.* You'd think the aftermath of a wedding would be a little more graceful—something a bit cleaner, a bit softer. But nah. That was wishful thinking.

We'd spent the entire day cleaning up after last night's reception at Mission Beach, and it was worse than I had expected. And it wasn't just me either. Rather, the whole crew—all eight of us PLUS our manager—had spent the past 10 hours slogging through the wreckage, like it was some kind of post-party war zone.

The empty beer cans crunching under our boots had made it challenging to pick up the wasted wedding cake that had been left to melt into the sand. And let's not forget the dehydrated white roses shriveling in the sun like forgotten offerings.

Yup, it was all there, along with the spilled champagne and shattered glasses buried just beneath the surface, just waiting to catch someone's bare foot and make it bleed.

Did I mention the cigars still smoldering on the cinderblocks, like someone had just walked away mid-thought? How about the gum smeared across tabletops like a careless signature?

And the worst part had to have been that sour puddle of vomit on the asphalt, just baking there in the noonday sun, right in the middle of everything. I had to step over it more times than I could count, hauling bags to the dumpster and back again. The stench stuck to me and got in my throat, to a point where there were moments when I thought I might lose it myself.

YICH!

There's now absolutely no question: cleaning up a mess like this is one hell of a lot lonelier when you don't have someone to talk to during the process. Usually I get to chat with Sofia while I work, which makes the time pass faster and softens the edges of things for me.

Only she's been gone for the past two weeks, and it's not like she's off on vacation or anything. From what I've heard, her house was destroyed - just wiped out in an instant—and she was now trying to settle into some kind of temporary living situation with extended family...at least until they figured out a more permanent solution for her and her family.

I felt really awful about her situation, too, and didn't even know how to help her—hell, I didn't even know how to reach her anymore. Not really. She hadn't said much to me lately—hadn't really talked to me at all—and I didn't know what had changed, or if I had said something wrong.

She may have just shut down a bit, and I can't say I'd blame her if she had.

People around here kept telling me to give her space. And maybe that's all I could do—back off and be around if she ever wanted to talk; a presence, but not a problem.

But it's all fuckin' weird! I mean, first there was that explosion at her house, and then that bizarre bleach incident at the regional center while she was there. I tried calling and texting to see if she was okay, but all I got back was a short, sharp "I'm fine."

Jeez, it's not like any of it was *MY* fault! But she can't fool me. Not Sofia. She tries acting tough, but I could feel it through the screen—she was still in shock and maybe unraveling a bit, even if she wouldn't admit it.

Again, who could blame her? She'd been through so much in such a short time. My reaching out probably felt like just another unwelcome noise in the chaos.

It's wild, isn't it? Summertime is supposed to be easy. Sunlight. Longer days. Lots of laughter, and maybe a little romance if the stars line up properly. Right now I'd be happy just to see her again, and to know she's really okay.

♦♦♦♦♦

I walked past my housemates without a word, heading straight to my room and closing the door behind me. Normally I'd burst in with a loud "HELLOOO!" to show lots of energy, even when I'm running low. But today? Today begs for silence. Decompression. The illusion that the rest of the world doesn't even exist.

Plopping onto my bed, I sighed, then melted into the soft mattress. It felt nice to kick off my work boots and just *be*.

Lying there, I shifted onto one elbow and opened my phone, figuring to jot a few notes into one of my online documents...just to get it over with. I knew I could wait, but was so fried I'd probably forget everything if I didn't do it immediately.

Do the brain dump while the thoughts are still fresh.

Besides, what's the point of checking my texts? Sofia's disappeared, and what am I going to read? A reminder from my mom this morning about bringing sunscreen?

12 hours later, that's not exactly relevant anymore.

So I lazily pecked away on my phone and did my homework. The strange thoughts about today's events kept replaying in my mind, but there wasn't much I could do about that, either.

♦♦♦♦♦

Mid-summer's usually a good time of the year. Despite the scorching sun, there's something about the way the breeze slips in off the bay that makes the work bearable. The flower beds around the city are in full bloom, spilling color across sidewalks and park borders. It's beautiful, even if you're sweating through a city work shirt with a trash grabber in one hand and a bag of empty beer cans in the other.

That's where I come in. People like me keep the parks and beaches clean while everyone else flies kites, swims, or snaps selfies for their little highlight reels. I don't mind the work, really—it's honest and it keeps me moving...only something's shifted lately. You can feel it in the air. The community vibe is jittery, and people are oddly hesitant. It's like there's something creeping just under the surface of normal life.

Take today, for example. We were out by Belmont Park doing a beach cleanup. I'd just picked up a shattered glass bottle half-buried in the sand when I overheard two girls at a nearby picnic table. They looked like sorority types, with their tan legs, loud sunglasses, and margaritas sweating in their hands. Their Delta Delta Delta shirts were tossed onto the bench beside them, glittery and proud, and at first I dismissed them as the kind of girls who major in "networking" and were looking to get their MRS degrees by the time they turned 25.

But then one of them mentioned an accident at the Midsummer Fair, and how they were starting to target regional centers. My ears perked up and I slowed my pace, pretending to check the trash bag for a hole while leaning just a little closer.

I know; I'm not supposed to eavesdrop, but I *had* to. Because this wasn't just gossip, but more like a warning.

The girl closest to me—the redhead with the pug nose, olive skin, excessive red lipstick, a sky-blue blouse, and cutoff jean shorts—was leaning into her drink like it held all the answers. Her voice cut through the coastal air, sharp and casual all at once.

"I mean, don't you think it's a little strange these accidents keep happening at the regional centers?" she said, twirling her straw like she had some kind of nervous tic. "They obviously don't have anything to do with the events the centers are hosting. But still, they don't seem to have much security either. These places are being targeted, girl!"

Her friend—curly black hair, copper skin, chartreuse sundress, matching sandals, and a kind of glazed-over patience that said she'd heard this routine before—rolled her eyes with a smile. "You're overthinking it. The way you say it makes it sound like a conspiracy. You're starting to sound like a true crime influencer."

But the redhead just shook her head, lipstick catching in the sunlight. "Think about it. First, La Mesa explodes from some so-called 'gas leak.' Then suddenly the same kind of thing starts happening at the regional centers. Coincidence? I don't buy it. It's way too clean. Like...strategically messy, you know?"

Her friend shrugged. "Yeah, but La Mesa wasn't even a regional center. Why would that rundown place be a target?"

And though I wanted desperately to stand there raking that one spot and catching every shred of their theories, I heard my boss calling to me. Hoping that the two women hadn't noticed me snooping on them, I scurried back to our main location and shook my head. I'd been told before to not do that—to not even listen to conversations I wasn't a part of—and I knew better than that.

This time I couldn't shake the feeling that the redhead was right. Something was going on. Something more than what was being shown on the news. And whatever it was, it was circling closer.

♦♦♦♦♦

So yeah, hours later those words were still bouncing around in the back of my brain like a rubber ball in a concrete box. I couldn't shake them, and they were messing with my head enough that I couldn't even type a single line into my document app to finish homework: a short poem for writing class.

I'd been staring at the screen for what felt like forever.

Maybe it was writer's block again. Or my brain just didn't want to sit still long enough to be creative. Either way, a break was definitely called for.

I switched over to YouTube, hoping to find something decent—maybe a horror two-reeler or some creepy low-budget gem that might jolt my imagination back to life. Instead I just ended up scrolling. And scrolling. And scrolling.

Influencers faking their way through another personality quiz. Product placements disguised as "spontaneous" reactions. Animations with overstimulating colors and inappropriate messaging and imagery targeted to five-year-olds. People teasing their dogs or getting smacked in the face with rakes. And maybe the occasional video of tourists getting chased by a bison in Yellowstone after they annoyed it by getting too close.

More of the same carbon copy brain rot.

And now, on top of it all, every other scroll was plastered with ads for scammy AI apps and pyramid scheme fitness programs. I sighed and kept scrolling, trying to find something—*anything*—that felt real...or at the very least, unsettling enough to wake me up.

That was until my thumb slipped and accidentally clicked on a news video. And just like that, my brain snapped into focus as the news anchor's voice filled my room—smooth, precise, and dropping details that sounded like they'd come straight out of a Wes Craven film.

> *"Yesterday, a 40-year-old woman, identified as Paula Dulce, was found dead in the women's bathroom at the Midsummer Fair near Solana Beach. Doctors were baffled when an autopsy revealed strong evidence of bleach in her system. Speculators say this marks the third incident involving chemical accidents and regional-hosted events throughout San Diego County. Many in our local community are beginning to question if their families are safe during this summer season."*

"W-what?" I blinked at the screen, my pulse skittering.

The anchor continued, face solemn behind her perfect makeup:

> *"The San Diego County Regional Nexus Center shares its condolences with the Dulce family. Since the tragic explosion in La Mesa, there has been a rise in online speculation and misinformation with internet sleuths doxxing groups like 'Plant It Around' and other local organizations. Law enforcement warns this kind of speculation could cause more harm than good. The creators behind the Midsummer Fair said because of the incident and the ongoing investigation, they may need to shut down earlier than expected this year."*

♦♦♦♦♦

I sat there stunned, the words reverberating in my skull. This was the *fourth* time this summer something like this had happened. First the La Mesa explosion. Then that "gas leak" at Sunset Coast Regional. And before that, the Creative Minds Center event in La Jolla. And now THIS?

These couldn't be isolated accidents, and I wasn't buying that argument anymore. It felt like there was a thread running through all of them being pulled tight by some invisible hand. The idea made me more paranoid than I wanted to admit...even to myself.

The news had already pivoted to a story about a car crash that caused an eleven-car pileup at the junction of I-8 and I-805. The anchor was describing how a school bus heading south on 805 had plunged into the guardrail and landed smack into oncoming rush hour traffic heading west on 8, all in a cheery voice as images of bodies strewn across lanes were shown in the background.

It was the kind of gruesome spectacle that would have usually grabbed my morbid curiosity, but I wasn't listening anymore.

Instead I sighed and felt a sour taste in my mouth. The way the news just jumped from one tragedy to the next, smoothing over horrors like they were minor hiccups, made me sick. I wouldn't be surprised if they would then cut to a summer cookout segment or a story about puppies right after that news story to lessen the shock for viewers.

Tossing my phone onto the bed, I got up, deciding I'd rather listen to the silence of my room than the sanitized chaos spilling from the screen.

I wandered over to my desk and stared at the clutter piled there: papers, half-dead pens, random scraps of notes. This was as good a time as any to start cleaning my room; something I'd been putting it off for weeks with the promise I'd get to it eventually.

The truth is I get distracted a lot, and today my brain was practically screaming for an escape.

♦♦♦♦♦

Sorting through a scatter of random knick knacks, countless scraps of paper, dull pencils in need of sharpening, and assorted trash that should have been pitched ages ago, I suddenly realized my baphomet plushie was missing from my desk.

This little idol, half-human and half-demonic in form, had the body of a man and the head of a goat. Made of black faux fur, yellow button eyes stitched on crooked, red thread carefully tracing the mouth, nose, and curling rings that marked the horns, it was something I'd always kept close since the day I got it. It wasn't just a plush; it was mine. Familiar. Comforting.

And now it was gone.

Who could have taken him? And come to think of it...where were my latest drawings—the sketches I'd spent hours on—of Kali Ma, the fierce and protective goddess, her necklace of skulls hanging heavy with defiance. And what about Dracula, regal in his sweeping cloak, his fangs catching the shadows?

They were gone, as was my journal—*MY JOURNAL*! All missing.

What the hell? Could I have misplaced them?

No, more likely the answer was that someone had been in my room, invading my private space. My things had to be somewhere, but they certainly weren't where I'd left them. Because my room might look like chaos to someone else, but I always knew where my things were. Always. I could have found them blindfolded.

♦♦♦♦♦

"Damian."

I glanced up as Ren's voice cut through my spiral. He was standing in my doorway, one hand resting on the frame as if to keep me from bolting.

"We're having a meeting in the kitchen," he said.

"I—yeah, that's fine, but...have you seen my journal? Or my Baphomet plush? I can't find them anywhere."

But Ren was already turning away, calling back over his shoulder, "We'll find it later, Damian. This meeting's important."

I stared at his retreating back, annoyance and unease knotting tighter in my chest. Slowly, I got up to follow, a restless dread crawling along my skin as I glanced around my cluttered room one last time.

Where the hell did my stuff go?

♦♦♦♦♦

Leaving behind my barely-cleaned-up room, I wandered out through the doorway, still turning over possibilities in my head.

What was this meeting going to be about this time?

Maybe someone was pissed that their clearly labeled yogurt vanished from the fridge. Or maybe one of my housemates was about to launch into a tirade about money going missing—again. Nothing would surprise me around here anymore.

My shoes scuffed the floor as I headed down the hall, each step making the old wood creak and squeal under my weight. When I stepped into the kitchen, the first thing that hit me was the brightness.

Two strangers were seated at the table, both dressed head to toe in blinding, virginal white. There wasn't a speck of color anywhere on either of them, and it was almost theatrical...like they'd walked in from a detergent commercial.

I scanned the faces of the other housemates, hoping someone might give me a heads-up what was going on here...only everyone else looked just as blank and clueless as I felt.

♦♦♦♦♦

Ren stepped forward and cleared his throat. "Alright, guys, we have some guests here today."

He gestured toward the two strangers, who sat smiling serenely, looking like the proverbial cat that swallowed the canary.

"Everyone, meet Mune and Brady from a small non-profit organization called the Purity Syndicate."

I waited for more, arms folded tight, the name rolling around in my head. The Purity Syndicate. Odd. Pretentious, even.

Some dusty corner of my memory sparked—reminding me I'd read about a group with the same name back in the early twentieth century. A bunch of corrupt industrialists, if I remembered right.

And I knew there was a Purity Syndicate mentioned in the online combat game. But there was no way these guys were connected to any of that. Probably.

Still, there was something about them that made the hair on the back of my neck go up...though I was damned if I knew why.

I guess it was the smug look on both their faces that rubbed me the wrong way. Sitting there grinning, they looked like they'd won some invisible game.

It certainly wasn't the kind of smile my boss or Ren would give me; one that said "Hey, we're all in this mess together."

No. Their smiles were too polished...TOO white...like masks that were hiding something. Behind those gleaming teeth, our "guests" looked more like wolves than humanitarians, biding their time for the moment they'd lunge for the throat of an unsuspecting sheep.

My instincts screamed to stay the hell away from them.

Was I just overthinking it? God knows my brain tends to spin out after a full day baking under the sun. And I couldn't even remember the last time I'd stopped to grab a bottle of water.

Yeah. I was probably just being judgmental and reading too much into it.

Then came the sales pitch. "Hello friends, it's great to see new faces this evening, and we're so excited to show you all this presentation. My name is Brady and this is my good friend Mune," the blond man said, gesturing to his partner—the guy with whose skin was as pale as his clothing, making for an odd contrast to his dark hair and freckles.

Mune spoke in a similarly chipper tone, almost as if he was a mall elf telling children Santa will soon be coming to bring them gifts. "We have some very good things to bring for all of you, all made in our humble abode. And I'm sure it would help you immensely with the daily struggles you all face."

My insides were twisting in horror at the idea of even sitting at the same table as these guys as alarms blared inside my brain. Still, the questions remained; was I just being paranoid?

♦♦♦♦♦

My skin crawled each time they laughed. They both made a chortling sound that felt too loud, too rehearsed. And the way they kept talking down to us like we were a bunch of clueless kids just grated on my nerves.

In fact, their attitudes were a little too la-di-da for my tastes. I stood there with my arms crossed, trying to keep my expression neutral while my mind churned.

"It can be disheartening, can't it?...Yeah, it can." That was Brady, speaking *at* us rather than *to* us. His tone was syrupy, steeped in false sympathy and that brand of condescension that makes you want to break something.

Then, like some game-show reveal, they brought out a tray lined with bottles. Each one dark-tinted, glinting under the fluorescent lights, and labeled in bold letters:

Miracle Tap.

There was barely any other information on the labels—no ingredients list, no warnings, no description. Just that name.

This product had a rather odd name for a dietary supplement, even though it was simple enough to stick in your brain. Each bottle looked slightly different—one crammed with pills rattling around inside, another a dark, viscous liquid that could've passed for castor oil or cough syrup.

My mind rebelled. These guys didn't know me or anything about me or my health. Who the hell were they to be pushing supplements like THIS on me, or on any of my friends?

Something about this whole visitation—and the obnoxious way they were presenting it—was fishy.

I glanced back up at the pale dressed duo to listen to more of their so-called presentation, and wondered if this was actually a sales call or some kind of public dressing-down.

Something about their message suggested they were operating in an autism = demons mentality. Assuming I was right, this was the LAST kind of shit we needed around our household!

"Our team has developed something that is sure to help you all out. It's been tested extensively, and proven time and again to help you deal with the overstimulation you're facing every day."

♦♦♦♦♦

My brain went blank, checking out as the two of them droned on endlessly. Their voices blurred together, especially once they started talking about "the spectrum" like we were either dim-witted or Neanderthals. Fuck this shit! They were framing us like preschoolers who needed babysitters, rather than as adults capable of living our own lives.

And it wasn't just me. A quick look around the room convinced me that my housemates were confused and irritated by the weight of the condescension these guys were slinging. The uneasy, sideways glances my friends were sharing all asked the same question; who invited these clowns?

"I'm sure some of you kids—" Brady caught himself mid-sentence, backtracking with a syrupy smile, "I mean, some of you lovely people have faced discrimination. After all, you all have trouble regulating sensitivities, don't you? Isn't it just part of life in this household?"

The words hung in the air like someone had farted. Bella shifted in her chair, soft-spoken as always, but said what so many of us were thinking. "Um...no, I think we're doing fine—"

"Furthermore," Brady spoke louder and stomped all over her answer with an interruption that was sharp enough to make her flinch.

Rude didn't even begin to cover it.

Mune's eyes flicked over towards me, and he gestured like he was presenting me to the class as the topic of Show and Tell. "Everyone's on the spectrum, of course," he said breezily, as though this was just a casual truth about all of humanity. "Some look like us," he added, gesturing to himself, "others have verbal and cognitive functioning issues."

He swept his hand toward Roberto, sitting in his wheelchair with confusion plainly written on his face. Roberto couldn't speak, but he didn't need to; his expression said it all. He was a person, not a prop.

And just when I thought things couldn't get more grotesque, Brady leaned in. "Many parents—usually single parents—always have to keep their precious ones in line." His smile curled at the edges like it hurt to hold it in place.

Then Mune, with mock gravitas, reached under the table and pulled out something familiar. My chest tightened. He held it up like a prosecutor revealing evidence to the jury.

"Even drawings of oddities like this."

My stomach dropped as I saw him sharing my unfinished drawing of Kali Ma.

Then he pulled out my Baphomet plush, presenting my personal belongings as if they were confiscated items from a police raid.

I gasped, eyes snapping wide. Why the hell was my picture being displayed like that? An "oddity"? What's that supposed to mean?

And how had it ended up here—in the kitchen—in Mune's hands? Who the hell had been rooting around in my room, taking my things? For that matter, who gave it to these two interlopers? Or were they the ones who had taken them?

"You mean Kali Ma?" I blurted out before I could stop myself.

That got everyone's attention. The whole group turned toward me, the air thick with confusion and curiosity.

"Pardon?" Mune said, blinking at me like I'd just spoken fluent Martian.

"Kali Ma," I repeated, more firmly now. "The goddess of time, preservation, creation, and destruction. She's a benevolent goddess in the Hindu religion—often called the dark mother. She destroys evil to protect the innocent."

Brady and Mune just stared, wide-eyed and silent, as if I'd suddenly sprouted antlers right in front of them.

I raised an eyebrow. "I've studied a lot of science, mythologies, world history, and writing...in case you're wondering how I know this."

♦♦♦♦♦

Brady scraped his thoughts together, his voice cracking faintly at the edges. "You're...very knowledgeable." The words sounded clumsy, like he couldn't decide if he was supposed to be complimenting me or finding a polite way of saying "Pipe down, kid!"

His unease was obvious in the way his eyes darted to Ren, as though silently asking him to handle me. Then, with all the subtlety of a middle-school bully, he tossed my drawing aside like it was a piece of trash. My stomach twisted with indignation at the sheer audacity.

"Yes, Damian is very knowledgeable," Ren cut in smoothly, his voice pitched just high enough to plaster over the tension. He gave a faint chuckle, as if to soften the mood, but the sound stung—it felt like he was humoring me instead of backing me up. "He's got a real passion for world history and different religions. This is a guy who loves taking trips to Balboa Park, just to see the museums. He's always reading about all kinds of science and history."

Ren laughed again, light and airy, though it sounded more like he was gently patting me on the head. Like I was a kid blurting trivia at the wrong time, rather than someone making a valid point that deserved to be taken seriously.

I glanced at Ren and whispered, hoping to not bring any more attention to our conversation. "Okay, but who put my artwork there? It was in my room."

Ren shrugged, "I-I don't know, Damian. Let's talk about this later."

I bit my lower lip and huffed through my nose. Not wanting to argue, I decided to just be quiet, still eyeing my drawings and other things on the table and trying to discern who had snuck into my room uninvited.

Living in a group home, I'm very protective about my things. The fact that these two cretins took my possessions from my room without any repercussions *REALLY* irked me. Yet in the interests of peace I sat, reluctantly watching, listening, and anxiously waiting for them to leave and for me to get my stuff back.

♦♦♦♦♦

As our "guests" droned on, my mind temporarily shifted to autopilot, remaining fixated on how my things mysteriously migrated from my room to the table as their presentation about the so-called Miracle Tap continued unabated. Bottles of their so-called cure sat lined up in neat little rows, though I couldn't have cared less. More importantly, I sat preoccupied and lamenting the loss of my old copy of The Cockroach That Ate

Cincinnati, which I'd watched so many times the VHS had worn it down to nothing.

Their voices blurred into white static and self-satisfied nonsense, until Jenny's voice cut through my fog. "Does this have any side effects?"

Mune didn't miss a beat. "Maybe a bit of spit-up, and certainly nothing more than a slight case of the runs. But that's just your body getting used to it. Give it a day or two—three at the most—and you'll be fine."

He looked at her with a dazzling smile that was all teeth and sparkle; the kind of cinema smile that makes people swoon. Jenny actually blushed, like he'd slipped her a diamond ring instead of a line about diarrhea.

I, on the other hand, wasn't buying a single word of it and instead focused on his use of the phrase "Spit-up." This HAD had to violate some kind of FDA regulation. Spit-up meant vomit, which no legitimately approved supplement or medication would cause. And the runs? That's just a polite way of saying you'll be chained to the toilet.

Why would anyone willingly swallow something guaranteed to make them hurl or sprint for the bathroom? Or both.

♦♦♦♦♦

Leaning in closely towards the bottles lined up on the table, I squinted, trying to spot an ingredients list, nutrition facts label, or anything else remotely official.

There was nothing: just bold lettering saying THE MIRACLE TAP.

My gut twisted, with everything about this whole episode screaming "Snake Oil Salesmen!" And I wasn't about to let these two strangers sell this crap to people I cared about.

"So, which of you wants to volunteer so we can demonstrate?" Mune asked smoothly.

My stomach dropped. What, exactly, were they going to demonstrate?

Glancing at the others, I prayed that someone else felt the same unease I had crawling over my skin. Only nobody spoke. There wasn't a single protest; not even a cough to break the silence.

And then...Pedro raised his hand.

"God, not him!" I thought, closing my eyes and rocking back and forth.

My pulse spiked as they settled him into what looked disturbingly like an anesthetic mask, the rubber pressing over his mouth and nose.

Ren finally piped up, his voice tight: "And how does this work exactly?"

At least I wasn't the only one with alarm bells going off.

♦♦♦♦♦

I watched, pulse hammering in my throat, as one of the men in white unscrewed the cap on one of the bottles and poured a bit of its contents into what looked like a humidifier they'd adapted for these purposes. My heart slammed against my ribs, with every instinct screaming that this was not right.

"So we'll only add a small amount to the device—like so." Mune's tone was gentle, coaxing, like he was explaining how to water a houseplant. He poured a tablespoon of clear liquid into the spout as Brady flicked a switch.

The machine whirred to life with a thin hiss, and a faint vapor began to rise.

It quickly became obvious that this Frankenstein prop anesthesia rig belonged in a bargain-bin horror film, rather than administering "assistance" to my friends.

Still wearing that too-perfect smile, Brady spoke directly to Ren. "By using this machine while someone sleeps, Miracle Tap will, over time, help your residents behave in ways that are much more preferable to general society. In a week, they'll even find there are no more stims..."

My stomach dropped like a stone, and I couldn't stay silent any longer.

“I have a question, though,” I cut in, my voice louder than I intended. “Why are you all talking about us as if we don't know how to function ourselves? Do all of us really need this?”

You could have heard a pin drop in that room as every head turned toward me, their eyes wide and blinking. But as far as I was concerned, this bullshit was a total farce and at the moment I didn’t care what any of them thought. I was too pissed off, too fed up with this freak show presentation to feel embarrassed.

Besides, I genuinely wanted answers. Who the hell were these people? Why were they here peddling this so-called “miracle cure”? Were they clueless do-gooders—or were they predators looking to cash in on vulnerable people?

Whatever the truth was, I knew one thing for certain: I didn’t like any of it.

“People need to protect their kids from all sorts of dangers today, and no cost is too high to protect your loved ones,” said Mune. “Think of it this way; if you had a child, wouldn’t you want the best for them?”

I stopped him. “That’s all well and good, but none of us here are children. We’re adults trying to live our own lives, and we don’t need a couple of strangers telling us what to do. We all have our thoughts.”

“Besides,” I snarled, "children AREN’T property!”

Brady looked up brightly, looking to help his partner. “Children are under the roof of their parents, and legally the parent has every right to make decisions for them.”

“Does that include curing them for illnesses they don't even have?” My stare challenged them as I tried to bore holes into their eyes. “You’re trying to cure people of things that can’t be controlled.”

“Damian, enough,” Ren tried to intervene, but I was having none of it.

“No, I’m curious. What are you trying to ‘cure’ here? Can our “conditions” be really cured by some liquid as you claim it would? And what are *YOUR* qualifications to come in here to ‘treat’ us?”

I hoped the air quotes I used around the word treat would help indicate I didn't believe a word of the tripe they were selling.

I continued, building up a real head of steam. "I read recently that it takes about 12 years to get a new drug evaluated, and this is obviously a new drug. So before we start swallowing your pills or inhaling your wonder solution, *please* show us the FDA approval. Because there's nothing wrong with us, and we have a right to know that this stuff you're peddling is safe."

The room fell silent, but before I could finish, Pedro slumped over in his chair. My heart dropped in my chest, and all I could think was *"Oh God, let him not be..."* I couldn't bring myself to add the word "dead."

"Pedro?" I called to him, "Are you okay?" Ren, dread washing over his face, rushed to Pedro's unconscious body slouching over the edge of the seat.

I watched as the others in the room also started running to him, and as I rose to follow suit, Mune stopped us. "Please, we know what we're doing!"

Ren angrily shook his head and screamed "What ARE you doing!? He's having a SEIZURE, for Chrissakes!" Ren pushed Mune away, sending him close to falling on his ass. Cursing under his breath, Ren gently shifted Pedro to the ground as Karen tried to guide the others away.

Jenny was shivering so hard I thought her teeth might chatter right out of her skull, as Bella—more wide-eyed than usual—darted between Pedro and the machine and asked with a trembling voice: "W-What's happening to him?"

♦♦♦♦♦

"How much did you put in there?" Brady hissed at Mune, voice sharp but low.

"I put the same amount Aeron said," Mune muttered, then turned to Ren, trying to calm him. "Sir, please, we—"

"You'd better leave before I call the police!" Ren snapped, his voice like a whip. He was as done with these clowns as I was, and I felt vindicated.

Brady panicked. "I—I think we should go," he stammered, grabbing the bottles and bolting for the door, Mune scrambling after him. My stomach turned when I saw something small tumble from his pocket onto the floor—my Baphomet plushie.

I began lunging forward, only to be intercepted by Charlotte—one of the volunteer coordinators, who quickly grabbed Mune's shoulder. "Hey! You can't just—"

Charlotte's words were cut short as Brady spun, wild-eyed, and pulled a canister of pepper spray from his pocket. In one deft motion, he sprayed her in the eyes and—as her scream split the room—the two men vanished.

The pepper spray burning fiercely, Charlotte staggered back shrieking, her hands clawing at her face in a desperate attempt at relief. The room dissolved into chaos as my housemates cried out, frightened and confused, their voices breaking into a chorus of panic. Ren and another coordinator rushed to the unresponsive Pedro and rolled him onto his side as they fumbled with the first aid kit. Brian guided Charlotte into a chair, her screams rattling the walls.

"I'll call for help!" my disembodied voice cracked as I sprinted back to my room, fumbling for my phone. Slamming the emergency button for paramedics, I tried to catch my breath, even as fury twisted my gut. I wanted to chase those bastards down myself, drag them back here and beat the hell out of them...but Pedro's limp body mattered more. I wasn't about to let him die.

Outside, screeching tires reverberated as Brady and Mune—those monsters in white—tore away into the inky night.

♦♦♦♦♦

Relief came only when the paramedics burst in. Pedro stirred faintly, eyes fluttering open, dazed but alive. They loaded him onto a gurney, their voices brisk and professional over the hum of panic still simmering throughout the house.

I looked at Ren, sweat streaming down his temples as he stood rigid, still shaking from what we'd all just experienced. "Who the fuck invited these people?" he muttered under his breath.

I didn't have an answer. None of us did. Whoever had welcomed those so-called "healers" into our home had just opened the door to a nightmare. And now that they knew where to find us, I couldn't help but wonder if they'd be back to finish the job.

Through the open windows I heard sobbing outside, and for the first time that night I wanted to cry too. Instead, I sank into a chair, clutching my knees and forcing myself to breathe.

The flash of red and blue lights outside told me the police had arrived. Ren disappeared into the glow, and was probably already being questioned. The rest of us just sat in the wreckage of fear and tears, wondering how close we'd all just come to disaster.

♦♦♦♦♦

There was to be no new fresh hell for us that night. The ambulance pulled away, its sirens fading into the night, and the police were done with this round of questioning. The heaviness of the day settled over me as my eyes drifted to the floor and caught on something small and white lying near the leg of a chair.

A business card.

Hands trembling, I picked it up, the glossy surface catching the light, and instantly recognized the simple logo of a dove, its wings brushing a small rising sun. Clean. Painfully simple. Something I'd seen very recently...on the bottle of Miracle Tap.

It represented the Purity Syndicate, and my gut twisted as I read "Mune Pentacle – Organizer/Mentor."

There was no phone number or email. The only contact information led you right into the lion's den. A single line at the bottom of the card read:

The Purity Mansion
7667 Marigold Water Dr.
Ramona, CA 92065

Ramona. Out in the mountains near Julian, about a half-hour northeast. A big question mark hung over my head as I wondered why they'd list an address but scrub off every other form of contact. Why not hand out their details like any other nonprofit would?

As Winnie the Pooh might say, "Curioser and curioser." Nothing about this was right. Nothing at all.

With the police already gone and everyone desperately hoping to settle in for the night, I slipped the business card into my pocket and forced myself to help Ren with whatever he was doing. Still, my thoughts spun like a pinball ricocheting off bumpers, careening from one fear to another.

How the hell was I supposed to tell anyone what I was thinking? If I said it out loud, people would probably look at me like I'd finally lost my mind...especially if my theory turned out to be true.

But one thing was unquestionable: those people in the white coats were bad news. Period!

♦♦♦♦♦

A sudden jolt of brilliance—a spark, like a lightbulb blinking to life over my head—hit me. Sofia would understand. Maybe I could tell her.

I paused, chewing on the idea. God knows I didn't want to dump my paranoia on her and make things worse than they already were. She'd already been through enough the last few days, and I certainly didn't want to compound her suffering.

Then there was the reality that I really had no clue what the "right" thing would even sound like. One wrong word, and I could end up hurting her—or driving her away entirely.

-PING-

Glancing at my phone, I half-expected it to be my mom checking in for the third time today.
But it was from Sofia. Was the universe trying to tell me something?

Blinking, I read the screen three times to be sure I wasn't imagining it.

Nope. Definitely her.

I opened the message instantly, eyes flying across the words:

"Hey. It's Sofia. Can I tell you something?"

My pulse quickened as I ducked out of the kitchen and hurried to my room, locking the door behind me for privacy. Fingers flying, I typed:

“Hey! It’s been a while. You doin’ okay?”

Almost immediately, her reply appeared. “Yeah, I’m fine. I just...I need to tell you something. And I’m hoping you don’t think I’m going crazy right now.”

“What do you mean? I don’t think you’re crazy!”

It was obvious she was tiptoeing around something big, trying to downplay whatever it was. Given what I’d just been through, nothing was going to sound crazy to me any more.

Besides, if I’m her friend I should be there to help her talk through whatever it is, right?

And while I was tempted to unload my own rant about the bizarre scene that had just unfolded in my living room, I held back and wanted first to hear what she had to say.

♦♦♦♦♦

A few moments passed before her next message popped up: “Something is happening, Damian, and I think I found how to prove it.”

My stomach tightened involuntarily. “You mean the explosion? Like some mastermind’s plot?”

Sofia texted back: “Not just the explosion. Haven't you noticed the rash of ‘accidents’ in regional centers lately.”

“Yeah.”

“I think I’ve figured out what’s going on.”

A pause hung between us, long enough that my fingers twitched over my phone screen. Dying of curiosity, I again typed: “Yeah?”

Instead of words, a photo popped up of a video cassette. Frowning, I thought “What the hell?”

Even as my fingers hovered over the keyboard, another text arrived:

“I found this old cassette, and—look, I know it’s weird to think this old musty tape holds some kind of clue, but I think this means something important.”

My head spun. A VHS tape? I didn't even know anybody still used those things. Swallowing the urge to be sarcastic, I responded, "So the mastermind's plan for all of this is...in there? You sure you're okay?"

Well, that didn't come out quite the way I'd hoped it would. Sofia quickly responded, "What's *THAT* supposed to mean?!"

I typed fast, afraid I had scared her off. "I...look Sofia, no offense, but doesn't it seem a little too farfetched that you'd find a videotape that solves this spree of disaster?"

Well, if I was trying to piss her off, I guess I'd succeeded. In an instant Sofia wrote back: "FINE! I'll stop bothering you about it if you don't want to believe me."

Gasping, I quickly wrote back. The last thing I wanted was to leave her hanging like this. "Wait! Don't go. I want to understand. Please. Tell me what you saw that could be the answer to this whole thing?"

♦♦♦♦♦

A video appeared in my inbox that she had recorded on her phone to share with me.

Clicking on it, I squinted to see the screen. It was dimly lit, and I had to work hard to make out the short clip amidst the whirs and still noise of the TV signal.

It was a room—no, more like some church setting where a sermon was being held. The presenter's name—Aeron Inochi—appeared on her TV screen. His voice was overly smooth, and the distortion from the aging VHS only intensified the dreariness of listening to him. And though the sound was muffled, I could kinda understand what he was saying through my phone speakers.

There was definitely a sales pitch going on here...something about finding an alternative to receiving help, and not being 'prey' to the healthcare industry.

I almost vomited when the next image - an array of sleek bottles, boldly showcasing the striking, colorless title: The Miracle Tap - appeared on the screen. Surrounding the bottles, cheerful cartoon flowers animatedly swayed in the corners of the screen, adding a playful charm reminiscent of some old Tex Avery animation.

The video was cut short there, but I was speechless. There was no fucking way!

“Can you just meet me somewhere? Like my house?” Sofia suddenly texted back, “I can show you more of the video over there.”

My eyes widened with excitement at the idea that she was inviting me over to her home. Whatever this cryptic tape was that she had discovered, it had to be serious.

Selfishly, a tiny thrill ran through my body. Sofia wasn’t someone who invited people into her personal space lightly, and I hoped her family wouldn’t object to my showing up unannounced and so late in the day.

“Okay, sure. I don’t mind. Where and when?”

The response came quickly. “10076 Sur Mesa Blvd., Lemon Grove. And as FAST as you can get here.”

I bit my lip as a rush of adrenaline flooded through me. Joy. Rapture. She’d actually sent me her address. She wanted me there. Needed me there. “Of course,” I typed back, adding “I’m on my way.”

I hit *SEND*, grabbed my hoodie, and bolted for the door.

Chapter 16 - What's Truly Perfect?

-Juniper-

It was incredibly hot last night, and I didn't sleep much. The dormitory has neither heat nor air conditioning—Aeron says such things weaken us—and sometimes it seems like a sacrifice. Especially in winter, when temperatures in the low thirties are fairly common around here.

Still, this is what Aeron wants, and we're all dedicated to following his word. So is the occasional sleepless night really that big a deal?

And because it was Aeron, and he has arthritis, we all overlooked the small heating/air conditioning unit he kept in his private room.

♦♦♦♦♦

Around 5am I opened the stained glass window, taking a moment to admire the image of the oversized dove of peace and the olive branch it held in its beak.

The window hinge squeaked as I gently pushed the frame. Countless species of succulents and flowers lay in a carpet beyond the room I'd called home for the past several years. In the midst of this carpet squatted a pure white fountain decorated with cherubs grasping pan flutes and maidens playing lyres. Spewing from this fountain was an endless stream of water from nearby Lake Cuyamaca that circulated twice each day between the catch basin and our reservoir, always ready to be pumped back through the plumbing, repeating the cycle again and again.

I smiled looking at the fountain, both for its beauty and because I remembered the day we'd snuck into the park facilities at the lake. "Water should be free for everyone," Aeron had explained to us as we sat near the front gate. So he sent Amber to distract the overweight middle-aged man sitting in the booth taking entry fees, instructing her to first remove her bra, unbutton her shirt and tie the shirt at her navel. So attired, she chatted the man up, smiling and flirting and asking if he'd come by to visit her once she had her tent popped up.

She kept him going a solid ten minutes while six of us—each carrying two covered five-gallon buckets—ducked into the park and Aeron sat at the wheel and kept our van out of sight. Then she returned a half-hour later with more questions, touching his knee and scratching the top of her breast by pulling her shirt open and giving him a good look.

And boy was she outrageous! After an extended scratching episode, she even asked him to do her a favor and look closely at one spot that was now red. "Does this look infected to you?" she whimpered, her eyes tearing.

The poor guy was so fixated on her pretty face, the chance to look at her nipples, and the idea that he might be spending a chunk of the evening with this beauty that he ignored the six of us—each lugging two 40-pound Home Depot buckets filled with lake water - as we left the park in full view and headed down the road towards Aeron and the van.

It was a scenario that we repeated every month after that, typically going in after dark when the front gate was closed, the guard gone for the day, and the water available for the taking.

♦♦♦♦♦

Under the waning moon I spied trees bearing the lemons and apples that we'd use in the kitchen. This coming mid-summer weekend it was obvious this would be a bountiful harvest indeed.

There, sitting on the electrical lines, were a pair of mourning doves cooing their way through the breeding season. This pair wasn't yet sitting on a nest, though they looked eager to start a family. Behind them the sunrise approached, painting the sky a golden orange hue. It was obvious that, from the scrub jays calling boldly from the trees to the never-ending chirping of the crickets, a glorious new day was upon us.

It was just another day in paradise, and it felt incredibly welcoming.

The truth was it always felt welcoming. It was just one reason I loved waking up here.

Only something just felt off today—like the air itself was holding its breath.

I wanted so badly for it to be a good day. But not even the cooing of mourning doves in the courtyard or the gentle spray of water dancing from the fountain could drown out the memories gnawing at the back of my mind. I just felt numb.

Not good. Not okay. And definitely not perfect like I used to pretend I was.

Then again, what does perfect even mean? It's a question that had been echoing in my head lately, circling back on itself like some tired riddle with no answer. A concept I kept picking apart until it unraveled into nothingness.

And there was just so much swirling around up there. Too much. I needed to talk with someone RIGHT NOW!

"I'll speak with Aeron," I told myself. He was a reasonable guy, after all, and I was sure he'd understand why I had questions about where exactly our "family" was heading.

♦♦♦♦♦

Sitting back on the bed, I brushed off the quilted comforter that the girls had made for my birthday a few years back. I brushed my fingers through my hair, feeling a few loose strands fall off and settle on my neck.

The recent stress made me increasingly aware of how much of my hair was falling out. True, a few lost hairs was a minor inconvenience when compared to everything else going on around me, but still...

Dressing in my usual attire—a blinding white blouse with a jeans skirt—I reasoned it was summertime and the day would almost certainly get hot.

Because despite everything the tourist bureau says, San Diego county is in a desert and sometimes it gets hot. I mean HOT, with typical temperatures in the 80s or 90s, and the thermometer climbing into triple digits isn't at all unusual. There's no humidity, almost never any rain, and practically no breeze...at least up in the hills where we were.

Today it was deathly still.

♦♦♦♦♦

The mirror beckoned for me to examine myself more closely. Grooming oneself can be challenging under the best of circumstances, but it's not unusual to be reflected in your complexion when you feel miserable.

Stroke. Stroke. Stroke. I brushed my hair gently, trying to encourage the golden highlights brought out by the sun without pulling out too many additional strands. Clipping my burgundy bow clip into place, I added a soft shade of seafoam green and teal eyeshadow and, just for grins, some mascara to bold my eyelashes.

Ever hopeful, I put on some strawberry lipstick. It's the shade I like best, and I know it's also Aeron's favorite, so I figured perhaps I'd have a chance to share it with him in a kiss. Completing the ensemble, I put on my white knee high socks—the ones with the cute kitty faces on them—and my strawberry red shoes, tightening the buckles to make them fit just right.

♦♦♦♦♦

Heading out the door, I left the safety of my cozy chamber behind with more than a touch of trepidation. Walking along the patchy trail caused me to focus on not slipping on the little river stones lining the bank and poking out from the edge of the green pasture.

My eyes followed the rocky road and a few of the blue-eyed beauties and marigolds that Mune had planted recently in an effort to make our sanctuary more colorful. I looked forward towards the head temple—more like the mansion of our sanctuary and worship—that was decorated in a maze of rosemary and lavender bushes.

The detailed Spanish tile that comprised the bulk of the path pulled the casual visitor towards the temple and showed as vibrant as ever under the morning sun. The twisted vines hanging from the towering white pillars on the far side of the path seemed to want to grab you, even as you admired the grace of those same pillars casting long shadows over the oversized mahogany door that provided the only entrance into the temple. California honeysuckles bloomed from the vines, attracting bees and hummingbirds and all buzzing a steady tune. Reverently, I entered the mansion, appreciating the chocolate brown clay tile that helped keep everything inside dark and cool.

Inside was as luscious as the outside; evidence of the care and the expense invested in making this a temple worthy of a man like Aeron. The beauty of the marble floor was overwhelmed only by the pearl white staircase spiraling down from the second and third floors of the home. To the left was a wall of succulents, and to the right a wall of water that almost certainly wetted the visitor from head to toe if they got too close.

This was where the main magic happened; our community's holistic worship for the man who had envisioned and created it all. It was all I could have asked for in life; a stable home within a loving community, with a family to spend the rest of my days with.

There is absolutely nothing like unconditional love to ensure one's happiness.

♦♦♦♦♦

The kitchen, full of copious amounts of food, was always one of my favorite places in the entire community. Any hour of the day or night I knew I could wander in and find a wide variety of cereals and whole foods, ready to cook or be eaten raw.

But eating didn't seem appropriate right now. All I wanted to do was find Aeron and talk with him.

That was until I saw Mune and Brady sitting there, nervously explaining to Aeron about...well, I wasn't really sure what they were talking to him about.

I did catch two snippets of the conversation as Brady blurted out: "One of them found out about what we're doing and exposed us." This was quickly followed by Mune's suggestion "We may have to lay lower than we thought we should before we catch more attention than we want to."

That was when Aeron exploded. "What do you mean? You were CAUGHT? By a fucking RETARD?"

♦♦♦♦♦

The three men stopped talking the moment they saw me draw near. "I'll talk with you two later," Aeron told the two boys, turning to look at me with that familiar smile. "What's going on, Junie?"

I had always liked the nickname he had given me, and it made me smile despite my concerns. "Yeah, uh, I wanted to talk to you about..."

"Will it take long?" he said abruptly.

"Well...maybe. I..."

Aeron sounded more on edge than usual, and he cut me short. "I'm sorry, Junie, but I don't really have time for anything in-depth right now." He gestured towards where Mune and Brady were sitting and gave a look of disgust. "It looks like I'm going to have to deal with a bigger issue first."

"Oh," I said, trying to hide my disappointment. "When do you think you'll have time for me?"

"Around 12, I suppose," Aeron said over his shoulder as he walked away with Mune and Brady. "I'll be back."

♦♦♦♦♦

Blinking, I was unsure what had just happened. I watched the three of them hustle towards the exit and thought how odd it was, him acting that way. Perhaps he was stressing about one of the new members. Or maybe donations were down, making it difficult for us to pay the mortgage for our community.

That would mean we'd all be turned out into the streets, because the bank would insist on getting paid, and those guys are notorious for not having a sense of humanity. Yes, it was just like Aeron to put all his focus on something that important, worrying for the rest of us while we went about our lives unencumbered by the concerns of daily events.

He was so heroic. It was probably best to just give him some space and for me to have some breakfast, like he said.

Still, how could I be so selfish and just eat when I knew he had taken on the burden of not only caring for our growing family, but also was so distracted making sure we all had a place to sleep.

Oh Aeron...why won't you confide in me and let me ease your burden? You and I both know how much help I could be to you...

♦♦♦♦♦

By the time I sat down at the table, I was convinced that my dear Aeron was losing sleep over the very future of our family and our community. Having reported for her shift in the kitchen, Beatrice cooked a nutritious breakfast for me, frying two eggs and toasting some homemade sourdough bread, which she then topped with avocado and sprinkled with bagel seasoning. To this she added a side order of hash browns made with sweet potatoes, toasted garlic, and a garnish of alfalfa, all of which were grown in the garden just outside the kitchen door. Even the eggs were homegrown, coming from our own chickens.

All this was joined by a glass of fresh orange juice from our small orchard growing just beyond the garden. Ah, fresh orange juice! A classic, and to my mind the best way to start any day.

Beatrice was probably the best chef we had when it came to breakfast. As she put the plate before me she smiled, noting "These are Matilda's," indicating the eggs. Only Beatrice would name the chickens and identify the eggs, helping us all to develop closer relationships with our sources of food. I guess it was one of those circle of life things she was always talking about.

And as always, breakfast tasted great and left me quite full. Still, as I sat chewing my eggs, my mind floated back to Aeron's quick exit from our conversation and my inability to engage with him. Something was obviously going on, and he wasn't happy about it. "I have to find a way to help him," I said out loud, though to no one in particular.

Beatrice looked at me oddly, said nothing, and continued bustling about the kitchen.

♦♦♦♦♦

Recognizing it was probably best to ask Aeron about such things in private, I considered my options for where I should speak with him. In his office...or maybe his personal lounge?

Yeah, that should be a great place to talk. After all, the lounge is where he has really opened up to me in the past, venting about his 'divinity' Ruby Ridge. At least that's what he usually called her.

I really hoped he would get to see her again one day, even though I'm pretty iffy if there is a heaven or not. But Aeron believes there is an afterlife...just not the one that the Holy Bible describes.

Of course, the family I used to live with didn't even read the entire Bible, preferring to cherry pick the verses that best suited their beliefs of the moment.

Aeron, though, had always given the impression that he believes death leads to a state similar to dreaming - an ongoing, shifting inner world built from memories, emotions, and imagination. And assuming he's right, he'll be able to create his own version of eternity and the peace it will provide him.

♦♦♦♦♦

Aeron has had such an enormous impact on my life. He's taught me countless skills I'd never have picked up on my own—practical things that seem simple to other people but always felt impossible to me. Without him I wouldn't know how to pay my bills, speak at a conference, fold clothes properly, or even recruit new members for our cause.

But Aeron's influence hasn't just been practical; it's also been personal. Because without Aeron, I wouldn't know how to dress for any occasion. I wouldn't know how to dance or sing. Or how to kiss, or to please a man while maintaining my virtue.

His stubble used to scratch my skin when he kissed me, leaving my lips and cheeks tingling and raw. But he persuaded me that this was a good thing to learn about. That it was important for me to know how these things felt.

Naturally, I believed him. Because if Aeron wanted me to understand something, it meant it was important.

Admittedly, the kissing and the other stuff he had me do made me uncomfortable, but I figured it was because I'd never done anything like that before. I was scared and nervous. It was outside my comfort zone, and I was terrified I'd mess it up somehow. What if I did it wrong?

But Aeron always reassured me. He told me I didn't have to worry—that he'd handle everything, and all I had to do was lie back and relax.

"This is good for our cause and for our family," he had told me often.

Then he looked me in the eyes and asked me to prove my faith and my trust in him, "Just this once."

He made it sound like an honor; like I should be grateful.

And of course back then, when I was 14 and brand new to the family, I didn't understand how what he was doing could possibly be connected to the cause. I couldn't put the pieces together.

But Aeron was so gentle...so caring. Or at least that's what I told myself at the time.

I remembered the first time we ever really talked. Aeron leaned close to me and said, "You seem like you're looking for something deeper from your life...I see that in you." And the thing was he was right.

♦♦♦♦♦

Over the next few days he surrounded me with warmth and praise. He made me feel seen in a way nobody else ever had. He listened to me like I mattered—like my thoughts were important.

Coming from a broken home, I supposed I'd been grieving. At this vulnerable point in my life I was lonely, disillusioned, and spiritually hungry for something—anything—that felt bigger than myself.

I mean, people always say teenagers are "finding themselves." But hell...show me even one 14-year-old who actually knows who they are.

So when Aeron told me, "I've never met anyone like you. You belong here. We've been waiting for someone *just* like you!" I fell headfirst.

I was in love.

Then one night he lowered his voice like he was letting me in on a cosmic secret. "I prayed last night and I saw your face, and I knew you were part of the prophecy. You and I are the only ones who see the truth of the world, while everyone else is asleep."

That was when I knew Aeron was the only source of truth and love I'd ever want or need. Which is why I'd require his approval for what I did with my life. Because without him, I was terrified I'd disappear back into the nothingness I'd come from.

The last thing I ever wanted was to go back to that empty, gray life I'd had before I became part of the family.

And when he whispered "Your body is a vessel ripe for awakening. This is sacred, not shameful," I believed him. I thought it meant I was chosen. Special. Holy, even.

I convinced myself that letting him touch me was part of my spiritual growth. That it was Aeron channeling divine will.

And that's why, back then I happily did anything—and everything—he asked of me. Because I thought it meant I belonged.

♦♦♦♦♦

One thing I always appreciated about Aeron was how he treated me like an adult.

Back home, I was constantly talked down to, like I was some clueless kid who needed babysitting. But Aeron? He looked at me like I was a grownup. Like I was a lady, even.

Sometimes, though, I'd catch myself wondering whether I was really a lady at all. Or even a woman, for that matter.

The questions came from this small voice in the back of my head that wouldn't shut up, whispering questions about who—or what—I really was.

My issue, of course, is that I never felt like a man OR a woman. It's this inconvenient debate that bounced around inside my skull for a good long while now, and I've never been sure how to resolve it.

But then I told myself that Aeron probably wouldn't care either way. After all, it's my essence he loves, right? That's what he always says. It's who I am on the inside that matters to him.

It's not like he'd suddenly hate me if I turned out to be a boy instead of a girl.

♦♦♦♦♦

Aeron almost never gets angry. Sure he gets stressed sometimes, but not angry.

Sometimes I think maybe I'm just imagining it all—that uncertainty about who I am—like it was some kind of internal identity crisis. Somedays, when I'd put my hair up and wear my overalls, I'd feel more masculine. But when I started prepping myself for a meeting or for a sales pitch with a prospective new member, I'd dress in the fanciest gown I had. At times like that I never felt feminine enough.

Heck! Even with lipstick and the sweetest perfume I have, it just wasn't enough to feel as feminine as I should.

I dunno...maybe I'm still confused after growing up in a house where I was always told what I should be. How I should act, or dress, or speak.

I mean, nobody—*NOBODY*—ever asked me what I wanted. I was just told what to do, and I was expected to do it. Period. Full stop.

Is it possible that I learned to question myself so much in those days that now I can't stop?

♦♦♦♦♦

There are other times, though, where it feels bigger than just mere confusion. That's when I feel a soft, pulsing ache under my ribs—a feeling that I'm not wrong, exactly, but that the words people use to describe me don't quite fit properly.

It's like I'm wearing clothes that almost fit, but pinch in weird places.

Sometimes I think maybe I'm both a boy *AND* a girl. Or that I'm neither. Or that I'm something in-between that nobody has a word for yet. Those thoughts make me nervous, since the world doesn't seem built for people who live between the lines.

When I have moments of questioning and insecurity, I remember how Aeron would hold my face in his hands and say "You're perfect just as you are. You're mine, and that's all that matters."

For a while that made me feel safe. Because if Aeron said I was perfect, then maybe all the other questions didn't matter.

And I'd be fine living my life like this...except for that little voice—that DAMNED little voice—that seemed to pop up at the most inconvenient times and whisper that maybe Aeron only loves the parts of me that served his purpose.

I hated myself for thinking that...because Aeron was everything to me, even when he made me feel like my body wasn't my own to control.

♦♦♦♦♦

My attention kept getting drawn to the clock hanging just above the potted succulents on the shelf across from me. The hour hand moved slowly, the minute and hour hands slowly inching along as they pursued their endless race around the clock's face. Absent-mindedly, I tapped my fork against the edge of the plate of half-eaten eggs, listening to the rhythm of the soft clanking of the porcelain against the metal utensil. I had bigger concerns than food, chief among them deciding how to bring up my questions to Aeron and how long I would really have to wait to speak with him.

There were always chores that needed doing in a community like ours. After waiting a solid hour before going in search of Aeron again, and having lost my appetite, I decided to kill some time by tending to some of the simpler tasks around the mansion that required attention.

After all, he'd said noon, but given the demands for his guidance and leadership, I recognized that probably meant more like 2pm.

♦♦♦♦♦

One of my favorite things to do in our community was tending to our flock of chickens and peacocks. I made sure they were fed, collected their eggs for Beatrice, and searched for loose feathers for us to use in our next art projects.

After that I visited the garden, watering the plants that produced strawberries, summer squash, apples, avocados, lemons and other seasonal crops. I even tended to the vibrant flower gardens, taking a moment to admire the irises, marigolds and african daisies. Having become permanently enamored of these flowers and the look of a bouquet of the three in one bunch, this seemed like the perfect time to pick them as a gift for Aeron.

Then, with a bunch of flowers in one hand, I collected an armload of the produce before heading inside. I had only killed about a half-hour and figured I needed to delay some more by tending to some personal tasks. Laundry, washing dishes with Beatrice, washing the windows...anything just to keep my mind and my hands occupied.

And I never minded keeping the mansion clean, figuring it was the least I could do. "After all, it's for Aeron," I'd keep telling myself.

As noon approached, I decided it was time to risk approaching him. Sure, he'd probably be running late, but I needed to risk it if I ever hoped to get some answers.

♦♦♦♦♦

I'll confess that I dawdled a bit, writing down some ideas for the next sermon geared towards our newer members. But to be completely honest, I was irritated and felt like I was the only one around the house besides Beatrice who was working today.

Seeing no evidence of Aeron's presence, I headed towards the taxidermy room; one of Aeron's personal rooms in the mansion.

Shortly after declaring me his favorite, Aeron had given me a special key to get into this room, and he and I were the only ones who could access it. I entered the room of burgundy walls, each decorated with a wide variety of stuffed animals that had been mounted, preserved and immortalized for Aeron to admire into eternity. Larger animals, frozen in various poses, were scattered around the room, sitting on tables or on the floor, simultaneously threatening and harmless into perpetuity.

Along the far wall sat a lowboy cabinet, perhaps eight feet wide, upon which sat a long row of perpetually grinning animal skulls. Many were rodents of various sizes and species, though the biggest head—at the center of the display—was an alligator's skull, its jaws pried open to show off its sharp teeth.

I glanced at the coffee table and noticed four cat skulls and a small deer skull with missing teeth, none of which I'd noticed on any of my previous visits to this room. Curiously, they were all polished and white, as if recently cleaned.

Of course I'd always known Aeron liked to collect animals, though the lack of any live ones around the community had seemed curious. Bones, fur, feathers was what I'd see the most, including the whole mounted creatures propped up like prized collectables.

Still, none of this really surprised me. Sometimes it was as simple as feathers, other times something as massive as the full-sized jaguar mounted in the corner, as if it were prowling for prey; an apex predator frozen in time.

These were sentimental items for Aeron, providing permanent memories of the animals and fond thoughts whenever he viewed them.

And I'd also noticed his keen eye for detail, both in the animal parts he owned and those he commented on or coveted. "Look at how sharp the claws are," he'd pointed out to me when I eyed a recently acquired raccoon. "They're perfect for gripping, climbing, digging...or tearing."

Aeron had smiled at this last part, as if he imagined himself as a raccoon. "Did you know that a raccoon can open jars, unlatch cages, or kill a chicken or a squirrel with one swipe? They're also strong, clever, and have really sharp teeth. But because of their camouflage, they blend into the environment. And movies have made them seem clever, funny, and mischievous, so they've acquired a lovable image."

"All of which adds up to them being overlooked when something bad happens. Sure, they may rummage through your trash or waddle through your yard, but they're usually not the first suspect when something goes wrong."

Of course, Aeron conveniently skipped the realities that raccoons carry rabies, can be very aggressive when cornered, and can cause serious injuries if provoked. But if raccoons seemed harmless while being very capable of causing harm, maybe envisioning himself as a raccoon would have made a lot of sense after all.

♦♦♦♦♦

Stepping closer to the newly-acquired animal skulls, I couldn't help but notice the unique detail in between the teeth of the deer skull. Portions of the enamel looked scarred by bits of soot or charcoal, leaving part of the skull grey. It was almost as if someone had placed a torch against the skull to burn it.

I wondered where Aeron had found these. Kneeling to the floor, I glanced at the cat skulls and noticed they, too, had a similar pattern. It was...odd.

"Hello Junie. What do you think of these new additions to my collection?"

It was Aeron standing in the doorway watching me. He looked as surprised as I was. Immediately standing up, I snapped my head around with a gasp. "I'm s-sorry. I shouldn't intrude."

"No, no, no, Juniper," he said calmly. "We've discussed this before, and many times. You are allowed to go into any rooms in the house. You've been here for over 10 years now, and I trust you completely."

He smiled at me and I responded with a weak smile of my own, nodding. "Right, right. Of course."

"After all, it's not like you're that lunatic Linda. She would go into my files and tear up papers or go through the trash looking for chicken bones she could chew on," Aeron said, staring off into space at the thought and speaking more to himself than to me.

But he had piqued my curiosity. This was a name I had never heard before.

"Linda?" I questioned, "Who's Linda?"

Shaking his head and sighing, Aeron explained. "Linda was one of the original members of the Purity Syndicate. She was here before you joined the family, and she was a very sweet lady. Some said she was the life of the party, always making sure everyone's needs were met. Especially mine," he smiled lewdly, licking his lips and winking at me.

He continued, "Linda made the best strawberry ladyfinger dessert this family ever had. But something went wrong in her brain. After a year or so with us, we found she was becoming irritable and couldn't string 10 words together into a coherent sentence. And then when Beatrice caught her trying to eat the raw chicken in the refrigerator..."

I stood silently, looking to Aeron for more detail.

"We found Linda screaming about how the food was poisoned and that 'they' were out to get us. I had known about her hostility towards others outside the family, but was now starting to suspect there was something more at play. She was increasingly unable to work, and everyone in our community at one point or another felt her paranoia turned on them."

"We were able to get her a variety of antipsychotics and antidepressants, but nothing seemed to help her. We eventually determined she was bipolar, but by then it was too late." He shrugged, "Maybe taking the wrong medication had worsened her problem. I don't know. I do know that she was later admitted to some psych hospital up north, and none of us have heard much from or about her since then."

Wow! Okay, I never expected that.

♦♦♦♦♦

Aeron gingerly opened the box of chocolate assortments we'd just made and that now sat on his desk. His fingers hovered over each one as if debating which one to choose. "It's really a shame," he continued. "She would've been saved by these."

Questions bubbled to the front of my brain, hot like a cauldron over a campfire. Finally I had to ask, "Um...how come we don't take them ourselves, Aeron?"

Surprised, he looked up. "How's that?"

"The cherry cordials. I mean, we've made them for ourselves too, haven't we?"

He sat and looked at me thoughtfully. "I'm not sure why we'd take them, Juniper. Nobody here that I've seen has the issues of so many people out in the community. Plus there's the possibility of contamination. You know how Nancy has that terrible allergy to cherries. Do you really think it's fair for the rest of us to enjoy these delicacies when she can't?"

I nodded. Having one of our members being allergic to cherries, it would be unfair for the rest of us to partake of these sweets. Still, I wondered whether the same thinking wouldn't have applied to Beatrice's peanut allergy that time we made those peanut butter & chocolate cookies. True, Bea wasn't there while the rest of us enjoyed the goodies, but still..."I mean we could always make our own..." I ventured.

"What do you mean?"

"I mean we could make a batch of treats just for us to enjoy. If not cherry cordials, why not chocolate truffles?" I suggested.

"That's a fair point," Aeron nodded. "We could do something for ourselves in an event. But we'll obviously need a recipe for that."

He looked at me kindly as I nodded in agreement. Then, as if momentarily forgetting that I was even there, Aeron reached over the coffee table to the wine cabinet tucked in behind the couch. From this hidden treasure chest he pulled out a bottle of La Crema chardonnay and a box marked "Waterford," from which he extracted a single elegant crystal goblet.

He struggled to unwrap the foil from the bottle, then fought with the cork to extract it from the bottle. At one point I even feared his frustration would cause him to just take the whole mess, fling it at the wall, and shout "Fuck it!" as shards of glass and wine sprayed everywhere.

♦♦♦♦♦

At last Aeron won his wrestling match with the bottle, allowing him to pour an apparently much-needed libation. He began muttering, the residue of the day's stress still etched on his face.

"Aeron? Did something happen today?" I asked.

He looked up, startled to realize I was still there watching his every move. As an afterthought, he invited me to take the dirty jelly glass from the corner of his desk and pointed to a half-open bottle of Charles Shaw wine sitting next to it. "Why don't you pour yourself some Chuck?" he suggested - an offer I politely declined. Why he called wine "Chuck" I was never able to determine.

Shaking his head slightly, Aeron took a sip from his glass and cleared his throat before he spoke. "Eh, something happened with a meeting today, something about some...'know-it-all' trying to destroy our little family."

"Why?"

He considered me for a moment, as if deciding whether to take me into his confidence. "Some people just don't understand the choices we make and all the good things we do for the people who live here and for the local community."

He set down the bottle onto the table and held the elegant glassware, swirling the pale wine and inhaling the delicate fragrance. He shook his head again and looked grim-faced.

"In their narrative we do bad things and hurt people. But the truth is we do more to help people than the government and the president have ever done, combined."

Aeron drained his glass and reached for the bottle to replenish his supply. Thinking about it from where he sat, I supposed he had a point. But as I opened my mouth to respond, he continued. "There are many perspectives, Junie...only some are more valid than others."

"More valid than others," I repeated softly. For some odd reason that statement troubled me. Maybe it was just that it sounded coarse. After all, everyone's entitled to their opinion, aren't they? That means there's no right or wrong when it comes to how someone wants to live their own lives. And as long as you're helping other people—or at the very least not hurting them—then what I think about how you live your life really doesn't matter, does it?

I continued to turn that over in my mind, recognizing that I didn't need to look any further than the mirror. There I'd see a girl with no education and a bad upbringing who was still capable of finding her own happiness. And I figured people should have their own meanings and perspectives, even if they're different from everyone else's.

♦♦♦♦♦

"What is truly perfect?" It was an odd question, but I needed to know Aeron's thinking on the subject.

He paused, his half-full wine glass just short of his lips, and looked at me curiously. Taking a moment to finish his portion, he lowered the glass and looked at me seriously. "Pardon?"

"I don't understand what is truly perfect." I fidgeted, twisting my hands in my lap and struggling both to understand and to not run out of the room crying.

"I've been thinking about that question a lot lately. For instance, I noticed at the Midsummer Fair last month that there were a lot of people at our booth who wanted to cure their children of...well, whatever their kids had."

I paused. "There seemed to be many reasons why adults were purchasing our candies for their kids. Things like autism, ADHD and diabetes. But there were also a few who wanted their kids to change their entire personalities."

Aeron raised an eyebrow. "Change their personalities? In what sense?"

"Like wanting their kids to be more well-behaved or just have their kids conform to whatever they're told to do." Running my fingers through my hair, I felt each individual strand tickling my fingertips. I was anxious to hear Aeron's answer, knowing he was wise and would decipher my meaning, despite my inability to speak clearly.

Continuing, I said, "And I'm kinda wondering about that; what is really perfect for the parent and...what is flawless for...us in general?"

Aeron bit his lower lip as he considered the question. "Hmmmm." He refilled his glass and swirled the wine, looking as if he was thinking deeply about that question for the first time himself. "THAT is a good question."

I nodded. "Yes, it's...confusing, to say the least. Mind-boggling, almost. I mean, how can you please everyone?"

"Perhaps..." Aeron finally responded. "Perhaps you can't really please everyone, and maybe you shouldn't really even try to. Yet despite that, I believe there can be a cure for even the most uncertain factors so that everyone can be happy."

He shrugged. "This is a flawed planet, Junie, and it's our duty to try making it a better place by fixing things. In Hebrew they have a phrase - 'Tikkun olam' - which refers to various forms of action intended to repair and improve the world. I figure what we're doing fits into that category. Because even the most tragic of upbringings can be fixed. And maybe our efforts can move things along to the point where everyone will be satisfied one day."

Confused, I tilted my head—still unsure what Aeron meant—and encouraged him to elaborate. "Okay, you know how you came from an unstable home in Escalon?" I nodded, feeling the dull ache of ancient resentments and grief caused by a home I'd long since abandoned. He came closer as he spoke. "You had seen the barbaric sermons, the baptisms and hypocrisies..."

"Yes..." I nodded, speaking softly as he knelt next to me.

"Well, I believe there are ways for that kind of horrible behavior to go away—to just vanish—and that is why I created this organization."

Aeron's hand had appeared, warm and comforting, on my shoulder as I eyed the soot stuck in the crevices of the teeth on the four cat skulls arrayed before us. His hand slid lightly down my back, the fingers brushing the lumbar vertebrae of my lower back as I struggled to focus. Typically I'd never allow anyone to touch me this way—or any way—but Aeron wanted to touch me like this, and I just let him do whatever he wanted to do.

♦♦♦♦♦

I closed my eyes as his lips grazed the nape of my neck—soft, practiced, and perhaps a tad too deliberate. I wondered, distantly, if this was meant to be another lesson. Another act of devotion. Another way to teach me what being a "lady" meant.

"Hey, Aeron?" I murmured.

He barely paused. "Hm?"

I felt the sharp point of his nose press against my skin.

"Do you think I'm...a lady?"

He stilled. "What makes you say that?"

"I don't know. Lately I haven't felt very...feminine. Does that make sense to you?"

"Juniper." Aeron softly chided me. He drew me tighter into the crook of his arm, anchoring me in a way that made it hard to tell whether I was being held or held down. "You are most definitely a lady."

I nodded intently, even though I didn't quite believe it myself. "Yes, of course."

But the words tasted false, even as they tumbled out of my mouth.

"My brain just gets noisy, that's all," I added. "Like...maybe if I had one of the cherry cordials, the thoughts might quiet down."

Aeron shifted. His arms loosened, and for a moment I thought I'd said something wrong. He cleared his throat, eyes flickering elsewhere.

"That won't be necessary, Junie," he said, his tone tightening like a noose. "You just need to remind yourself that there's nothing wrong with you. Nothing at all."

"I just thought—" I began, but he cut me off, his fingertip pressed to my lips.

"No more of that," he whispered.

Then, without warning, his body pressed harder against mine. It didn't feel reverent, sacred, or safe...just possessive.

♦♦♦♦♦

He reached up and brushed my hair behind my ear, tracing it with a reverence that felt hollow. "Sometimes," he said, voice thick with something I couldn't name, "you look just like her...only golden."

I didn't have to ask; he was talking about Ruby when he got like this. I so desperately wanted to believe I could be enough to make him forget her, to be what he needed and to give him peace. But I smelled the wine on his breath and the cigarettes he'd promised he'd given up. There was an ache in his eyes, and an insatiable hunger just beneath it.

He leaned in close—too close—and just as his mouth began to form my name—

BZZT!

Aeron groaned in frustration, pulling away to answer his phone as I remained on the floor, heart pounding furiously. His touch lingered on my skin like fingerprints on a window, though something about him felt off-balance today.

He paced the room, speaking quietly into the phone, his tone agitated and his words indistinct. Finishing, he turned to me with a distant expression.

"I have to leave," he said abruptly. "But Junie—don't ever doubt your femininity again, okay?"

"Y-Yeah," I whispered. "Sure."

And just like that he was gone.

♦♦♦♦♦

The room felt colder without Aeron in it, though maybe it was only now that I noticed how dim it had become. I sat in the middle of all the dead flora and sacred relics—offerings, trophics, bones of meaning—and tried to make sense of what had just happened.

Stunned, I stared at the floor while trying to collect my thoughts. Aeron's mind was definitely elsewhere today. Even the fact that he'd touched me was peculiar, probably because he hadn't really done that to me before...at least, not since I'd first shown up years ago.

Had he really meant to...?

No, that couldn't be. This was Aeron, and he'd never hurt someone he loved. I shook my head. There was no use thinking like that, and he obviously wasn't up for further conversation about it today.

Meaning I had two options: ask him about it tomorrow, or forget it ever happened.

A distant and unformed memory from Escalon conjured itself up in the back of my brain. A touch. A whisper. A locked door. I couldn't place it. I couldn't name it. But it was there.

And it felt a little too familiar—images of my "uncle" —cycled through my mind.

<u>Chapter 17: The Evidence</u>

-Sofia-

I waited anxiously for Damian, half-convinced he might bail on me. Given the way I sounded in my text, I wouldn't blame him if he did.

Yes, I knew my family would freak when they saw him at the door, but I honestly didn't care at this point. Let them ask their questions, as I was done always feeling like I needed to hide for fear of what they would think. I just needed someone to talk with. Anyone.

I needed someone who would sit across from me and not flinch. Someone who wouldn't try to explain it away, or tell me to get some sleep, or say "it could've been worse." Damian—convenient and safe—was the logical answer.

Because the truth is I'd been barely holding it together for a while now.

My head had been full of heavy, horrible questions that felt like they were eating holes in my brain. Questions like did I do something wrong? Is this some twisted cosmic punishment? What the hell did I do to deserve this much fear and death? The coughing and gagging—the incident in the regional center—it was all still ringing in my ears. And I replayed it, over and over, as if the pieces would eventually snap into place and make some kind of sense.

But they never did.

I'd just been sitting in the corner of a borrowed room, holding my knees and rocking back and forth. There was a nagging awareness that, really, I was just a guest occupying space in my grandparents' home. The only familiar things in my existence right now were the small handful of rescued stuffed animals from the ashy remains of my old house.

Everything else was buried with the flames of the fire, and I couldn't help but feel I should be dead right now.

I should be ash and nothing else.

I mean, HOLY SHIT! somebody tried to kill me—with bleach. BLEACH!

Someone I've never even met thought I was disposable enough to be erased with a cleaning product.

And I lived. I suddenly felt like Harry Potter: The Boy Who Lived!

♦♦♦♦♦

For my entire life, all I've ever done was to try and be good. I followed the damn Golden Rule like scripture: "Do unto others as you would have them do unto you." Be kind. Be decent. Be the better person.

And where did it get me? Nearly dead!

In fact, given that being kind and passive almost killed me, I started wondering what's the point? Should I keep living by that rule, even when the world spits in my face? Or would I be better off changing the game and becoming what the world seems to respect most: unfeeling, brutal, and untouchable?

I didn't have an answer yet; just flashbacks and nausea. I'd been haunted by these God-awful things I'd seen, and the overwhelming stench of bleach.

Because now I couldn't smell bleach without breaking into a sweat. It wasn't just the memories, but the recognition of the nastiness that coated my lungs and got inside me.

I mean, FUCK! I'm now panicking whenever my mother or my aunt start cleaning the house with it, that scent drifting through the hallways like some invisible ghost of what came so close to happening.

So I run away every time, neither stopping nor explaining. I just bolt out the door, down the steps, onto the porch—anywhere the air feels less poisoned.

And the worst part was the day my aunt—who means well, but just doesn't get it—actually asked me to help her clean the bathroom with bleach, like it was just another chore.

Gagging in the hallway before the words were even fully out of her mouth, I couldn't even make it to the sink. The bile came up so fast I barely had time to breathe.

I'd rather live in filth, sitting in my own swill for a week straight, than to ever get within a mile of that stuff ever again.

I know I'm being extreme, but almost dying will do that to you!

♦♦♦♦♦

It feels sometimes like there's no way anybody—not even to the most respected psychiatrist—could possibly understand what I'd been through. The experience was SO horrific that there was no use trying to even explain.

I mean, there are certain things in life—having a baby, losing a parent, and the like—where if you've experienced it, you don't need any explanation. And if you haven't gone through it, no explanation will ever truly suffice.

Without question, this was one of those things.

And given the entire scenario I'd just barely survived, how was I supposed to ever trust anyone again? Because it sure seemed like every time I'd tried trusting in the past, I'd crashed face-first into the wall, again and again.

Then there was my family. UCH! A colony of conflict avoiders so committed to silence, they might as well be their own religion. They'd always clung to peace like it's oxygen, terrified of confrontation while remaining allergic to honesty. If there was the faintest risk of raising their voices or bruising someone's ego, they'd fold, smile, pretend, and swallow it all until it festered.

Their universal fear of upsetting others was so deeply rooted in this group that they'd bottle up all their feelings, which would further increase the stress level in our home. They'd see it as protecting themselves from distress or trauma, while I'd see it as evading accountability for their actions and hiding their selfish behavior in a thinly-veiled effort to maintain their own self-image.

It was cowardice disguised as kindness.

And while all this is going on, they'd remain consistently blind to my needs and the wreckage of a life I was standing in. They wouldn't hear the way my head was still ringing from the screams, or smell the bleach that still clung to my skin, or see how much of me was buried in the fire.

They neither knew, nor cared to know. And so amidst their willful ignorance I was left alone with the devastation.

♦♦♦♦♦

Naturally, growing up in a house where conflict was poisonous, I learned to dodge it at every turn. I became the great compromiser, always ready to smooth things over or pretend mistakes weren't mistakes at all.

Yeah, I'd do anything to hold on to the fragile illusion of stability. But this—this was *WAY* too big. In my view of the world, you can't brush past someone trying to kill you and simply rationalize it away.

Something like this has got to leave you angry. Scratch that: terrified. The kind of terror that crawls into your bones and makes your skin feel too tight.

The kind of terror that you know you'll never forget until the day you actually die.

♦♦♦♦♦

The doorbell chimed, but I stayed frozen, paralyzed by the what-ifs. What had happened. What had almost happened. And were "they" at the door, looking to finish the job?

I was spent—overwhelmed mentally, emotionally and physically—as my mind silently swirled the drain. I knew—on some distant, rational level—that I was spiraling downward and losing my grip on perspective. But when you've come this close to being snuffed out, what's the benefit of sugarcoating?

Contemplating this mental vortex, I struggled to shift my focus to something more productive. My gaze snagged on the cursed cassette across the room, its cheap plastic casing sitting there like evidence of my unraveling. That grainy footage, the veiled threats stitched between its static—“It’s an illness, something that can’t be cured. Or at least it shouldn’t be.”—silently taunted me.

With every breath, the walls of this borrowed guest room seemed to close around me tighter. There were no cats curled at my feet, no journals for me to bleed my thoughts into, no fidget toys to ground me. Just a couple of salvaged stuffed animals watching me silently from the corner.

Comfort and distraction were a thing of the past for the likes of me. I had nothing.

♦♦♦♦♦

“Hey Sofia!” It was my Aunt Bruna calling from the living room. Her voice grabbed my attention as it invaded my swirling thoughts.

“I...yes?” I called out.

“I think you have a friend here who wants to see you.”

It couldn’t be...

"Coming," I whined, hiding the cassette beneath the pillow on my bed before exiting my room.

Boy, talk about surreal! Damian—wearing the same black sweatshirt, charcoal pants, and scuffed black Doc Martens he always wore—had actually appeared at the doorstep of my temporary home. Just because I’d asked him to.

I looked him up and down, smirked, and wondered why he always wore black like he was on his way to a casual funeral.

Sighing, I forced myself to smile so my aunt wouldn’t get suspicious.

♦♦♦♦♦

“Yeah, uh, this is Damian. We...work together,” I said through clenched teeth, praying my aunt wouldn’t hear the panic behind my voice.

"And, uh—" Damian jumped in, trying way too hard, "we also have the same chemistry class at college." His head bobbled like one of those dashboard toys, his nervous grin practically mirroring my own discomfort.

"Oh, that's nice!" Aunt Bruna beamed. It was instantly obvious how wild her imagination was running as she constructed some fantasy about young love blooming under her roof. "If you want, I can make you two some snacks. Maybe some sandwiches?"

Of course it had to be sandwiches. That was Aunt Bruna's one-size-fits-all solution for every social situation; make sandwiches.

Here she was making her annual pilgrimage from Fresno, living with my grandparents for a month or so, and she was all ready to insert herself into my "social life." No thanks.

Though you could argue that I should be grateful. After all, it was better for her to throw together a cheap charcuterie board than to try cooking salmon again. The last time she'd tried that little exercise, Auntie had nearly torched the kitchen.

Yeah, bread and cold cuts were definitely her strong suit!

I exhaled in relief that my dread and Damian's twitchy attempt at conversation hadn't really made an impression on her, even as my brain tripped over the possibility that she might think we were...dating.

Or worse.

"Great, that sounds perfect," I blurted way too fast. And before Damian could say another word, I grabbed his arm and yanked hard enough to make him yelp. My glare said it all: Don't ask questions; just move.

♦♦♦♦♦

Dragging Damian into my bedroom, I slammed the door shut and twisted the lock until it clicked. The silence was sharp, as if the whole house was listening to what would come next. I leveled a look at him that didn't need words: "Why are you here?"

"I just wanted to see if you're okay after—"

My words came out strangled. “I’m fine. Let’s not bring it up, okay? It’s bad enough I’m stuck here.”

Damian’s eyes flicked toward the locked door, then back at me. “She seems nice,” he said lamely, meaning my aunt.

“Yeah, they’re all nice when they’re not snooping or eavesdropping.” My voice curdled into a grunt as I added, “She has no concept of personal space.”

We just stared at each other across the room’s stale air as the blades of the rickety old ceiling fan swayed like some slow pendulum, cutting the silence into slices.

Finally, Damian cleared his throat. “So...about the cassette.”

“What about it?” My voice was ice.

“You said it could be proof of something, right?”

I rolled my eyes. NOW he believed me—now, after bleach and chaos, when the story was already too heavy to carry. “Yes.”

“Then why don’t we just take it to the cops?” he pressed. “And see if they can help.”

A shiver ran up my spine. The thought of dragging the tape out into the daylight, into their hands, into official reports—it was like shining a spotlight on everything I had already endured...like forcing a rape survivor to relive her attack in open court.

My voice had gone quiet. “Turn it in?” I asked, almost mocking him. “Do you honestly think they’ll take a look at some grainy VHS and not laugh us out of the precinct?”

“How so?”

“Damian, it’s a cassette.” I snapped the word like it was an insult.

It was bad enough he was here at all, sitting in my room like he belonged. I’d invited him, sure, but that didn’t matter now. His presence pressed in too close, and all I could think about was how little space there was between us.

Still...as much as I hated to admit it, what Damian said was arguably logical. It almost made sense. Just hand the cassette over and let the police deal with it.

But deep down I couldn't shake the certainty: no one was going to believe a grainy VHS of some lunatic "Purity Syndicate" sermon.

"So?"

"So?" I snapped. "Do people even *use* VHS anymore? Doesn't that just scream amateur? Like it's some practical joke?"

He leaned forward, refusing to back down. "It's still evidence. Physical evidence. If it connects to the attacks, they'll have to take it seriously."

I scoffed, shaking my head. "Like they'd ever believe me."

"Us," he corrected, steadying his voice. "They'll believe us. We're in this together."

I wasn't convinced. Not even close. "Damian—don't you watch those analog horror videos online? The police are just going to see this as some sick prank about a fake cult killing people like us. They'll laugh us out of the station, and then we've got nothing except humiliation."

The creaky fan above powdered the room with dust and silence.

♦♦♦♦♦

Convinced he was right, Damian shrugged, brushing aside what to him probably looked like the start of one of my meltdowns. "I don't see why they'd ignore what we have to say. This isn't a video of photoshopped monsters, Sofia; these are REAL people."

"There are real people in analog horror movies, too!" I snapped, my voice rising before I could stop it. My hands flew to my hair, ripping at the roots as though I could claw the anxiety right out of my skull. Damian flinched at the sudden outburst, but his face showed worry; not anger.

Somehow that made me feel worse. Heat, embarrassment and despair tangled in my chest and crawled up my neck to choke me. I mean, why did he even care? Why was he still here, insisting this could work, when all I could see was the inevitability of failure? Wasn't it obvious how hopeless this all was?

Admittedly, I'm always trying to control things and wrestle the world into my choice of shape, but this? This was *way* beyond me, and panic was quickly settling in. An overwhelming fear had pressed hard against my ribs, whispering over and over that nothing would work and I was screwed. "Better to not get involved; just walk away," whispered a voice in my left ear.

♦♦♦♦♦

I knew that voice wasn't Damian's. He stood before me, solid in his argument, his presence like a wall. He believed it MUST work, while I could barely believe it had a chance.

Tears—hot and traitorous—stung my eyes, and I bit my lip to stop myself from breaking down further. My face burned crimson, and I hated myself for trembling like this in front of him. I despised the part of me that wanted to collapse into his certainty, just to feel steady again.

Hot shit! Now I was having a meltdown, and in front of Damian, of all people. How embarrassing!

There was the gentlest tap on my shoulder, pulling me back from the spiral. I lowered my hands and found Damian standing there, holding something out like an offering.

It was a plushie. And not just any plushie, but a reversible Halloween plushie, stitched with an absurd sort of charm: wide, glittery anime eyes set into a black cat's round face.

The fuzzy black kitty reminded me of Lucky Minx; my scruffy little outcast with one eye, a chipped canine, and a clipped ear that had made him look half-phantom even when alive. It was all I could do to not completely fall apart.

The memory, and not knowing what had ever become of him, hit me hard. Imagining the worst for my four-footed friend, a low sigh escaped me as I accepted the plushie, the soft fabric brushing my fingers like a ghost of comfort. I flipped it inside out, revealing a goofy, grinning, bright orange cloth jack-o-lantern. Its ridiculousness drew out a sad, fleeting smile.

"It's going to be okay."

Damian's voice was both soft and fragile, and grounded me in ways I hadn't expected. I hated being this raw in front of anyone, and detested my emotions for threatening to spill into his hands alongside the toy. In that moment vulnerability was weakness, yet I couldn't deny the quiet reassurance in his words, or the fact that some small part of me was grateful for it.

♦♦♦♦♦

I clutched the reversible plushie in my lap, flipping it back and forth—black cat, goofy pumpkin, black cat again—my nervous hands betrayed the swirl of emotions I was experiencing. I kept my gaze down, unwilling to meet Damian's eyes, though I could feel him nearby: close enough to comfort, far enough away so I wouldn't feel like he was suffocating me.

"We can fix this," he said, his voice soft but certain. "And even if we can't do it ourselves, we can find professional help."

"It's..." my voice cracked, sticking in my throat. "It's so hard to believe that when I'm..."

He tilted his head, studying me. "Believe what?"

"...It's hard to believe anyone's really going to help me, or even take me seriously about this. Not after I've been let down so many times."

The words spilled out, wet and bitter. I blinked against the tears already blurring my sight, determined not to sniffle; not to let the dam break completely.

"Really?" Damian's voice lowered, and I sensed him stepping closer. His concern pressed down on me, but I ducked my head and hid behind a curtain of tangled hair. "Did something happen?"

"No one has ever taken me seriously," I muttered, the confession burning. "My family, teachers...even strangers on the bus. Not. One. Person. Ever."

The words stuck in my throat, each one more bitter than the last as I spat them out. Finally I forced myself to whisper the full truth.

"It's devastating to feel like you don't matter to anyone."

♦♦♦♦♦

I forced myself to continue, daring him to understand. "We might have similar scars, Damian, but in many ways mine are crueler. I mean, I'm almost 24, yet my mother doesn't even think I can live on my own because she says I'm too impulsive."

“Then there’s the way people react when they whisper about me. I’m standing *RIGHT THERE*, but it’s like I’m not even in the room...or like I’m not even human.”

“I feel like I’m a pariah in my own family, Damian. They treat me like a walking reminder of everything they don’t want to deal with in life. To them I’m not their daughter, not their blood. To them I’m just a child stuffed with unwanted baggage they’d rather shove in the attic and forget about.”

I glared at him through the wet strands of my hair, my throat raw with the effort of holding myself together. “Try living with *that*!”

♦♦♦♦♦

Still clutching the plush kitty, I let out a hard huff and dragged my eyes away from Damian until they landed on the one thing in the room that still felt like *mine*—my favorite poster, salvaged from the fire’s ruin.

“Periodically, my parents threaten to have the authorities arrest me or throw me in the “nuthouse” if I ever act up,” I muttered, my voice low but tight with heat. “They justify it by saying the world isn’t safe with someone like me to be running around.”

I turned on him angrily. “So what makes you think they’re actually going to help us, Damian?”

He said nothing, the silence pressing down heavier than the stale air spinning down endlessly from the dusty fan above us. I felt him weighing my words, confusion flickering across his face and concern etched deep as his eyes lingered on me.

Was he contemplating if my frustration could one day push me to the edge?

♦♦♦♦♦

This was probably the first time I’d ever cracked open the armor I’d built and said any of this out loud, and it was a strange feeling. It was bitterly ironic that Damian—the one person I’d spent so long holding at arm’s length—was showing me more genuine sympathy—no, *empathy*—than my own parents had ever been able to manage.

Finally he sighed, the sound heavy, his hand raking back through his messy hair. “Well,” he said slowly, “you’re certainly right about one thing. Not everyone is going to take us seriously. Not as people."

His voice had a tired weight to it that acknowledged a truth you wished didn't exist. "It IS frustrating," he admitted. "Especially when you're dealing with people who refuse to even try to understand. People who think 'different' means 'broken', and believe patience requires too much work."

He shook his head, lips pressed thin. "That sucks."

Then he leaned forward to steady his voice, making sure I didn't feel like I was being cornered. "But, Sofia, that doesn't mean everyone is out to get you, and not everyone is going to treat you like you're a danger to society."

I dropped my gaze and refused to meet his eyes. Still, his voice persisted, steady and unshaken.

"My mom used to try to make my teachers understand what I was dealing with," Damian said. "But they'd just brush her off. No matter how many times she reminded them, they wouldn't listen."

"They CHOSE to remain ignorant because it was easier for them than trying to recognize the issues I had in my life."

He went on, carefully trying to walk the line between a serious conversation and one that might push me further than I wanted to go. "And sure, there will always be people like that—ignorant and prejudiced—but that doesn't mean we can't find people who WILL believe us, Sofia. There are people who will help us."

♦♦♦♦♦

I studied him from under the curtain of my messy blonde curls. His concern hadn't wavered even once, and it was almost unbearable to see someone care this much for me. I clutched the plushie tighter against my chest, wishing his words were true—wanting to believe that maybe, just maybe, someone could be on my side.

The cynic in me kept whispering "It's a fantasy."

Still, for a split second, the idea of being helped—really helped, maybe for the first time in my life—felt like a spark trying to catch flame. My heart leapt against my will, only to have me smother it with caution and force myself into neutrality.

"How would I even know?" I finally asked, my voice flat but my throat tight.

Damian's expression softened. "I don't know much," he admitted, almost shyly. "But as flawed as people are, there's always someone who cares. Always."

♦♦♦♦♦

I inhaled slowly and tried to steady my breath. "Okay, let's say we find someone who cares. What happens then?"

My voice came out sharper than I had intended. "Do we just dump the cassette in their laps and let the cops sort it out? Because I don't want to have any more of a part in this nightmare than I already have."

I brushed the damp strands of hair from my eyes, trying to shield myself behind the motion. Damian didn't flinch. He just shook his head, calm but grim. "I can't say that I blame you. But yeah—that's exactly what we do; hand it over, and let the evidence speak for itself. All we have to do is explain where it came from."

"It's the only way they'll catch the sick bastard behind all this."

♦♦♦♦♦

I knew he was right, and just wanted this whole twisted mess to be over and behind me. Let the monster behind this nightmare get dragged into the light and locked away somewhere where he could never touch us—or anyone else—ever again.

Damian's logic was maddening in its simplicity: just hand over the tape. Let someone else carry the burden. Still, if that really meant I could finally wake up tomorrow without bleach burning in my lungs and nightmares gnawing at the edges of my mind, then maybe it was worth it.

Maybe. But even as I nodded, I once again knew the sting of that old truth—I would never be "normal" again. Not after this. My house was gone, my life was cinders, and no matter how many times I whispered and wished for it to be otherwise, I couldn't bring it back.

♦♦♦♦♦

I longed for the days when my life wasn't consumed by this chaos and opened my mouth to say something more when a sharp knock rattled the door. Probably my aunt with the "snacks."

Wiping my eyes quickly, as if that could hide the redness in my cheeks, I went to unlock the door. Sure enough, there she was, smiling faintly as she thrust the plate into my hands. I muttered thanks and shut the door before she could linger, but I didn't hear retreating footsteps.

"Bruna, please give us some privacy."

A pause, followed by her muffled voice: "How did you know?"

I rolled my eyes. "Because you're obviously waiting and listening at the door. Now go away!"

After a sheepish apology, her steps finally creaked away down the hall. I turned to Damian with an annoyed look that said as clearly as words: See what I mean?

The small plate of snacks sat between us—fruit slices, peanuts, a bag of chips. Damian peeled a tangerine, the citrus tang cutting through the stale air of the room.

"So," I began, "what happens now? Do we just...send the cassette to the police?"

He shrugged, casual as though we weren't talking about evidence that could stop the slaughter of countless innocent lives. "I don't see why not."

I let out a sharp sigh. "But how am I supposed to get it there? My only transportation is the trolley, and my mom doesn't even want me out alone since the La Mesa and regional center attacks. Maybe *you* could drop it off? You've got more freedom than I do."

Damian chewed thoughtfully on a slice of orange, then bit his lip. "Can you show it to me first?"

I blinked. "It's right here under my pillow..."

"No, no—I mean, I want to watch it."

My stomach sank. Of course he'd say that. "Are you sure?"

He nodded with unnerving seriousness. “I just...I just need to see it for myself.”

I dragged my fingers through my hair and let out another heavy sigh. Although deep down I didn’t want him entangled in this at all, I’d known it was too late the moment I’d texted him.

Looking at his steady eyes, I realized there was no way out but through.

Edging over towards the bed, I lifted the pillow hiding the accursed tape. The ugly black rectangle felt heavier than it should have, like it carried all the weight of my fear inside its spools.

My grandparents’ old VCR sat beneath the TV, next to a neat pile of Disney DVDs and weathered cassettes of vintage cartoons I hadn’t touched since childhood.

For a moment, I wished I could lose myself in one of those instead. But it wasn’t to be.

I pressed eject, the machine coughing up an old tape labeled *The Dreams of the Eerie*, and slid in the cassette that had haunted my nights. The mechanism clicked, whirred, and clanked as it rewound itself like some ancient beast grinding its teeth.

Damian and I sat together on the shaggy carpet, knees brushing, our eyes fixed on the static hum of the screen as the tape began to play.

♦♦♦♦♦

Damian watched the video as I watched him, with his expression shifting between curiosity and unease. The more the foul commercial played, his curious gaze looked more disheartened and full of dread.

I swore I even saw the hairs on the back of his neck stand up as the unedited part of this Aeron person explained to his associates how undesirable people like Damian and I are to his vision of society.

After all, this “leader” was explaining what he and his group would do eventually. Given the events of the past several days, he was obviously referring to what was going on in our world RIGHT NOW!

Damian's expression grew more uneasy as the scene with the mother and child flashed across the screen. The child's screaming had never stopped ringing in my head, and hearing the little tyke just reinforced the echo.

I wondered if Damian would react the same way.

♦♦♦♦♦

The tape finally clicked to a stop and he turned to me, his voice low but sharp.

"Where did you find this?"

I swallowed hard. "At the burned remains of La Mesa. Where the memorial was." My shoulders hunched. "Since then there have been more 'accidents,' and I think this has something to do with it."

His brow furrowed. "It wasn't damaged from the flames?"

"No. It was strange. It looked like someone had dropped it there after the accident." I looked up at the ceiling. "It kind of feels like fate that it ended up in my hands."

"Why didn't you say something before now?"

Anger bubbled up and my voice got shrill. "Do you think I could? You think I have a car to just drive over and drop this off?"

"I mean, I can't go anywhere! If I even tried, my parents would grill me about why I was headed to the police; then they'd just say it's me 'acting out' again. That it's grief, or anxiety, or that I made the whole thing up to get attention!"

♦♦♦♦♦

My voice cracked as I forced myself to meet his eyes. "So maybe...maybe you can take it to the police. You're a guy, and they'd be more likely to listen to you anyway."

"Me?" he blinked, startled.

"You have transportation," I pressed. "And maybe they'd believe you."

"What about you?"

“I...I don’t think they’d let me go,” I admitted, jerking my chin toward the living room where my parents sat like silent judges.

“But you’re in your twenties,” Damian countered, “They don’t control you.”

A bitter laugh escaped me. “They have conservatorship. That means they can say I’m unfit to make decisions or that I can’t be trusted. And the thing is it doesn’t matter what’s true. If they say it, they’re believed. My word means nothing.”

I gripped the cassette like it might dissolve if I let it go. “Please, Damian. I’m asking you—I’m begging you—to take this to the authorities. If they won’t believe me...maybe they’ll believe you.”

Chapter 18: Cordials in the Corridor

-Damian-

I was determined to help Sofia if I could. That evil video cassette now sitting heavy in my bag felt like the only chance I had to do right by her, and maybe even to protect her. If this was the proof she believed it to be, then it was my job to keep her secret safe while also putting it into the hands of someone who could do something about it.

Which meant only one thing: I had to bring it to the police. It was simple, clean, logical, and with a little luck would all be over soon.

For Sofia's sake I prayed it would be as if nothing had ever happened.

♦♦♦♦♦

The Uber hummed along the cracked road, taking me past the edges of Lemon Grove. Out here the ghost of La Mesa's destruction still clung to the air. Charred husks of buildings rose like broken teeth against the skyline with whole blocks sealed off with yellow caution tape, the scars of fire stretching wider than I could see.

I pressed the VHS tape tighter against my lap, my knuckles whitening as I held it close. After all, this wasn't just an old cassette, but rather a reminder of everything that had already been lost. The fire, the smoke, the lives erased. And the fact that Sofia's home was buried in all that ruin gnawed at me.

A flicker caught my eye as we drove past. I turned my head just in time to glimpse them: a cluster of figures standing on the street corner. A dozen, maybe more, and all dressed in blinding white.

At first I thought they were wearing hazmat suits, which would be fitting enough considering the wreckage around us. Only it was pretty obvious that these weren't government-issued outfits. There was no protective gear and no helmets.

In fact their clothing looked almost casual. Near as I could tell from a distance, these guys were all dressed in crisp linen. What they were wearing was the kind of thing you'd see at some Fourth of July lawn party in the Hamptons.

And here they were standing like pale phantoms against the ruins. They were out of place, and stuck out like a sore thumb.

As I craned my neck for a better look, the car made a sharp turn towards the highway and these pseudo-specters disappeared behind scorched walls and police tape.

♦♦♦♦♦

I couldn't get out of my mind the feeling I'd seen people wearing those kinds of clothes before. As they were neither hazmat suits nor uniforms, something about them nagged at me like an itch I couldn't scratch.

My primary focus remained on getting this VHS into the hands of the police. The nuisance was that the closure of La Mesa's constabulary after the explosion left me with no choice but to head for the San Diego County Sheriff's office in Lemon Grove.

Fine. It was closer to my home anyway.

♦♦♦♦♦

The Uber ride ended with the driver dropping me at a random corner, nowhere near the station. He probably figured I was a kid, so there was no need for him to be polite. And the moment I shut the door he bolted, like the devil himself was grinning at him from the rearview mirror. Of course, I didn't realize he'd ditched me in the wrong spot until he was already gone.

Yeah, that fucking figures! Too late, I realized I should have kept my eyes open to watch where we were going. But nope—I'd trusted him, and now I was the idiot with six blocks to walk and a tip to deduct from his night's work.

Guess who lost that round?

♦♦♦♦♦

The tape weighed heavy in my bag as I hitched it higher onto my shoulder and started the trek toward the station, sitting on Main Street near the edge of town. The sky was already dimming, the shadows stretching long across cracked sidewalks, and it always felt like sunset hit Lemon Grove too fast...like someone had flipped the OFF switch on the sun.

I could almost feel Ren dialing my number to ask why I wasn't yet home.

But the detour gave me time to notice the neighborhood. And Lemon Grove—even as it starts to gentrify—has still got its quirks.

Some houses kept their postage-stamp lawns green and freshly cut, while others had let theirs crisp into yellow hay. A few ditched the effort altogether, putting in fake grass or turning their yards into rock gardens with barrel cacti sprouting up like little desert altars. Flowers fought against the heat where they could, stubbornly refusing to wilt and bringing forth bursts of color.

Walking here was a harsh contrast to the coast. That difference of a few miles inland took you from enjoying a pleasant breeze to stepping into an oven. Cripes, it was easily 15 degrees hotter here, with the air thick and baking. Sweat trickled down my spine under the black shirt I'd stupidly chosen. Why the hell I wore black every damn time I got dressed was beyond me.

Hershman—my science teacher—always harped about how black absorbs light, while lighter colors reflect it and keep you cooler. I'd nodded like I was listening, but here I was practically roasting myself alive. You'd think I'd have learned by now.

Like Homer Simpson would say; "DOH!"

♦♦♦♦♦

7pm, 2 blocks from the Sheriff's department, and I involuntarily froze mid-step. I dunno...maybe I was meant to be in that place at that time, assuming you believe in that sort of thing. Heart hammering, I peeked out, half praying I'd imagined what I was certain I'd seen.

CRAP! No such luck! There, across the street in this seedy strip of Lemon Grove—where the rotting hulks of warehouses seemingly deteriorated as I watched them—two men strolled casually into one of the old buildings. They wore neither hazmat suits nor uniforms, but crisp, head-to-toe white; the same blinding vision of purity I'd seen before.

Mune and Brady...the same guys who almost killed Pedro during their visit to my home. I felt torn between nausea and rage at the sight of these two heartless asses, wandering around in public as bold as brass.

My brain was working overtime, trying to figure out why these two would-be assassins would show up here in the middle of nowhere, parading into some abandoned warehouse like it was Sunday services at church.

Shouldn't they be hiding after what happened with Pedro? Shouldn't they be *anywhere else* but in the middle of a neighborhood where one suspicious look could get them flagged?

Yet here they were, walking in like they owned the place. Without hesitation, or even bothering to lock the door behind them.

♦♦♦♦♦

My brain spun in a dozen directions at once, but kept returning to one key item: they didn't lock the door behind them.

I couldn't help but wonder how wise it would be to snoop around looking for evidence that would help prove what they were up to. The debate was between that or booking it over to the Sheriff's office, handing over the cassette, and washing my hands of this nightmare.

But if I did that, did I risk these two cretins vanishing into thin air?

Of course I could always just play it safe, call another Uber, get the hell out of the area, and pretend I never saw a thing.

Each of these options carried a risk. Should I walk straight into a potential death trap, or risk losing my only chance to expose the individuals apparently behind the horrors that had so recently been visited upon the innocents of San Diego county?

I felt the weight of the VHS in my bag pressing against my side like an anchor, grounding me in the middle of my spiral. Jimmy Buffett's voice popped into my head like a taunt: "Indecision may or may not be my problem."

I wanted to laugh, but my throat was too dry.

♦♦♦♦♦

My body screamed at me to turn around and run, but my heart dug in its heels. This was for Sofia. She was my friend—maybe even more than just a friend—and she needed help. If I bolted now, I'd never forgive myself. She might never forgive me either, and I wouldn't blame her.

So I snuck in the same door those two miscreants had used, intent on cautiously exploring the building and beating it before I was discovered. And like you'd expect in most old warehouses, there were piles of dusty boxes and rusted steel drums cluttering the place, which conveniently provided me with lots of darkened corners to hide in. The place reeked of dust and damp metal, and the air had that heavy, abandoned tang that clings to your throat.

The strangest part, though, was that just outside I'd noticed a riot of lantana bushes blooming in wild, neon colors—pink, orange, yellow—like someone had planted a garden at hell's doorstep. The memory of those flowers almost felt mocking now as I tiptoed deeper into the gloom. I even thought I also saw some spider lilies—those curling red flowers that symbolize themes of death, loss, and remembrance and often represent the connection between life and the afterlife—right by the doorstep.

Coincidence? I had to wonder.

♦♦♦♦♦

I scanned for cameras, motion detectors, or anything that would give away my presence, but found nothing more than sagging beams and a mesh of cobwebs strung together overhead like broken chandeliers. For one stupid moment I marveled at the spiders' craftsmanship, remembering how my art teacher once compared Saraceno's installations to galaxies strung in silk.

Shaking myself back to reality, I quietly tip-toed into the narrow hallway at the far side of the room. A few muffled male voices, low and steady, echoed off the walls from some hidden location. I caught the cadence, though not the words, and every step closer made the hairs on the back of my neck rise.

The problem, of course, was that this place was significantly bigger inside than it looked from the outside. The eerie, dusty—almost creepy—feeling blended with those ghostly voices coming from who-knew-where and put me more on edge with every step.

That open door at the end of the hallway may have been welcoming to some, but to me it just suggested some new fresh hell. At the very least it was some secret entrance to a workshop from Hell itself.

Amongst the shadows I spotted a flash light which, miraculously, worked! Carefully inspecting a side room I stood before, I found it to be little more than a pitch black bathroom that was as abandoned as the rest of the place. Still, I trod quietly, all but certain of doom and disaster if I was caught snooping and alone.

♦♦♦♦♦

A low humming sound came from an open hallway up ahead on the left, and I ducked into the darkened room, praying I wouldn't bump into anyone unexpectedly. But rather than Mune or one of his associates, I instead spotted something both unexpected and very familiar: a table full of the bottles brought into my group home earlier today!

Creeping towards the metal table overflowing with stained, crusted bottles, I spotted a few bits of scribbled notes scattered around the perimeter, tucked under the bottles' bases or hanging from cobwebs that had attached themselves to the table's lip.

Distance prevented me from making out what any of the notes said, but that little voice in the back of my head kept telling me to pick up one of the plastic bottles. Though this was the *last* thing I wanted to do, I somehow overcame my fear and reached for the nearest one.

It was very difficult to read in the near pitch black warehouse, and I reluctantly turned on the flashlight a second time, being sure to cover much of the beam with my shirt to barely eke out a thin beam of light. By squinting really hard, I was able to make out some of the words on the label.

It looked like a newer version of the label had recently been plastered on, which just added to my sense of unease. For one thing, this "product" still lacked any consumer information one would normally associate with something safe. Nothing indicated

FDA approval, instructions for using it safely, or indications of what problems it would fix. There was no outer box, either, or anything suggesting it was anything other than a home remedy that might contain virtually anything.

Even poison...

I dunno...call me old-fashioned, but I expect something more from any product I'm going to consume. Something still sat uneasily in my brain about all of this, and I scanned the darkened room in search of any additional clues that could potentially help me put the pieces of the puzzle into the right place.

♦♦♦♦♦

I had recently learned about Saint Michael the Archangel. He was leader of the heavenly armies, protector against evil, and the patron saint of police officers, soldiers, paramedics, and others who fight against injustice. To my mind this included detectives.

So I quietly said a prayer to him asking for help. Almost before I was done, I'd stepped on a small, crumpled ball of paper with a shopping list in sloppy handwriting. Only this shopping list was for various chemicals that someone noted needed to be replenished, including:

★ Extract of Stargazer Lily
★ Sodium hypochlorite
★ 25% sodium chlorite
★ Perfumes
★ Chlorine tablets

I stopped reading, struggling with the names of other reagents that I couldn't pronounce. Even my little bit of chemistry education made it instantly obvious that these were not ingredients you'd find in a "harmless product".

At the bottom of the sheet there was an obviously counterfeit FDA approval stamp with notations on how to improve it next time.

Thinking back to conversations with my chemistry teacher, I had a disturbing realization: this was a list of ingredients that could be used to make a chlorine bomb, and a powerful one at that.

FUCK ME! Were they *serious*?

These things were being repurposed for aromatherapy or consumption as fish capsules. And quickly shining my flashlight around the musty warehouse, I realized the dull smell I'd been inhaling was the air reeking of chemicals I couldn't name.

♦♦♦♦♦

I pulled up the collar of my shirt to cover my nose from the malevolent stench, and hoped I could get out of there without passing out or dying. How these guys hadn't yet been arrested was beyond me. I glanced down at the list again, then stuffed it into my pants pocket as possible evidence of whatever crime I had just discovered.

Cautiously exploring more of the area, I spotted tall, rusted industrial metal shelves a few feet away stuffed full of packaging and empty bottles. Seeing anything clearly in the dimly lit room was a challenge, of course, and I was reluctant to use the flashlight lest I be spotted. That forced me to step closer towards the wall, all the while dabbing at my eyes, which watered like an open faucet from the overpoweringly strong smell of what I'd concluded was a large room full of bad news.

This new set of shelves was full of bleach, vinegar, ammonia, and hydrogen peroxide. I quickly recognized that each of them by themselves posed absolutely no risk, and would typically be seen as a normal accumulation of household supplies.

But Chemistry 101 had taught me that mixing them together could create something FAR more sinister. Mixing bleach and vinegar could be fatal, bleach and ammonia could cause vomiting, and a cocktail of hydrogen peroxide and vinegar was guaranteed to be highly irritating to both the skin and lungs.

All in all, this room was increasingly looking like a disaster just looking for a place to happen!

Because lessons from Chemistry 101 persuaded me that these materials were explosive if not handled properly. Suddenly I held my breath, both from the crap surrounding me and because of the recognition that I was walking through a powder keg.

All of which forced me to ask why a group selling candy and nutritional supplements would have this kind of inventory? These were all chemicals that shouldn't be messed with casually, and NEVER be mixed! So what the hell?

And that was before I almost tripped over the oxygen tank. Yeah, something here definitely needed to be reported to the authorities!

♦♦♦♦♦

Another set of shelves further down the wall held more bottles, and above it were notes stuck to a cork board on the wall. Risking turning on the flashlight for the third time, I noticed that everything on the board looked to have recent dates. And there was a checklist with locations of...what the fuck?

- ☑ ~~La Mesa Farmer Market Fest (June 12th)~~
- ☑ ~~MidSummer Festival (July 5th)~~
- ☐ El Cajon (August 1st)
- ☑ ~~Kearny Mesa Sunset Coast Regional Center (July 1st)~~
- ☐ San Marcos Regional Craft Fair (August 7th)
- ☐ Poway's Autumn Fest (September 28th)
- ☐ National City Surf N' Art (September 30th)
- ☐ Chula Vista's Oktoberfest (October 17th)
- ☐ El Centro Regional Center Winter Party (November 11th)

Something in my brain snapped. These were major public events or locations of the regional centers in and around San Diego! The capital letters of *LA MESA* had scrawled next to it the words "*already bombed OR gassed,*" while next to the town *EL CAJON* it read in dry red ink "*to be blown.*"

I could come to no other conclusion: This *had* to be the origination point where the bomb was built to blow up La Mesa. True, it was always possible that the bomb had been built elsewhere and then brought to its ultimate destination, but right now did that really matter?

All I knew was that the trees and succulents in La Mesa and downwind had been wilting since the explosion, and the people there, from what I'd heard, had been suffering from severe breathing issues. Add to that the reality that all the roads and trails were still filled with dead animals, and...

♦♦♦♦♦

Trying to remain calm was challenging, given the number of questions and scenarios running simultaneously through my mind. This had to be one of the scariest moments in all my 24 years, and I was struggling to figure out my next move.

A sealed box full of assorted chocolate cherry cordials sat on the shelf just above my head. There was no label, nor was there any nutritional information. Given my surroundings, it was instantly obvious this was not a box of goodies one might buy at the local grocery store. And it struck me that these candies were—could it be possible someone might think so diabolically? —made with at least some of the items on that shopping list.

Poison packed within the chocolatey coating? Meaning the cherry liquor was not really cherry liquor, but something that could kill you.

HOLY SHIT!

I felt physically ill, horrified by the very idea...and recognized that I might be closer to the truth than not. Waves of nausea overtook every fiber of my being, and my body shook out of pure dread. It took every ounce of my will to keep from fainting, knowing if I did I'd almost certainly not survive the day.

Because if I was right, these chocolate candies were designed to be euthanasia pills...only covered in chocolate and packaged in a neat box.

And thinking back to the visit from Mune and Brady suggested they were made specifically to be given to people who...

People who were no different than me.

I reeled backwards, simultaneously trying to process my discovery, to not throw up at the idea, and to not make any noise that would tip off the would-be murderers who still sat talking elsewhere in the warehouse.

GOOD GOD, NO! Now I understood why Sofia had been so panicked lately. She knew more than she was letting on, and this could easily have been a big part of it.

Boy, if you'd told me when I woke up this morning that I'd be a mass of dread, panic, nausea, and confusion before the day was out – that I'd be fearing for my very life – I'd have laughed my ass off and told you, point blank, that you were crazy. And yet here we were!

♦♦♦♦♦

FOOTSTEPS!

Panicking, I ducked back into the main room and hid behind a large bank of metal cabinets. It was just one of a series of rows of cabinets, intermingled with rows of containers, labeled and containing God knows what.

There I struggled to make myself as small as possible, standing perfectly still and trying to not breathe, scream, or knock over anything from this hall of horrors.

Two men dressed in white had entered from the far side of the room as I watched quietly from my hiding place. Covering my mouth, I desperately tried to muffle any sound from my breathing, even as I strained to catch any snippets of their conversation.

What I hadn't known prior to that moment was how much sound gets absorbed by wooden beams, which explained why I couldn't hear what either of them were saying. Yet I found if I put my ear up against the side of the file cabinet beside me and held my breath, I could make out the two men laughing about something.

♦♦♦♦♦

"I also found this," one of the men said as he pulled something from his pocket. Peeking over the top of the cabinet, I saw him holding up a charred cat skull...probably the last thing I'd ever expected to see in his hands.

Then again, this day had already gone so far sideways, I guess nothing should have really surprised me anymore. Only he was also holding up a dried limb in his other hand, and I guessed it was almost certainly from the same unfortunate animal.

Were these people making sacrifices to the Devil?

I swallowed a sharp gasp. Sofia had had some alley cat friends before her house got bombed, and it broke my heart considering what she would think if she could see the scene that was now unfolding before my eyes.

“You think Aeron would like a cat better in pieces?” he chortled, holding the remains as if they were some sort of plaything. I thought it a sadistic, disgusting activity to hold a dead animal the way he did, but the other guy’s reaction was a simple shrug.

“Aeron hates cats.”

“That ain't true. He loves animals, but only if they're dead.”

I heard them both laugh derisively before they stopped to look through the papers on the desk. Swallowing hard, I watched them shuffle the papers and hoped they wouldn’t notice anything was amiss.

“Shouldn’t we get the boxes ready?”

My blood ran cold. “Boxes” implied there were more than I’d seen, and there being two men to prepare them suggested there were a lot of boxes. Even if each box only held a dozen “*chocolates*”, that was a lot of lives that were in danger. And my gut told me each box held more than a dozen of these deadly messengers.

Part of me figured I’d already seen too much and didn’t care to learn any more right now. Plus I still needed to get Sofia’s videotape to the Sheriff's office on the next block, so maybe it was time to beat a hasty retreat.

Slowly and cautiously I stepped back, trying to keep as quiet as possible as I took delicate steps on the concrete floor. I padded my way towards the door, carefully staying behind the chemical—and explosive-packed—shelves. I’d heard enough to convince me these were rotten people, and I needed to get out of there immediately!

The doorway beckoned, offering me freedom from this nightmare I was experiencing. Slowly...slowly...the two men continued laughing, talking, and moving things as I hit the door softly.

♦♦♦♦♦

The massive metal door groaned on its hinges, dragging a harsh, metallic screech through the air like nails across a chalkboard. The rusted joints let out a deep, grating GRRRNK! as the door finally gave way, echoing through this warehouse of death.

"Creeeaaaak...kreee-eeeek..." it protested as I pushed open into the sunlight. The two men dressed in white snapped their heads around at the sound, and that was when I gave up all sense of

decorum and made a break for it. Bolting out through the hallway, I swore I heard yelling from that storage room that echoed through the halls.

All I could think, over and over, was “SHIT! They know I’m here! I GOTTA GO!”

And as I sprinted out of the building and felt the sun’s warmth hit my face, the door slammed with a violent metallic "BANG-CLANG-krk-krk!" It sent a shuddering echo through the cavernous space behind it, and the rusted hinges gave a final, reluctant rattle—like chains dragging on concrete—before falling still.

“STOP HIM!” screamed a voice that echoed throughout the hallway from the outside.

♦♦♦♦♦

Baseball giant Satchel Paige once said, “Don’t look back. Something might be gaining on you.” Tempting advice—except I knew, right then, something was gaining on me.

I ran harder, lungs burning, as two figures tore after me. My sneakers slapped the pavement, the sound of my own heartbeat louder than the chaos of the street. Faces turned as I passed—neighbors, strangers—some frowning, some curious, most completely oblivious to the nightmare unfolding just a few feet away from them.

I veered toward Lemon Grove’s main street, cutting sharp corners, doubling back, ducking into alleys and out again—anything to throw them off. But every glance over my shoulder proved it useless—they were still there. Closer. Always closer.

I was dead—or would be soon.

Then, up ahead, a staircase rose on the far side of the street like a lifeline. Through my gasping breath I repeated it like a mantra: Must...get...to...the...stairs...

Traffic blurred past, horns blaring, but I didn’t care. I darted between cars, my chest heaving, pulse hammering so hard it felt like my ribs would crack. The staircase loomed closer. If I could just reach it...

♦♦♦♦♦

Brady, the blond-haired man, was right on my heels. My heart slammed against my ribs as I ran, faster than I thought my legs could carry me. Then came the noise—"*SKREEEEEEE*—" "*HOOOONK*!" "*WHUMP*!"

I risked glancing over my shoulder. His white robe was now filthy as he lay sprawled in the street, struck down by an oncoming Buick. The impact had been brutal, and I saw a red stain seeping into the fabric.

And though he was probably seriously injured—or perhaps even dying—I couldn't let myself dwell on it. My survival was the only thing that mattered now, and I knew it was going to be them or me.

I opted to be selfish and forced myself forward, lungs burning, legs screaming, while listening to the footsteps behind me quicken. This guy Mune was faster than he looked, running like the whip of his master was driving him ever harder towards me. The sheriff's office was no longer an option—I just needed to get out of here...to get home...to get anywhere safe.

♦♦♦♦♦

Silence. I crouched behind some trees at the stair landing, desperate to catch my breath, when the bushes behind me rustled. A hand clamped onto my shoulder, yanking me upright. Panic. Adrenaline. Instinct.

I kicked, punched, and twisted in a desperate effort to free myself. The impact jolted his leg. He felt the contact—flesh, bone, fabric, air.

My efforts were greeted by a grunt, a sharp cry, and the sickening sound of a body falling over the concrete wall and tumbling down the concrete stairs.

The man's expression flickered in that instant: surprise, then pain, then nothing as his momentum carried him backward. His feet left the step. Time stuttered, before gravity did its job.

Thump. Crack. Clunk.

The man fell hard, bouncing and twisting down the concrete steps. A sick rhythm of limbs and stone followed—shoulder, hip, back, skull. A jangling of keys, a muted shout cut off mid-tumble. He landed at the bottom like a dropped sack of bricks...and didn't move.

For a second, the air went silent except for the hum of the power line. A dog barked somewhere far off. No cars. No one was watching.

I froze, shuddering. Mune—or what was left of him—lay crumpled at the bottom of the staircase.

"That's gonna leave a mark," I muttered, voice shaking as I clutched the bag with the VHS tighter. My only thought now was getting the fuck out of there.

♦♦♦♦♦

Mune lay unmoving, a crimson pool blooming from the back of his head into the cracked asphalt of the parking lot. My stomach lurched. Relief and horror crashed together inside me like two speeding trains. I wanted to keep it together—God, I desperately wanted to keep it together—but my whole body trembled.

Some small, decent part of me whispered "You're responsible. Go back."

Another voice, sharper, colder, snapped "Screw him. You'd be dead if they caught you."

I listened to the second voice and bolted, ducking into an alley and pressing my back to the brick wall. My lungs burned; each breath coming ragged and shallow. My heart hammered against my ribs like it was trying to escape.

What now? My brain spun in circles, a cyclone of fear and options: back to Sofia's? Home? The police? Anywhere but here, where every scenario ended with the same image—white coats closing in, hands grabbing, and some unthinkable fate.

♦♦♦♦♦

I forced myself to move, stepping out onto the street to get my bearings. "HEY! WATCH IT!" a woman in a beat-up Chrysler convertible barked as I practically walked in front of her efforts to park.

I muttered an apology and stumbled on, clutching my bag and the VHS tape as if it were a talisman. My mind reeled as I stumbled on in a trance, as if on autopilot.

The big question, of course, was what was my next move? Going home didn't make much sense, since Ren wouldn't believe me and would try to take the videotape away from me.

Besides, the house was already in a state of chaos, with everyone rattled by what had happened this morning. And poor Pedro was in the hospital.

Though I'm not a very religious person, I'll admit that at that moment I prayed for him.

So if I wasn't up for dealing with the police, and going home wasn't an option, there was really only one place I could find sanctuary: Sofia's house. Considering it from every angle, I recognized that she was really the only person who might understand how deep this whole thing ran.

♦♦♦♦♦

"THUMP!"

The middle-aged woman with the arm load of groceries was RIGHT behind me as I turned towards the street. Her grocery bags scattered across the sidewalk, and she snapped, "Could you PLEASE look where you're going!?" Her eyes were tired and sunken, and she looked like every day was a chore for her to get through.

"I—I'm s-sorry..." My knees gave out and I dropped onto the concrete, gasping like a greyhound at the finish line. My heart pounded more fiercely than I'd ever heard it before, threatening to explode from its cage inside my ribcage.

Her anger melted when she saw how pale my face was, and she stopped chasing the three rolls of paper towels that had landed in the middle of the road. "Oh my gosh—are you okay?"

I wanted to shout *NO!* I wanted to tell her I'd just witnessed something out of a horror film that wasn't supposed to happen in real life. But nothing came out. Just the sound of me panting, hands trembling, the world tilting at the edges.

Everything I'd read about in books—the secret operations, the "accidents"—none of this was fiction anymore. It was happening right under our noses, and no one had noticed.

"Hey, it's alright. Just breathe," the woman murmured, kneeling down to my level and putting a hand on my shoulder.

I really tried hard to relax, but my breathing came out jagged and uneven. My brain was feeling scrambled, and panic gnawed at my chest like a squirrel locked in a tiny dark room and wildly trying to escape.

"Here!" she held out a plush toy—a black kitty with anime-wide eyes and white paws. It looked like something she might have just bought for a child, and I took it and held it close, like a security blanket.

The plushie was absurdly soft and warm under my trembling fingers, and the texture helped ground me. My breathing steadied, if only a little, as I took in my surroundings through the haze of paranoia.

"Th-thanks," I whispered, glancing at the spilled contents of her bags lying all around us: boxes of spaghetti, oranges, apples, bananas, some canned goods, those paper towels, flowers scattered in every direction, and a huge white teddy bear. "I'm...I'm sorry if I ruined your..."

"Don't worry about it," she sighed, brushing her hair from her face. "I'm the one who should be apologizing for shouting at you."

"It's fine..." I said, finally pulling in an even breath. "I shouldn't be running like that. And you're obviously hauling gifts for someone's birthday."

She let out a hollow laugh. "Actually...they're get...well gifts for my kids."

My heart sank. "Oh. I'm sorry." I glanced at the black cat plush in my hands. "Here, I can—"

"No, no. Keep it," her voice softened. "You look like you need it more than they do right now."

I stared down at the plush and felt guilt crawl up my throat—not just for bumping into her, but for everything I'd seen today.

She stared at the daisies and roses scattered across the street, now ruined as their petals drifted into the dusk. "I don't even know if my kids are comfortable smelling flowers right now. It hurts for them to breathe."

"...Hurts to breathe?" I asked carefully.

Her eyes glistened. "My kids were...attacked by monsters. The same ones causing these horrible accidents." Her voice cracked on "monsters."

My stomach dropped. So I *hadn't* been imagining it: this shit was real.

"I'm...I'm so sorry..."

She gave a bitter laugh. "Why are you sorry? You're not the cause of this."

She sat next to me on the curb, the both of us staring at the dirty disembodied petals vanishing under the passing cars. Streetlights flickered on overhead, throwing long shadows across her face. "I just don't understand why they haven't been caught yet. And why my kids, and not me..."

"I read that the police are on the job, trying to find these guys," I started.

She snorted. "Yes, I know all about the police investigations. But the reality is these guys are still out there, and the police don't even know where to start."

♦♦♦♦♦

I swallowed, unsure how to comfort her...until my hand brushed the hard edge of the VHS cassette inside my bag.

"Maybe I can help you—"

"How?" she said, voice flat and skeptical. "We don't even know where they are, let alone know how to prove what they've done.

They could be anywhere. Hiding in the forests of Idyllwild for all we know, or halfway to Yuma."

"I have evidence!" The words tumbled out before I could stop them. "I know a witness...but I need to convince her to come forward."

Her head snapped toward me, eyes widening, wild hope flickering in them. "W-who?!"

"My friend Sofia. I've been trying to get her to talk—"

She was instantly torn between exuberance and cynicism. "And you have evidence? Like what?"

"We found a videotape where these guys admit to what they've been doing."

♦♦♦♦♦

"Why haven't you turned it in to the police?" she blurted, her tone a strange mix of excitement and despair. The sudden intensity made me flinch. "You have evidence. What are you waiting for?"

"Well, she wanted me to go to the station for her and—"

She leaned closer, her voice urgent and raspy. "You and your friend may have what it takes to stop these horrible people. You have a videotape. You have a witness. You need to talk to the authorities. *NOW*!"

She stood up abruptly, her demeanor instantly changing from exhaustion to determination. "I can even take you to the police station. Let's go!"

As she gathered up her belongings from the street, the woman lifted her head and, in a no-nonsense tone, said "Come on. We're going now...unless you want more innocent people to get hurt."

Unsure how to respond, I swallowed and nodded. This was a woman on a mission, and it was pretty obvious nothing was going to stand in her way. I wondered what had happened to her children.

"Yeah, I can do that but..."

"But? But what?"

"I....kinda need a ride..." I glanced back as I heard sirens blaring, making their way closer to where two men in white robes lay dead or dying in the streets.

"Like I said, I'll be happy to drive you to the police station RIGHT NOW!" she insisted. Only I needed to get back to my own home to gather my thoughts before I went to the cops. Because now I was party to the "accidental" death of two men, and there were sure to be a ton of questions, my name would be in the newspapers, and...

UCH! All I wanted was to just get away from this neighborhood, and all the shit that had just gone down.

My hope was that things had calmed down at home and Ren was probably wondering where I was. I already have a few messages from him, unread, on my text feed, and I was sure he was understandably worried. Plus my budget just couldn't handle one more Uber ride right now.

"But...but..." the woman protested. I knew she was upset about her kids, but she sounded like a motorboat and I had to suppress a smile.

"Tell you what," I suggested. "Take me home now so I can get some rest. I'm a mess, and I wouldn't be of much value to the police like this. You'll know where I live, and you and I can go to the police tomorrow, bright and early. I'll be ready to go any time you like."

"That" I continued, throwing her a bone, "will give me a chance to connect with my friend Sofia and try to persuade her to also come forward."

There was a great deal of truth in what I suggested, knowing we'd need to have more witnesses for the investigators to lean into this case as far as it would undoubtedly require. I didn't believe the cops would just take what I said at face value, and really had no idea who this woman was.

Besides, I really didn't want Ren to know the real reason why I was out this late, and telling him I was going to a police station wouldn't sit too well, either.

♦♦♦♦♦

The drive home was pretty quiet. I gave her directions to get me back to the group home, but otherwise the air was still. My levels of paranoia and anxiety had lessened, despite being driven home by a complete stranger.

Finally I pushed myself. "So..." I said, trying to make simple conversation. "How old are your kids?"

"...Claudia, my daughter is 12, and my son Jason is 16" she answered quietly. I felt bad, and realized I didn't even know her name.

"I'm really sorry miss...um."

"Madeleine," she answered.

"Madeleine," I repeated, trying to remember it like I was adding a name to an internal phonebook in my head. I still grasped the VHS in my hand, and recognized I'd failed to do one simple job. Sofia was gonna be *PISSED*!

Now I was returning back home, anything but triumphant. There was no way this could end well. Police in the morning, an angry Sofia, a stranger driving me home.

YEESH! How had I gotten myself into this?

Briefly, I considered hitting the bus station and leaving town. Because for all I knew, the rest of the so-called Purity Syndicate could be looking for me in the streets if I got anywhere near that warehouse...let alone Ren nagging to determine where I was, and probably asking my mom about my whereabouts.

SHIT! It all sounded so wrong. I'd already gotten my hands tied by saying that Sofia was a witness to the crimes. It was a dumb move on my part talking about Sofia when I was only told to turn in the tape.

But it was also now impossible for me to back out.

“So you’re going to talk with Sofia about testifying and showing that evidence, right?”

Yeah, Madeleine wasn’t about to let me off the hook. I’d made a commitment, and she was the type to hold me to my word.

“I– yeah, tomorrow,” I nodded, wincing and internally kicking myself. Terrific! How was I supposed to convince Sofia’s parents when they inevitably asked why I was asking her out?

I was *such* a wreck. Still reeling from what had happened in the warehouse, then on the stairs during the chase. Sure, I had calmed down a bit, but I was really backed into a corner. I continued speaking; “I’ll bring her to the police station then.”

Chapter 19: Resentment

-Sofia-

I sat at my desk, anxiously waiting to hear from Damian that he had turned in the VHS tape to the police. He left my house last night shortly before dusk, and here we were at lunchtime and I had bupkis. No text. No call. No nuthin'!

He could be dead for all I know.

Yeah, I had to admit it—there was a heavy sinking feeling in my chest, as if something bad had happened to him. I mean, I couldn't believe I was saying this but I was really worried for Damian, and cursed myself internally for sending him to the police station to turn in the VHS by himself. I know my paranoia is usually what gets the best of me, but something in my gut told me my anxiety might not be so wrong this time.

Maybe I should have faced this with him. After all, I had been the one to find the video tape...

Through my bedroom door I heard a muffled knocking. The last thing I wanted to do was to be sociable, so I hoped whoever it was would go away.

"Sofia, your friend is at the door!" Aunt Bruna called out.

Thank God!

♦♦♦♦♦

I surprised myself at how briskly I got up from my bed, practically running down the hallway to get to Damian standing in the now open doorway. "Sofia!"

I all but jumped on the poor guy. "Hey, Damian–" I yelped as he quickly grabbed my hand and looked me dead in the eyes with such a lingering urgency, making my stomach drop. Still holding my hand, he urgently whispered, "Come with me."

It was obvious that something big had gone down yesterday. I nodded meekly as we both headed to my room, leaving behind my confused aunt and not caring in the slightest. We had bigger issues to deal with at the moment than her nosiness.

I closed my door and turned to him. "Did you turn in the..."

"I didn't," he answered before I finished my sentence.

My heart sank. "But...why not?" Part of me was filled with dread, knowing that the one piece of evidence that could point a finger at these monsters was still floating in a state of limbo. And I had to admit it was mainly my fault for not having taken care of the whole thing sooner.

How many people were needlessly suffering because I'd dawdled?

Damian swallowed and briefly looked at the closed door behind us. He was panting, as if he'd run a great distance. "Something...happened yesterday. Honestly...you have *every* right to be paranoid, Sofia..."

"What are you saying?"

"It's..." he shifted nervously. His eyes told me he was desperate to talk about whatever had happened, even as he was at the moment painfully uncomfortable. "There are people...horrible people. They're trying to make this all look like a series of accidents."

He looked deep into my eyes. "I found something that sounded a lot like what they were talking about in that tape you discovered...only the shit I saw was for real!"

♦♦♦♦♦

Damian pulled a crumpled piece of paper and a business card out of his pants pocket. I sat, puzzled, as he laid out before me what he had recently learned. "There's this whole group planning domestic terrorism all around the county, specifically at major events and regional centers..."

I blanched and felt my heart drop to my stomach as I read down the crumpled list. Moaning, I knew that—horrific as it seemed—this was real. It was happening, and had been going on for who knows how long.

Damian shook as he continued his tale. "Hell, I was there, and barely got away. I was really scared, Sofia, and I felt like they were going to hurt me if they caught me."
"I'll tell you one thing, though; I'm not sure who these people are, but they really wanted to stay hidden and completely out of sight. They know what they're doing, and they know it's wrong."

"People?"

Wearing a face that proclaimed he was dead serious, Damian nodded slowly. "Yeah, people, like plural. This is not the act of one person, but a group of them. And they're very organized."

He clutched the bag holding the VHS. "Two of them chased me, and I'm happy to have gotten away with my life. There were a bunch of them, and I honestly fear that they could still be searching for me now. I even called in sick to work today and missed my classes. I'm scared shitless that these guys are still out there."

"Worst of all, the two who chased me know where I live!"

Damian's hands were shaking, and I was pretty sure it had nothing to do with the cold coming from my room's air conditioner. I felt awful that I had pushed him to go alone and do this without me. Whatever had happened to my friend—for indeed, I now saw him as my friend, or at least my ally—was my fault.

And now he may have people associated with this Aeron Inochi guy after him. *Now* what?

♦♦♦♦♦

I started "Maybe we can call the non-emergency police line..."

Damian stopped me before I could finish. "Someone already did."

I blinked. “Who?”

“Some lady I met last night...her name’s Madeleine, and she already called about the evidence we’re supposed to turn in.”

“What? What do you mean ‘we’? I told you I don’t want to be involved...” I paused and looked at Damian’s face. He was looking away, which could only mean one thing.

“Damian...don’t tell me.”

He winced. “I...may have told her that you were one of the main witnesses and had been the one to find the evidence.”

“Damian!”

“I’m sorry! I was in a panic and I wasn’t thinking clearly. It just kinda came out of my mouth before I could stop it. Besides” he whined “the minute you found that videotape you got involved, whether you wanted to or not.”

He huffed, “Look, it really doesn’t matter. We just need to turn it in to the police, with no questions asked.”

♦♦♦♦♦

“The police...” I shuddered.

My parents had instilled in me a fear of the unfettered authority that police officers had in the city. They’d heard so many stories about how the police force would tackle an autistic person and hold them down until they stopped breathing, not caring about what condition we were dealing with.

And I knew that we can’t resist the law. My problem was feeling that they won’t see us as humans...especially if we’re having a meltdown, when we might be having problems thinking straight.

Maybe it was all conjecture. Maybe it was real. But either way, dammit, my parents had drilled this all into my head, and now even the thought of talking to the police scared me.

♦♦♦♦♦

“I can’t.”

Damian was both curious and slightly frustrated. “Why?”

"Why what?"

"Why are you so insistent that you not be involved? Do you really think everyone is the enemy here?"

I was stunned at this accusation; defensive even. "It's not as simple as you think! What I said yesterday was true. I don't have as much freedom as you do. I wasn't taught the social skills I wanted to learn. And because I'm in conservatorship, my family has a say about what I can and cannot do. Hell, I wasn't even allowed to talk to boys for such a long time."

I huffed in frustration. "I doubt you live with a family that cares more than mine does about reputation being more important than authenticity. I mean, I was raised in an environment where I was forced on countless occasions to watch films whose only goal was to make people feel good. These were movies about perfect families raising autistic children, and these kids were used as props to make the main character have a sense of hardship, rather than as equal members of a loving family."

"That's the kind of family I've had all my life, Damian; people who see me as a hardship they must endure, rather than as an equal member of a loving family. So how do you think that has made me feel?"

♦♦♦♦♦

There was a pause that felt like it lasted nearly a half hour. The rickety fan and the air conditioner's low hum were the only noises in my small room.

"You know," I said sadly "I wanted to be a poet or a great writer, just so I could get out of this place. I figured if I could show that I was more than what I'm already seen as, I would be able to prove my worth to a larger universe of people."

"But I've sometimes wondered if my pride and sense of self-worth are all in my head. Maybe..." I looked at him earnestly. "Maybe it's all just a fantasy to keep myself from going insane."

He sighed and continued looking at me. "Do you...do you really want my honest opinion?" Damian asked in a surprisingly serious tone. I looked at him, bewildered and wondering what this guy before me had to say. I heard him sigh again before he spoke.

"I...I just think that you tend to overthink a lot about yourself...and maybe..."

He hesitated, obviously concerned he was going to offend me. "Go on," I urged, half-afraid he'd say it and half-afraid he wouldn't.

"Well," Damian went on "Maybe it's made you resentful towards everyone, including yourself. I mean, based on the way you've behaved and the things I've experienced in my group home, usually people like us tend to hold ourselves back. We don't want to try or we're too scared to try because we fear everyone else's opinions. And I'm not blaming you entirely, but you..."

The air was still as the plushies and I awaited his final verdict. "Well, you haven't really planned out much, have you?"

"Don't get me wrong," he hurriedly continued. "I don't mean to put you on the spot here. You claim you want to be a great poet and think you know better and yet...you typically cower away. And I get it; your family is kind of a bunch of narcs, but...well, they kinda have a point."

I was getting more steamed the longer I listened to his words. "Because if you really want to prove to them you can be better than they'll ever be, then why cower away from the challenges you're facing? And why are you cowering away when it's our lives that could be on the line because of this cult?"

"Besides, if you really want to prove it to them and the authorities, then you have to take that risk to stop these guys. Because if you don't, we – you and I – may not be alive long enough to create the things we were meant to."

♦♦♦♦♦

I was genuinely speechless. It had never occurred to me that Damian could be so aware, and that he could see right through me the way he just had.

Sure, what he said had hurt – it cut me right to the quick – but I couldn't help but think that he was more right than not.

And I – we – were seeing the patterns. We were connecting the dots and seeing the similarities of so many people dying from 'mysterious causes.' It was obviously not going to go away on its own, and between us Damian and I might even be in a position to help bring this horrible nightmare to an end.

Because these guys were nothing less than a death cult, and the messages I heard coming from him were simple, honest, and true: "If not us, then who? If not now, then when?"

♦♦♦♦♦

I swallowed before I meekly responded. "I…it's not that simple."

"I know," he nodded. I was shocked that Damian – a guy who I had recently found to be incredibly annoying whenever I was around him – could be so understanding. Guilt gnawed around the edges of my consciousness as I considered how I had previously misjudged and mistreated him.

"Sofia, Madeleine is helping us." Damian assured me. "She already called the police station's non-emergency line and gave them a heads-up about what was going to be coming their way. If you'd like, you and I can go in together. And she said she'd be happy to give us a ride if we wanted."

"Do you want me to speak with your parents?"

I sighed. "I wouldn't know where to begin talking with them. I mean, the last thing they would want me to be doing was to go out anywhere with a guy. I told you; they don't trust me, and they're going to automatically assume we would do God knows what."

I shook my head in frustration. "They always assume the worst."

As I considered the possible consequences to my friends at the regional center if we didn't do something, the answer became clearer.

Finally nodding, I reluctantly agreed. "I guess we can do that. But the only way that I can do that is when I get to work. We'll hand the evidence to the investigators and police later."

Damian grunted. "Sounds like a plan to me." He pulled out his phone and started typing in numbers. "I'll let Madeleine know."

♦♦♦♦♦

I watched Damian's fingers fly and debated whether I would actually go to work today. Deep inside I knew that I wouldn't go, even if I told everyone else I would.

The truth was I really didn't want to go to work today, even though I'd been out for several weeks. All I wanted to do was to get this damned VHS into the hands of the police...and to be done with it!

After that? Well, maybe I'd hang out in the coffee shop or something...with Damian, of all people.

Never thought I would see the day!

♦♦♦♦♦

Aunt Bruna was calling me from somewhere on the other side of the house. Knowing I had a boy over as company, she'd most likely made some snacks again.

Lovely. As long as she didn't make any heart-shaped mini sandwiches this time.

"Yeah?" I called out.

"Can you come into the kitchen, please? Your mother wants you to see this."

"What now?" I groaned. Did I not put the dishes in the proper alphabetical, color, or size order? Maybe I left a single sock on the floor again. In my current mood, with such important things on my mind, the last thing I needed was to be subjected to another lecture about something ridiculous and petty.

I mean, really...why should their OCD behavior be *my* problem?

Plus there was that strange feeling that Damian might have to follow me out there, and I figured I'd have to sell it to him. "C'mon," I turned to him. "She probably has more snacks made with cheap cheddar."
I headed towards the kitchen with Damian following closely behind me.

"Oh there you are," Bruna greeted me with a grin. "Your mother brought some supplements that she figured could help you."

♦♦♦♦♦

My blood froze. One glance at the bottle she was gripping and I was ready to run, screaming, into the street. My mother and my aunt—my own flesh and blood—were sitting at the kitchen table,

Bruna busily prying off the cap of a bottle of The Miracle Tap, completely oblivious to what she was suggesting.

I blanched at what they were suggesting, then glanced at Damian, who instantly recognized and understood my horror. Aunt Bruna walked towards us grasping the fatal elixir and jovially reported, "Everyone's talking about how this can fix all kinds of health problems. I insist that you try some," she smiled.

"See? I told you," Damian whispered to me. "These guys are lying, telling people who don't know better that autism is curable. And I can only imagine how many people they've already poisoned!"

Speechless, I stood there feeling like a deer in the headlights. My mind went blank and I struggled to find my voice, meekly asking, "Oh...um...where did you get that?"

My mother answered, "I got them from some nice ladies at the farmer's market." Bruna added "They said they were fundraising for two of their friends who died yesterday."

♦♦♦♦♦

Damian cursed under his breath at that last part. I swallowed and asked, "Are you...sure that would actually help me? I mean, what makes you sure you can trust a couple of strangers at a farmer's market? Surely you can't trust a lot of people these days."

Damian nervously jumped into the conversation in an effort to try and change their minds. "Y-yeah. And we aren't really sure if it's FDA-approved."

Bruna continued pleasantly, "Well, we were at the fair recently and saw lots of people buying these. I was going to bring you along that day, but I figured you wouldn't like the crowds."

"Oh Christ!" Damian muttered.

My mother stood up and walked towards the living room, calling over her shoulder and making it quite clear she was annoyed with me. What else was new?

"There's no need to panic, Sofia. Just do what you're told and everything will be fine."

♦♦♦♦♦

“I’m not panicking. I just...think it's a little weird that there's a product that claims to cure autism,” I called, struggling to keep my voice level.

I hated when she’d project her pain onto me. I mean, that woman is emotionally immature, and that’s always been HER problem....only lately she’s increasingly been making it my burden.

After all, the ego is a fortress, albeit a fragile one. My mother and aunt see themselves as survivors, yet they trap me into their stagnant atmosphere—a place I never wanted to be a part of, and spend every day working hard to avoid.

Which explains why what should be pleasant conversations with my mother regularly turn into defensiveness on her part, and screaming matches prompted by her fear of me leaving the home to interact with “more mature” minds.

Only the really fucked up part—that she’s legally in control of my actions and my life—leaves me trapped in a heavy schedule of the mundane, without my having any kind of a significant say over my very existence.

♦♦♦♦♦

“You always make a big deal out of the littlest things, Sofia.” She was still carrying on, not listening to a word I was saying. I’d run away, except I have no resources, no plan, no prospects, and no place to go. This leaves me being held hostage by my own mother.

Lovely!

“Can you just listen to me for once?” I pleaded, “Don’t you think it's very odd that there's a product like this? I mean, is there any evidence that it even works?”

“Then try it,” my mother stated flatly. Once again, she wanted what she wanted, and my needs or desires - despite the fact that I was the one who would be most immediately impacted - were being ignored.

“NO!” I said firmly, standing my ground.

“Sofia.”

“No. I’m NOT taking it!”

She pointed at Damian. "Are you just saying that because he's here?"

Suddenly in the spotlight, Damian flinched. My mother's lips curled into a slow, knowing smirk, her eyes narrowing as she suggested "Do you two have a thing going on that I don't know about?"

"Mom!"

She turned on him like a python. "YOU! GET OUT!" she snapped. "She already had enough trouble before you showed up. Get out of here now, before I call the police."

Recognizing how unwelcome he was in my home, Damian glanced at me. I felt awful for the position I'd put him in, and angry about the wild accusations she was making towards him. "Mom, he's not..."

"No. No, it's fine." Damian volunteered. "I guess I've kinda overstayed my welcome."

He backed away from me, giving me a worried look that silently begged "Whatever you do, do NOT take those things." And I could see he was torn; part of him feeling he had to get out of there, part of him nervous to leave me alone in this tense situation.

My mother made the decision for him. "Then *GO*!" she snapped.

♦♦♦♦♦

"Right. Sorry." Damian nodded. He nervously slunk out of the door, glancing at me to mouth "Please text me" before closing the door behind him.

I glared at my mother. "Was that *REALLY* necessary? He didn't do anything wrong."

"You didn't tell us you were bringing a visitor here," she scolded. "You're here to do what we say is best for you. *NOT* to do whatever you want."

And here we go. Suddenly I was on the defensive for some imagined infraction.

"I didn't think he was going to come over today. He's a friend who was having an emergency!"

She didn't miss a beat, throwing it back in my face. "This sounds more like a conspiracy!"

"Would you *STOP*?! Not everyone I meet is some weirdo!" I argued.

My mother was just getting warmed up, ready to hurl a steady stream of verbal abuse until I did whatever she wanted just to shut her up. That was when my father stepped in.

"What is going on here?" he huffed. "I could hear you two arguing from outside."

Before I could say a word, my mother jumped in with her wild accusations. "Sofia is freaking out about these supplements we got her from the fair. I don't see the issue."

My dad took the pill bottle and inspected it closely, his bushy eyebrows furrowing as he read the label. He turned the pill bottle over and around, carefully examining it for directions or nutritional information.

He found no details regarding facts about this dietary supplement. No percentages of daily values of vitamins, no list of ingredients, no cautions for pregnant women or temperatures that the package should be stored at.

No nothing, and I hoped my father would see reason and listen to me. He turned to my mother and Bruna. "And...what are these pills supposed to be for?"

Bruna spoke up "They're supposed to help people like Sofia with their autism. That's what the nice people at the fair told me."

"As if I didn't have enough 'help' already," I muttered under my breath.

♦♦♦♦♦

My dad unscrewed the bottle, making my heart jump into my throat. "Let's see what we're dealing with," he said as he dropped one pill on the table. He opened the silverware drawer and pulled out a steak knife. Turning to me, he smiled. "I'll make a deal with you. I'll take one half, and you take the other half. We'll both benefit, and I'm sure it won't be so bad."

The gel capsule sat unmoving on the table as he placed the edge of the sharpened knife against it. "Thunk!" It was split in two as the liquid oozed out. Trying to show me how harmless it was, my dad reached for one of the halves and popped it into his mouth.

"Wait, Dad..."

I was too late, and his reaction was fast. Immediately tasting the bleach, my father gagged and dashed to the sink, sputtering as he spit out the pill and washed out his mouth with running water. Bruna and my mother looked on, confused as he repeatedly rinsed his mouth.

All I could do was wince from the gagging and sputtering. I stepped back, feeling vindicated.

♦♦♦♦♦

"What? What is it?" My mother was understandably confused. "It shouldn't taste *THAT* bad"

My father gargled and spit for the fifth time, then turned on her, outraged. "Not that bad!? It's BLEACH!"

Everyone froze as my father glared at Bruna, "Are you sure these aren't supposed to be cleaning capsules?"

"N-No," Bruna shook her head nervously, "They said it was for children"

"Children!? This would *KILL* somebody!"

My mother was clearly unpersuaded. "Don't all pills taste bitter?"

My father was obviously torn between outrage at my aunt, horror at what had almost happened to me, and disgust at my mother's refusal to recognize what was happening before her eyes.

"*THAT* is not bitter! *THAT* tastes like metal dipped in cherry syrup!"

He was *PISSED*, and I was secretly delighted. Finally there was someone in a position of authority who was listening to me.

He huffed angrily. "Are you trying to get our daughter killed? She nearly died from the bleach incident at the Center, and now you're trying to feed this shit to her?!"

♦♦♦♦♦

My mother wasn't convinced. "You're not believing all this bleach attack nonsense too, are you? These are all clearly accidents. Everyone on the news says that, and I believe them."

My dad was now firmly on my side. "How would you know!? You didn't experience what Sofia went through, and I would think a firsthand experience would have much more credibility than some moussed news anchor who is just reading off a piece of paper!"

Hearing them argue like this, I backed away and retreated to my room. It was bad enough that my fears had just been confirmed, and I didn't also have the head space for a screaming match.

I mean, someone out there had convinced my aunt to buy something for me that they claimed would help "my condition." And she was naive enough to buy their snake oil, or more accurately snake venom.

Worst of all, there were a lot of naive people out there who thought that autism was something that needed to be cured, like it's a common head cold.

♦♦♦♦♦

I needed to escape from this place. The conversation had quickly gone downhill, and my family was now only interested in arguing. I felt like my head was going to explode from the stress.

But my father "got it" now, my aunt was perpetually going to freeze the moment anyone challenged her, and my mother would chronically argue with anyone who remotely disagreed with her...and she'd go to the mat to defend opinions she swore by, despite her lack of evidence or credibility.

She regularly reminded me that she was incapable of seeing things from anyone else's perspective.

Sidling down the hallway again towards the heated conversation, I ducked left and snuck out the front door. My grandparents sat in the living room, my grandfather snoozing on the couch while my grandmother sat and watched Family Feud on television. She was another one, never noticing the real-life version going on eight feet away from where she sat.

I chased down Damian, who stood a half-block down the street waiting for his ride to arrive. I called out to him, and he glanced back, stunned and relieved to see me.

“Sofia?”

“I’m going with you! I need to get out of there.” I said firmly, wiping away a tear that had leaked onto my cheek.

“But what about your parents?” he asked cautiously. “You’ve got to know you’ll get into trouble just by being out here...”

I cut him off. “I don’t care! They’ll be arguing with each other for hours, and probably won’t even notice I’m gone until morning. I left my door closed, and SHE won’t even think to check on me.”

Damian shot me a concerned look.

“So...is it always like that...at home?”

I laughed bitterly, “You have no idea!” I straightened my jacket. “But I don’t want to think about that right now. We have evidence to turn in and bad guys to try and stop. The only thing that matters to me is for this mess to be over.”

Damian nodded. “Noted.” He glanced at his phone. “Madeleine says she’s around the corner and will be here in about three minutes. Which means it won’t be long until this is all history.”

He shrugged, and I was happy to know we wouldn’t have to worry about it anymore. “It’s not like anyone could track us down after this,” he mumbled.

“I sure hope not,” I said softly, more to myself than Damian.

Chapter 20: The Rabbit Hole of Aeron Inochi

-Whitney-

I was filing papers at the police station, waiting for José to deliver forensic results. Hours had already slipped by, but I wasn't really surprised. It'd been weeks since we'd gotten any kind of a break in this case. Since the La Mesa explosion, there had just been problems, bad news, and more bad news.

My phone buzzed with a text from my wife sending a gentle reminder to eat a decent meal. She always worried during cases like this, and over the years she'd noticed my habits all too well—skipped vitamins, another cup of joe swapped in for real food, and operating on about three hours of sleep every night for as long as it took to solve the damned puzzle in front of me.

There was no question about it: I was obsessed with my work, and black coffee had become both my fuel and my crutch.

Yet I couldn't help but notice—even through the fog of caffeine—that I hadn't heard anything from Madeleine. No calls. Not even a quick hello or the half-hearted thumbs-up emoji she used to send.

I worried about her more than I admitted out loud. She was a mother gutted by pain and hollowed out by grief, working 14 hour days to distract herself...or maybe to keep herself from doing something she knew she'd later regret.

Still, I couldn't blame her if she wanted to take down the bad guys with her own hands. God knows I sometimes felt the same way.

♦♦♦♦♦

I drained the last of my fourth cup of the day, the bitterness scratching my throat. The jitters were back. My wife had told me to switch to that mushroom coffee she swears by, and maybe she was right. Obviously, I needed to do something to stave off the headaches and eye twitches that came with drowning myself in caffeine.

Something moving by the front desk caught my eye. Two young people—barely into their twenties, I figured—stood talking to the clerk. The guy, tall and kind of geeky looking, wore dark, alternative clothes and had kind of a goth look to him. His friend, a nervous-looking woman, wrung her hands like she was reporting a stolen dog or some petty theft.

Nothing really made them stand out of a crowd, and I barely glanced at them. With bigger and more important things to deal with, I filed them in my mind as background noise.

"Whitney!"

My head snapped up as Jimmy called to me from the other side of the plate glass wall. He gestured to me to follow him into the office. Inside, José waited with Jimmy and four other investigators, all wearing that tight, hungry look you see when a case finally coughs up something worth chasing. Next to the kids at the front desk was Madeleine, of all people. Did she bring them here?

Jimmy held out a battered VHS cassette, the label smudged and bleeding ink. His voice was flat but electric:

"A couple of kids just dropped this off. They said it's connected to the case."

I blinked, stunned for a beat. My mind flicked back to the two twenty-somethings I'd seen talking with the station clerk just minutes ago. I hadn't thought twice about them then, but now all I wanted was to chase them down, shake their hands, and say "Thank you."

I was also dying to ask them a coupla hundred questions, but knew the desk sergeant would have their contact information. Seeing that tape, and determining how much of value was on it, was MUCH more important right now.

♦♦♦♦♦

I stared at the cassette, feeling like I'd been transported back to another era. "C'mon, Jimmy—nobody uses VHS tapes anymore," I muttered, skeptical. "Do we even have a player for this thing?"

Jimmy smirked, about to answer, when Amelia walked in—swagger in her step and a dusty old VCR player tucked under her arm like a trophy. Her hot pink and fire-orange hair clashed spectacularly with her crisp navy-blue uniform, but on her it looked good.

"We're way ahead of you," she said, full of self-assurance.

Amelia tinkered with the VCR, plugging it in and pushing buttons. She moved a few cables around to ensure they were in their correct spots and the connections were good. After a few false starts, the screen flickered blue, the VCR humming and clicking like a mechanical heart warming up.

♦♦♦♦♦

Amelia slid the tape into the unit, and a moment later the screen cut to black. Then came the sound—an ear-splitting burst of distorted organ music, warped by decades of wear. It crawled under my skin.

On the screen, a man appeared, standing at a pedestal, mid-sermon.

"Wait—WAIT! Pause it!" Jimmy barked.

The frame froze, a grainy portrait of the man's sharp features and self-satisfied stance.

I leaned in to get a better look, "Aeron Inochi?" I asked. I knew the name, but not much of the history, and wondered what this guy had to do with any of it. "What about him?"

Jimmy didn't hesitate. "This piece of trash has a rap sheet as long as your arm. He was a local conman back in the 2000s. He caused loads of trouble for years before that in Palm Springs. This dipshit was in an anarchist gang when he was a teenager, spray-painting walls, smashing storefronts, and even robbing a convenience store at gunpoint. We arrested him in '91, but some hotshot lawyer got him off with probation after he spent one day in a jail cell. I always felt he had potential to do a lot worse, but could never prove anything."

He continued "At the end of the day, all we were ever able to nail him for was the robbery, but I've been waiting for him to show up again. This guy is dirty. Trust me on this; he's very dirty."

♦♦♦♦♦

I watched the sheriff adjust his glasses as he continued. "But he did try to 'redeem' himself—if you could call it that—during his college years. He did some community service, and helped some organizations around the Palm Desert area. You know—easy stuff, like cleaning up the park."

Jimmy walked across the room to a metal file cabinet. Bending over, he reached into a drawer, pulled out a file, and returned to place it on the table. Opening the pale folder, he revealed over a dozen photos from over the past few decades, all showing the same man on the screen.

The photos were passed to me, one-by-one, and they didn't paint a pretty picture to the practiced eye. There was a mugshot of a teenage Aeron Inochi. Then a bunch of images as an adult over a period of years. This guy looked like a creep, though I recognized that looks can be deceiving.

Jimmy continued "He tried to run for office once, too. I mean, this guy is smart. He learned all about the law and politics, and saw that the real opportunity was to be in a position of power. He said he wanted to make changes for the better, but really all he wanted was a chance to stick someone else's money into his own pocket."

"And how did that go?" I asked sarcastically, even though I already had a feeling it wouldn't be good.

"Not well. The man was practically chased out of the city after he was raving about a 'cleansing' of people whom he deemed to be undesirable," Jimmy explained. "There was never a formal determination whether this was a psychotic episode or if he genuinely meant it."

I shook my head in disbelief, muttering "My bet's on the second theory!"

Sitting up as the words sunk into my brain, I turned hard towards Jimmy. "Undesirables? Like ethnic cleansing?" I asked.

"Just about," Jimmy replied, rubbing the back of his head. "This guy wanted to get rid of people with disabilities—autism, deafness, blindness...even amputees. The man was a perfectionist when it came to how he saw human beings. If you didn't measure up to what he thought of as perfection, he claimed you were a waste of skin."

"In other words, you're telling me he's a sociopath."

♦♦♦♦♦

Slowly I shuffled through the stack of photos, carefully examining every detail of Inochi's face, dress, bearing, and surroundings. Whenever he had a companion in an image, I'd pay particular attention to the way they were interacting; the men who were helping him, and the women serving him as if he were their superior.

There were no clues in his clothing, ranging from grimy to suits, but there was a smugness in his visage—a haughty, holier-than-thou feeling that emanated from his every pore—that made me angry. Choking, I spit out "How did a dirtbag like this get away from the authorities?"

Admittingly, I was more than a little annoyed that no one over at the desert city had bothered to set the guy straight long ago.

The answer I got wasn't very satisfying. "Well, the bottom line is the guy didn't cause legitimate harm to the people he had discriminated against at the time, so nobody in a position of authority had any jurisdiction to arrest him."

Leaning back and tilting my chair against the wall, I looked at the freeze frame of this creep and listened as Jimmy gingerly handed me a few more files.

"Inochi *did*, however, have a reputation of being a conman back in 2010. That was when he sold some 'holistic' healthcare items which actually caused someone to be taken to the hospital. But again—well—let's just say he got a good lawyer and got bailed out of the situation."

"And how did this piece of shit happen to have the money to hire that lawyer?" I wondered aloud.

"His family owned a successful succulent business a while back. I think it was called *Dry Bloom Botanics*, or something like that. His parents died—oh, I don't know—probably 12 years ago. They were driving a truckload of barrel cactus up from Cardonal down in Hidalgo state in Mexico and their truck got stuck on the train tracks right down the road here at Spring Street. The story that I heard was that they figured it was the middle of the night and they were worried about getting their merchandise to the shop for the weekend rush. I guess they forgot about the freight trains that run at that hour."

Jimmy shook his head sadly. "After the funeral it came out that he had inherited everything. He was the only child, and he got the house and the business and who knows what else. Next thing you know, from what we heard, he'd sold the lot and sunk it all into the old Sully Knight property up in Ramona."

"Why there?"

"Dunno. After Sully disappeared, it looks like Inochi just set up shop as if it were his own."

♦♦♦♦♦

José wasn't done, and offered me a business card to look at. "Those two kids who dropped off the video—they said this was the place it came from."

I grabbed the card and read it slowly: '***The Purity Mansion, 7667 Marigold Water Dr., Ramona, 92065.***'

Purity, my ass! This guy had "*dirty*" written all over him!

I still remembered the words that Madeleine's daughter had barely whispered in the emergency room. That small, weak voice quavered as it asked *"...Am I pure yet?"*

The unnerving phrase kept echoing and bouncing around the back of my head, and I steeled myself. "We need to send a unit up there fast. And let's get the wheels in motion to get a search warrant. How quickly can you prepare a probable-cause affidavit?"

"Well," Jimmy said, stroking his chin, "This is a complex case, but we're not really going on a fishing expedition. We're looking specifically for biological evidence, right? Anything else we find is a bonus, but you've got reason to believe this guy is tied to the bombings?"

"That, and maybe a couple of other things that have been going wrong around here. I'm looking for anything that ties Inochi to large supplies of bleach."

" Whitney, ya gotta figure it's gonna take a coupla hours just to prepare the affidavit. Then the judge could easily take a few hours on top of that, if he's got it in his mind to be difficult for any reason."

"We don't have time to be mucking around here, Jimmy. Who's the duty judge?"

"That would be Judge Weinberg," Jimmy replied.

"I know him," I smiled grimly. "He's a good guy, and he'll see reason in this case."

"Okay," he responded. "But you've got to figure it's gonna take us half-a-day to get the warrant in-hand. We'll call the Sheriff's office out in Ramona and give them a heads-up on what's coming, then ask them to send a car once the warrant has been issued."

I nodded, already anticipating we'd probably want to have more than a couple of cops there for the questioning. Besides, given this shit-for-brain's track record of slipping through the cracks, I didn't want anyone taking any unnecessary risks that they might get ambushed.

One thing I knew for certain was there'd be no funny business this time, and Aeron Inochi was going to explain himself. There was no question in my mind that lives were on the line.

Like me, it was just as personal to find enough evidence, lock up this guy, and throw away the key.

♦♦♦♦♦

Aeron Inochi's track record showed a derelict who was slippery. This meant stopping whatever he was doing was sure to be more difficult than we'd originally estimated. I stopped by to see Theresa at the station's research desk to see what else I could learn.

After the usual pleasantries, I outlined my challenge to her. "Do me a favor, would you?" I finished "and see what you can learn about this guy."

♦♦♦♦♦

Even as Theresa dug into the project, there were certain things I already knew. This was a man who would deny everything and blame the system or make it appear as the fault of the victims. I wouldn't be shocked if he still had money to buy a good lawyer, too.

I studied his profile a bit further. He was obviously very charismatic, so it seemed like a safe bet that Aeron Inochi had a lot of followers already under his spell. He was a real Svengali, this guy, and he reminded me in many ways of Charlie Manson back in his Helter Skelter days.

Now Manson - THERE was a nut case! Intensely charismatic, exerting extraordinary psychological control over his followers, and with an uncanny ability to read people, mirror their desires, and project authority, spirituality, and belonging. Anyone coming in contact with him was struck by the way he "persuaded" people using speech, music, and emotional manipulation. And his followers were so deeply loyal, they were willing to commit murder just because he asked them to.

What a bunch of fuckin' loonie tunes!

Yet like Manson, my guess was Inochi is able to persuade complete strangers to become loyal followers, ready to cover his backside despite any pain, turmoil or deceit his actions created.

And if the contents of this videotape were to be believed – and I was certain they should be—he was now tricking desperate parents into filicide—the unintentional killing of their own children.

Yeah, they apparently didn't get any lower than Aeron Inochi!

♦♦♦♦♦

Those words about the "cleansing" kept nagging at me. My gut told me this situation was sure to get worse than anyone was suggesting, and we needed to jump on this whole thing sooner, rather than later.

One thing I was certain of was that this wasn't some scammy product thrown together by some crude conman selling snake oil, but rather the actions of a pathetic and very sick man with ill intent. "Where did they find the tape, anyway?" I asked.

"Madeleine called and said that the girl—the nervous one who was in here a while ago—found it in the ruins of La Mesa. The girl said it felt to her as if someone intentionally set it there." José shrugged. "She wasn't sure how it got there either. She just asked us to play it, and said that she hoped it would help."

"Madeleine?"

Jimmy nodded. "Yeah. She's the one who sent them here, and even drove them over to ensure they'd get here. The woman did everything but hold their hands and walk them inside."

I was puzzled. I mean, how in the world did she find these kids? The last I'd seen her, she was taking care of her kids at the hospital, and now she's out playing Nancy Drew.

Then there was the tape itself. These kids drop out of nowhere with such a great clue to this mystery. It almost sounded *TOO* convenient.

"Not to mention the guy in black, who claimed there was an incident yesterday morning in a group home where two men from the same organization poisoned a friend of his," Jimmy continued, adding "This tracks with a report we got from Sharp Hospital that they had a patient with traces of bleach in his system, mainly affecting his lungs."

♦♦♦♦♦

It's a funny thing about criminal cases and conspiracies. Sometimes they resolve themselves, with the criminal "mastermind" doing something stupid, thinking they're smarter than the average bear, and virtually shouting from the rooftops who they are and what they've done. Other times it can take years before all the pieces add up and you're able to break the case wide open.

Then—every once in a great while—it seems as if someone is watching over us, virtually begging the police to get to them...and *fast.* Like someone trying to commit suicide, knowing full well they'll be stopped before they're successful, this kind of a situation seems like a cry for help.

And so it appeared here—that someone affiliated with this guy Inochi was leaving us a trail of breadcrumbs to help us stop him cold.

♦♦♦♦♦

"Should I continue with the tape?" It was Amelia asking, snapping me from my deep thoughts.

"Yeah, play the tape," Jimmy responded. We watched her press the play button and again started following along with the sermon. The man on the screen spoke like he was promoting a new laundry detergent, like those telemarketing ads you see late at night that keep telling you to "Call now!" and repeating a toll-free phone number so you can buy their product for $19.99.

And true to form came the product shot, showing the different sizes of the products that resembled vitamin bottles. It was available in pill or liquid form, in a bunch of different flavors, and they wanted you to buy today.

I made a mental note to call my friend Stephen at the FDA.

The screen shot cut to a woman standing at an ironing board, her toddler playing behind her. I leaned closer trying to identify the child on the screen. This kid looked eerily familiar, but I couldn't quite put my finger on why.

"Emmy Anise?" I blinked, I felt Jimmy and José next to me, I heard José gasp slightly and Jimmy grumbled "Yeah...that's her."

♦♦♦♦♦

The case of Emmy Anise had been a cold case for some time now, and Jimmy had been trying to solve it for almost five years. The poor kid had been found in a garbage can up in the Twin Oaks area, just north of San Marcos, and this video had obviously been shot prior to that.

Unfortunately, Emmy didn't survive the trip to the hospital, and the report was that she'd died under the care of the paramedics.

Jimmy had always suspected it was a crime planned by her parents, but there just wasn't enough DNA evidence to prove his theory. And it was odd that she was declared dead, since there was no blood or bruises. In fact, there were no scratches or wounds of any kind.

However, according to Jimmy the morticians had reported that she was inordinately pale and smelled of bleach.

Suddenly it dawned on me; Madeleine's kids, both lying in the hospital, had both reeked of the same chemical. Both of them had eyes with dull looks, as if they weren't "all there". Yet Madeleine's two children had somehow survived the attack.

As for Emmy Anise, she hadn't made it, and I felt ill the more I thought about how this strategy - killing people deemed "inferior" for some reason or another by those hardly in a position to make such a call - had been going on for such a long time. Worst of all, it had all been RIGHT under our noses, but we had never seen it.

That was the bad news. The good news was that we finally might have all the dots connected and be in a position to stop this horror show.

Jimmy briefly punched his fist into the wall, trying to control his outrage. "Dammit!" he hissed. He was understandably angry, wishing Emmy would've gotten more justice sooner.

"Jimmy," I called to him gently.

"The bastard's been doing this shit for YEARS!" he screamed. "She was a *CHILD*, for Chrissake! A fucking child!"

"I get your frustration."

"Frustration? I'm LIVID!" he yelled. "The judge released a convicted felon known to be a disability-hating weirdo, and this piece of shit turned around and killed a kid. Who could have seen THAT coming?!"

I understood the source of Jimmy's sarcasm. "I mean if that's not evidence, then I don't know what that is. Emmy's mother needs to go down, and so does Aeron."

I tried talking him off the ledge. "We don't exactly know if she was aware of her daughter being poisoned. Even if she did, we'd still need more evidence to prove it in court."

♦♦♦♦♦

Silence fell upon the room as we all stared at the photo of the child who had died too soon, though I took some comfort knowing that—even if we couldn't necessarily prove Emmy's mother's guilt—we most likely finally had Aeron Inochi locked up.

Either way, it was definitely time to have a chat with Mr. Inochi.

"Damn fucker, that's a child..." Jimmy mumbled.

I turned to José. "What else do we have?"

José shrugged. "Other than this tape, we've got nothing." José looked at the recent pictures he had plucked from a newer folder he had—pulling out a crumbled old paper. "But I think one of the kids—the goth kid who came with the girl—found a warehouse near Main Street in Lemon Grove. He said two men chased him out of there, but he managed to snatch this list. Only we weren't sure if it meant anything."

I leaned in to decipher the messy writing, made worse by the crumpled paper. It was a list of chemicals and extracts, making me even more eager to search that particular building.

"We may need to look in that place to see what else turns up." I stated. "I'm guessing we'll find some clues about the recent chemical attacks around the city."

"Y'know," Amelia added, "There was some reporter nosing around here recently about the La Mesa explosion. He was talking about doing a newspaper story, but decided he needed more after he had seen a video recording from that day."

"He give you a name?"

"Pete Ross," she said blandly.

"That sleazebag from downtown?" Jimmy questioned with his brow raised. "What footage did he see? What have we missed?"

"It was from a security camera that we had overlooked," Amelia shrugged. "He said something about people wearing white might've planted the bombs. He was suggesting it was some purity cult who might've caused it all."

♦♦♦♦♦

Running over my conversation with Madeleine's daughter, I realized that people wearing white was definitely a pattern to this whole thing. Now I really wanted to see that footage from the explosion. "Do we have the footage for that?"

"We do, but it's currently in Kearny Mesa at the Crime Laboratory," José responded, "Some of the film is damaged from the heat of the explosion. And the imagery is so disturbing that none of the media is willing to release it to the public."

My sense of urgency was taking over, feeling how close we were getting. "Let's hotfoot it over there; I want to review that piece of evidence NOW!"

Jimmy nodded. "I won't be surprised if Aeron's a part of this too."

"So, Aeron Inochi is expanding into other areas," I ruminated. "Isn't that charming?"

Chapter 21: True Intentions

-Juniper

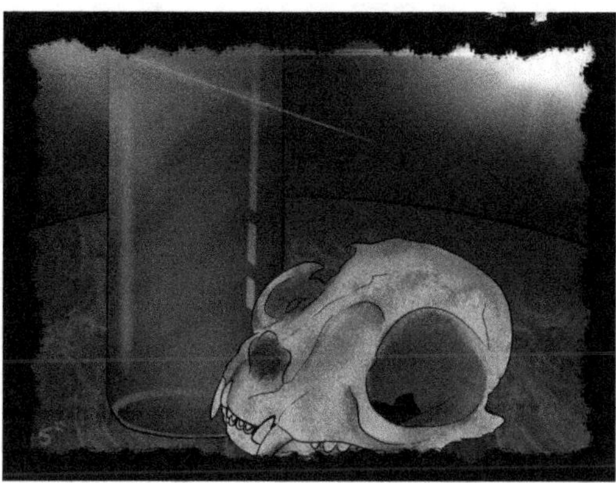

"It's getting late. Where *is* he?" I muttered as I waited for the rest of the family to return to our sanctuary. Aeron and the others were out longer than I had expected, and it was practically dark out.

They were most likely making funeral arrangements for Mune and Brady, I figured. Or maybe the police had picked them up for more questioning?

Who could say for certain? All I knew was they were supposed to have been back here around 7pm, and here it was almost 9 and they were nowhere in sight.

This couldn't be good!

I rubbed my fingers on the texture of the paper, and...

"Ow!" Damned paper cut! Instinctively pulling my hand back, I sensed the nick in my skin as blood started rising from the small wound.

There were too many distractions for me to focus properly. What was Aeron up to? Were we doing the right things? The shock from both Mune and Brady's deaths yesterday.

I mean holy shit, what the hell was going on here?

Jasmine walked by, her face plastered with as much worry as mine was. Knowing Aeron had spoken with her earlier, I called out "How is he?"

She sighed and ran dainty fingers through her hair. "It's hard to say. I haven't seen anything like this before."

A door slammed open, startling us both. Already on my feet and heading towards the front door, I cried out hopefully. "Aeron?"

My shoes clapped against the porcelain tile as the large front door came into sight. WHAT a relief to have him back. Only he looked dog-tired and totally drained, and I was almost tempted to say that Aeron—my beautiful Aeron—looked TERRIBLE!

My smile faded. "Aaron? Is everything all right?" I suspected he'd been drinking again. Then again, given the stress from yesterday's events, who could have blamed him for needing some kind of release?

Aeron swallowed. "No..." was all he said.

♦♦♦♦♦

I wasn't sure what else to do. Poor Aeron had started his day with the cops coming by to pepper him with several dozen questions. They'd kept him in a locked room for over an hour, harassing him about a video he had made years ago.

I mean, who do these guys think they are? Here he was dealing with the loss of two of our family members, and these bastards couldn't even let him grieve. Whatever it was they wanted to know, you'd think it could have waited for another couple of days.

It's not like Aeron was going to leave town or anything. He just wanted to live his life in peace, and share that peace with others around him.

"They died a few days apart from when..." he swallowed, a tear at the corner of his eye. "The anniversary of when Ruby passed..."

I hadn't made that connection, and felt my heart shatter. "Is...is there anything..."

He shook his head sadly. "No. There's nothing you can do at this moment."

"Please, Aeron," I pleaded "You need to know I'm here for you. I want to help you."

He slowly looked at me with weary eyes; drunk, heartbroken, and reeking of cigarette smoke.

Funny...I thought he had quit smoking a long time ago. Still, this tragedy of losing our members must have taken a bigger toll on him than I had realized.

"Maybe..." he croaked.

"Yes? Yes, anything!" I was practically begging to do anything possible to make sure he didn't spiral out of control.

Aeron took me by the hand, his knees unsteady. "Only I'm not sure you're ready for this..."

"Please! I *am* ready! I will do whatever you need me to do!"

"Anything?"

"ANYTHING!"

Aeron paused before forcefully grabbing my hand. This was very unusual for him, so I knew whatever it was had to be very important. "Come with me," he said, leading me into the taxidermy room.

Jasmine stood there watching us head down the hall as Aeron closed the door behind us and locked it. He whipped a lighter from his pocket and lit the incense on the table, as if he'd known this moment would come and he wanted to be prepared. The scent of cheap Egyptian musk and jasmine burning filled the air as Aeron gestured for me to sit on the sofa. Turning down the lights, he sat inordinately close to me, fumbling in his jeans pocket for something he obviously wanted to share.

Aeron took my hand and lay it on top of his knee. Into my open palm he pressed a pill and, with a sickly grin, instructed me, "Swallow this. It's like nothing you've ever felt before, and you're going to love it."

As I reached for a cup of water conveniently placed on the side table, Aeron picked up a remote and turned on Barry White on the nearby stereo.

♦♦♦♦♦

It didn't take long for the little pink pill to take effect. The music grew louder, the colors in the room more vivid, and my body began to feel weightless. I think I giggled, my cheeks flushing as I sank into the plush couch cushions. Aeron sat beside me, his eyes never leaving mine as he leaned in close. "Just relax, let it happen," he murmured, stroking my hair gently.

It was puzzling, but my limbs soon felt like they were made of jelly. Those tingling sensations washing over me didn't quite make sense, but I was struggling with blurry vision and couldn't quite concentrate as Aeron's hand moved from my hair to my shoulder, his fingers tracing patterns on my skin that seemed to set my nerves on fire. I squirmed, unsure of what to do or say, my mind racing with a mix of excitement and confusion.

He was closer to me than anyone had ever been, and I was on the verge of panic, even as my brain absorbed him repeatedly saying "relax." His breath, sour and hot, coated my skin like smoke in a sealed room. When he touched me, my first instinct was to pull away, but he was stronger, heavier, and his hands clamped down on my arms like iron.

♦♦♦♦♦

My brain kept telling me to get out of there fast, but Aeron was having none of it. His touch grew bolder as his hands roamed all over my body, providing me with a strange mix of fear and curiosity. I wanted to protest, but coherent thinking seemed to be a thing of the past. I weakly asked, "Aeron, what's going on?" though my words must have gotten lost in the pounding bass of the music.

Aeron leaned in closer, his breath hot against my ear. "It's okay, Juney. I'll take care of you," he whispered, as he began unbuttoning my blouse. My heart hammered in my chest with a dull throb that seemed to echo through the room. The panic was rising now, a cold hand squeezing my insides, but I couldn't push him away. My body was a traitor, responding to his touch despite the screaming inside my head. It was like I was in sleep paralysis, except the shadow demon was real—touching me—and I couldn't fight back.

There were no words that I could conjure to describe what he was doing to me at that moment. Nothing that my mind could understand to explain why my body ached and my insides wailed for help, even though my mouth couldn't seem to make any sound at all. The mush that had until recently been my brain tried to make sense of it. Was this how people showed anger? Or grief? Was this some kind of punishment? What had I done wrong?

♦♦♦♦♦

Aeron continued undressing me and my thoughts were a jumbled mess, his hands moving with a confidence that I just couldn't comprehend. I'd never been with anyone before—though my inexperience was a secret I had always guarded fiercely—and I was happy that way.
And an understandable horror swept over me as I realized I was about to lose my virginity to someone I had trusted to protect me. Sure, I had told him for years that I loved him, but he'd always been happy with the way I pleased him. I hadn't wanted this with anyone, and had always managed to successfully sidestep this moment.

But here I was trapped in a nightmare where I couldn't cry out, couldn't fight back, couldn't even move. I thought back to the times he'd kissed me when I'd first shown up in the community, always telling me how I was his favorite and how important I was to him.

And yeah, I'd been both a little hurt and confused when he'd chosen one of the other girls to share his special gifts with, even though I was secretly relieved that I didn't have to deal with "*that*."

But now he was acting much more aggressively, and his gentle kisses were nowhere to be seen, now replaced by sloppy kisses that were less of passion than of something feeling darker and more predatory. He was taking what he wanted without regard to whether or not I wanted it too; forcing himself on me, bruising my lips and knocking my teeth with his own. I was trying to pull back from him, and he was hurting me, holding me in place much harder than I'd ever been held.

Why, Aeron, why? Can't we just go back to the way things were before?

♦♦♦♦♦

As Aeron pushed me further into the couch, I could feel the weight of his body pressing down on me, the fabric of his jeans rough against my bare skin. My eyes widened in terror as I tried focusing on anything but the cold, hard reality of what was happening. My thoughts scattered like frightened birds, and I went somewhere else in my head, somewhere quieter.

I stared at the poster of a serene waterfall on the wall, the sound of the rushing water seeming to drown out the horrors now facing me at the hands of my beloved Aeron. Then I glanced at the animal skulls right under the poster; dead creatures kept as trophies, their bones frozen in time. To keep my mind off the reality that I was being taken against my will by this man who had always been my everything, I tried looking at every detail and texture of each bone.

It was no use.

The pain was too much to ignore. Aeron's face was a twisted mask of lust above me, his eyes glazed over as he whispered sweet nothings that were anything but. And I felt my mind disconnect from my body, floating somewhere above the room, watching the scene unfold as if it were happening to someone else.

It was the only way I could survive the agony. The minutes stretched into hours, or so it seemed, as he used me in ways I'd never imagined nor thought possible. My clothes lay in a pile at the foot of the sofa as he climbed atop me, his pants around his ankles scratching my bare legs. He was going to take everything from me because he wanted to, and that was the end of the discussion.

Each thrust brought a fresh wave of pain, but both my brain and my body were too numb to feel anything but a dull ache. My thoughts grew distant, a haze that hovered around the edges of consciousness.

Aeron kept muttering. "Oh Junie," and "You look just like her." The longer he went on, the faster and harder he pushed into me. My pain, my fears, my feelings, my involuntary tears...none of these seemed to mean anything to him.

All he felt was an animal urgency, and all I felt was devastation. And when it was finally over, all I could do was to lay there, trembling and violated. I lay still, as if pretending not to exist might make it all untrue. And I'll admit that I didn't cry—not because it didn't hurt, but because I didn't know that crying was an option.

♦♦♦♦♦

His breathing heavy and sated, Aeron finally pulled away.

I lay there feeling like a significant portion of my very being had been stolen from me. The room tilted, with colors bleeding together into something nauseating and unreal. My body felt like the remnants of a Salvador Dali painting, rather than something that belonged to me. My very essence had been ripped from my soul, though I didn't have the right words to describe it.

Only the ache and the absence.

Laying there, bereft of a will to live, I knew my world had just been changed in ways that I never could have imagined. Aeron—the one person I had trusted more than anyone on the planet—had just robbed me of something that could never be given back.

I suddenly hated him. It was my final thought as I felt a chill wind pass over my exposed flesh. Aeron was up and around doing heaven knew what and just left me to pass out on the sofa; naked, vulnerable, and feeling decidedly alone.

♦♦♦♦♦

There was a pounding in my head as I woke up from the sudden blackout. God, I felt so sick!

Questions swirled through my brain as I struggled to focus and determine what had happened in my ordered little world. Why had I awakened on the sofa in Aeron's private room? Why were my clothes torn and lying on the floor? And why did I feel so ill, so numb, so dizzy and disoriented?

It was incredibly dark outside, and the lights in the room were as dull as my mind, leaving me with zero idea what time it was. In the shadows I could see Aeron's collection of taxidermied animals, their still faces staring at me. Did I detect pity in their glance at whatever I had just endured?

"Don't worry, she won't remember this."

It was Aeron's voice, wafting over to me from somewhere across the room. He was talking to...gosh, I couldn't even tell at first...but the voice sounded vaguely familiar. "*Tom,*" I thought, struggling to place it.

"Are you going to leave her here?"

"No, I can move her back into her room. But for now we need to figure out where that damn tape was." There was a lot of clinking and clattering as things were getting shoved around, as if Aeron was anxiously searching.

"What do you mean?"

"The cassette. The video I made back in the early 2000s about the prototype for the miracle cure. It's not in my files. Who the fuck took it?" Aeron muttered angrily.

"Odd. Do you think someone misplaced it?"

"Fuck, I don't know!" Aeron was obviously frustrated. "We can't let anyone find that tape. It has the raw, unedited footage of the original commercial..."

♦♦♦♦♦

Despite my dazed state, Aeron had piqued my curiosity. With my body too heavy to move, I sunk into the seats of the cushions and focused hard on every word and every sound being made. Aeron obviously figured I was still unconscious, making this a perfect opportunity to eavesdrop.

"First, one of those people from a group home chased away Brady and Mune—that little turd might even be responsible for them both dying—and now this!" It was the angriest and most belligerent that I'd ever seen him, and his next statement confirmed what I'd begun to suspect. "If that cassette is examined by anyone from the outside world, our community will be ruined!"

Ruined? There was an interesting choice of words.

Tom was further considering the situation. "Hopefully it didn't go far, Aeron. I'm sure that Juniper can help you find the document when she wakes up, and..."

At the mention of my name, Aeron's tone grew cold. "It's a videotape, not a document. And Juniper doesn't need to know about this. She was already confused enough about the explosion we did in La Mesa, I'm not even sure if her strategy of spreading the word about our cause is working anymore. I don't want her to question it further like Linda did..."

"If you insist. What's our next move, then?"

Aeron paused. The silence in the room was thick as he mulled over the options.

"We'll just have to find whoever speaks out against us and deal with it ourselves." Looking over the back of the sofa, I watched Aeron take a swig from the glass of wine he was holding. He cleared his throat before continuing. "The way I see it, the worst case scenario is we'd have to destroy everything and start over from scratch. Besides, there's a good chance the cops could be arresting folks soon."

"Then perhaps," Tom suggested, "now would be a good time for us to find a new home."

The two men rose, Tom following Aeron as he stormed out of the room to make a hasty search for the missing videotape.

A cold, dark look had passed over Aeron's face, and for the first time in all the years I'd known him he'd completely lost the friendly, cozy, comforting look he always reserved for every member of our family. His warmth had instead been replaced by an uncompromising disdain, and it suddenly struck me that this organization—indeed, our entire family—perhaps wasn't as welcoming as I'd always considered it to be.

Tom turned out the light, leaving me lying there on the sofa—my limbs splayed for all the world to see—as I sunk back into the sweet oblivion of sleep.

♦♦♦♦♦

The next morning I found myself waking up in my room, as if I'd been teleported there from the sofa or last night's experience hadn't actually happened. But my awful nausea couldn't just be explained away, and my head pounded. Added to my body aching as if I had been hit by a freight train, and all I could figure was that Aeron had carried me back to my room as he'd suggested to Tom.

Today my room felt colder and less vibrant than usual. Glancing at my phone as I heard a '*PING*' —I groaned in pain. The sound gave me a headache, and the sudden jerking of my head made me feel like someone had ripped my brain out of my skull before casually tossing it back into place.

I'd definitely had better days.

Sluggishly, I reached for the device and looked at the notification. It was from Beatrice.

"Hey Juniper! Me and our new recruit Andy are going to head down near Spring Valley today. We're going to meet two people today and bring them back here! You wanna join us? I could use the help."

Slowly, I sat up. Every cell in my body was on fire, letting me know it was *not* happy with me and how I'd behaved last night. And now this. I mean, how was I supposed to respond to that? Of course I would come along for the ride, and try to be as cheery as always...though I was pretty sure I wasn't going to be happy about it.

And yet I felt so awful that I just knew I'd vomit the moment I sat up. My reality had been shattered, and my heart was broken. Listening to Aeron and Tom last night, I now recognized the lies I'd been spewing on the family's behalf for the past ten years. My commitment to the Purity Syndicate didn't mean anything, and the way Aeron had treated me last night proved I didn't mean anything to him either.

This was a bitter truth—one that was hard to swallow and for me to accept. For now I recognized the truth of the entire situation: the Purity Syndicate was actually no different—no better—than the horrid Baptist church that I had run away from so many years ago.

One could even argue it was worse!

♦♦♦♦♦

I texted back to Beatrice, "Yeah, of course, just give me a few minutes," even as I struggled against the lurching in my stomach amidst my difficulties in standing up straight. Part of me wished I could say '*no, sorry, but you'd better go without me*' so I could just take the day lying in bed and recovering.

But after a decade I knew that nobody was ever allowed to be idle around here. We all had to always be moving the family's needs forward, and sloth wasn't allowed under any circumstances.

Besides, after what had happened last night, I didn't want to be around Aeron. It's not that I was afraid of him, but I suspected I'd say or do the wrong thing and make him angry at me. And even though I knew I hadn't done anything wrong, I still didn't want to make him angry.

Slowly I sat up, afraid to move too fast lest I retch onto my comforter. With Beatrice waiting for me, it would be hours before I'd be able to clean up a mess like that, and that was the *last* thing I needed right now.

So I forced myself to stand, slowly pulling on my nice denim jeans and my spotless white dress shirt, and appreciated the irony. Because after last night, I suddenly didn't feel qualified to wear white anymore.

I'll confess that prior to that moment I'd never thought I'd hate the color white, but now it had taken on a whole different meaning for me. Tightening my leather belt, I pulled on a pair of lace socks, suddenly feeling gross as I realized how infantile they looked.

And in a heroic effort to look normal, I brushed my hair and spritzed on some strawberry perfume. That was something else I was starting to hate, and in an act of defiance I refused to wear my usual strawberry lipgloss, convinced that just putting it on would probably make me gag.

Staggering a bit, I made my way out the door. It felt awkward to walk outside in this condition, pretending as if nothing in my world had changed. And fortunately, I didn't see Aeron before I left. I didn't know where he was, and at the moment I didn't really care.

♦♦♦♦♦

The 45-minute drive felt a bit awkward. This guy Andy was new, and I didn't want to be bringing up difficult subjects in front of him. Besides, I didn't know how to bring up what I now knew or suspected...or if Beatrice would even believe me.

Given my state of mind, I was in no mood to be talkative in the car. The passing cars were enough to hold my attention, and I pleaded having a headache when Beatrice tried to engage me. Watching the motion of the buildings and vehicles sliding by was more than enough for me to handle.

From chaparral to small towns to the highway leading to the heart of San Diego, I had little to say to either Beatrice or Andy. All I could hear was the gentle hum of the car moving, buzzing under their idle chit chat and giggling. My responses were limited to small periodic smiles, hopefully timed to make it appear that I was actively listening to everything going on around me.

We finally stopped at a place that looked abandoned, and I was pretty sure I'd never be able to locate it on a map. Stepping out of the car, I took a deep breath, felt nauseous, and tried to hold it together and just get through the day. 'Is this place part of Spring Valley?' I wondered.

As I stood there, Beatrice began unloading several items from the car's trunk. Ropes, a bottle of some clear liquid, and some other stray parts I couldn't identify. Glancing around, I recognized some of the apartment buildings and abandoned storefronts from the nearby suburbs, which looked strangely like pictures I'd seen in the news.

We were in Lemon Grove...but why?

"Um, Bea...this isn't Spring Valley," I said.

She nodded. "Aeron told me we should drop off a few things," Beatice replied curtly. I blinked, confused less by the errand than by the location. Beatrice picked up the bottle and the rope, indicating three canvas bags that needed to also be carried. "Get those for me, will you?"

Andy picked up two of them, the contents straining the seams of the bags, while I grabbed the third one. Beatrice was already 20 feet ahead, heading down the hill to some unknown destination.

♦♦♦♦♦

A warehouse appeared around a corner, its facade framed by flowers making it look like something from a movie set. The door stood ajar, as if waiting to swallow us up for lunch. Unhesitatingly Beatrice walked in, giving the distinct impression she knew exactly what she was doing and where she was going. Andy sauntered after her, struggling to keep the bags upright and saying "OW!" every time one of them banged against his legs.

But I thought it odd that this was a building I'd never seen before. Apparently, I wasn't completely in the loop on what was going on in the family, and there were things someone felt it was better for me to be ignorant about.

♦♦♦♦♦

It was cold and musty inside, and cobwebs hung from the ceiling like some eerie lace ribbons and thin threads. Clutter was everywhere, and a desk stood in the corner covered with papers. Shelves with tiny labels, cans, bottles, and boxes were everywhere, and a historian might have said it looked like we were preparing for the invasion of Normandy.

A pang of desire to clean the place up and make it look nice nudged the back of my brain, though I forced myself to ignore it.

Beatrice hadn't stopped until we reached a storage room on the far side of the warehouse. It was full of oxygen tanks and countless gallon bottles of clear liquid, all tightly sealed. The room reeked of bleach, and was instantly identifiable the moment I got near the building's entrance.

My eyes were tearing from the stench of bleach, and I couldn't walk the last few feet. Sitting at the desk, I left it to Beatrice and Andy to retrieve the rest of the supplies from the car and carry everything—including my burden—into the store room.

♦♦♦♦♦

I sat with my eyes closed, thinking some fresh air might be nice...if only I had the energy to get up and walk outside. However, inertia had taken over and I just sat there, staring without focusing.

Beatrice and Andy returned and she came to my shoulder to whisper in my ear. "Are you okay?" I nodded. "You sit here. We won't be long," she reassured me.

Andy patted my shoulder, prompting me to open my eyes. That's when I saw the receipts for bleach, sodium hypochlorite, and a bunch of other chemicals. Several samples of FDA approval stickers sat on the table before me, with notations on how to make them appear more authentic.

Next to these was a note with a list of locations, some of which—including "La Mesa" —were checked off. In purple ink was a handwritten note of the same date the "accidental" explosion had happened.

Ready to vomit, I jumped to my feet, stumbled back and instantly knew the truth. This group—my family—was nothing more than a bunch of murderers. And our entire objective was to promote OUR group, regardless of whose lives we ruined along the way.

HOLY FUCK! How messed up was this?

♦♦♦♦♦

Andy tapped me on the shoulder, interrupting my train of thought and causing me to jump. "Hey, Juniper, we need to hurry up. We don't want anyone else to see what we're doing here."

Beatrice was eyeing me with concern. "What's going on, Juniper? You don't look so good."

I turned towards their confused faces. These were people I thought I could trust, but suddenly I wasn't so sure I could trust anyone. Do I confront them? Did they even know what was going on here, or were they just playing messenger for Aeron's nefarious tasks?

As I opened and closed my mouth like a fish trying to breathe out of water, we were interrupted by unfamiliar voices.

"This is where you found the chemical and those notes?"

"Yeah. It's weird that they don't even lock up their things–"

At the open door stood three people, framed by the daylight pouring in through the warehouse's entrance. We looked at each other across the expanse of the room like we were frozen in time.

My eyes adjusted to the bright light to show me an older man wearing a rumpled sports jacket. With him was a twenty-year-old goth guy dressed in black from head-to-toe and a girl about the same age with soft boho colors.

"Ooooh shit," the goth guy muttered.

Chapter 22 - Nabbed

-Damian-

We all stood there, frozen in our tracks. It was like deja vu all over again...only worse.

The other three people glanced back at us. One of the girls wore jeans, but the other two were fully dressed in white, so that kinda tracked. Given our earlier experiences, both Sofia and I knew we weren't safe from these freaks after all...no matter how nice a face they tried to put on things.

The evil memories made me gulp as we looked across the chasm of the warehouse room at a guy and two girls about Sofia's age, or maybe a bit older. They stared back at us, and the room held its breath as the guy clumsily pulled a gun from his belt.

One of the girls stopped him, glancing back at us with a forced grin plastered on her face. Her reaction was obviously put on expressly to smooth over a tense situation, and was the furthest thing from sincere that I'd ever seen. "Hello," she chimed, "We didn't expect visitors. My name is Beatrice, and this is Andy and Juniper."

The guy—Andy—waved nervously with his left hand as he shoved the gun back into his belt with the right. The girl with the jeans looked like she would have rather been getting a root canal than standing in this room.

"Visitors?" said the guy in the rumpled sports jacket, cocking an eyebrow. His name was Robyn, and he had come along to guard us, taking notes every step of the way. The guy was definitely a cop, and I gathered he was friends with Madeleine. When I had told him about the abandoned warehouse I was chased out of, he had only said two things: "Could you find it again?" and, when I said I could, he simply said "Let's go."

So here we were, the three of us. We'd wandered through the streets of Lemon Grove as I tried to find my way back to that horrific place where two men in white had tried to kill me the day before. And we walked around aimlessly until I remembered the stairwell where I'd met Madeleine, and Robyn brightened up. "I know that stairwell," he reported.

Half-pulling, half-pushing, he led us to the stairwell, and from there it was relatively easy for me to retrace my steps. Not a half-block away I spotted the correct building which—interestingly—had its front door ajar. And with these three characters inside, I began to understand why.

♦♦♦♦♦

Even as he kept a careful eye on the guy with the gun, Robyn addressed the girl who appeared to be the leader. "Is this some club of yours?"

"Well, yeah," said the guy, a little too eagerly. "We are part of the Pur..."

"A club. Yeah, we're a club!" Beatrice interrupted. Andy gave her a sidelong glance indicating his confusion at being cut off. After all, wasn't the whole idea to get the word out about what they were doing?

Beatrice continued. “We’re a community that helps the needy, homeless and the people with addiction.” Despite her bright expression, it seemed pretty obvious she was hiding something—perhaps quite a bit.

To my mind she was a terrible liar. There was a lot that wasn’t being said, though I decided to leave it to Robyn to suss it out.

“Uh-huh,” was all that Officer Robyn said. Yeah, he was no more convinced than I was. Something definitely stunk in this place, and it wasn’t anything that could be cured by breaking a bottle of perfume.

“It’s odd,” Robyn continued, “to have an abandoned warehouse be the location of your club meeting. I mean, this is literally the middle of nowhere. What’s the name of your group?”

The woman ignored his question. “Think what you like, but we belong here and you don’t,” she said, getting agitated. “We’re just here to take out a few of our belongings, and we will be on our way.”

It was more than I could bear. “What are you taking?” I asked suddenly.

She turned to follow the sound of my voice. “Just some boxes of candy. My boss has an insatiable sweet tooth, and he’s found that if he keeps too much of this stuff around the house, he’ll eat it all and get fat.”

“Of course,” Officer Robyn smiled. “This makes perfect sense. So you’re helping your boss to moderate his behavior by enforcing some portion control.”

“Exactly!” she responded, visibly relaxing.

Robyn walked in front of us by a few steps. Even as I prepared to follow him, Sofia stayed behind and tugged on the back of my T-shirt. It was almost like she sensed an attack about to happen.

“It’s funny that you would store your candies in a place where you have all these chemicals on the shelves. Aren’t you afraid the candy could get damaged?”

Beatrice put on her most charming face. “Nah. We keep everything safely separated. Besides, those aren’t ours. A guy my boss knows runs this place, and we just keep a few packages here.”

“I get it,” Robyn responded, turning to me and Sofia. “Well then, we should be on our way. Miss Madeleine is going to be waiting for us.”

Robyn indicated the open door with his eyes and started to ease us back out into the outside world.

-POP-POP-

The moment Officer Robyn had turned his back, Andy pulled the gun and shot him in the leg. Sofia shrieked as she heard the noise and Robyn crumpled to the floor. And in the time it took for me to realize what was happening, Sofia and I found ourselves staring down the barrel of the same gun.

We froze. Sofia hid her face as if she was praying this madman didn’t shoot us.

I started to reach for the radio. “I need to call for an ambulance,” I suggested, but the crazy in white was having none of it. Instead he pointed the gun at my face and waved the barrel away from Robyn. His message—for me to back off—was quite clear.

The blonde girl in the jeans shrieked at the guy with the gun. “ANDY, WHAT WAS THAT ABOUT!?”

"I just did what Aeron told me to do!" Andy shrugged.

"I- WHAT!? When did he tell you to start shooting?"

"He told me there were to be no witnesses. I trust what Aeron says." He then turned to her suspiciously. "Don't you?"

♦♦♦♦♦

I was desperate to flee, but felt frozen in place. The weapon was pointed at us once more, and with Robyn on the floor and in danger of bleeding out, we were trapped.

Sofia's eyes brimmed with tears and looked desperately for a place to hide. I kept glancing at the walkie-talkie at Robyn's side, knowing full-well that one wrong move and we were all done for. My heart threatened to explode from my chest, and I increasingly regretted bringing Sofia into today's mess.

"So what do we do with them?" It was the blonde one speaking in a shaky voice. "We can call the ambulance so we..."

The other woman shook her head hard. "No. We have to take them with us. We can't have any bodies here at the warehouse. *He* wouldn't like it."

"How do we keep them from bringing more attention?"

It was Andy, but before anyone could answer the blonde tried again. "Or maybe the ambulance?"

"No, he's right," the other one coldly replied. "We can't have anyone else notice what's going on."

The blonde looked at the two of them as if they had suddenly grown multiple eyes. "We can't just leave a cop bleeding out here!"

The other woman was done being patient. “Juniper, please! We *HAVE* to do what Areon says!”

Andy approached us, stepping over Robyn while cocking and uncocking the hammer of the gun. Fuck! I’m only 20, and this was how I was going to die?

Only while Andy was focused on us, I heard Robyn weakly croaking into the walkie-talkie. “S-sheriff, we need b-backup...suspect with a gun and keeping our witnesses hostage”

-POP-

“AH!” I heard Sofia scream as she clutched onto me. And without warning I felt something pressed onto my face—a cloth that smelled sweet and odd. And even as I flailed under the tight grip holding the cloth to my face, I got dizzy and everything went black in incredibly slow motion.

The last thing I heard was Sofia screaming my name, then someone above her seemed to apologize, as if giving Sofia comfort.

“Please...forgive me...”

Chapter 23: Getting Out Of Dodge

-Sofia-

The first thing I tasted when I woke up was blood on my tongue. I took a deep breath as my eyes snapped open, confirming I was both wide awake and bound by rope. The firm fibers clung tightly to my flesh, digging in and burning my skin. Thrashing, I realized my ankles were also bound, either with a zip tie or duct tape. My sides hurt, and I kicked...only to land on something soft.

A muffled scream reinforced my suspicion that I wasn't alone. It also confirmed for me how difficult it is to yell for help when one has a gag in their mouth.

Another muffled shout echoed and I listened carefully, only to realize it was Damian's voice. I made a mental note to apologize for kicking him, provided we ever got out of this alive.

For now, though, we were trapped...and by the feel of the air we weren't in the warehouse any longer. Lifting my head as far as my bonds would permit, I saw a series of taxidermied animals staring at me, their black, beady, lifeless eyes making me feel like we were the prey.

Damian's muffled panting through his nose told me he was okay, though perhaps a bit panicky. I yelped, the sharp burn from the rope going up a notch as he tugged, both of us realizing his wrists were tied to my ankles...and vice-versa.

Whoever had tied us was evil, putting us in a tug of war and unable to stand, sit, or roll. All that was left was for us to lie there, for fear of hurting each other.

♦♦♦♦♦

To this day I still don't know how Damian was able to work the handkerchief out of his mouth. He must have chewed, pushed it with his tongue, then chewed it some more while ripping it with his teeth. Some of it no doubt got swallowed.

All I did know for certain, though, was that he was suddenly going from making completely unintelligible sounds to speaking clearly, albeit with an obviously sore throat.

"Sofia!?"

The only sound I could make with that damned gag in my mouth was "Hm!?", though for all Damian knew, I could have been reciting the Declaration of Independence. I yelled with the handkerchief and must have done something right, because my twisting, turning, and physically rebelling loosened the handkerchief enough that a piece of it fell off my mouth. I didn't know if it wasn't tied on well or the material of the cloth was weak, nor did I particularly care. All that mattered was that we could now communicate.

"Damian? Where are we now?"

"Dunno..." he said as we both glanced around the room. It was dark outside, the faint lamp lights from outside only dimly lit up the colored glass windows. We were prisoners, or hostages, or whatever you wanted to call it. All I knew was I had no idea where we were, Robyn was dead, and we were in deep shit.

Panting through my nose, I tried to hold it together. This was *NOT* how I wanted to go out; not like this!

"Sofia, wait. Hold on!" Damian whispered urgently, as we both heard noises from the outside. Some people were arguing, or maybe it was a sermon. The blood was pounding so loud in my ears that I really wasn't sure of anything anymore.

I was also pretty sure that Damian didn't know what was happening, either. I glanced at the windows again, watching the gathering gloom. It seemed like it had been hours since our capture, and something—there was that damned little voice in the back of my head—told me that calling for help at this moment would probably have the exact opposite effect.

Tears came to my eyes as I sighed "Perhaps this is it, huh?"

♦♦♦♦♦

Damian didn't answer for a few seconds. "Maybe..." he said, sounding kind of defeated. "I just feel like shit for dragging you into this."

Part of me wanted to agree with him, to agree bluntly that it was all his fault that I was lying here about to die.

But the smarter half of my brain recognized that Damian had just wanted to help. So rather than busting his chops, I instead remarked "Well, at least the cops believed us."

Damian couldn't look back at me and just stared at the ground instead. "Do you think they know where we are?"

"I'm guessing not. Those bastards shot Robyn." I swallowed.

That horrid memory flicked in my brain to the moment that had happened too quickly. I could still see Robyn lying on the floor of the warehouse, bleeding from his leg, and hearing that last bullet as he tried calling the sheriff before going silent.

That was before the chloroform, the ropes, the gags. It felt as if they had been prepared for us; knew we'd be there and wanted to make sure there were...

What had that guy Andy said? "He told me there were to be no witnesses."

Fuck! *WE* were witnesses!

♦♦♦♦♦

There was no way this ended well for us, I figured. Pausing, I swore I heard...gunshots?

That's when I wet my pants!

Were they practicing? Or was there someone in that other room who also saw stuff they shouldn't have seen? "You hear that too, right?" I whispered to Damian.

"Yeah..." Damian's voice cracked in a higher decibel. We both lay there, expecting members of this fraternity of death to barge in and kill us any second. The floor pressed incessantly into my hip as I tried shifting my weight, only to have Damian do the same and have me end up exactly where I'd been seconds before.

We both stared silently at the blank white door. There was a glow from outside, but the cool breeze suggested it was the middle of the night. A light peeked in the curtains. Could it be that dawn was coming? "Can you see what time it is?" I called over my shoulder.

"Yeah. There's a clock over here with a snake skull on it," he responded. "It's 12:32."

Tick. Tick. Tick. The device kept announcing that we were running out of time. Damian shifted in his ropes again, making the rough and fringy twine burn into my skin.

We lay there helplessly for who knew how long before Damian broke the silence. "Y'know, I kinda want to ask you something."

"Like what?"

"...It's something I wanted to ask before, well, before any of this happened. Did you...enjoy having me around?"

Really? We were about to die and he just decided that now was the time to ask me how I felt about him? I mean, this is the kind of shit you see in movies, but this—*THIS* was real life! And frankly, I wasn't in the mood right at the moment to have a heart-to-heart talk.

Of course I could lie and say I always enjoyed having him around. That would make him feel better, and he'd go out on a positive note, as it were.

I chose instead to answer honestly, as if this were a confession at church. "At first no."

"Was it because of my obsession with horror?"

"It's not just that," I replied. "To be completely honest, I've been annoyed with everyone and everything these days. I mean, there's my family, and they just argue with me and with each other non-stop. Then there are the people I deal with at work. And at school. And anyplace else on a daily basis."

I continued; "I mean, I'm stuck in a dead-end job, cleaning up after people who are too self-absorbed or too lazy or too stupid to even see the benefit of keeping their own city clean. Worse yet, this wasn't the job I signed up for, but it was the only job that was available for me that pays halfway decently. I haven't got a ton of education, which means I can't get a better job and am at the mercy of a boss who doesn't give a shit...and I haven't even gotten a raise in a long time."

I looked over my shoulder, but was too tied up and stiff to be able to see his expression. But I did hear him say: "I guess that makes sense."

"Yeah. And I know it's dumb, but that's how I saw it. Truth be told, I'd recently begun questioning the way I've always treated you."

"Oh?"

"Yeah. I was wondering if I'd been too harsh on you. And I was thinking about all these internally hateful thoughts I typically have about other people, and whether they've actually been trying to help me. I found myself wondering if it was all because I just don't like them, or actually resented the fact that I had no choice but to to be around dumbasses and hypocrites. But after you helped me and believed in me, I started thinking maybe I had judged you unfairly."

Damian laughed bitterly. "Well, I may know chemistry, history and horror, but I've got to admit I was the dumbass dropout who walked into that shed and got us into all of this."

"Dumbass? No, I don't think you're a dumbass. Crazy to go in there, maybe, but certainly not dumb."

♦♦♦♦♦

What was going on here was what threw me. I mean, we were actually bonding...something I never thought I'd see. And figuring none of this would matter in an hour anyway, I continued: "Y'know, knowing what I know now, I kinda wish I had had a friend like you when I was in grade school."

"Really?"

"Yeah. Other kids looked at me like I was weird, taking my books and smashing them into the mud because I had the audacity to say I didn't like action figures. And when I got pissed off, I'd push back at these kids, throwing their stuff into the mud too."

"Only because I was 'different,' I would be the one who got punished for it by the adults. But that's not the point. You're a great person, and I've concluded you're better than me. And I'm sorry for the way I've treated you before."

"I appreciate that," Damian said. "Other kids weren't very nice to me, either, because I was quiet all the time. I used to draw a lot, too, and the others thought I was weird."

I was curious now about this side of my new friend, and briefly forgot where we were. "You used to draw?"

"Yeah. Actually, I still do, but not as often as I write. But between the bad economy and the stupid AI coming around, trying to sell your original creative work can be discouraging."

Well, I'll be damned! After all this, it looked like Damian and I were more similar than I'd realized. In fact, I was genuinely enjoying the conversation, and was about to ask another question to just keep the conversation going when I heard footsteps marching in our direction, coming closer with every step.

My heart lurched into my throat once more, the reconciliation depleted as the door suddenly swung open.

♦♦♦♦♦

An angry, wild-haired man shoved his way in through the door followed by the blonde who had helped capture us earlier. He was obviously agitated, and she was pleading with him. "Aeron, this is NOT what we talked about!"

"And I don't want to have to change the name of this group and start over again somewhere else!" he screamed.

I snapped my mouth shut, shuddering on the floor as my mind reeled. This guy was obviously the cult's leader, but I was stunned—*STUNNED*—to recognize him from the video. This was Aeron Inochi in the flesh—older, but just as loony as when he was standing on the dais touting that crap in so many different flavors.

At a glance, we could see that Inochi was still a man who was physically unimposing yet visually arresting. Short and slight, with a narrow frame and hunched, prowling posture, he seemed coiled with nervous energy. His eyes were his most striking feature—dark, sharp, and constantly moving, capable of locking onto a person with unsettling intensity. And it was instantly apparent that he used those eyes deliberately, staring without blinking to dominate conversations.

Aeron's face was lean and angular, deeply lined and with an ageless, feral look. Long, stringy hair that probably hadn't been washed in ages framed his face, then blended into a thin, uneven beard. His ragged, countercultural clothing—fringed jacket, denim, bare feet—set him apart from the rest of the community in their white uniforms and helped him cultivate a prophetic, outlaw image. Yet everything about him shrieked a sense of menace.

He rummaged through a desk drawer, pushing massive amounts of paper and loose items from his desk. A wine glass dropped to the floor, exploding into a hundred glass shards. But like that and everything else, he ignored the hurricane of files flying through the air as he focused on finding something.

His eyes wild, Aeron sweated and screamed, making him even more terrifying to behold.

"Aeron," the blonde said desperately "you're *NOT* thinking straight! Tell me this isn't what the plan was all along."

The two argued loud enough for Damian to urgently whisper "We need to figure out how to escape - and fast!"

“How? Our situation hasn’t improved any in the past hour. How are we supposed to cut through these ropes?” I whispered back.

Damian rolled onto his belly to give me a clear view of the window. “I don’t know, but we’d better figure it out somehow. Look outside!”

There was an unnaturally panicky tone to Damian’s voice, and I looked towards the colorful glass window. The dove design was a darker shade of gray than was natural, and the shading kept shifting. It looked like an angel flying out of the inferno, only...

Inferno. It looked like hell out there, and given that it was still the middle of the night, this could only mean one thing: They were burning the place to the ground to get rid of any evidence.

I was nauseous, my panic rising as I made a valiant effort to pull my arms out of my bonds.

It was hopeless.

♦♦♦♦♦

“Ow! Easy!” Damian whispered urgently. My flailing had tightened the ropes on his side, giving him rope burn. “Let's try this slowly and steadily. And maybe I can free my arm first—”

A bell rang. No...that wasn’t right. The sound was wrong and it was coming from too close by. It was more like the sound of a bowl reverberating after it had been struck.

Sure enough, the blonde had dropped a large metal bowl, which landed just millimeters from my nose. She’d obviously caught wind of the smoke, which was now seeping in under the doorways. Or perhaps it was the flames, now readily apparent through the dove on the window.

And she freaked out, as you’d expect any normal person to do. “Aeron!? WHY is the front garden on fire? What’s going on out there?” She started heading towards the door as he grabbed her arm.

“Don’t worry about it,” was all he said. His tone was cold, his gaze level. He was in charge, and may well have even struck the match himself.

Both angry and scared, the blonde tried wrenching her arm away from his iron grip,

"What are you DOING?" she shrieked. "You can't just set things on fire because you're angry or in a bad mood! Why can't we just talk about this like we used to?"

He was leaving no room for discussion as he looked at her like one might consider an insect. "I've burned down trees and buildings and my taxidermy collection many times. It's my operation, and I decide when it's time to fold the game."

"It's time," he said flatly. Indicating us, he added "I'm having Jason come in to clean up these two loose ends."

♦♦♦♦♦

No matter how you sliced it, this wasn't going to turn out well for me and Damian, and we both knew our minutes were numbered. And to her credit, the blonde was going to bat for us. "Look, why don't we just let these people go and explain..."

Inochi roared. "Like HELL I'm letting them go! They caused this problem! If these two meddling kids had kept their noses out of our business, we wouldn't have to close up shop. *THEY* are the reason we're in this mess!"

"How do you figure?"

"They came poking around our warehouse. They told the police. They're the problem, and Jason is going to fix that part of the problem in about five minutes. Go tell Jason I want to see him."

The blonde stood there looking at Inochi before turning to look at the two of us. Then she looked back at Inochi. "No."

Inochi's eyes grew to slits. "What did you say?"

"I said no. I won't get Jason."

Inochi set his jaw and smacked the blonde so hard she flew back a good two feet. Without another word, he stormed out of the room bellowing "Jason! Jason! We have three problems I need you to take care of. *NOW*!"

♦♦♦♦♦

The blonde had been shocked by the force of the blow, but she was still conscious—at least, conscious enough to have heard her former mentor calling for her execution. She shook off the stunning betrayal, slowly rose to her feet, and ran over to where Damian and I lay bound to each other. Grabbing a large chunk of the broken wine glass, she quickly sliced through our restraints.

We both moved slowly, stiff from hours of bondage and atrophied muscles. She squatted in front of us, breathless. "You guys have about 45 seconds to live unless you run. Now. Go. *GO*!"

I opened my mouth to thank her as Damian grabbed my arm. "Thanks, we gotta go," he said, already moving. I nodded in agreement, recognizing there was no time for cordiality and zero reason to stay a moment longer than necessary. I mean, the building was on *FIRE*, for Chrissake! And with Jason probably en route to put a bullet into each of our heads, there was absolutely no time to waste.

We sprinted to the door, the blonde grabbing a rag on the way to open the overheated doorknob. Outside the building, the massive blaze was growing and we took off, heading towards the left and what we hoped would be the exit. The blonde ran right, and quickly got lost in the shadows.

♦♦♦♦♦

I grasped my vermillion sweater in one hand, and grabbed onto Damian's with the other as we ran through the hallways trying to find a way out before the walls burned down around us. We glanced back, only to see a rapidly spreading fire set off by the lunatic who was obviously intent on making sure anything identifiable was burned to ashes.

CRAP! Every turn we took was cut off by fire or an impenetrable wall of smoke. Jason was out there hunting us, and there could be no question we were in a ridiculous amount of trouble. The idea of escape was evaporating as quickly as a pan of water in that heat.

"This way!" Damian said, gesturing towards the right hallway. He tugged at my hand, then put his hand behind my shoulder blade, half pulling and half pushing me along. I stumbled, struggling to follow him and letting instinct take over in a desperate attempt to escape this fiery hellhole.

♦♦♦♦♦

Like the rats that Aeron fed his "special cure" to, we were stuck in a maze. Every corner we turned became a dead end, or a storage room, or had a light coming out indicating someone was inside. And were those footsteps I heard behind us? Maybe they were echoes of our own journey, or figments of my imagination?

Either way, they freaked me out!

My mother had warned me there would be days like this, but I always thought it was just a figure of speech.

From somewhere above I thought I felt cold water from an automated sprinkler system—water that turned to steam as soon as it hit my body and hair. "Wet and cool is good," I reminded myself as we ran. But the horrors expanded as I realized we were running right into the storage area full of bleach.

"Cover your nose. Try not to breathe," Damian shouted at me. "Bleach and ammonia or alcohol is poisonous, or could even blow up."

"Let's get the fuck out of here!" was all I could say, turning abruptly to find...

♦♦♦♦♦

Aeron. Whether he'd heard us in our search for freedom, or discovered our escape from the taxidermy collection, I didn't know. All I could see was his rage at the prospect that we'd get away from the so-called justice he sought to mete out, and his intent to stand between us and the only door into or out of this room, holding us there until Jason arrived with his pistol.

Damian started shifting left, nudging me right in an effort to outflank Aeron. But the idea of Damian sacrificing himself so that I could get out of the room was unacceptable. Damian was now my friend, and I wasn't going anywhere without him next to me.

Moving faster than I realized was possible, I lunged for the shelf full of bleach and grabbed a gallon jug. Twisting the cap off, I held my breath, even as I started to throw up in my mouth. Memories of the Center flooded over me, threatening me with a blackout.

"Twenty seconds of bravery," I muttered to myself "and it'll be over one way or the other."

♦♦♦♦♦

Aeron was backing towards the door and trying to block our way. "Jason!" he called over his shoulder. Silence. "Jason!" he called again, his voice a bit more shrill. "Where is that dipshit?" he muttered to himself.

As the madman turned his head, Damian spotted what I was doing and reached for a jug of ammonia on his side of the room. Locking eyes with me, he twisted off the cap and waited to see if Jason would come.

Nothing. Damian nodded to me and we both turned to our captor. "Hey, Fuckface! Here, have a drink!" I hollered, swinging the bottle of bleach at him and getting it all over his shirt, face and hands. As it landed, Damian threw his bottle at Inochi's feet, the contents swelling over him like a geyser.

The results were instantaneous, and Inochi grabbed at his face. Recognizing the buildup of toxic gases in the tiny enclosure, Damian shouted "NOW!" and the two of us barreled into the doorway, knocking Aeron over and back out into the hallway, now sodden from the sprinkler system's never-ending streams.

Many of the doors in the hallway were now open, with members of the community searching for Aeron or heading for the exits. A warm breeze was blowing from the hallway down and to the left, and Damian—without a word—grabbed my hand and pulled me in that direction.

♦♦♦♦♦

The open door and the bright flames were seemingly just inches away from us when Jason appeared at the end of the hallway behind us. Beatrice was behind with Andy calling for Aeron as Jason pointed his pistol at the back of Damian's head.

"Beatrice," he shouted "GET DOWN!" She glanced up at him and saw the pistol, turned to grab the front of Andy's shirt, and pulled him down onto her in the middle of the hallway. And I felt the bullet fly through the back of my hair as Damian yanked me outside and into the surrounding brush.

Laying on our bellies, we stayed there—way too close to the burning embers but too scared to move—and held our breath, hoping against hope that we wouldn't be spotted amidst the insanity taking place around us.

And by the time Jason clambered over Beatrice and Andy and made his way to the door we were low enough in the tall grass that he couldn't see beyond the bright light of the fire and make us out.

"Hasn't anyone seen Aeron?" was the call coming from several directions. And seeing the search for us was at this point probably hopeless, Jason instead went in search of his boss, still lying in a pool of chloramine vapors.

♦♦♦♦♦

It was Jason who found him, too. "Aeron?" he said as he practically tripped over the prone body of his leader. "You okay, sir?"

Aeron grunted in response as Jason picked him up and hoisted him over his shoulder. Ten strides down the hall, a sharp left, four more strides and Jason was laying Aeron out on the ground outside to breathe the spark-filled air.

It took a minute or so for Aeron to be conscious enough to engage in conversation with him. "What happened to them?" he rasped.

Jason didn't answer at first, figuring Aeron wasn't really in any condition to have a serious discussion. Aeron sat up and looked at him sharply.

"What happened to them?" he said, his voice once again commanding.

"In all the turmoil inside the building, they got lost in the crowd. I'm sorry, Aeron."

Aeron staggered to his feet, waving away Jason as he ran over to help. "I'm going after them," Aeron growled angrily. "Give me your gun."

Jason unflinchingly handed it over. "How many bullets have I got here?" Aeron asked.

"Counting the bullet in the chamber? Four."

Aeron considered the Sig Sauer 9mm V226 handgun for a moment before turning to Jason. "Thank you," he said calmly, pointing the barrel at Jason's forehead and pulling the trigger.

"Apology accepted," he said before setting off around the campus.

Damian and I watched in horror from the weeds as Aeron strolled calmly through the burning community and gathered his flock. Surrounded by flame, they looked like a scene from the movie Carrie, all seated in a circle on the dirt as their world burned around them.

Aeron stood before them—all 50 of them—preaching as he had in that video so long ago. "I want you all to go into the cafeteria," was all we could hear him say as he added "I'll explain why when you get inside."

The group funneled into the only building not yet on fire and, as Mara—the last person in the crowd—edged inside, Damian and I snuck up to the window. A voice in my head told me we should be running to get the hell out of there, but morbid curiosity had taken over. I, for one, just *had* to know what would happen next.

Chapter 24: A Fateful Gulp

-Sofia-

The cups were already lined up when Mara entered the hall. They formed a careful arc on the long table—white plastic, identical, their rims catching the lantern light like a row of small moons. Someone had wiped the surface clean. Someone always did. Order mattered here, especially when the whole world outside was falling apart.

The air smelled wrong, especially given the raging fire around them. But inside it smelled sweet. Almond-adjacent, though Mara couldn't have said how she knew that. She had never tasted almonds like this. She told herself it was just a bowl of punch. That's all they ever drank in the community was punch, with the exception of the occasional glass of wine that Aeron forced himself to drink for medicinal purposes.

Aeron stood at the front, barefoot as usual, his white robe brushing the dirt floor. He looked smaller tonight, somehow, but his voice—his voice filled the room the way water fills a crack. "Family," he said, and the word landed with weight. "They're coming. It is time."

A murmur passed through the crowd. Not panic, but more like recognition. As if the sentence completed a thought they'd all been carrying around unfinished for weeks.

Mara felt Eli's fingers tighten around hers. He didn't look at her. He was watching Aeron the way people watched storms roll in: alert, reverent, and afraid to blink.

"Those who live outside our community don't understand us," Aeron continued. "They never have. They'll separate us. Take the children. Rewrite our story until everyone thinks we're monsters."

Janet stood near the front and began to cry quietly. Someone shushed her—not unkindly, but firmly.

Mara scanned the exits. Two guards stood in front of each of the doors that used to stand open to all. They each casually held a rifle, as if this were a drill.

Aeron continued preaching. "We have built something clean here, something free. And freedom scares the people in the outside world. They don't know what to do with it, so they demonize those who do."

He smiled then, a tired smile, like a parent explaining a hard truth.

"So tonight, we choose. Because the outsiders will paint you as a villain and put you in a federal prison for the rest of your life. There you will live a life engineered to grind you down slowly, without ever quite finishing the job. Every day the lights will snap on before dawn, merciless and absolute, stripping away sleep as if it were contraband. They'll count you several times a day; not to check on you, but to remind you that your body is owned, inventoried, and confirmed by them. And they'll feed you a breakfast that tastes of starch and resignation, eaten fast, eyes forward, because lingering invites attention and attention invites trouble."

"You'll have no privacy in prison, as your every movement will be watched and every word weighed, every moment of every day. You will learn to amputate parts of yourself—like your humor, softness, curiosity—because these can and will be used against you. Silence will become your armor, and you'll respect those around you not as a courtesy, but because you'll risk threats and punishment if you don't.

Any mistakes you make will echo for years. And there will be violence against you by those who are bigger and stronger. Even if it doesn't happen often, the possibility of violence and danger will always hang in the air, constant and instructional."

"And even if you survive all of that, you'll never have a moment's peace like you do here. There will be a steady stream of work details that will keep you occupied, though they'll do nothing to restore your dignity. "

"I promise you, my friends, that anyone going to jail will find their remaining time on this planet to be stretching cruelly inside every single day, only to collapse without warning into lost years. Anyone you knew in the outside world will forget you even existed, and their lives will happily continue without you."

"What other choice do we have?" cried Janice from the back of the room.

"We choose to live out our lives on our own terms," Aeron said, lifting a cup. The word "choose" echoed, bounced off the tin roof, and came back thinner as he hoisted his cup towards them. "Come, my friends. It is time."

♦♦♦♦♦

Mara's heart began to pound. How many times had they rehearsed this scene—nights when they'd laugh afterward, relieved, and were told it was only a test. She remembered how the tests kept coming. How each one took something small from her: a doubt, a question, a night's sleep.

"Make two lines," Aeron said gently. "There's plenty for everyone. No rushing. No fear."

A line formed on either side of the table as family members around her murmured with excitement. Eli pulled her forward. "It's okay," he whispered. "It's what we talked about."

Mara opened her mouth to answer and found nothing there. The hall seemed to tilt, the lanterns swimming. She saw the cups more clearly now—some already filled, liquid dark against white plastic.

A child laughed somewhere, high and confused. A mother hushed him with a kiss pressed too hard to his hair.

When it was their turn, the server—a girl Mara had taught to read—wouldn't meet her eyes.

"Drink together," Aeron called. "So no one is alone."

Mara took the cup. It was warm. Her name was written on the side in careful marker, the letters rounded and familiar.

She looked at the certainty on Eli's face. Belief had smoothed all the sharp edges from him, and all she could think was "This is what loyalty looks like."

She hoped she was as worthy as he was.

♦♦♦♦♦

Somewhere behind her, a chair fell over. A voice said, "Wait—" and then was swallowed by applause. Encouraging. Relentless. Aeron raised his own cup.

"For dignity," he said. "For love."

Mara held the cup at her lips.

And in the space between breath and action—thin as a thread—she wondered whether love was supposed to taste like this.

Chapter 25: A Death's Hymn

-Aeron-

I swallowed my cup of water as the rest of the family drank their punch. One. Two. Three. Four.

At five I saw the first body hit the floor, then two more, then a dozen. I'd heard that cyanide acted quickly, but this was even faster than I'd thought possible.

By the time I'd counted to 20, only Andy and Beatrice stood before me, having held off on drinking at my request. Only...

Looking around at the bodies sprawled across the floor, there was one person notable for her absence: Juniper. Her riot of blonde hair was nowhere to be seen, and that just wouldn't do.

"Andy," I smiled, as a spider might smile at a fly caught in his web. "Andy, go outside and find Juniper. She needs to join the rest of the party. And Andy...keep an eye out for those two strangers, please."

Without a word, Andy was out the door searching for our errant messenger. Beatrice stood close to me, ignoring the fires raging at our door and making small talk as if nothing was different from any other day.

Through the window I saw a glimpse of Juniper. Our eyes locked for a moment before she took off like a scared rabbit, heading pell-mell for the woods along with those two heathens that had escaped. Only by the time I'd be able to climb over my fallen family members, I knew they'd all be long gone.

♦♦♦♦♦

It had been ten minutes by my count when Andy returned. "Sorry sir," he said, closing the door behind him. He stood there, palms up, indicating he'd come up empty and couldn't find Juniper or those two strangers.

"Padlock the door," I instructed, watching him do so before I addressed his lack of results. "It's disappointing that you failed," I muttered. Smiling at Andy, I said "Thanks for trying," then pointed the gun and pulled the trigger.

The bullet hit his left shoulder and he looked at me, confused. "Why?" was all Andy could croak.

"Because you don't want to spend a lifetime in prison," I responded, pulling the trigger again to finish the job.

♦♦♦♦♦

There were sirens in the distance, getting closer by the second. Whether they were from police or fire equipment I couldn't say, though I guessed both were en route. The helicopters flying overhead confirmed my instinct that we were done here, and we all knew it.

I stood there, shaking and watching as everything fell and burned around me. The room was now on fire, and the distinctive wail of sirens coming closer and from several directions was unmistakable.

Added to this was the nearby barking as the K-9 force approached. I glanced around me, only seeing my family members dead in growing puddles of blood. And I jumped at a touch on my shoulder. Glancing around I saw not Juniper there, but Beatrice.

"Aeron?" she said, a quaver in her voice. "Aeron, let's get out of here now while we still can."

I said nothing, but gazed down at her and smiled grimly.

BAM!

The gun had amazingly little recoil as I watched her fall backwards to the floor, grasping her mid-section and the gaping hole I'd just made in her. Beatrice lay there wordlessly mouthing something and I leaned down to put my ear against her contorted face. "I love you," she said as she went limp, and I took that as my cue to bring the pistol to my own temple and pull the trigger.

Only I'd used my last bullet already. *"FUCK!!"* I screamed, throwing the empty weapon onto the wall.

♦♦♦♦♦

I was losing my mind. The one thing I'd wanted—to go out on my own terms—had now been denied to me. Grabbing a handful of hair in frustration, I pulled it from my scalp and shrieked. How could I have failed? How could Juniper—that traitorous bitch—have done this to me? After all the love and support I had given her? I'd made her my girl, and she'd turned on me.

At that moment I knew with certainty that she'd also had something to do with the missing video tape.

I glanced at the fires from the outside, burning down the years I'd invested building my sanctuary from the outside world. The panic. The fires. The sirens. The dogs. My heart was pounding in my ears. How could everything have turned to shit so quickly? It was all Juniper's fault. I'd escape and track her down and make her pay...that fucking cunt!

I screamed. "I can't go back to prison; THEY'LL NEVER LET ME OUT!"

There was no way out.

♦♦♦♦♦

I glanced at my desk. There, sitting innocently, was the prototype box of cordial chocolates we'd made to teach the others what the display should look like. The creation that brought nothing more than death to anyone who didn't fit my image of perfection. Those seemingly innocent treats that were meant to change everything, for good and all.

I had no choice, and grabbed the candies, immediately shoving three of them into my mouth. My face contorted as the taste of the bitter dark chocolate mixed with the awful chemical aftertaste and hit my tongue.

"The bastard's in here!"

They were yelling outside, trying to knock down the door or blast off the locks, and I laughed at them. They can't arrest me if I'm dead, I thought as I stuffed another couple of the chocolates down my gullet. Only one thing mattered right now: making sure I'd eaten enough to do the trick and deny the police their prize.

Because there was no way I was going back to jail. That crap lawyer the last time hadn't gotten me out fast enough from that hellhole I'd been in, with the beatings, the rapings, and the solitude. After all I'd done, I'd end up with a shiv in my back before long and would spend every minute until then watching over my shoulder in fear. Or I'd be everyone's bitch the moment I ever stepped foot into a cell again.

No; I'd much prefer to take the easy way out.

♦♦♦♦♦

I gagged, coughing up the remnants of the chocolate from the back of my throat. The aftertaste of chemicals and chocolate coated my tongue and made me want to puke. But despite the burning from my throat all the way to the center of my guts—despite the metallic taste of my blood rising in my throat—I was determined to keep it down. This was important, and I needed to finish what I'd started.

My breathing was raspy, and my voice grew hoarse as I tried to call out to Juniper to tell her I loved her and to show her what she'd done to me. That bitch—that obnoxious little pest who had brought me—*ME*!—to such a horrible ending. She should be the one who's dying. Dying alongside all that I had built for her; dying for the cause. Dying beside me.

I shouldn't have ended my run this way. The world needs me and my ideas. They need my leadership...and they all know it.

♦♦♦♦♦

PING! There was a terrible burning sensation in my right shoulder. I looked up to see three cops spilling in the front door and another dozen behind them.

And it was bad enough that I'd been shot, but getting shot in the shoulder meant there was no way I could shoot back. Of course, having tossed my gun away probably wasn't the smartest move, but if I'd had any bullets left, none of this would have mattered anyway, right?

I looked for someplace to hide or get away, only to realize it really didn't matter anymore. I was just minutes from my own death, and nobody could stop that now.

I looked for something to throw at this fuckers. Staggering to my feet, I leaned against the wall behind me. Stumbling, I hit the floor with a hard thud, wincing as my head bounced off the ground. Dizzy. Couldn't see straight. Chocolates worked better than I'd realized.

Blood began pouring into my eyes from a gash on my forehead, though it was a minor discomfort compared to the intense burning in my stomach. My intestines were screaming at me for what I'd decided to subject them to, and I desperately wanted to vomit.

MUST...HOLD...IT...DOWN!

Coughing. Choking. Couldn't decipher if I was tasting chocolate or my own blood. Maybe they were the same thing at this point.

The cops were yelling, their sounds blurred by the incessant ringing in my ears. That stupid thing that hangs in the back of my throat—a uvula, the doctor called it—was swelling up and clogging my airway. My entire throat was closed as I struggled to breathe. Can't see. MAKE IT STOP!

My brain felt like it was on a merry-go-round set on high-speed, and I was feeling more lightheaded than ever before. My mouth was all swollen and burned, my stomach perforated and begging me to upchuck. Shock, infection, organ failure...yup, there could be no question that my body was shutting down.

As the police moved closer and a coupla medics brought in a gurney, I could barely feel my chest rising and falling. Yeah, I'd never see the inside of a hospital, let alone a jail cell. Mission accomplished!

I watched myself, as if I was an outsider sitting a few feet above watching the wretch who sat in deadly judgment of so many others finally meeting his own maker. Before long I'd become an inanimate object and a feast for the worms. My breathing was slowing even more, my pulse rigid and fading.

♦♦♦♦♦

The saddest part was that not long ago I had one of the top minds in the world, so vibrant and animated that others auditioned to be my companion. Now it was expelling its last few thoughts like sparks spitting out from a dying fire. I watched, helplessly, as my life force was denied the admiration and attention that once clamored to fuel it. I could no longer thrive on being the center of the universe, and my energy would no longer come from the validation I got from others. No longer would I be in control of my environment and the people around me, nor would I feel powerful and significant.

In truth, I would now feel nothing.

All my life...all my bodily activity...*everything* would soon be gone. Intellectually I understood I was no longer going to be here. My story...my life...my journey would end miserably in this room, in an instant I couldn't predict and had no control over.

And yet this instant felt so slow and agonizing as my internal organs failed one after another, all thanks to my own creation—the Miracle Tap—doing its sordid work. It was painful, yet I found it welcoming as I greeted death. I'd be gone, but I'd know I'd gone on my own terms, and the rest of the world—with their phony morals and their repressive justice system—could go fuck themselves.

It hurt so much, going this way, though my mind still couldn't be at peace. The time for me to move was past and I was lying in my own blood, piss and vomit. It was poignant, in a way, that my brilliant mind would go this way, watching helplessly as the flames and the cops both crept closer.

Who would have ever thought death would be both terrifying and soothing to the dying mind?

And as I lay there awaiting the infinite, all I could see in my mind's eye were brief flashes of past memories, both real and imagined. It was a haunting reminder of how short my life really had been, always striving to bring order to the chaos around me and now wondering if I'd ever made any progress.

Laying there, drifting into oblivion, I realized I'd never had any positive impact and my life ultimately meant...nothing.

♦♦♦♦♦

They'd hoisted me onto the gurney and were hustling me into the ambulance when I heard the Emergency Medical Technicians talking. "That's the piece of shit who killed all those people?" said one.

The other responded; "That's him. Hey Charlie! Drive real slow to the hospital. In fact...why don't we stop and get a donut first?"

Of course, one could legitimately ask if any of that really matters when death crowds in to take over the mind, the body, and the soul. This was to be my final moments on earth, and frankly I didn't give a shit .

Finally, I closed my eyes for good. The pain in my chest finally stopped, and the beating of my heart slowed down into silence. There would be no more pounding, and I was finally going to be at peace.

And that last thought—Oh, Ruby, my *deadly divinity*...I hope to see you again...

And again...

And again...

Only nobody will ever know.

Chapter 26: The Living Nightmare is Over

-Whitney-

"Yep, he's dead, alright," Jimmy said nonchalantly as he dropped the limp arm that had once directed the deaths of dozens. Eyeing the blackened ooze that had been either blood or chocolate and now trickled from the corner of the corpse's flaccid lips, Jimmy added venomously, "This piece of shit took the coward's way out."

I sighed, a mass of mixed feelings. Sure I was pissed that the man responsible for all the pain and horror visited upon so many innocents—including Madeleine's kids—had killed himself to avoid being arrested and having to face proper punishment. But I was more relieved that he wouldn't be hurting people anymore, and that he'd been permanently put out of business.

I looked around the charred remnants of the warehouse, coughing a bit from the curls of dense smoke streaming up towards a hole in the roof. It had been just a month since the summer festival, but it felt like years had passed. The summer winds came in off the ocean, carrying away the acrid smells and, hopefully, the bitter memories associated with this fucker who would be king.

The timing of the breeze was telling, I guess, given that La Mesa—just 13 miles from the beach—doesn't get much breeze because of all the hills and urban heat. Of course, sitting up at a higher elevation probably doesn't help. Perhaps the universe was trying to tell us that it was time to move on from this nightmare.

It was a thought that left my mind as quickly as it had entered, though. Because as I considered the possibilities, I knew that this was a story that wouldn't soon be forgotten by anyone in San Diego County. Even as the media moved on to the next big story, I knew it would be burned into over three million minds for a long time to come.

Of course, the news would milk the story down to the bone, connecting the bombing of La Mesa to the compound burning to Aeron Inochi's suicide by bleach poisoning. From the memes to the online influencers talking about it, this was a story that would be hot for weeks before finally fading into the old news category.

And the chances of finding any new witnesses or surviving cult members was slim, though there was always the chance someone could be turned up by the inevitable Dinesh D'Souza documentary. And there was sure to be a ton of grief from the elected official crowd unless investigation could turn up any survivors first.

Of course, given that Inochi was no longer a threat, there would probably more likely be a call of "Case Closed!" and an urging to move on to the next crisis. And neither José nor I had any interest in pursuing those, thank you very much.

Regardless, for as long as I lived I didn't think I'd ever be able to forget the horror this piece of shit was responsible for.

♦♦♦♦♦

The firetruck sirens blared as first responders rushed towards Ramona. Trucks from Santa Ysabel, Julian, Poway, and other front-line emergency apparatus operating under the San Diego County Fire Protection District umbrella screamed towards the destruction that had taken place around the spot where I now stood.

The gardens, still ablaze, were being whipped by the wind and were feeding upon themselves, and airtanker aircraft from CAL FIRE's Ramona Air Attack Base—about 2 miles away—were reportedly already en route to drop fire retardant on and around our position.

I prayed they'd get here before the fire spread to the dry brush in the acreage that surrounded us. And I listened as the chickens, frantically clucking as they fled the 20 foot wall of orange, tried to outrun the bleating goats, desperate to escape into the darker brushes and prevent themselves from being added to the casualty body count.

♦♦♦♦♦

Once more outside and breathing clean air, we dodged the paramedics, struggling to do our jobs while staying out of their way. I kept a watchful eye out for more corpses in the area, careful to not trip over those already draped with the white sheets. Triage teams lined up the dead in anticipation of the arrival of the coroner's "meat wagon."

The more I watched, the more I realized how little these people—these poor, misguided people—had known about the cause they were supporting or the man they were following.

They were still people after all – ordinary folks who had been sadly tempted into joining the cult of a deranged lunatic when they were at the lowest and most vulnerable point in their respective lives. Pressures from their troubles had persuaded them to join a garden of belief that was poisoned from within. Their faith, weaponized into fear, had become a paradise turned into a prison, and a case of salvation twisted into damnation.

And just like Jonestown or Heaven's Gate, what had begun as hope for so many had ended in horror, with a mass delusion masquerading as deliverance and love for the leader turning into a noose around their necks.

The more I considered it—the more I looked at the disaster Aeron Inchon had been responsible for creating—the more ill and depressed I became. For his was a doctrine that demanded everything: money, mind, body, soul...and eventually, life.

Jimmy patted my back, as if sensing the flood of emotion that was overwhelming me despite my best efforts at stoicism. "We did all we could, Whitney," he mumbled, muttering under his breath "At least Emmy has gotten some justice out of this."

♦♦♦♦♦

He was right, of course. Not just about Emmy Anise, but Aeron's other victims, too...both living and dead. *All* the families impacted had seen deserved justice served, helping them to get some closure and, in time, to heal. By morning a team of therapists would have the information they needed, and counselors would quickly be dispatched to community centers to help their clientele.

And because I was their man on the inside, Madeleine and her children were already getting the help they so desperately craved. Some of it was coming from state-run victim assistance programs, of course, and there were nonprofits and support organizations like Jewish Family Services who could also be counted on to step up.

But recognizing how screwed up the healthcare system is altogether, I knew Madeleine and the others were going to have to pay out-of-pocket for a good chunk of this, and that would be problematic for many of them. Ultimately, it was pretty obvious a crowdfunding campaign would be needed to help lend a hand and pay for their much-needed therapy for a while.

I made a mental note to send in a healthy contribution.

♦♦♦♦♦

I'd spoken with Madeleine a couple of days ago when she reported that - other than lingering aches - both her kids were healing...at least physically. Of course, the three of them will have to deal with these traumatic memories for the rest of their lives, and wouldn't be able to "just get over it", like the callous or unimpacted members of the community were already advising.

I made another mental note to stop by their house on the way home to drop off some dinner. I'd stop at D.Z. Akins and bring them a couple of corned beef sandwiches, I decided, knowing how much Madeleine loved their food.

As for my sweet tooth, even with this case resolved I knew I'd never be touching *any* cherry cordials again. And to think how many of them I had scarfed down over the years.

Probably better for my diet, too.

♦♦♦♦♦

The paramedics pushed a steady parade of gurneys, and it was like watching shoppers checking out at Costco on a Saturday afternoon. I observed them carrying the remnants of limp corpses, lifting them with care into the seemingly endless supply of body bags before placing them on each gurney and pushing them towards their temporary destination: the morgue. Many still held their personalized plastic cups gripped in their hands, now destined to be buried with them courtesy of stiff fingers as rigor mortis started settling in.

Yet despite the parade of pallbearers, there simply weren't enough of them to collect all the corpses at once. And I already had the itch, knowing the news outlets would be rushing in momentarily searching for their next big headline, even as the pools of blood congealed around them throughout this cursed place. Damn, where was the police department and their Public Information Officer? These guys really needed to take control of the situation, and I didn't want to be there any longer than necessary.

I was eager to call Madeleine to tell her that the man she'd been looking for was no longer a threat. And that the cult that had attacked her children was now also history. Gone. Kaput! Completely up in smoke.

Yeah, I had serious doubts that there were any other current members left alive. Good luck to the media to find any of the family left living to interview them for their news stories, or to find an accomplice...

♦♦♦♦♦

This seemed like a logical conclusion for about 30 seconds...until I saw two people approaching us not far from the burned brush and the curtain of ash blowing around us. There was a guy and a girl, covered in ash and limping, holding each other up. The guy—tall, thin, and dressed all in black—looked familiar, though I couldn't quite put my finger on why. Jimmy nudged me in the ribs when he spotted them too.

"Isn't that the two kids who dropped off the video at the station?"

Holy shit, he was right! Jimmy and I dashed towards them, even as medical personnel started coming at them from both our left and our right.

And as I got closer, I saw her. It was a young blonde woman, probably in her early twenties, and she was also covered in ash and more than a few blood stains. Her face resembled a mask that was half horror at what she'd done and half believed it wasn't her fault.

Whether her apparent reaction was caused by trauma, shock or willful ignorance I couldn't say, but there was absolutely no question in my mind that she was a cult member. I allowed the other two to be led away by the medics, knowing they'd be in good hands now and with the police. I made yet one more mental note to check in on them later.

Turning my attention to the blonde, I put up my guard again, knowing her boss was dead but unsure how committed she still was to the cause.

Three other police officers on site had also noticed her, and with a look I cautioned Jimmy to hold his fire as she slowly approached.

♦♦♦♦♦

Jimmy clicked his taser, ready to press it into service at a moment's notice, and I knew I needed to move faster than he could. "Stop right there, young lady," I called out, "and identify yourself."

Jimmy kept his hand on his belt, ready to jump into action as she stopped about 20 feet away. He and I exchanged glances while I remained unsure if she was relieved or dismayed that the whole thing was over.

She glanced at Jimmy, his hand on his weapon, before turning her full attention to me. "J-Juniper..." she said, her voice little more than a whisper. I looked her over from head to foot. She wore an ankle-length, flowy, modest dress; a headscarf; and simple sneakers, all of which seemed to have been until recently pure white, though now she looked more like a refugee who had just gone through a war. It was difficult to see where she stopped and her filthy clothes began, and a healthy portion of dirt and dried grass, ash from the fire and more than a bit of blood all walked with her.

As she stood there waiting for a reaction, I wondered if there were any other surprises still waiting to emerge from the woods. Though I mourned the loss of life, I crossed my fingers that the rest of this morbid troupe was dead.

Chapter 27: The Fate of the Syndicate

-Juniper-

I'd watched Aeron supervise the passing of the family, standing there grinning broadly as everyone drank their punch. There was more than enough cyanide to do the job, and within seconds my friends—one by one—collapsed at his feet.

Then he spotted me at the window and I knew it was time to beat it out of there.

My last view of Aeron was him standing atop a small podium, his arms outstretched as he invited the entire community to relinquish their mortal shells and leave life on their own terms. "It's GOT to be better than a lifetime in shackles," he exhorted them.

As the bodies fell, I ran for my own life with Sofia and Damian—the couple I'd helped keep out of Jason's grasp—hot on my trail. Because despite whatever Aeron said, I wasn't brave enough to take my own life. Without question what the Purity Syndicate had done was horrible, but I'd have to live with the guilt and the knowledge of the terrible things I'd helped make happen.

♦♦♦♦♦

Somewhere behind us the door slammed open and Andy was on the hunt. "Lay low," I instructed the other two, for good measure adding "don't make a sound," before I snuck off into the darkness behind us.

On the far side of the cafeteria there were several half-empty metal drums that Beatrice used for capturing used vegetable oil, and Sam and Gregg had been tasked with turning that oil into soap and fuel for our truck and our generators. The drums were out of sight from the door Jason had just come out of, but from my new hiding place I could see them just fine.

WHAM! The rock I tossed landed perfectly atop the drum, and a loud echo came forth. I then ducked back into the darkened woods and cut a hard left behind the burning trees, coming out on the other side of the cafeteria. 100 yards away I could see Jason as I tossed a handful of pebbles at the window behind where Beatrice stood talking with Aeron.

She started to move, then stopped as Aeron said something. They'd look out the window and see the police starting to move closer, the dogs from the K-9 unit barking ever louder, then go on with their conversation.

Jason stepped into the open air, gun at the ready and obviously frustrated. Lying in the overheated dirt, I pitched a handful of larger gravel and heard one of them strike the window pane next to Aeron. Sticking his head out of the door, he hollered "Jason, she's over here," before ducking back inside.

By now I was on my feet and moving back to the metal drums, telling myself "rinse and repeat," only to bump into Damian and Sofia launching a handful of rocks over the roof. Knowing Jason would have figured it out by now, I instructed the other two to split up and run deep into the woods, then lie on the ground and remain still. "With luck," I told them, "we'll all get out of here alive."

♦♦♦♦♦

It was a deadly game of hide-n-seek that we were playing, but with Aeron's extra victims now out of the way, it was just a matter of me avoiding Jason until he tired of the chase. And after 10 minutes of the back and forth, round and around, he finally said "Fuck it!" and went back in to report to Aeron.

With the fire roaring, the police radios crackling, and the dogs barking, it was difficult to hear much from inside the cafeteria. The sirens and the helicopters didn't help either.

Andy, Beatrice and Aeron all seemed to have come through the evening in one piece, even as every other member of the community lay in a decaying heap around them.

Meaning I now faced a choice: Run away and hope I could just blend into the crowd; confront Aeron, meaning I'd probably be executed before I could even open my mouth; or take responsibility for my own actions, put this life behind me, and go face the music.

Yeah, maybe what Aeron had said about spending the rest of my life in a jail cell was right, but we'd hurt people—a LOT of people—and something inside insisted I put on my big-girl pants and do the right thing.

♦♦♦♦♦

I considered my options a bit more, ready to run for freedom, only to think about how I'd spend the rest of my days looking over my shoulder expecting to find Aeron. "He's not the type to break over something like this," I muttered, looking around at the fiery compound. "He'll bounce."

And did I really want to have him chasing me for the rest of my life? At least if that was going to be my fate, I wanted to first make some amends for the horrors I'd helped to cause.

As I watched the police barge into the cafeteria, I stood and turned back towards the woods and followed them to the top of the hill. From there I began to walk down, my dress, headscarf and sneakers all covered in ash, dirt, dried grass, and more than a few blood stains. What had started as my day dressed in white was now anything but, and while part of me was horrified at what I'd been a part of all these years, another half believed it wasn't my fault.

It was all Aeron, I kept telling myself, even as I knew my life was as much of a mess as my clothing.

Up ahead I saw Damian and Sofia going off with the medics, but I headed towards the guy who looked like he was the leader of the cops. There were five of them—three in uniform, and these two others who could have easily passed for civilians.

As one of them clicked the taser on his belt, the other guy—the boss—put up his hand. "Stop right there, young lady," he called out, "and identify yourself."

I stopped about 20 feet away as the two cops in plain clothes exchanged glances. Contemplating the second guy, his hand on his weapon, I turned my full attention to the head cop. "J-Juniper..." I whispered.

They all looked at me as if they couldn't believe what they were seeing. Given the wreckage I'd just left at the top of the hill, neither could I. But, unlike all the rest of the cult, at least I was still alive.

♦♦♦♦♦

I half expected to be gunned down when I walked up to the police. But that guy – what was his name? Oh yeah...Whitney—he'd stopped the other cops—the trigger-happy ones who would have put me out of my guilt and my misery—and sat me down on a bench with a bottle of water and a blanket around my shoulders, and he talked to me. He was respectful and treated me like a person—a real person—and certainly better than Aeron ever had.

So there I was, far from the burning fires of what I used to think of as the home that I had belonged to. For the only time in my life I'd actually had a community around me that I wanted to be part of forever.

Forever was now a thing of the past for me, and everything I'd known had been destroyed. Memories and remnants of my life felt like they were flying away by the second, the ashes of the past 10 years disappearing on the same breeze that carried away plumes of smoke into the night sky. I watched as everything I knew was snuffed out by the dark skies and the bright sparkling stars. It felt like the wind had blown out the fire of a candle, leaving behind an atmosphere around me that was the same sickly red that La Mesa's sky had once been thanks to me and my "friends."

I didn't even know what to feel anymore. Sadness? Betrayal? Anger? Bitterness? I wallowed in all of these things at once, unable to even begin to define this feeling beyond the numbness in my chest. It felt so odd.

And the sky—muggy with soot and smoke—was choking, making me feel as claustrophobic as I had that night Aeron stole my virginity.

It was all Aeron. His organization. His vision. His evil plans. The rest of us were his stupes—his innocent victims. I hoped they'd put him away in jail for the rest of his life, all right, and I'd be happy to testify against him and tell the police everything—*EVERYTHING*—in a faint effort to regain my life, my honor, and my self-respect.

♦♦♦♦♦

I thought about that young couple I'd saved, their panicked faces still burned in my memory, and hoped they could one day forgive me for what had nearly happened to them. In my mind I was asking for forgiveness for all the deaths the syndicate had caused. And for what we did to La Mesa. And to the wider community of San Diego County.

I thought about that woman in the bathroom at the fair. If only I had known sooner what this so-called familial group really was. If only my eyes had opened sooner to what a monster Aeron really was.

I knew now that I couldn't blame much of what had happened on the rest of his followers, because they didn't know any better than I did. Still, if we'd really been paying attention we'd have recognized that making chocolates laced with bleach is going to hurt people EVERY SINGLE FUCKING TIME!

If we'd been paying attention! But "if" was the biggest word in that sentence. It's like my first grade teacher, Ms. Tweedy, used to say; "If an apple had teeth, it would bite you back."

Nope, I'm pretty sure everyone in the family was just as convinced as I was that we were doing a good thing, and now I felt like I was coming out of a fog. Reality was seeping in, and I was going to have to get used to things others considered normal, like silence, free time, and making choices without someone else's permission. Emotions flooded over me—grief, rage, relief, shame, joy—and it was overwhelming.

As I considered the shock from seeing my found family die in front of me, I began crying, screaming, and feeling numb.

Maybe…maybe I'd have been better off just confronting Aeron and getting it over with after all. After all, what was done was done, and sitting here, unable to do anything to change the past, or the present, or presumably the future, wasn't going to accomplish anything.

♦♦♦♦♦

A touch of reality settled in as my mind dissociated itself a bit from the memories of the people that I had just lost. I thought I could have trusted them with my life, and would have done anything for them. Anything for Aeron. Only…I didn't.

Maybe that's what had me so confused. I had loved Aeron since I was a young girl and had pledged my life to him. But when push came to shove, I took that video from his desk and planted it where it was sure to be found.

And here we were. Was I angry at myself for betraying him, or pissed at him for putting me into that horrible position in the first place? And which of those five stages of grief was I in? Denial? Anger? Bargaining? Definitely depression.

It suddenly struck me that I was struggling with every part of grief except acceptance, because it was so damned hard to accept what I had been a part of and the horrible things we'd done—that I had done. I was in physical pain, recognizing what a God-awful person I had willingly become and unable to accept that or know what would come next.

And now, having walked down the hill instead of disappearing, I didn't even know if it would ever be possible to get a clean break, start over as if it had never happened, and live a normal life. Wouldn't my face be inextricably linked on social media as the public spokesperson for the Purity Syndicate? Wouldn't any potential employer look up my name and have that jump out at the top of the pile?

I wondered if I had any of those chocolates left…

I mean, even just getting a job as a waitress in some tiny town out west would still require a social security number. Even if I changed my name—which was probably not a bad idea—it would involve all kinds of layers of bureaucracy and spending money I didn't have on lawyers and such.

Yeah, getting to that new chapter in my life was going to be complicated, if not impossible. But now I was determined to get my life back. I was done with the real family I'd grown up with, and now the Purity Syndicate was a thing of the past.

But I knew that 24 was too young to stop living, and it was time to stake out my own vision of my future...whatever that might be. And no matter how I pulled it off, I'd learned one incredibly valuable lesson: to *never* be used again as a toy to be manipulated by anyone else.

I needed to come clean. Right now.

♦♦♦♦♦

One thing that being the spokesperson for The Syndicate had taught me was how to present myself well. It was this innate ability that had led Aeron to make me his PIO—his Public Information Officer. He even sent me to classes so that I'd learn how to speak with the media and manipulate our message, always keeping The Syndicate in the best possible light.

And as the last surviving member of what KFMB-TV had called "The perpetrators of this disaster," I was going to have to use every bit of that skill now.

Only this time it wouldn't be for Aeron. No longer was I going to try and tell people how wonderful he was. From what officer Whitney told me, Aeron had taken the easy way out and swallowed the chocolate cordials, leaving whoever was left behind to bear the brunt of public anger.

That meant me! And though in my innocence I had longed for a better world and he claimed he would take us there, it didn't take a genius to look at the thick smoke and the blaze turning the darkened clouds a ruddy red to recognize that this had been nothing more than the fantasy world conjured up by the twisted mind of a dead man.

So I was going to use every bit of that public speaking skill in a desperate bid to avoid the hangman's noose. Today I would be speaking for myself, and would happily throw any of my former compatriots under the bus.

Hey, if I ended up in prison, maybe I'd even write a book about it to ensure my side of the story got told.

♦♦♦♦♦

A large spew of water gushed from a firehose being carried by firefighters to put out the still-raging flames. Another emergency team nearby looked like police and medical technicians. There were no sleazy journalists in sight, unlike the last time I'd participated in a scene like this.

Ah, but I was sure I wasn't done with that vile little beetle of a man—Pete Ross—who would have no doubt already heard about our little party. And when he did I knew he'd tear himself away from whatever peephole he was looking through to come reeling into the charred area while the chaos of fire was still full-blown.

I resolved there would be no more tricks or treats. I would speak for myself this time instead of for a cult that was no different than the church that I was raised in. The mosquito of an intrusive thought would no longer be buzzing around endlessly in the back of my brain.

I was the last surviving member, and I needed to testify. Ultimately, it was the least I could do, and I owed it to all the innocents who had suffered.

♦♦♦♦♦

So I set my teeth, prepared to speak for the people I'd claimed to care about for so long. And though I froze as I saw the gurneys being pulled out from the countless ambulances that had parked on the road leading down to the burning mansion, I pushed myself.

I had to go forward and pay the price for our cruelty and *my* stupidity.

Whitney stared at me, as did his partner, and all I could think was "I must look a sight!"

All the second in command could say was "Now we'll finally get the real story of what happened."

Chapter 28 - The Courthouse

-Juniper-

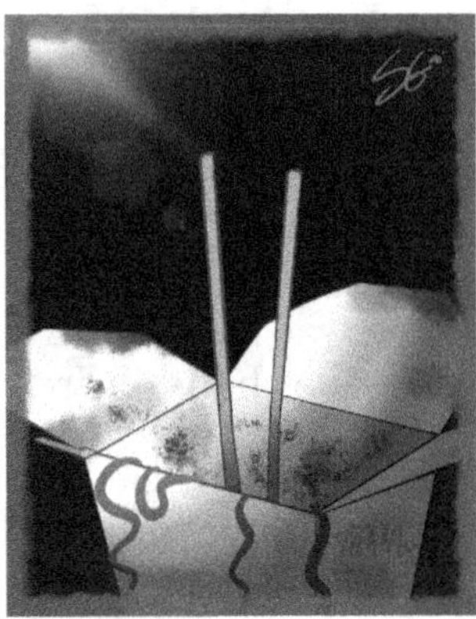

I was cleaned up by the medics and taken to a motel that night to shower and get a meal. Imagine my surprise: I thought I'd spend the night behind bars, and instead I was given a clean, private room and told to wash up. The officer standing outside my door even had a fresh set of clothes sent in for me, though the pants were a bit loose and the shirt a bit tight.

I cried some more standing in the shower, unsure what would happen next.

Another detective—a woman named Rocky, who had blond hair and a tan—bustled around the room while I ate some mediocre Chinese food. "Sorry about that," she smiled, "but it was the only place around here still open."

It was my first meal of freedom, of sorts, and I wasn't complaining. And when I asked her what would happen to me next, all she would say was "Don't worry, honey. Just get some sleep. You've got a big day in front of you tomorrow."

♦♦♦♦♦

Morning came way too soon and I quickly found myself sitting in the long corner of the San Diego County Superior Court in El Cajon. From the few snippets I was able to pick up, I was being arraigned in the courthouse with jurisdiction over La Mesa, and since that was where the first significant crime—the explosion—had taken place, they got me.

I'd started my day with a McMuffin from the local McDonald's and, thanks to the detectives, a donut. Then they brought me to the courthouse where I came in through a side corridor, hoping to avoid the gaggle of reporters at the public doors out front of the building. The hall smelled faintly of old paper and bleach and I smiled at the irony of finding myself here in a place scrubbed of emotion by routine. My wrists were cuffed—not painfully, but firmly, as if the metal itself had already decided that I was guilty.

The courtroom was smaller than I expected. No grand speeches lived here; just wood worn smooth by decades of elbows and hands, a seal on the wall, a judge's bench raised only enough to remind everyone who controlled the room. The gallery murmured when I entered, then went quiet, like a held breath.

The officer told me where to stand, and I was introduced briefly to a guy named Austin who said he was with the public defender's office.

♦♦♦♦♦

They read my name aloud, slowly, carefully, as if the syllables might explode if rushed. It sounded wrong to me—too official, too solid—since for years I was called something else. Sister. Vessel. Chosen. Or just Juniper.

But then they said my full name—"Juniper Marie Cox" —well, it felt like a coat I hadn't worn in a very long time.

The judge asked if I understood why I was there. "Yes," I said, though the only thing I really understood was that everyone in this room had already decided who I was and that I was guilty of all kinds of heinous crimes.

The word *allegedly* floated around the charges, but it landed without weight. Murder. Conspiracy. Abuse. Deaths counted in numbers too large to picture without breaking.

My attorney leaned close to whisper: *Answer only what you're asked. Speak clearly. Don't explain.* I nodded, though explaining was the only thing I wanted to do. Not too long ago I would have testified for the truth—Aeron's truth—until his truth hardened into a pile of dead bodies at his feet.

♦♦♦♦♦

The prosecutor read the charges like a grocery list, and each count landed with a soft thud. I struggled to not react, knowing that reaction would be seen as a kind of confession.

And when I was asked to enter a plea, the room sharpened. *THIS* was the moment everyone recognized from television; the hinge where stories turn.

"Not guilty," my attorney responded.

The words felt borrowed, and I didn't know yet what 'guilty' meant in a world that no longer included Aeron's prophecies of a better tomorrow.

♦♦♦♦♦

The judge set my bail at $250,000—a number I couldn't possibly afford—and it was spoken without cruelty or mercy. Dates were scheduled and motions were made. The machinery had begun to move, patient and unstoppable, and I was informed of my rights, each one delivered like a lifeline I was only now allowed to notice.

As they led me away, I looked around once—just once—at the empty space where the others would have stood. Aeron's chair. The circle. The certainty. All gone.

All that remained of the Purity Syndicate was me: a woman in shackles, a courtroom that didn't care what I had once believed but only what I had done, and a future reduced to calendars and case numbers.

For the first time, no one is telling me what God or Aeron or anyone else wanted. The silence was terrifying, and—impossibly—it was also the first honest thing I had felt in years.

Chapter 29 - Avoiding The Hangman's Noose

-Whitney-

Austin was able to cut a deal with the District Attorney, and I was invited to be part of the conversation as well. "She'll testify to everything the Purity Syndicate has done over the past 10 years," Austin had assured us. "She was one of Inochi's top lieutenants, and she knows how everything worked."

The District Attorney was standing firm. "20 years," was all he said.

Austin had worked with the DA before, and had seen this dance. "You know that number won't survive trial."

"Twenty is generous given the body count she's responsible for."

"Not if the jury hears who gave the orders. Not if they see who benefitted. My client wasn't the architect—she was the filing cabinet. You know Inochi was the guy behind everything, and he's the only one who benefitted."

"And he's conveniently dead, so there's nobody to punish. Besides, she enforced it."

"She documented it, Spenser. That's why she can give you dates, methods, locations, and names you don't have yet. She never bought a bottle of bleach, and she never picked up a gun. She's anything but responsible."

The District Attorney paused as Austin slid a piece of paper across the table. "These are notes my client drafted last night from a diary she kept."

The DA read the notes carefully, skeptical and debating his options. "What do you think, Whitney?" he said, turning to me. "Are these notes real?"

I nodded. "Based on what I've seen of this case, Spenser, this girl is telling the truth. I think we need to give her some incentive to help us tie up a bunch of loose ends. Twenty years just won't cut it."

Austin pushed "Those notes are legit, all right. And that's just the appetizer. She'll testify to financial channels, coercion techniques, and post-event cover-ups. She puts intent where you currently have inference."

The DA remained unconvinced: "Six months doesn't match ten years of harm."

"I disagree. Six months matches the value of certainty. You want a story that puts it all behind us with a narrative locked down. You want to stop guessing, and let the hyenas in the press move on to bother someone else."

I nodded as Spenser threatened "If she lies just once..."

"I know...the deal evaporates. She knows that too, and she's terrified enough to be honest."

The DA paused. "County time. No early release. Full cooperation. Recorded debriefs. Ongoing availability. And no press interviews."

Austin confirmed "Six months, county, full cooperation, immunity limited strictly to disclosed acts."

The District Attorney exhaled. "Draft it. But if she's holding anything back, I will bury her."

"That's fair."

Chapter 30 - Meeting The Judge

-Juniper-

I glanced at the clean, fresh cut newspaper on a bench across from me. The bold text of the title practically jumped off the page, screaming.

> ***PURITY SYNDICATE RESPONSIBLE FOR LA MESA'S DESTRUCTION?!:*** *How a small close knit group sewed destruction and terror across San Diego county.*

It was the same stuff I'd been seeing for days. Every TV channel, radio station, and blogger was talking about the horrible people who had been responsible for death and destruction. Memes cheering DING DONG, THE WITCH IS DEAD! with my face as the witch had been all over Instagram and Facebook.

Except I wasn't dead, of course, and I'd now have plenty of time to figure out my next move and where I wanted to live. Maybe I'd go work in a coffee shop in some little town in New England...

♦♦♦♦♦

Austin had made it simple for me: "You can go to trial and they'll put you away for years. Or you can sign this deal and in six months you'll be free and can move on with your life."

There really was no choice. I was damned if I was going to take the fall for Aeron, and six months – well, I'd been told you could deal with anything if you knew there was an end to it - so I'd know going in that after 181 days I'd be done.

Like I said...there really was no choice.

♦♦♦♦♦

This was all too surreal, knowing that until recently I had been part of the Purity Syndicate cult and their misdeeds. That's what that obnoxious Steve Ross had called them; misdeeds. Please! What an understatement. Now I'd woken up from the nightmare, only to discover I was actually in a bleak reality.

Yeah, Ross tracked me down in my temporary jail cell for an interview. I guess it wasn't too tough for him to figure out that I was the same girl he'd met after the La Mesa explosions. And since he knew my address...at least for the immediate future.

And my personal feelings about him aside, I couldn't really say that I blamed him. The guy had a job to do, after all.

"I'm not allowed to give any press interviews," I told him when he came to see me in lock-up. Those were the terms Austin had me agree to, and I was determined to stick to it. "How would you feel about writing a book with me, then?" he leered, just before I invited him to leave.

After Aeron, Steve Ross was the *LAST* person I wanted to talk to.

♦♦♦♦♦

The hearing where we signed off on the deal was fairly uneventful. My lawyer showed up, his brunette hair slicked back with too much gel. He was clean shaven and wore a spotless black suit and azure tie, spic and span and approaching me like he came straight out of a commercial from one of those ambulance chaser law firms.

All I could think of was that under normal circumstances I'd have admired such cleanliness. But today...well, today the very idea of clean was making me more uncomfortable than I'd ever have thought possible. Still, at least he wasn't wearing white!

Austin was all formal and professional today, unlike the last time when he'd at least tried to make me feel comfortable. Today everything was brusque. "The court will be ready shortly. You'll be asked a few questions. Answer them honestly, then they're going to take you back to your cell. I'll come by later and we can talk some more," he said, waving off any additional questions I might have had.

I nodded, and stood before the mirror examining myself in my orange jumper with SD Jail in big black letters across the back. "This," Austin said, observing me, "is the color that everyone wears during the transportation and intake process. Because even though you've been behind bars for the past two weeks while we've been negotiating with the District Attorney, you're not yet part of the general prison population. They use the orange uniform to instantly know you're still a newbie."

"What color will I get when I'm inside?"

"Depends," he responded. "My guess is blue, since you're going in for a relatively short sentence and will be considered low-risk."

Well, ultimately none of that mattered, I knew, since I was just counting the minutes until I'd get out.

♦♦♦♦♦

As we sat down at the defendant's table inside, I considered how much I honestly despised Aeron at that moment. I was glad he was dead, and just wished he could have been punished too. To distract myself, I sat there doing math in my head, waiting for the judge to arrive. *There are 24 hours in a day times 181 days equals 4344 hours,* I told myself. *Multiplied by 60 minutes in an hour means 260,640 minutes, and...*

I was stopped from adding up the seconds when I saw a little door open up behind the raised podium and the judge—all dressed in black robes – stepped into the courtroom. "All rise!" called the—what do you call the guy?

No matter! We stood up while the guy with the big voice while Judge Weinberg took his seat. My case number was announced and I heard my name, but didn't really follow most of the rest of it. Instead I focused on the judge, who was much older than I, with silver hair and loose skin. The look on his face said "I mean business, don't screw around."

Austin had already explained to me that there would be no jury, since we'd cut a deal. "Your Honor," the other lawyer interjected,

“Our office has come to an agreement with the defendant, the conditions of which are before you.”

The judge nodded and looked down at me and Austin and the lawyer at the other table and asked us to confirm the details. Yes, I was Juniper Marie Cox. Yes, I’d been part of the Purity Syndicate. Yes, we’d done all those horrid things. Yes, I was going to fully cooperate with the District Attorney’s office to help tie up all the loose ends from my previous activities. And yes, I was going to County jail for a period of six months.

“This all seems fairly straightforward,” the judge observed. “Is there any additional business before this court?”

Austin spoke up. “Just two items, your Honor. My client has been completely cooperative at every step, and has already served 14 days behind bars. We would ask that this time be credited against her sentence.”

The judge nodded. “That seems fair. So ordered. And your other item, Mr. Deaver?”

“Your Honor, my client has made it abundantly clear that she was duped by the decedent, Aeron Inochi, and the District Attorney has shown he obviously believes her by agreeing to the term of incarceration. Given her expectation to be a model citizen while behind bars, we would ask that she be assigned to the kitchen, where she could learn a skill that will help her upon her release.”

“I’m not in a position to dictate any prisoner’s work assignment, Mr. Deaver,” the judge said dryly, adding “I will, however, make this recommendation to the warden.

“Thank you, your Honor,” Austin said. And with that I was put into handcuffs and led to a bus which would bring me the 15 minutes back to Santee’s Las Colinas Detention Facility. On the way back I kept myself occupied, thinking *of just 167 days to go. That’s 4008 hours, or 240,480 minutes, or...*

The bus pulled up and the door opened. “Everybody off,” the driver shouted. It was probably just as well, because by the time I could have come up with a number of seconds, the answer would have immediately been obsolete.

Chapter 31 - Inside and Outside

-Juniper-

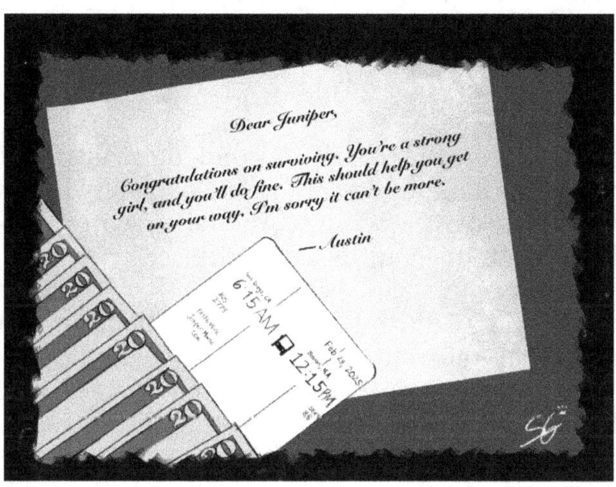

Six months is not a jail sentence you do. It's a season you inhabit. By the time the door closed behind me, I'd already learned the first rule: nothing moves fast except fear.

The intake room smelled like disinfectant and old breath. Disinfectant...like bleach. How ironic! Shoes came off. Bra came off. My hair tie was surrendered like a confession. A woman with tired eyes read my name wrong and never corrected it. That became my second lesson: names are flexible here.

My bunk was top-tier, near the vent that hummed all night like an insect trapped in a wall. Sometimes I'd lie awake, listening to it and counting how many times I'd inhale and be convinced that if I fell asleep something permanent—and bad—would happen.

It didn't, and morning would always come. I'd go out of my way to not piss off anybody, and to see how I'd fit into the hierarchy. My lawyer came by once in my six months and talked with me for about 10 minutes, so I was basically on my own.

♦♦♦♦♦

The days arranged themselves quickly. There was a body count, then breakfast. Dayroom. Count again. Lunch. Programs or nothing. Dinner. Count. Lights dimmed but never dark.

At first I'd mark the days in my head—day three, day seven, day ten—but numbers became unhelpful. Getting a job in the kitchen helped—good ol' Judge Weinberg! —until I was told I'd have to exchange my blue uniform for the white kitchen uniform.

Some fucker up there in the universe has a *really* perverse sense of humor!

The first time I forgot what day it was outside really freaked me out. I didn't bother making any phone calls, mostly because I didn't know anyone on the outside. And lacking any money...well, nothing for me from the commissary, I guess.

♦♦♦♦♦

Whenever I ate, the food would arrive in plastic trays with compartments that never quite fit what they held. I'd eat because there was nothing else to do. The soy protein tasted like damp cardboard, and bread was currency. Peanut butter was power, and coffee packets could buy silence.

I learned how to tuck little items into my sleeve to help bribe other inmates and get what I wanted. And I learned who to sit near and who to avoid. The woman who talked too loudly about her innocence? Nothing doing. The one who cried quietly at night and pretended she wasn't? No thanks! The one who has done this before and walked like the floor belongs to her? I cultivated a friendship with her with a package of Doublemint gum.

Privacy was non-existent, violence rare and discomfort constant, but the secret to success was always who you knew.

♦♦♦♦♦

By the second month I'd stopped flinching at doors. I had also stopped checking my reflection for changes, both because mirrors were limited and unkind.

The job in the kitchen was repetitive, which was the point. I was there to wash dishes, and had no great aspirations beyond that. My mantra became *Just let me make it through today,* kind of like the folks at Alcoholics Anonymous. Dirty dishes became predictable in a way life never was. Focusing on my raw hands drowned out the need to think about what a disaster my life had become.

At night I'd write letters to Aeron and Beatrice that I knew I'd never send. It helped me to work through my anger, and taught me that emotion, like contraband, was safest when hidden.

The TV would play constantly, with daytime court shows bleeding into evening news, which in turn would bleed into reruns of old sitcoms. I didn't really care what was on, so long as it filled the space of my days.

Someone taught me how to play cards. Someone else taught me how not to trust anyone who teaches you anything too quickly.

Yeah, I'd already figured that one out!

♦♦♦♦♦

Month three was when jail stopped feeling temporary. I realized one morning that I could recite the schedule without thinking. My body would awaken before the lights would dim, and I'd figured out which officers would ignore small rule-breaking and which ones would write it up just to feel taller.

It began to feel like the life I'd known before had been a television show I used to watch and grew bored with. Conversations with other inmates would repeat themselves. "How are you holding up?" became a question without an answer, and I started replying, "I'm fine," because it was easier than translating the truth.

Oh yeah...and I started dreaming of rooms without doors.

♦♦♦♦♦

By month four, I was finding every sound to be too loud and every rule felt personal. I'd snap at a woman over who got to sit on a particular chair, then spend the entire afternoon replaying it in my head. As confused as I was when I came in here, I recognized even less of myself now.

I circled my release date on a scrap of paper and hid it in my locker like a fragile thing. I was halfway there, but had gone from counting the minutes to counting the weeks. It seemed easier, somehow.

But I also noticed kindness when it appeared: an extra fruit cup slipped across a table, a warning whispered before an officer rounded the corner, a hand on my shoulder during count when my chest tightened for no obvious reason.

These moments mattered more than they should, but I knew I'd never forget them. They made things more survivable.

♦♦♦♦♦

Month five stretched out before me, with seemingly everyone asking how long I had left. Saying six weeks made me feel lighter somehow, and it was less permanent than 42 days. I was impatient, checking the calendar too often, and time fought back by slowing down.

Now I had a different fear—not of staying, but of leaving. There was nobody out there to even notice that I'd been gone, and I was once again comfortable with having a routine in my life.

At night I'd imagine walking through automatic doors, sunlight landing on my skin like something earned. I'd imagine noise that wasn't controlled and choices that weren't rationed.

♦♦♦♦♦

Finally came the month of my release, when paperwork became the new obstacle. I packed, then repacked my few belongings, and said a few awkward goodbyes. Some of the women hugged me, others nodded, while still others pretended to not see me at all. Everyone was hoping this would be them next.

On my last night in prison I couldn't sleep, thinking this was the moment of truth. My bunkmate a couple of months back told me about how she'd liked living in Springfield, Massachusetts, and how pretty it was during the fall. I decided that was as good a place as any for me to set up shop, and just had to figure out how to get across the country when I didn't know anyone and had no money.

Listening to the vent hum one final time, I realized it had become familiar and almost comforting. For some reason I found that thought more unsettling than anything else.

♦♦♦♦♦

Release morning was procedural. Sign here. Wait. Sit. Stand. Count again. I was dealing with the county Sheriff's Department, and all I was getting was an envelope with my old clothes in it. That dress and scarf, still covered with grass and mud and blood. I almost vomited when I saw those horrible clothes and a tsunami of memories washed over me. *Wait, can I keep the jumper that says SD Jail on the back? It's GOT to be better than returning to this hell!*

There was no money for me, no transportation, and no place for me to sleep that night. No food either. All these guys wanted to do was get me out of there, and they didn't really care how abrupt or disorienting it was. It was a classic example of "Here's your hat. What's your hurry?"

I contemplated the transition and my next move when the guard saw my clothing and called to me. "Cox? Stay here," before she returned with a plain t-shirt, sweatpants, and a pair of cheap sneakers. She looked at me and added "There's something else here for you."

Puzzled, I awaited permission before stepping forward to claim it. Inside a plain white envelope was a typewritten note.

> **Dear Juniper—**
> **Congratulations on surviving. You're a strong girl, and you'll do fine. This should help you get on your way. I'm sorry it can't be more.**
>
> **Austin**

Attached was a one-way bus ticket to Boston and ten twenty dollar bills.

♦♦♦♦♦

A door opened that I had never walked through before, and the outside air felt aggressive. Colors were louder than I remembered them being, and my shoes felt wrong on my feet.

I stepped forward, though nothing dramatic happened. There was no music, no applause, and no sense of closure.

It was just my feet as they moved me towards the bus station. At least I knew where I'd be sleeping for the next few nights; on a Greyhound bus.

♦♦♦♦♦

I arrived in Springfield the way unwanted things often do—quietly, without ceremony, and at an hour when no one was awake enough to notice. Though my ticket was for Boston, I decided to give this a try first. At this point, I truly had nothing left to lose.

The Greyhound hissed to a stop just after dawn, brakes sighing like it was relieved to be done with me. I remember standing when the aisle cleared, joints stiff, head buzzing from three days of bad sleep and worse air. The only thing I carried was the paperwork from my release, which I promised myself I'd put into a safe place and hopefully never need to look at again. I put down *The Royale* - a mediocre pulp novel I'd found on the seat and that I'd stopped reading somewhere in Arizona. Here I was, dressed very inappropriately and in desperate need of a shower and a hot meal.

I had $137.50 left to my name. Enough for a sandwich and coffee while I debated my options, though I decided to hang on to my money for now. Sleeping on the streets of Springfield, Massachusetts in the dead of winter didn't sound very appealing.

The station smelled like old coffee and disinfectant. I was no longer threatened by the smell of bleach; just tired of it. Looking around, I realized this was the kind of place that had seen a lot of people arrive believing this would be the place where things turned around.

Outside, Springfield was gray and undecided. The buildings were brick and solid, as if they had been here long enough to stop expecting explanations. The air was colder than I'd prepared for. California had been warm even when it was cruel. This cold felt personal.

♦♦♦♦♦

I walked, both to stretch my stiff muscles and because movement mattered more than direction. I followed the streets until the station was behind me and the silence changed. The city woke up in pieces—delivery trucks, a woman unlocking a storefront, a man smoking outside a convenience store like it was an obligation. No one looked at me twice, which was both a relief and a warning. My eyes scanned every storefront seeking a HELP WANTED sign.

By midmorning hunger had made itself impossible to ignore. Stopping in a bodega, I bought a dollar pastry and a coffee that tasted burned and thin, paying with crumpled bills that I counted twice before letting go of them. Sitting by the window, I let the heat from the cup thaw my fingers. Outside, people went to work while I sat inside trying to look like I belonged among them.

My day was spent learning the geography of exclusion. Libraries where you could stay if you were quiet enough. Parks where you could sit as long as you didn't lie down. Bathrooms that required a purchase. Shelters with waiting lists that spoke in weeks and months, not days. Every "maybe" came with paperwork. Every "*not today*" came politely, but nonetheless firmly.

But by late afternoon my legs ached, and I stopped at a bench near the river to watch the water move like it knew where it was going. It struck me that I couldn't think of the last time I'd been so unobserved. In jail I was counted several times every day, while here I was optional.

That night I slept badly. A cheap motel near the edge of downtown took half of my remaining cash in exchange for a room that smelled faintly of bleach and old smoke. The lock worked. The bed sagged but held. I showered, then lay on top of the covers fully dressed, sneakers still on, listening to voices through the walls—TV laughter, a couple arguing, a door slamming once with conviction.

I dreamed of buses that never stopped.

♦♦♦♦♦

My second day in the frozen tundra began with resolve. I woke up early, checked out without conversation, and stepped back into the cold with less money and more clarity. This was not a place that would come to me, but I would have to move toward it, piece by piece.

I found the government employment office after asking twice, and the waiting room was full of people who knew the routine way better than I did. At least I'd be spending a chunk of the day inside.

Forms slid across a counter, and I filled them out carefully, handwriting neat, answers honest but strategic. I was "between housing." I had "recent gaps." I was "available immediately."

They gave me pamphlets and a number...but no job.

At noon I ate half a sandwich and saved the rest, folding it carefully like it might be needed later. And by three pm the weight of arrival had settled in. This was the part no one warned you about: not the danger, not the fear, but the emptiness after motion stopped. The way momentum abandoned you all at once. The way you had to invent reasons to keep standing.

I walked some more, past triple-deckers with peeling paint. Past a school letting out, kids loud with the confidence of having somewhere to go. And that night I found myself back near the bus station, sitting on a bench and no better off than when I'd arrived. The sky darkened, the city thinned, and I counted what I had left and stopped when the number felt too small to say out loud.

Two days in and Springfield had not saved me, nor had it harmed me. It had given me space and silence and the burden of choosing what came next. Boston wouldn't be much better, I knew, and would mean starting over again.

I moved inside, knowing the building closed at 11 and hoping I could talk my way into staying longer. Tomorrow will be better. Tomorrow I wasn't going to stop until I found a job.

Besides, whatever I was dealing with here couldn't be much worse than what I'd already lived through.

Chapter 32: In the End...

-Sofia-

It's been a coupla' years now...

I don't even know how much time has really passed, nor do I care. That horrid summer ended, and my 15 minutes of fame are behind me. I'm good with that, too, and much prefer the anonymity of my life today.

The seasons have quickly shifted from summer to autumn, and soon to what will pass for winter in San Diego county. It's close to Halloween, and I don't even know yet what I'm dressing as. My parents moved into a new place near El Cajon, and I remain at the library pecking away at the keyboard, typing my book and saving each chapter on a thumbdrive I always keep in my pocket.

Yeah, it took me a while, but I finally feel motivated to write more and more. Though the more I think about it, this may be more like two books; one for poems and the other for a novel.

Is it possible I bit off more than I can chew with this project? Given that I tend to multitask a lot which, in turn stresses me out, I'm going to go with *"Probably!"* as an answer.

♦♦♦♦♦

Still, I'm not as stressed out as I would have been before, and I can thank Damian for that. Yeah, he's become probably my very first human friend, and the only one I can count on besides the street cats.

Shocking, right? But I can now say with confidence and without question that Damian is my friend...and a GREAT friend at that! Despite—or perhaps because of—the whole *'cult trying to kill us'* incident, we've grown close. Not a romantic thing, mind you, but he's more like the brother I never had.

It's weird that my mind even goes there. I mean, this guy I once had zero use for has been supportive and helpful with some of my writing, as I've been with his. We've become each other's strongest supporter and fiercest critic.

♦♦♦♦♦

I shift in my seat and lean back to see the words I've just written. The first few paragraphs of the novel's third chapter stare back at me. This writing process is unquestionably a slow process, though I've gotten a solid start. I must keep reminding myself to not push too hard, lest I get *another* writer's block.

Each time I start writing, I find my narrative drifts over to the events of what happened that summer, so I'm going to stop struggling against it and write what I know. Of course, I'm kind of tweaking it a bit to make sure it's not too on the nose about some of the details. It strikes me that going too in-depth about the explosions and poisonous candies and related details might be a bit insensitive to those who suffered the most.

And while it might be helpful to get some insights from that blonde girl—the one who survived and went to jail—I heard she got out and disappeared to who knows where.

For my novel, instead of having people in the story, I've decided to use anthropomorphic animal characters. The two main characters are a fox and a raven—both outcasts as the other critters see them as being evil or bringing bad luck. It's an homage to one of the poems I wrote a while back, and when someone asks me about the genre, I tell them it's a...well...fantasy horror kind of thing, with a bit of mystery. Where two outcasts of the town find a way to save the people in the area as they search for clues of who's the villain poisoning the locals in different cottages. Kinda like a furry homage to Sherlock Holmes kind of thing. Except with a bit more scary themes of some psycho poisoning the crops of the local farmers' markets.

I print out the pages I've just typed, save the file, and head home.

♦♦♦♦♦

Sitting at my desk at home, I lean back to reflect on my work and notice the calendar before me. My dad recently gave it to me to replace the one lost in the fire. I look at my scribbles and a few sticky notes here and there. Tomorrow is October 27th, and I'm supposed to meet up with Damian for some Halloween party...which my parents are *now* okay with.

They're even okay with my plans to walk around the neighborhood and grab a coffee in the cafe on Halloween night. True, I don't have a costume yet, even though Damian already has his Dracula costume, including cape and fangs.

I'll figure it out.

I stand up to look through a bunch of old outfits hanging in my closet and belonging to other family members, and wonder if I can use any of them for a costume. Nothing looks very appealing, leaving me with a box of my own stuff—shirts, shoes, and pants—sitting under my bed.

Tucked under some ratty jeans is a headband with black cat ears on it, conveniently sitting atop a black shirt and a black tail. I forgot that my parents kept some of my old stuff from early years tucked away in a storage unit. These things had obviously been spared when the explosion hit.

Maybe I should be a black cat this year. It reminds me of Lucky Minx, after all, and I really do miss that cat.

♦♦♦♦♦

I set my clothes on my bed, then walk back to the calendar. Everything seems to be taken care of for the month, though I realize the book contest—now an annual event—is supposed to be happening pretty soon. As I am no longer a La Mesa resident, that contest's off-limits to me, but somehow that doesn't matter anymore. Something else will come up, I'm sure.

What's depressing is knowing I'll never get my old home back or see my cat friends again. I'll never walk the same walkway to the old trolley that too was blown away from the explosion. Things that I cannot rewrite or replace, but will always retain in my memory.

Writing has become a form of therapy for me, and it's helped me a lot more than I thought it ever could. And maybe, even if I don't become a world-famous author, I can use writing to become more content than I was before. At least now I feel like I have more control, more confidence, and certainly more support than ever.

Plus I have support for my first, genuine friendship...and that's good enough for me for now. Perhaps things will go well for me after all.

♦♦♦♦♦

The song *Cruel Summer* by Bananarama is pouring out of my stereo speakers. I must have zoned out in my writing, failing to notice my phone is still playing music. I'm still not sure why, but the more I think about the simple title to that mid 80's song, the more I believe that all that heartache, horror and traumatic memory that I'm still working through means that really was a cruel summer for me...for Damian...for everyone in San Diego County.

I lean forward on my desk as I listen to that vintage tune, hearing the upbeat sounds and catchy lyrics, enjoying it a little despite the themes of a darker side of summer, the scorching heat not by the summer sun...but raging fires of ill intent.

Even if I feel more content now than ever, the anxiety has never gone away. And I realize now that the turmoil of that summer will never fully fade from my memory. No matter how many poems, tales or therapeutic novels I write to make me feel better. The memory will NEVER go away.

Even the foul scent of bleach will haunt me forever.

♦♦♦♦♦ ♦♦♦♦♦ ♦♦♦♦♦

About the Author

Welcome to the darkest recesses of my mind, where my psyche is scary...and in many cases tragic.

For most of my life it's been my dream to create stories for everyone to enjoy. Most of them have been niche themes, tiptoeing around fantasy and horror and addressing fears and phobias that have brewed in my head, seemingly forever.

I got into writing and creating artwork to help me process my thoughts and feelings that otherwise couldn't be fully explained. I'm exhausted by the merry-go-round of life, seeing it more often than not as a rickety tilt-a-whirl that can give you chronic whiplash, rather than a pleasant carousel ride.

For entertainment, I've been known to convert existing franchises, redrawing otherwise lovable characters and placing them into horror scenarios. Or I'll read a good book during a nice day, followed by an all-night classic horror film festival.

My cat Amalia watches all this, unsure what to make of me.

You're holding my first novel; a reaction to my fears of cults, fire, poisoning, and the like. As I spent the past two years working with the team at Write Away Books and wending my way through the writing process, I discovered it also allowed me to confront my internalized ableism and horrors that have otherwise held me back.

It would be legitimate at this point to question why someone with PDD-NOS does such a thing, and the reality is I want to be neurotypical. It annoys me that many "normal" people look at neurodivergent people as children. This effort is to demonstrate that I am not a child and am worthy of success and a great career.

Sadly, and like so many others, this means dealing with the reality that I'm sometimes used in my job, getting uncomfortable in groups of people I otherwise dislike. I've come to recognize the desire to live a simple life in someplace quiet, without noise or constant yelling or arguing from family members.

But the therapeutic process of writing this book has helped me recognize that, though I've internalized ableism and (for a time) become my own enemy, I've come out stronger on the other side.

With that said, I invite you to meet Sofia, representative of my bitterness, resentment and inner fears; Damian, who embraces both darkness and positivity; and Aeron, the source of so much of my angst. Writing *Deadly Divinity* helped me prove to myself that I can do the things I've always wanted to do. No longer will I allow fear and anger to hold me back. And no longer will I live my life by "What if...?"

Finally, my thanks for coming on the journey with me.

Sierra